A PLUME BOOK

THE LITTLE BOOK

SELDEN EDWARDS began writing *The Little Book* as a young English teacher in 1974, and continued to layer and refine the manuscript until its completion in 2007. It is his first novel. He spent his career at several independent schools across the country, and for more than forty years has been secretary of his Princeton class, where he also played basketball. He lives in Santa Barbara, California.

Praise for *The Little Book*

One of "Ten Things We Love This Week," *Entertainment Weekly*'s "Must List"

"As you might expect, *The Little Book* is anything but little. This is a wide-ranging novel of grand ideas, of the promise of the new century, now so far behind us. It is a story of fathers and sons, to be sure, of the bygone days when an American aristocracy held the reins of power. And it is a tale of books within books, and their influence upon history. But Edwards has a wonderfully subversive way with all this; along with the great men of the era, he creates astonishing female characters. The Burden women, who marry into the family after living rich, full lives of their own, have their tales to tell, too. All this swirls around in a graceful waltz of a book, spinning at times at dizzying speed, but leaving behind a haunting, unforgettable melody." —*The Times-Picayune* (New Orleans)

"Delightfully mad . . . *The Little Book* is presented with undeniable brio. Enthusiasts of Vienna and narratives of time travel are in for a thrilling adventure." —*San Francisco Chronicle*

"Inventive, bracing, poignant, and well written. Despite the title, there's nothing little about it. *The Little Book* is such an elegantly crafted story, it should be at the top of everyone's summer reading list, especially for those who love a good plot with an emotional punch. This is among my favorite novels of the year." —*Tucson Citizen*

"Selden Edwards's *The Little Book* is a wonderful novel and I think it has a chance to become a famous one. I've never read a novel like it. And I felt like my life was changing forever as I savored its many delights and mysteries." —Pat Conroy

"Selden Edwards's impressive debut novel is richly inventive, woven tightly with incident, and fully engaging. It is also superbly humane and readable." —Richard Ford

"Take a pinch of Mitch Albom's *For One More Day* and *The Five People You Meet in Heaven* (for an impossible chance to make amends or peace), draw a little from Madeleine L'Engle's *A Wrinkle in Time* and H. G. Wells's *The Time Machine* (for the potential of a twist on the physical universe as we know it), on the upscale side borrow a bit from Michael Cunningham's *The Hours* (for clever paralleling of extremely different contexts), hark back to E. L. Doctorow's *Ragtime* (for commingling historical and fictional characters), and throw in a heady dollop of romantic mooning à la Robert James Waller's *The Bridges of Madison County*, and you will have an inkling of the ingredients pulped together in *The Little Book*." —*Chicago Tribune*

"*The Little Book* is quite the twisty not-so-little novel. Everything is connected, we are told in *The Little Book*, and indeed it is in this tale. Caught up in an eternal loop, as well, though the book does come to a tender close, but only to start up again in the mind's eye. It's hard not to be thoroughly taken with such an approach to both the real and imagined past." —*New York Daily News*

"B+. *Back to the Future* for the intellectual set." —*Entertainment Weekly*

"*The Little Book* shows the rich imagination and the intellectual fire of the first-time author. . . . It would not be surprising to see this book become a classic." —*Deseret News* (Salt Lake City)

"Required reading." —*The New York Post*

"Rich, thoughtful, and clever. Edwards has been working on *The Little Book* since 1974, and it shows. He's created a complete world, one that's a pleasure to enter." —*Bloomberg News*

"*The Little Book* is unlike any novel I have read. In its historical scope it resembles Anthony Powell's wonderful series *A Dance to the Music of Time*, but with the introduction of the fantastic, through the device of time travel, and myth, through the arts and psychology, it delivers a very different and rather more modern experience. With so many volumes published in such a wide variety of styles today, it's hard to tell if any new book will survive for even a year, never mind gain literary immortality. But this novel, rooted in the work of more than thirty years, has as good a chance as any in recent memory of withstanding the test of time and becoming a classic." —*Santa Barbara Independent*

The Little Book

SELDEN EDWARDS

A PLUME BOOK

PLUME
Published by the Penguin Group
Penguin Group (USA) Inc., 375 Hudson Street, New York, New York 10014, U.S.A. • Penguin Group (Canada), 90 Eglinton Avenue East, Suite 700, Toronto, Ontario, Canada M4P 2Y3 (a division of Pearson Penguin Canada Inc.) • Penguin Books Ltd., 80 Strand, London WC2R 0RL, England • Penguin Ireland, 25 St. Stephen's Green, Dublin 2, Ireland (a division of Penguin Books Ltd.) • Penguin Group (Australia), 250 Camberwell Road, Camberwell, Victoria 3124, Australia (a division of Pearson Australia Group Pty. Ltd.) • Penguin Books India Pvt. Ltd., 11 Community Centre, Panchsheel Park, New Delhi – 110 017, India • Penguin Group (NZ), 67 Apollo Drive, Rosedale, North Shore 0632, New Zealand (a division of Pearson New Zealand Ltd.) • Penguin Books (South Africa) (Pty.) Ltd., 24 Sturdee Avenue, Rosebank, Johannesburg 2196, South Africa

Penguin Books Ltd., Registered Offices: 80 Strand, London WC2R 0RL, England

Published by Plume, a member of Penguin Group (USA) Inc. Previously published in a Dutton edition.

First Plume Printing, June 2009
10 9 8 7 6 5 4 3 2

Copyright © Selden Edwards, 2008

All rights reserved

℗ REGISTERED TRADEMARK—MARCA REGISTRADA

The Library of Congress has catalogued the Dutton edition as follows:
Edwards, Selden.
The little book / Selden Edwards.
p.   cm.
ISBN 978-0-525-95061-5 (hc.)
ISBN 978-0-452-29551-3 (pbk.)
1. Rock musicians—Fiction.   2. Time travel—Fiction.   3. Vienna (Austria)—Fiction.
4. Austria—History—1867–1918—Fiction.   I. Title.
PS3605.D8985F56   2008
813'.6—dc22   2007045785

Printed in the United States of America

PUBLISHER'S NOTE
This is a work of fiction. Names, characters, places, and incidents are either the product of the author's imagination or are used fictitiously, and any resemblance to actual persons, living or dead, business establishments, events, or locales is entirely coincidental.

The scanning, uploading, and distribution of this book via the Internet or via any other means without the permission of the publisher is illegal and punishable by law. Please purchase only authorized electronic editions, and do not participate in or encourage electronic piracy of copyrighted materials. Your support of the author's rights is appreciated.

BOOKS ARE AVAILABLE AT QUANTITY DISCOUNTS WHEN USED TO PROMOTE PRODUCTS OR SERVICES. FOR INFORMATION PLEASE WRITE TO PREMIUM MARKETING DIVISION, PENGUIN GROUP (USA) INC., 375 HUDSON STREET, NEW YORK, NEW YORK 10014.

For Gaby

Contents

PART THREE · THE LAST BURDEN

This is the story of how, through a dislocation in time, my son, Frank Standish Burden III, the famous American rock-and-roll star of the 1970s, found himself in Vienna in the fall of 1897. It is a complicated story, full of extraordinary characters and wild improbabilities. Rather than dwell on those improbabilities or the parts that require more thought and explanation, I will simply tell you what I know exactly as I know it and let you sort out the pieces for yourself, forgiving a ninety-year-old woman her various lapses of memory. As an aged poet once said, "I do not remember all the details, but what I remember, I do remember perfectly." And you will forgive this very subjective narrator her need to describe herself in the third person, as just another character in this remarkable tale. It is, after all, my son who is the center of this narrative. The world, of course, knew him as Wheeler, a name he acquired in the early 1950s, playing boys' baseball in the Sacramento Valley of California, exactly how we will come to later. So Wheeler it will be, as I reconstruct for you his story.

Flora Zimmerman Burden
Feather River, California, 2005

PART ONE

The Connectedness
of All Things

1

Arrival

heeler Burden did not think of visiting Berggasse 19 until the third day in Vienna, or at least there is no mention of it in the journal he kept with meticulous care from almost the moment of his arrival. The first days he spent adjusting, you might say, to the elation of newness and the spectacle of this city he knew so well in theory but had never actually visited. Then the practicalities settled on him, followed by a deep feeling of displacement. Wheeler was a long way from home with no means of either identification or support. But before the gravity of the situation set in, he was almost able to enjoy himself. Much of the first day, of course, he was busy marveling at his mere presence in such a magnificent and imperial city. It was 1897 Vienna, after all. The first hour, we learn from the journal, he spent clearing the fog from his mind and pulling himself painfully back to full awareness, emerging from the miasma of what seemed like a long uneasy sleep, and from the catastrophic precipitating event he was nowhere near ready to remember.

In the first moments Wheeler could only stare vacantly at the handsome men in dark coats and top hats, finely adorned women in long dresses with tightly corseted waists and well-defined *poitrines*, military officers in ornate and colorful regalia, workers carrying lunch boxes. Everywhere there were horse-drawn carriages of all sorts, and tall, elegant marble façades of the grand buildings for which Vienna at the end of the century had become renowned.

You do need to know that Wheeler Burden had never been to Vienna per se but had traveled there many times before in his mind. He could speak German as a result of a natural fluency with languages, and he had a general grasp of the manner in which a young man in fin de siècle

Vienna was expected to carry himself, both a result of what now seemed like careful training in the hands of his wise old mentor, the Venerable Haze, whom we will encounter momentarily. In fact, after some reflection, you might conclude that, as with so many heroes who are invited on extraordinary journeys, Wheeler's way had been prepared.

Some time after his mysterious arrival, in pulling together his initial impressions, Wheeler would detail in his journal his first moments on the Ringstrasse, the broad and magnificent boulevard that encircled the city, as awaking from a great sleep, floating between oblivion and consciousness. Anesthesia was an experience he had been through twice—once having his tonsils removed as a child and once in adulthood in 1969, during surgery to repair a spleen ruptured by an angry Hell's Angel at a well-publicized rock-concert riot. This time he was not lying inertly in a hospital room blinking at sterile walls and unfamiliar nurses, but rather coming to his senses walking along a magnificent, wide boulevard, gaping at finely dressed passersby and massive, grandly detailed buildings.

His first recollections were ones of ambling aimlessly, smiling, gazing absently at these spectacular edifices with awe and elation, as if the mechanism that had delivered him to this fabulous place had carried with it, like anesthesia, the complete dismantling of any worldly concern.

He must have entered, he figured later, somewhere near the Danube Canal and circled half the old city before enough consciousness descended to demand a verification of place and time. Wheeler found himself drawn to a newsstand, where he picked up his first newspaper. It was then that he realized there was no other city it could have been, really. All of the impressions that led to this inevitable conclusion were rooted in the Haze's vivid descriptions of the time and place, preserved in his famous "Random Notes," but of course Wheeler was at the moment much more concerned with practical matters than he was with the peculiar coincidence of winding up in exactly the time and place that he had heard described so often.

First, he had to do something about his clothes. He was staring at the Viennese, predictable given his circumstance, but they were staring back, which, again given his circumstance as a stranger in a strange land, was not good. People staring, you might know, was certainly nothing new to my son. With his long hair and Wild Bill Hickok mustache, Wheeler Burden was on *People* magazine's ten most recognizable list five years running in the mid 1970s, and, in the words of one of his grammar school teachers, had been "something of a spectacle" all his life. The Viennese focused their suspicious attention on him as he passed, not recognizing him specifically, as strollers in the 1970s would have, but simply wondering what a man in his late forties of his appearance, dressed as he was, was doing on the Ringstrasse. The style of the times and the crisp morning air made being out in shirtsleeves inappropriate, not to mention uncomfortable. This attention was giving him a deep sense of foreboding.

Since strangeness, not notoriety, was drawing the unwanted attention in this situation, one in which anonymity above all was to be wished, at least until he had his bearings, he decided that doing something about appearance was his first priority.

No matter how much a more cautious person—his mother, say—might have advised looking before leaping, he felt he had to act. So, just as he had made his way around the Ring to the area of the opera house, he was drawn into his first action, a fateful one, one that set in motion everything that was to follow and established him indelibly as the central character in this story.

Across from the opera house, near the grand entrance of the Hotel Imperial, Wheeler was stopped by the sight of a small serving man struggling to remove a heavy steamer trunk from a curbside carriage under the unsympathetic supervision of the trunk's owner, a stern and athletic-looking young man in his early twenties. The young man drew Wheeler's attention immediately, first because of his offensive manner and only secondarily because he was a fitter, more compact, and younger version of himself, almost exactly Wheeler's size and build.

Oblivious to Wheeler's attention, focused singularly on the unloading of his possessions, the young man burst out, "Hurry up, for god's sake. I haven't all day, you know." His accent was clearly American. He thrust some bills at the struggling man and a note onto which he had written some large numbers. "Here. Have it delivered to four thirty-three," he said with a contempt that made him immediately unlikable. "I've an hour's worth of business at the American consulate," he said under his breath, intending not to be understood. "That ought to give even you enough time."

Wheeler was not sure if it was more the man's abrasiveness or his own desperation that brought on the suddenness and audacity of his next move,

one that would solve his immediate problem and—it must be added—
create far worse ones. But however it was, he quickly left the scene in front
of the Hotel Imperial, found a back entrance to the hotel, and strode confidently up the broad service stairs. An expert at secretive entries and es-
capes, Wheeler had learned long ago that assertive confidence always
masked inappropriate entry.

On the stairwell, he passed a maid in a white and black uniform.
Wheeler saluted her and flashed a confident greeting; then as soon as she
disappeared around a corner he picked up a bundle of soiled bed linen
and carried it up the stairway. He explored until he found his way to the
fourth floor stairwell within eyeshot of room 433 and watched through a
crack in the heavy door until the little man with the dolly and trunk arrived.

He slipped into the room unnoticed and into the large hall closet while
the man fussed with the luggage. Suddenly, as he heard the door click
behind the exiting servant, Wheeler was alone in the spacious hotel room
with the large upright steamer trunk, and—because the young man
seemed to have packed for a good long stay—with a large wardrobe to
choose from. Remembering the "hour's worth of business at the American
consulate," he took his time, laying out clothes on the bed. He chose the
shoes, trousers, shirt, vest, and coat that seemed the most conventional
from his brief walking tour of the Ringstrasse. As he finished dressing and
was choosing a tie, he noticed on a trunk shelf a neat pile of five envelopes, each with the name of a country written on the outside. He chose
"Austria" and found inside a stack of paper currency, which he began to
pocket, then returned respectfully to its place. Wheeler Burden had been
known to bend the rules, but he was not a thief.

Suddenly, a key sounded in the lock, and the door swung open. The
young man, seemingly in a hurry, walked in with his head down and was
fully into the room before he looked up and saw Wheeler, now well
dressed, standing at attention beside the trunk. The young man let out an
involuntary grunt of surprise as his steely eyes did a quick appraisal of the
situation. The two men stared for what seemed an interminable moment,
the younger one's face reflecting a quick evolution from stunned surprise
to unmistakable indignation.

Had Wheeler known then what he wrote in the journal later, he would
have seen in the young man's eyes a familiar, smoldering intensity too

deep for either man to recognize. "And what do we have here?" the young man said, collecting himself, his nostrils flaring, absorbing the very essence of the intruder and sensing something primal that defied words and civility. As his words hung in the air unanswered, the two men remained transfixed, both taking in details of the other.

Had the younger man been less taken aback, he might have sprung forward and attacked, but in that instant of surprised paralysis Wheeler seized his advantage. Before the eyes of his startled new adversary, he reached for the Austrian envelope and, deftly snatching it, brushed past him and stepped through the door and out into the hall. The young man paused for an instant, giving the intruder the slight advantage he needed, then, recovering from his momentary paralysis, darted out into the hallway.

As Wheeler reached the service exit, he swung the door shut with a mighty force, then wedged it closed with a wooden stopper. He descended four flights to the back alley, the sound of the haughty young American banging on the door fading as he went.

Quickly, he reached the Ringstrasse and adjusted his stride to match that of the average passerby. He crossed the broad boulevard near the opera house into the dark narrow streets in the heart of the old city, past St. Stephen's Cathedral, well removed from the scene of his crime. He was now comfortably and appropriately dressed, with Austrian currency in his pocket, all but a shave and a haircut away from looking like a Viennese or at least a turn-of-the-century American tourist. He felt quite pleased with himself. After he was settled, with some at least temporary means of support, he would try to find the man and make amends, but for now he had Vienna to think about.

Wheeler Burden was a new man. He gave little thought to his old twentieth-century clothing, which he had left like so much shed snake's skin in a pile beside the steamer trunk in the American's hotel room. He felt such immeasurable relief at being comfortably clothed and in cash, with no one staring, that, for the moment at least, he was able to disregard the fact that he was friendless, still without passport or any means of identifying himself, and that on this, his first day in 1897 Vienna, he had acquired a mortal enemy.

2

No Ordinary Journey

hen he instructed the Viennese barber to cut his hair short and shave the Wild Bill Hickok mustache, Wheeler finished the transformation to anonymity that his borrowed clothing had begun. He now looked "shockingly normal," his long-time friend Joan Quigley would have quipped, had she been able to see him now in Vienna. "Now, you look just like everyone else," he could hear her saying, disgusted and amused. Joan Quigley, wife of a prominent federal court judge and social power in Pittsburgh, where her husband had grown up before becoming a Harvard football star, had given Wheeler his first sexual experience back in 1959. She had remained his secret and passionate love for fifteen years. "Wheeler Burden is fifty-yard famous," she had told him one day in San Francisco shortly after his injuries in the Altamont catastrophe, exasperated, referring to him in the third person. They were in Golden Gate Park, outside the de Young Museum, and she was trying for the umpteenth time to have a serious conversation about their future together. "I mean, he's not first-sighting recognizable like Ringo Starr, say, or Robert Redford, or Mick Jagger, oh no, but definitely in the second tier. After walking fifty yards, in New York or San Francisco or Atlanta, you can bet that someone is going to come up and shake his hand and ask for an autograph or ask about Woodstock or whether Shadow Self will stay together." This time she was especially peeved. "It gets damned annoying, you know, especially when one is trying to have a serious conversation about the future. And he doesn't do anything to prevent it. It's that damned Wild Bill Hickok look," she continued, knowing Wheeler would never settle for anonymity. "No one would recognize you with a shave and a crew cut."

But people noticing Wheeler on the street had started a long time before the Wild Bill hair and before Joan Quigley had rolled him in the hay at Harvard in 1959. It had been somehow a natural consequence, Wheeler's mother, Flora Burden, always figured, of having a famous father and an eccentric, no-nonsense mother. That and the fact, incomprehensible to Flora's English sensibilities, that at age twelve or so their small Sacramento Valley town discovered that this young man could throw a baseball faster than anyone they had ever seen. So it was that his mother became pretty accustomed to having people point and stare as they walked down the street and then come up and want to talk about his future plans.

Whenever Wheeler thought back on his life and its extraordinary trajectory and looked for causes, he inevitably credited being the son of a famously heroic father or perhaps just being generally blessed by benevolent gods. Whatever it was, he could pretty much pinpoint the moment it all started—his epiphany day, he called it—that day at age ten when he pasted the sparrow hawk with the rock. At least that was when it became clear about the throwing-arm part.

In the fall of 1951, Wheeler Burden—then known as Stan—was ten, a fifth grader, walking with his mother in the bottom forty acres near the Feather River, the part of their farm inside the levees that flooded nearly every winter and was suitable only for row crops. Flora loved the bottomland, with its large open bean fields and thick stands of cottonwoods and isolated pothole lakes where you could scare up wild ducks and pretend you were lost and alone. There was a calm wildness to it that was like nothing she had known growing up in London. In the long tormented days when she first arrived after the war, the walks with her son were her salvation.

This one afternoon, he was giving her, as was the custom on those walks, a detail-rich and seamless version of the latest chapters of *Ninety-Three*, the Victor Hugo novel he was reading, or rereading. For young Stan Burden, his mother always conjectured, talking was discovery, so she would just let him ramble as she lost herself in figures from the recent prune harvest. She knew he was eccentric, flamboyant even, and she liked that. His free flow of ideas kept her good company, and she figured the outpouring was good for releasing all the pent-up male energy of growing up without a father.

She walked and listened as he recounted all the vivid details of Hugo's heroine, a mother hauling her children through the ravages of the French

Revolution and the Reign of Terror. Wheeler had no idea of the events that she had worked to keep secret: that when he was very young his own mother had made a very similar odyssey hauling her own infant son through newly-liberated northern France after the invasion, searching for her Resistance-hero husband, the boy's father, the legendary Dilly Burden.

As Wheeler told the Victor Hugo plot, he noticed with ten-year-old fascination a sparrow hawk hovering at about a one-hundred-foot distance. Without thinking, and definitely without breaking stride in his narrative, he picked up a smooth stone and winged it straight at the bird, striking it squarely in the chest. The bird fell like an overripe peach and hit the ground with a thud.

Wheeler's story stopped midsentence, his jaw dropped, and boy and mother stood watching the fallen bird as first it lay inert on the bottom-land's rich alluvial dust, then struggled to raise itself, shaking the cobwebs out of its tiny brain.

"Look what you have done," his mother said without a trace of either awe or humor, after it was clear that the bird was not dead and might in fact revive. "And for no reason."

Wheeler's mother had a well-earned reputation as a no-nonsense pacifist. Five years earlier, in 1946, her husband already dead in the war, she had made the unlikely move with her five-year-old son from their bombed-out London neighborhood to the small family farm in far-off California. Wheeler's father's family, the Boston Burdens, had given it to Wheeler's mother outright. It was a way to buy her off, to get her out of the way, a recompense for what she had been through, and a place to raise the family's only grandson, the last of the Burden line. Wheeler's mother, ravaged by war herself, had been glad to leave the gloom of her own and her country's loss, and the Boston Burdens had been glad to have her out of sight. The family, at least Wheeler's grandfather, had never accepted Flora. Regardless of how desperately she had loved his son and how she had left England to search for him almost as soon as the Allies landed in Normandy, it was clear to Flora that to the old patriarch Frank Burden she was little more than that English Jewess his son had gotten pregnant.

What may have appeared to the world and even perhaps to Flora Burden as exile was for a London-born American boy a dream come true, the ideal surroundings for an upbringing. From his earliest years, Wheeler roamed the bottomlands with his friends, carefree and uncomplicated.

Now, watching the wounded bird fluttering on the ground beside his mother, who understood little of what it was to be a ten-year-old rural California boy, Wheeler could only stammer. He thought of explaining to Flora the entire history of boys and rocks and incredible long shots, but for once in his short life he was speechless and even at the age of ten realized the futility of some tasks. "It was far away—" he began, still feeling the magic of the stone leaving his hand. "I never thought I'd even come close." The sparrow hawk stretched out its wings.

"You were trying to hit it."

"Well, yes," Wheeler stammered. How do you ever explain to your English mother how an American boy throws rocks at just about everything, not really expecting to hit anything? And this English mother, Flora Burden, was about the most uncompromising woman Wheeler would meet in his life. She drove a hard bargain in buying goods for the ranch. She knew exactly whom she wanted as friends and whom she did not. She was single, celibate, self-assured, and intended to stay that way. She was considered beautiful, granted, but her commitments ran too deep. "I'm an eagle," she would say to Wheeler. "When I chose your father I mated for life." And her commitment to pacifism also ran deep. She had been a life-long disciple of Bertrand Russell, Albert Einstein, and, most important, Sigmund Freud, whose seminal works she had embraced early and whom, at the end of his life, she spent time with when he emigrated from his Vienna home to London in 1938. She certainly did not want to be raising a young warrior, and, perhaps most important in this case, she knew nothing about ten-year-old arms and throwing range except that what began with throwing rocks ended with mighty armies going at each other.

"I didn't think I'd actually hit anything," he stammered again, still amazed at what he had accomplished.

"Well, now you know," she said, her way of pointing out what she hoped would be a life lesson for Wheeler, that such tiny and thoughtless acts of violence were exactly what eventually caused the huge consequences of global war. She never forced him to promise anything. She had complete faith in her son's rational powers, and saw no reason to explain or ask for an explanation. "Well, now you know" was for her all that was necessary. She had the utmost confidence that he would hear it, absorb it, and make the necessary attitude changes.

The sparrow hawk collected itself one last time, flapped its wings, then rose haltingly and flew to a nearby stand of cottonwood trees. Wheeler watched silently and recalled again the sensation in his right arm as the stone had left his hand. His fingers seemed to follow the trajectory of the stone to the fluttering target in one beautifully unified motion. Wheeler looked down at his hand, opening and closing it. He looked up at the position in the sky where the hawk had been hovering; then he looked back at his hand, then up to the cottonwood where the bird was regrouping. It was hard to explain, but something began to dawn on the boy in that moment. He had felt for just an instant the connectedness of all things.

It was, you would have to say, a life-altering moment. Wheeler's was going to be no ordinary journey.

3

The Venerable Haze

hen asked the most important influences in his life in the now-classic 1969 interview in *Rolling Stone* magazine, just after the disastrous Altamont concert when he was nearly killed by a pool-cue-wielding Hell's Angel, Wheeler Burden gave three: Victor Hugo, whose seven novels he had read for the first time by age thirteen; Buddy Holly, whose music he first heard in the Sacramento Valley when he was fifteen; and his Boston private school history teacher and mentor, Arnauld Esterhazy, indeed a most central player in my son's remarkable story, whom three generations of boys had called the Venerable Haze. Esterhazy, the Haze, had taught history to the boys at St. Gregory's School, Boston, for more than forty years before Wheeler's arrival, naïve and impressionable, at age sixteen in 1957 for his high school junior year, what St. Greg's called the second class.

Esterhazy had grown up and spent his early adulthood in Vienna at the turn of the century, and while recovering from shattered nerves and injuries in the Great War had settled at St. Greg's, where he became a legend. The two unlikely characters, the undisciplined boy from the California provinces and the old Viennese aristocrat, met in 1957 and formed a cohesive bond when family peculiarities brought them together. The relationship became a most formative one, even for the old man. Somehow, almost magically, the two—old master and young student—had liked each other from the start. "We have much to learn from you, Herr Burden," the old man had said in their first meeting, then pausing for effect, "as we begin writing on your tabula rasa." In his first week in the strange environment of his new school, the sixteen-year-old boy had written home about the eighty-year-old man, "Mr. Esterhazy and I seem to have known each other all our lives."

The Haze had taught and been close to Wheeler's war-hero father Dilly Burden in the 1930s, the reason why, everyone assumed, the old man had fixed such fierce attention on the boy from the moment he arrived. The old man did indeed begin a two-year process of filling the blank slate. It was the Haze, then nearly eighty, who so affected Wheeler's psyche that all other influences paled in comparison. That period from 1957 to 1959 was—Wheeler said later in that famous *Rolling Stone* interview—when two of his most important influences, Esterhazy and Holly, coincided, although the two never met nor for that matter knew each other existed.

Holly, himself a mid-twentieth-century American music icon, had spent his boyhood in Texas with no connection to Vienna. The Haze, a St. Gregory's icon, had never been to Texas, but had spent his boyhood in Vienna, witness to a most extraordinary pinnacle of culture and, simultaneously, the decline and fall of just about all the essentials necessary to preserve it.

The Haze was tall, thin, and indelibly cultured. His eyes burned with a blue intensity that when fixed on his young impressionable male audience lent the kind of urgency to his classroom observations about history that stuck in the minds of his students. He spoke with an accent more civilized and theatrical than Germanic. His dress was elegant and simple, all his clothes tailored wool and the finest cottons, having taken on that worn comfortable look of a prep school master, with a scent of a rich old talcum. "He smells like old Europe," an old boy told Wheeler.

And there was little doubt that it was the old man's kindly gentility that made Wheeler's otherwise disastrous transition to St. Gregory's bearable. As the young man from a farm in California sat in his totally unfamiliar blazer and tie among sophisticated boys in their totally familiar blazers and ties, he focused on his fascinating teacher instead of on his feeling of displacement. As Wheeler listened to the elegant descriptions of historic Europe, he focused on their compelling charm rather than his own deplorable lack of sophistication and classical education. And the daunting task of initiating the young man from the California farmlands was one with which the old man seemed strangely comfortable.

As a young man himself, Arnauld Esterhazy, descendant of one of the Hapsburg Empire's most prominent and aristocratic families, had received a superb education, had been part of the rich intellectual life of the Viennese coffeehouses, and had himself published a few *feuilletons*, the tight little highly personal essays in Vienna's famous liberal newspaper, the *Neue Freie Presse*. He had considered careers in both journalism and academia before being lured to America in the early 1900s, recruited by an anonymous admirer and St. Gregory's patron, to teach European history and academic German to prep school boys, which he did—at least according to legend—with immediate flamboyance and eventual popularity. Actually, his initiation had not been easy, his refined Viennese manner being perceived as haughty and arrogant, and it was not until he returned to Vienna at the start of the Great War and then came back in 1920, humbled by injury and nearly wrecked by the harrowing experience, that he began to work his way into school legend.

Then, in 1957, the old man's history lessons, those rich historical vignettes—"Hazings" the St. Greg's boys called them, "the world according to the Haze"—had an unexplainable appeal and did indeed begin filling the young Herr Burden's blank slate.

More than a teacher, the Haze was like an evangelist in his prime, delivering the good news. He was a one-man cultural force in St. Greg's boys' educational lives, three generations of them, who knew their European history cold, especially his proprietary corner of that history. Essays in his classes were called *feuilletons*, and the group of the most talented students who gathered about him perpetually he called, with a flourish, *Jung Wien*, after the artists and intellectuals who gathered in the cafés of his beloved city. Those talented young protégés went on to Harvard mostly, and then to distinguished lives of business and service. St. Greg's boys knew their European history, for sure, but most of all they knew about Vienna. Too many eminent Bostonians to number credited those Hazings as the primary inspiration for their luminous careers: one former governor of Massachusetts, a former U.S. senator, a museum director, a former Massachusetts attorney general and state supreme court justice, a novelist, countless Boston financiers, and many university scholars, to mention a few. The relationship with this charismatic old man accounted for the beginnings of Wheeler's knowledge of Vienna and, one might say, for his yearning to travel there, his desire—matched by hundreds of St. Greg's boys—to see for himself. "It was a time of delusive splendor," the Haze would say alluringly, "a whole glorious way of life teetering on the edge of the abyss, totally oblivious to its own nearness to extinction. But what splendor!"

&@&

Every St. Gregory's boy knew cold the gospel according to the Haze. And Wheeler was no exception. In his early days in 1897 Vienna, we know from his journal entries, Wheeler felt strangely well prepared for this bizarre experience, the lectures echoing in his mind as if his beloved mentor walked the Ringstrasse alongside him, narrating. He found himself so able to identify dress styles, buildings, parks, and landmarks that he knew exactly where he was, and exactly when, well before actually stopping at a kiosk in front of the opera house to read the title *Neue Freie Presse* and the day's date on one of the myriad newspapers.

The Haze's version went like this. In the 1850s, in a burst of civic liberalism, the Viennese, under the leadership of Emperor Franz Joseph, had decided to tear down the fortifying walls that had totally encircled the inner city since the early Middle Ages. And in place of the ancient barriers they constructed a broad and majestic boulevard, giving the city the burst of vitality and life that defined the end of the century. The resplendent Ringstrasse, one of the wonders of Europe, a monument to science, industrial superiority, and rational order, opened officially in 1865. The magnificent surrounding buildings, unmatched anywhere in the world, were begun and completed by the 1880s.

The wealthy industrial middle class came to power and established a constitutional regime identified with capitalism, industrialists, and Jews, who streamed into the city, finding release from the oppression they had endured elsewhere, as well as equality, opportunity, and aesthetic stimulation. The wealthy bourgeois city fathers shared their power gracefully with the aristocracy and the imperial bureaucracy.

The expansive magnificence, lined with plane trees, glorious in all directions, was too broad to be plagued by the crowded bustling of other European cities. "The Ringstrasse," the Haze would exclaim. "Here paraded indeed a most astounding variety of elegant humanity. Riding in carriages, bustling or strolling casually, brightly dressed military officers in an endless variety of colorful uniforms, handsome men in silk top hats, and women, the beauty of whom legend had not exaggerated." And St.

Greg's boys had no trouble imagining such a scene. All because of their Venerable Haze.

No one in the St. Gregory's academic community could explain the usefulness of knowing so many details about just one of the European cities, especially a second-tier one for those who favored Paris and London, but St. Greg's boys knew them nonetheless. "The best-dressed army in history," Wheeler remembered the Haze saying with a touch of irony, "poised on the edge of ignominious defeat. One could go nowhere in Vienna—a café, a restaurant, a table in the Prater, the city's expansive public park—without being surrounded by military uniforms. In colorful dress and puffery they led the world, with the emperor himself dressed most grandly of all."

Now, dislocated in time, Wheeler Burden stared in amazement as he walked past the spacious greens and the grandeur of the enormous public buildings and the new magnificent apartments, the whole area burst with life, the intended ideal. Now, in the Haze's Vienna, descriptions and musings from the master's precious "Random Notes" seemed to leap into Wheeler's brain, not as abstract curiosities for understanding modern history, but as details for survival. To this visitor from another time, the city whose splendor and vitality had existed only in fantastic stories and the perorations of his eccentric old prep school teacher spread out before him in vivid reality. Here before him stood the massive and ornate marble-façaded buildings, nearly all constructed in the last thirty years and representing that burst of confidence and cultural energy unparalleled in the rest of Europe. The very air of imperial magnificence and bourgeois grandeur that the Haze had described so many times now appeared before Wheeler without irony, with absolutely no sign of anything gone awry, provided one stayed out of the city's depressing and grimy poorer quarters.

During his forty-plus years at St. Gregory's, the old Austrian eccentric had kept a loose-leaf binder of reflections about Viennese life in the waning years of the Hapsburg Empire that he called his "Random Notes"—a collection of *feuilletons*, you might say—that he was constantly refining and reading to his students. "If you understand fin-de-siècle Vienna," he drummed into three generations, "you understand modern history." His eyes would then dart around the room to make certain that every boy's attention was fixed where it ought to be. "It was the *grandeur* that was important," the Haze would intone, imbedding that word in his audience's collective psyche. "It was the *grandeur*."

In moments of special poignancy and drama, the Haze would produce his prized source, the "Little Book," he called it, a slim and aged black volume from which he would read with great reverence. "This is from the fin de siècle," he would say admiringly, and then read a passage that to his mind perfectly captured the flavor of turn-of-the-century Vienna, every student hanging on every elegant phrase. "Writing gets no better than this," he would say in concluding and closing the book, often with tears in his eyes. The formal title of the sacred slim volume was *City of Music*, by a Mr. Jonathan Trumpp, but no one ever remembered the title; it was simply the Haze's revered "Little Book." And how every St. Greg's boy knew, loved, and quoted from that book. He would hold the volume in his slender artistic fingers and open to a predetermined page. "Let us see what our eloquent Mr. Trumpp has for us," he would say, or, "Let us enjoy the magic of the 'Little Book,'" and then he would read some perfectly delicious description of the cultural life of turn-of-the-century Vienna. "Isn't that writing absolutely exquisite?" And over the years his *Jung Wien*, sophisticated private school boys who could be cynical about so much in their lives, rarely directed any of their derision at the "Little Book."

It all made Vienna at the turn of the century a fascinating place to witness what turned out to be the decline from cultural heights into chaos. "Fascinating," said the Haze to young intellects, the children of Boston Brahmins, only beginning to grasp his message. "For an impressionable young idealist," the Haze added, in a piece of self-deprecating biography, "it was horrifying."

By the time of his actual visit to the great city, Wheeler's knowledge of the Haze's loose-leaf binder, his "Random Notes," was greater than what one could have expected of the rough-hewn and eccentrically informed adolescent from the provinces he had been in 1957. Before the Haze's death in 1965, the old man had inexplicably willed the notebook and all his other books and papers to Wheeler Burden. Exactly why no one really understood, especially considering all the illustrious St. Gregory's alumni and avowed Haze disciples he had to choose from.

"What ever happened to the Haze's 'Random Notes,'" alumni would inevitably ask, "and what ever became of his marvelous 'Little Book'?" Then someone would have to explain that all of the Haze's "papers," books included, ended up in the hands of that strange Burden kid from California. After Wheeler became famous, the bequest made a little more sense, but still not much. In fact, it remained a complete puzzlement, until, that is, the 1988 appearance of the great book.

Five years after the Haze's death, in 1970, Wheeler, by then a rising rock music phenomenon, showed the black binder to an imperious young editor from the small Athenaeum Press in Boston, who had made a special appointment and a special trip to San Francisco. "Have you read this?" the editor said, pointing to the bulging pages of the binder, as if its contents were outside the bounds of a Woodstock star's comprehension.

"Of course I've read it," Wheeler said. "I have lived and breathed it."

The editor looked wide-eyed, having discovered in one casual reading what every St. Gregory's boy had discovered over an entire prep school career. "There are a lot of parallels here," he said, failed by words. "The music, the arts, the radical politics of turn-of-the-century Vienna feels like today—Woodstock, antiwar protests, the rise of the arts." He paused, as if it were more than the mind could encompass. Then, as if reading from some preordained script, he offered, "We want to give you a contract. We will publish it, and we want you to be the editor. It's a big job." And Wheeler committed to work on pulling together his beloved mentor's scribbled observations, a task that would come to consume almost fifteen years—in fact, the last fifteen years—of his life. And for some unexplained reason, Athenaeum Press waited patiently.

So it was that in the late 1980s, years after the passing of the Venerable Haze, the "Random Notes" finally appeared in print. What had been for prep school boys the collected reflections and reminiscences that inspired the beginnings of an understanding of modern history became, when pulled together in one volume, as the *Boston Globe* reviewer said, "the poignant and prescient descriptions of the end of an era, profound and detailed reflections of a remarkable observer who spent the first third of his life thinking his culture a fantastic pinnacle of civilization and the remaining two-thirds uncovering exactly how it was all the cruelest of illusions." The lessons of these essays, it was agreed by most critics, were ones for our own time. Partially because of the book's timeliness and insight and partially because of the fame of its editor, Wheeler Burden's refashioning of the Haze's "Random Notes" became a national best seller. It brought with it a renewed fame and notoriety for a reclusive rock-and-roll icon, a "second coming," as his mother called it, that would become fatal.

For the title of the surprise 1988 hit Wheeler chose simply *Fin de Siècle*.

4

Young Vienna

n 1683, the last mighty Turkish army, the Muslim scourge from the east, attacked Vienna and laid siege for six months. It was a horrible affair that took the walled city to the point of near-starvation before the invaders saw the approaching Polish army and fled home, leaving behind bags of green beans the Viennese thought to be camel food. To an enterprising Pole, a man of the world named Franz Georg Kolschitsky, who had risked his life to summon the savior army, the city owed a favor. Kolschitsky had traveled in the Ottoman Empire and, knowing what the bags were, asked for and was given the seemingly worthless beans. He roasted them. With his personal spoils of war, he organized a small shop to sell the brew from those beans, and the first coffeehouse was introduced to Vienna and Western Europe.

At first, the sensitive Viennese thought the dark Turkish brew bitter and offensive, but when Kolschitsky thought to add sugar and sweet whipped cream to the mix, he created a new Viennese addiction. In the years that followed, Kolschitsky's establishment, the Blue Bottle, became the gathering place of the intelligentsia, and in time it spawned numerous imitators. At the close of the nineteenth century, in a city with a long-standing housing shortage, clean, well-lighted places to congregate were highly valued.

Two hundred and some odd years after that final siege by the Turks, Wheeler Burden, new to Vienna himself and with no place to go, found the famous descendant of Kolschitsky's coffeehouse, Café Central. For a vagrant, it was a godsend. And from his first day, he staked out his territory. He was tired of walking and was beginning to feel lost and out of place. The moment he entered he knew he had found a home. The air was warm and carried the rich fragrance of fresh coffee. The tiled floor and marble tables were the prototype from which so much of the American sense of first class derived. Everywhere he looked were well-dressed, intellectual-looking men and a scattering of women, either in groups or alone, reading the abundant newspapers or talking animatedly. "There were no fewer than forty-five newspapers in Vienna," the Haze would say, "and a well-appointed café, of which there were too many to enumerate, would subscribe to all of them. And for the small price of a cup of sweetened coffee or mineral water one could pass an entire morning catching up on the news."

Wheeler chose a table and sat, picking up the newspaper in front of him. A friendly young man at an adjoining table motioned to him. "Are we English?" he asked with a thick Germanic accent.

"American," Wheeler replied.

The group of four at the table laughed and poked each other with good-natured elbowing that reminded Wheeler of his mean-spirited schoolmates his first year in private school in Boston. He smiled back guardedly, "But I speak German," he said in their language.

The young man looked at him cheerfully. "Then you must have heard us," he said. "My friends insisted you were English. I thought you were French, and von Tscharner there"—he pointed to one of the smiling faces—"thought you were a Czech nationalist. We see Americans so rarely here in our men's club," he said, gesturing to the expansiveness of the café.

"Except for your famous countryman Mark Twain, who seems to be filling our newspapers these days," one of the young men added cheerfully. Wheeler was reminded suddenly that the famous writer had indeed moved with his family to Vienna for a year and a half sometime around the turn of the century.

"You are our first unfamous American," another said. "We didn't know what to make of you."

"Perhaps tomorrow you will join us." He held out his hand. "My name is Ernst Kleist. I am the would-be world-renowned painter of the group."

Wheeler took the hand. "My name is—" He paused. "Harry Truman." Why he said it he was not sure, but the words were out before he could stop them.

"Would you join us then, Mr. Truman? There is always one or another of us at this table. We do have our business to do, believe it or not, to make livings or earn our degrees, but we gather here whenever we can."

He gestured to his friends. "Those are the new generation of Viennese, a quartet." He laughed. "We represent the four points of the great Viennese intellectual compass. Karl Claus there is the visceral one, a writer. You know how they are. Always finding connections. He engages the world through his feelings and is forever finding and defending causes." The young man at Kleist's left smiled and stuck out his hand, acknowledging the description.

"Von Tscharner here is the tinkerer, the pragmatic one. He is our architect, redesigning the atrocious inner city. For him, if it works, it is good." The young man named von Tscharner took Wheeler's hand and shook it vigorously.

"And Schluessler over there," Kleist continued, "is our scientist, our Cartesian: he thinks, therefore he is. He is a university student, a genius in physics, rewriting Newton's laws of the physical world. For him, everything has to be rational."

"And you, Herr Kleist?" Karl Claus inquired buoyantly. "How do you describe yourself?"

"I am the intuitive one," Kleist said without hesitation. "I guess you'd say the one who jumps to conclusions and is a mortal annoyance to Schluessler and his rationalists because with no apparent reasoning I am more often right than not."

Schluessler jumped in. "Annoying, yes, but Herr Kleist and his friends are rewriting the rules of oil and canvas to make the world forget the Parisians. He and his friend Klimt."

"Ah," said von Tscharner the architect, "but he is better than Klimt, for sure."

"When this group gets too serious," Kleist said, "I am the one who adds the leaven to the loaf." He looked around proudly. "We represent all stations." He paused and patted his chest with a broad mocking smile. "We are the *Jung Wien*, the Young Vienna, you Americans would say."

Wheeler stared. These were the sons of the *haute bourgeoisie* that the Haze had talked so much about, the famous aesthetic offspring of the parvenu industrial giants and bankers, the ascendant liberals of Vienna who had built the Ringstrasse over the past forty years. Raised by their parents in affluence and materialism, surrounded by works of art, music, and literature, these cultured sons shunned the financial world of their forebears and took up the creative and intellectual life. The grandfather was a peddler from Kiev, who thrived after the establishment of the constitutional monarchy in 1848; the father built the business into an industry; and the sons were born into the luxury it created. Those sons grew up in interesting homes, with fascinating houseguests and dinner conversations, surrounded by art. Having very little interest in the business practices of their rich and powerful fathers, for them aesthetics were everything. It was they who made famous the Viennese coffeehouses, and it was from their ranks that emerged the great intellectual and aesthetic movements that so distinguished Vienna at the turn of the century. The Haze himself took enormous pride in having been a latter-day member of this prestigious group, *Jung Wien*, he also called it.

"I would be honored to join you during my stay in Vienna," Wheeler said.

"I look forward to getting to know you, Mr. Truman." Ernst Kleist looked back over his shoulder.

A young man came bursting through the door, as if late for an appointment. "Aha," said Kleist, "our last member. Here is the one who brings it all together, our glue, our Renaissance man, our multifaceted genius, too eclectic to pin down to any category, if he can remember to join us. Herr Truman," he said with a flourish, "may I present our philosopher, Herr Egon Wickstein."

Wheeler fixed on the young man with wild eyes and rumpled hair, carrying a small leather portfolio overstuffed with papers. "Wickstein?" He stared involuntarily. "That's Egon Wickstein," he said without thinking.

"You know Wickstein?" Kleist said, surprised.

Wheeler caught himself from bursting out with an *are you kidding?* and paused to collect himself. "I know his family," Wheeler said hastily, struggling to take his eyes away, "very indirectly."

"Egon," Kleist said, "this is my new American friend, Mr. Harry Truman. He knows your family, *very indirectly*." The young man looked at him distractedly, awaiting an explanation, and offered his hand. Wheeler took it and found himself staring into the eyes of the most famous philosopher of the twentieth century.

Wheeler felt a rush of embarrassment. Could he ever explain how he knew this young man, how he would grow up to be a sensation, an intellectual giant, how he had nearly gotten Wheeler thrown out of Harvard College? He shook his outstretched hand. "Actually," he said with confidence, "I had just been told that you were someone to look up if one were serious about philosophy."

The young man seemed a little surprised, but satisfied with the explanation. "I'm glad to meet you, Mr. Truman, and glad that at least someone thinks me serious. It's not easy being a university student in this city"—he pointed back to his friends behind him—"surrounded by all these self-appointed highbrow critics."

Kleist slapped him on the back with a good-natured laugh. "My friend is modest, Mr. Truman. He is our best student. The rest of us peck away at ideas. Egon brings the encyclopedia with him."

As the men chattered amiably around him at the table in the coffeehouse, Wheeler began to piece together all he remembered of the famous Egon Wickstein, whose life would end tragically. Years later, posthumously, Wickstein would enter significantly into Wheeler's life, when a young Harvard professor would accuse him of plagiarizing a paper from the famous philosopher. And here he was standing by his table at the Café Central. How close he had come to making a huge faux pas. And it was then, at that moment, that Wheeler had the first inkling of the thought: how easy it would have been to have blurted out something unthinking, as he almost did by simply recognizing the name with such enthusiasm. How easy it would be to say something to the young man that he would never forget, to plant a seed that might change the course of his life and change, even if only minutely, the flow of European intellectual history.

What effect would it have, he began to conjecture, if he walked up to this rather pretentious but charming young Egon Wickstein and told him he was destined to be famous, as both a thinker and a martyr? Would it not change the course of his life? Would it not change his actions just enough to alter imperceptibly the course that was to eventually carry him to his fate?

Such power, Wheeler thought lightly as he returned to the rich aroma emanating from his newly filled coffee cup. Wheeler felt elated, a new man in a new city, with a new lease on life. But, he knew now, he would have to be careful.

Wheeler would have thought more about this idea of changing history if he had not suddenly noted a disturbing turn of events. The stern young man whose clothes he was wearing had entered the café and was heading directly toward his table. Wheeler lifted the newspaper and hid his face in it as the man chose a table only a few yards from him. The man motioned imperiously to the waiter, then looked around the café, his eyes passing over Wheeler's buried face, then ordered his coffee and reached for a paper of his own. A cold shudder ran through Wheeler as he thought of the look in the young man's eyes. He rose, with his back to the man, then checked furtively over his shoulder to see if he had been noticed. The man seemed intent on his paper, but periodically looked up expectantly as if watching for someone. He had not seemed to notice Wheeler. Perhaps the shave and haircut had altered his appearance enough that he wouldn't be recognized, but he wasn't going to test the idea. With his head down, he said good-bye to his new friends, committed to returning tomorrow, and then abruptly left.

As Wheeler got to the door of the Café Central, apparently unnoticed, he paused for a moment and looked back to see his young adversary joined by a handsome, well-dressed man in his fifties. The two chatted familiarly, then sat down together and began what appeared to be a comfortable continuance of a conversation. The threat of being noticed by his new enemy and the unexpected excitement of meeting Egon Wickstein were too much on his mind for Wheeler to pay much attention to the meeting of the two men, a fateful one.

5

Wheeler-Dealer Kid

 oys' organized baseball, called Little League, was just starting up in the rural Sacramento Valley in 1953, the year
that Wheeler turned twelve in sixth grade. Walter Hefley,
who owned the Standard station on B Street and who sold
Wheeler's mother the gas and oil for the ranch, was coaching one of the
inaugural teams, the Indians they were to be called, and talked her into
letting Wheeler play. "Hear the boy has a pretty darn good arm," he said,
as he showed her the oil level on her dipstick. "I'll drive the lad home after
the practices on days you can't." Fair enough, she decided, but not without taking the opportunity to remind her son, realizing that it would be
totally lost on the very literal Walter Hefley, that after the brutalizing the
American settlers had done to the native inhabitants in the last century,
Indians did not seem an appropriate name for a group of impressionable
American boys.

"Only a game, Mrs. Burden," Hefley said when she asked, reinserting
the dipstick.

"It's only a game, Mother," Wheeler reiterated back home, preoccupied with loosening up his father's old glove, which he had found among
some military clothes and mementoes in a trunk in the attic. "Did Father
have a pretty good fastball?" he asked.

Wheeler's mother had no idea what a fastball was, let alone if her late
husband had possessed one. She had met Wheeler's father before the war
in London. Fresh out of Harvard Law School, he was recruited by the
U.S. Navy as a representative to the early version of Lend-Lease, before
American entry. That had been after he was a prep school and college
sports hero and before he was the legendary Rouge Gorge, hero of the
French Resistance, who had preserved the secrets of the Allied invasion

and inspired a generation with his heroic death at the hands of the Gestapo.

"I'll bet he did."

Flora Burden was shameless in her ignorance of American culture and
sports. "Is it something important?"

"A fastball? For an American boy," Wheeler said patiently, "it is."

"Well then, I am sure he had one. Your father was splendid at everything."

That was good enough for Wheeler. "My father had a great fastball,"
he would say convincingly, as if he had seen it himself. "I will have one
too."

Before the season Frank Standish Burden III had been Standish to his
mother, Stan at school. That first season with the Little League Indians
was when he got his name, and when he first learned to throw the prongball. Bucky Hannigan, who would become his great friend, was the
catcher. Bucky would have been pitcher, but he had lost one finger and
part of a second on his right hand playing with blasting caps in fifth grade.
The day before the first game Walter Hefley said to a group of boys, "Who's
going to pitch for us?" And Bucky said that the skinny English kid could
throw the ball pretty damn hard. "Let's watch our language," Walter Hefley had said, and wrote down "Mrs. Burden's lad" in the starting lineup.
Coach Hefley wasn't much with names.

The first pitch Wheeler ever threw in a game was the next day. It left
his small slender hand opportunely, you might say, and flew over the
heads of the batter, the catcher, and the umpire, who showed his inexpe-
rience behind the plate by yelling, "Look out!" as the ball whizzed past
them. The last pitch Wheeler Burden ever threw, eight years later, was
legend and many say it was one of the finest pitches ever thrown, regardless of age group and league. That last one, it is said, traveled at more than
ninety miles an hour, headed for the upper inside corner of the strike
zone, then dropped two to three feet and caught the lower outside corner.
"Willie Mays would have had a hard time with it," a baseball writer for the
Boston Globe would write. Such baseball history was not foretold, however, by Wheeler's second life pitch, nor his third, both of which sailed,
similar to the first, far from the intended target and ended up at the backstop. The third errant pitch caused Coach Hefley to take the first walk of
his life to the pitcher's mound.

"This is new to all of us, son," Walter said with the ball in his large hand. "You might want to rein it in just a bit." He was aware of the large responsibility he had laid on a twelve-year-old boy's shoulders, but he wasn't sure what to do about it. And he placed the ball back in Stan Burden's small preadolescent hand. Walter had never coached a team before, and had barely played the game himself. He had no son of his own. He was a widower who spent most of his time at the gas station, where he had to haggle mercilessly with Wheeler's mother over the bulk price of his product every year when the ranch's gasoline and diesel contract came due.

By contrast, Bucky Hannigan seemed to know exactly what to do. Baseball was new to everyone, it seemed, except Bucky, who now imagined himself a major league catcher, Roy Campanella of the Brooklyn Dodgers being his inspiration and model. Bucky knew his job was to settle down his pitcher. He was in his crouch behind the plate, waiting for the pitch. He spat on the ground, rubbed his crotch, and called out in a nasal twang that Stan's mother figured was a tradition for American boys. "Chuck to me, wheeler-dealer," Bucky Hannigan called out, since he too had not yet learned the skinny English boy's Christian name. "Chuck-fire, kid. Chuck fire, wheeler-dealer kid." And the English boy focused on the mitt with hawklike eyes, pulling himself in from wherever it was he had traveled. *Concentrate*, he said to himself. When he threw the ball this time, it was with sufficient accuracy and hardness that it made a popping sound in Bucky's catcher's mitt. Walter Hefley smiled and nodded in the direction of the boy's mother.

The more Bucky would call out his "chuck-fire, wheeler-dealer" litany, the more Stan would throw the ball to the center of the mitt. "I think we've got ourselves a pitcher here, Mrs. Burden," Walter Hefley said after the game, with a broad contented smile. Flora Burden was still wondering if the team couldn't have chosen a more appropriate name.

On the way home in the car Stan Burden had a hard time containing himself to the front seat. "That's the answer," he said, as if his mouthful of a three-part Boston Brahmin family name had been the question for him for a long time. "Wheeler-Dealer Kid. That's my new name, all right." And he looked over at his mother in the way an early Christian saint might have looked when he was receiving the stigmata. "From now on I will be called Wheeler." And so it was.

Although totally unfamiliar with this strange American sport of baseball in general and the new youth version of it in particular, Flora could
recognize immediately the enchantment in her son's eyes as he played,
and she loved it. She adjusted quickly to watching him throw the baseball,
the *fastball*, she concluded, and imagined her son's father as a boy in Boston doing the same thing.

The other thing that stuck besides her son's name was the prongball.
He learned it late in the season from Bucky Hannigan, who had always
imagined himself throwing it and would have, had it not been for the
misfortune with the blasting cap. "Hold the ball like so," Bucky had said,
making a fork with the two good fingers of his left hand. "Lay some good
wet ones on the spot just between the label and the stitching. Here." He
dropped a huge gob of spit onto the ball. "You keep working that spot, if
the ump don't catch you, which he won't 'cause you're just a kid. When
it's good and slick, the ball pops out between the two fingers like a watermelon seed, with no spin." He squeezed his fingers and let the ball pop
out. "With your speed and no spin, the ball'll hop all over the damn place.
No one'll ever hit you."

"Let's watch our language," Wheeler said.

The first game he tried it, he walked ten batters. Bucky, whose job it
was to catch the erratic pitches, was ecstatic. "You see that thing jump
around?" he exclaimed as Wheeler was coming off the mound after a wild
inning.

Seeing the erratic trajectories and thinking the boy had lost his stuff,
Coach Hefley moved Wheeler to the outfield and put in Robert Collins,
who gave up three home runs on five pitches. That was the last game of
the season, and the Indians lost to the Pirates twenty-three to three.

"Now what'd you go and show him that for?" Coach Hefley said to
Bucky after the game, when he heard about the new pitch. "Here's a kid
who can throw the ball straighter an' faster'n anyone's ever seen, and now
he'll be experimenting all the time." He paused, scratching his head. "You
know the way he is."

"A historic day," Wheeler declared on the way home, his head still full
of impressions of the ball snapping out like a watermelon seed between
his two slathered fingers. "Didja see that thing move?"

His mother looked back at him blankly, her own head still full of the incongruity of pirates playing baseball against Indians and wondering suddenly if perhaps Dilly's old friend Winston Churchill would have known what on earth her son was talking about.

Winston Churchill, son of an American mother and genuine admirer of many things American, most definitely would have.

Wheeler, his remarkable pitching arm, and his ancient glove gained notoriety in the Sacramento Valley during the next few years, a notoriety that would persist through Wheeler's sophomore year at Feather River Union High School.

Walter Hefley, who retired from coaching after that first year of Little League, usually mentioned Wheeler when he pumped Flora's gas. "The boy's a wonder, Mrs. Burden," he would say, and then she knew what was coming next. "If he could just be a little more conventional."

But being conventional, she knew, was just not in her son's makeup, a fact she rather relished. When he was in that same sixth grade year, he decided he was going to call the governor of California to give him his opinion on capital punishment. He asked the local operator to put him through to Governor Earl Warren, but she got only as far as the lieutenant governor's office. At that point, Wheeler began speaking for himself, and he got through to the lieutenant governor, a man named Goodwin Knight. The two of them had a long series of conversations about politics that stretched over the next ten years until long after Earl Warren had moved to the Supreme Court and Goodwin Knight had become governor of California himself. "You're the only kid I know," said Bucky Hannigan, "who if he don't like what's going on, he calls the goddam gov'ner."

"Let's watch our language," Wheeler said.

Sometimes in the middle of a ball game, Wheeler would tap his glove and walk over to first base and ask the opposing player how he had hit his pitch. Or he'd stop by third base at the end of an inning to ask an opposing coach what he thought about taxation or birth control or the role of religion in Western history. Most people were amused by him, and nearly all marveled at his ability to throw the baseball. That single and extraordinary talent gave young Wheeler Burden a lot of leeway.

"He's got lots to say" was his high school coach's way of explaining why Wheeler couldn't just pitch and keep his mouth shut. "Nobody cares about all those ideas, son," he'd say. "They just want you to throw the ball."

Once, when he was on a road trip to Bakersfield with a summer all-star team, he placed a call to Chet Huntley, the famous newsman, after an evening *Huntley-Brinkley Report*, talked his way through the switchboard, and conversed for almost an hour, running up a whopping bill for his hotel room. When his coach asked him about the call the next day, Wheeler said, "I thought he was wrong about Venezuela oil."

Wheeler made the all-county baseball team his sophomore year in high school, the first Feather River boy to do that since Ray Webster, who ended up with the real Indians in the major leagues. Now the most famous kid in town due to his fastball and a few minutes' illicit instruction from Bucky Hannigan, Wheeler's way in life seemed assured. No one in the town understood what happened next.

"His mom—she was English, you know—come up with sending him off to that fancy school in the east. Wanted him to go to Harvard," his best friend and catcher Bucky Hannigan said years later when asked to explain to the *Rolling Stone* reporter what had happened to Wheeler's world-class fastball and major league promise.

"Sometimes, God's gifts go to the wrong people," said his old high school coach in the same article. "It was all that mythology and Victor Hugo crap that ruined the boy. Wheeler Burden was always a first-class flake. But, jeezus, could he throw hard."

It was right about that time that his mother's extraordinary book was born. On one of their long walks in the bottomland, Wheeler began talking mythology, one of his favorite subjects at age twelve. His grandmother in Boston had given him a copy of Edith Hamilton's *Mythology* for his ninth birthday with a note: "My dear Stan, I think you will find this according to your tastes," and of course he had devoured it, in between Victor Hugo novels, and for a time, he could not have a conversation, see a movie, or read a newspaper article without referring to one Greek myth or another. One day, in the middle of one of their walks, he said, "Why doesn't anyone think of Persephone's side of the story?" His mother, long accustomed to the stream of thoughts that came from her son if she simply asked a prompting question or two, said, "What exactly is Persephone's side of the story?" and out came a most remarkable string of thoughts that Flora went home and immediately wrote down in her notebook, not realizing at first the conversation's critical role in her own life.

The young mythologist's point was essentially that Persephone, the beautiful young daughter of Demeter, the goddess of the harvest, when forcefully abducted by Hades, the god of the underworld, and taken away to his dark kingdom, is put in an awful fix. When her mother goes into mourning, the world is thrown into dark infertility, perpetual winter. Zeus gets involved and strikes a deal. Persephone can return to her mother for part of the year but will stay in the underworld as queen for part of the time. "She's in a very bad position," Wheeler said. "She has to be a little girl for her mother half the time and a big queen for her husband half the time. I don't think anyone has been too interested in her side of the story."

Over the course of the next few walks, Wheeler and his mother explored the subject in more depth. On each return to the house Flora wrote more and more in her notebook, until she and her son had pretty much exhausted Persephone's point of view.

One day, not long after, Flora Burden had one of the strangest visits of her life. She was sitting in the ranch office, working on the books, when a man in a dark suit and tie came in asking for her. He introduced himself as Smallwood or Woodcock, or some such, and said he represented a small academic press on the East Coast. He had heard that she had been a student of Sigmund Freud in London and asked if she might wish to write a book derived from the experience. Flora explained that she had not actually been a student of Freud's per se, but that she had been a psychiatry student in general, had been an admirer of Freud's work, and had been in the inner circle of Londoners who had arranged for his move there in 1938.

"Did you actually meet him?" the man asked.

"Of course," Flora answered a little dismissively, and she could see a look of genuine admiration on the man's face. "I would not have missed *that*."

"Well then, would you consider writing a book for us?"

At first, Flora insisted that there was not a book in her future. "I'm not that sort," she said. "Thank you very much." But then she saw the fat

Persephone notes sitting on her desk. "There's just this," she said quickly, and handed it to Mr. Smallwood or Woodcock or whomever, who was staying the night at a local motel.

He came back the next day with a wild look in his eye. "This is it," he said. "This is the book we were hoping for."

And so Flora Burden worked for a year refining the ideas in her notes that Persephone represented the plight of the modern woman, raised by a patriarchal society to be the dutiful daughter, but expected by the responsibilities of the changing world to be the independent sovereign of her own life. "The counterweight to Freud's Oedipus complex," a reviewer in *The New Yorker* would say, "modern woman taking charge of her own destiny." After much struggle with herself and further conversations with her son, *Persephone Rising* was born, published in 1955 in a thin volume under a pseudonym. It was Flora's first literary effort, and it established her, a few years later, as one of the first voices, along with Betty Friedan's *Feminine Mystique*, in the American feminist movement. More than forty years later the book was still read on college campuses, and the pseudonymous Flora Standish was still getting speaking invitations, most of which she turned down, at places like Berkeley and Northampton, Massachusetts, and Montreal. In all the times she appeared to talk about her book, as an act of motherly protection, she never really credited her main source, a somewhat erratic and hyperkinetic twelve-year-old boy who did little to control the stream of ideas that came when walking with his mother in the Sacramento Valley bottomlands. And she never talked about or explained the book's dedication: "For Dilly."

6

Going East

he idea of Wheeler's going east for his last two years of high school had been something of an armistice between his mother and his Boston grandmother. The grandmother had wanted young Standish to come board at St. Gregory's, where his father and grandfather, her husband, had gone. Wheeler was, after all, the last male to bear the Burden name, and he ought to get some sense of the family tradition. But the grandmother seemed to accept Flora's argument that selfishly, perhaps, she wanted her son and only child near her during the impressionable years of adolescence. Actually, Flora wanted her young son to have nothing to do with the Burden family as long as the cruel and bigoted old grandfather was around.

Wheeler's mother had never liked the Burdens, St. Greg's, Harvard, or Boston, for that matter, knowing very little about them except for their influence on her husband, who—in spite of the fact that she had loved him desperately—had been very poorly served, she thought, by the combination. In fact, she had thought the whole business of schoolboy heroics, preserving tradition, and rigid sense of duty a dreadful influence that had probably contributed to his heroic and totally unnecessary death. All that duty and honor had taken a perfectly nice and bright young man and convinced him that he had to give his life for some cause. She did not like it, did not want her son to have any of it, and she put up stolid resistance.

But when the stern old grandfather Frank Burden died in 1956, during Wheeler's freshman year in high school, Flora changed her mind about her son's receiving the benefits of a cultured education in Boston. And when it came right down to it, she had always found Mrs. Burden thoughtful and considerate, and—very much like Flora herself—a generally nononsense sort of woman. It was just the thought of her being married to that awful man that soured Flora's every impression. Now, the specter of him out of the way, the proper Mrs. Burden wanted Wheeler to learn Latin and German and wanted him to get some European history. She had always wanted him to be near her, a thought she had been expressing delicately and faithfully every month in letters. Flora, a woman famous for her resolve—sometimes thought of as stubbornness—finally relented. "There is only so much a single mother and a small farming town can do," she said to Wheeler in putting forward the plan. "And there is more to education than reading all of Victor Hugo and throwing the baseball."

Wheeler, who had suddenly and surprisingly added popular music to his narrow range of passions, had agreed to the plan not because he wanted to learn German and Latin, or because, as the last Burden, he wanted to be closer to his New England roots, but for the simple reason that he thought he would be near his new hero.

It was in the fall of his sophomore year, at a dance in the Feather River Union High School gymnasium, when he'd had another one of those life-altering experiences. The band, brought in from out of town, was playing music Wheeler had never heard before: country-and-western music with a rock-and-roll rhythm. Wheeler listened for two hours, barely able to concentrate on anything but the lead singer's twang and the skip in his voice and the way he wiggled around as he sang. After the dance, he told Bucky Hannigan that the singer was a pure original and a genius. Bucky laughed and looked at him cross-eyed. "He's just copying Tex-Mex," he said. "Sucker's just a poor fella's Buddy Holly."

It was the fall of 1956, when most of the world was going wild over Elvis Presley and had never heard Holly's name. Bucky had family in Lubbock, Texas, and had heard the local star three times. He took Wheeler to the local radio station where the DJ had a tape of Tex-Mex groups and let Wheeler hear the real thing. Wheeler immediately retrieved his father's old Martin guitar from its dusty case in the attic and began learning chords and picking out what he could remember of the songs.

In the spring of that school year when two Buddy Holly songs had made it to the Valley radio and to the national pop charts, he knew that Holly had traveled from Texas to New York City. Having an undeveloped sense of geography and how prep school students spend their time, Wheeler thought a Boston prep school would become a good launching pad for meeting his hero.

Frank Standish Burden III was out of place at St. Greg's. In the words of his dorm master, a hockey player from Bowdoin College, "His classical training is flawed, he can only barely write a coherent sentence, and he has read next to nothing. Would that he could master more than the Frisbee."

The Frisbee remark derived from one of Wheeler's great discoveries upon arriving at St. Gregory's. From the moment he saw a group of the younger boys throwing the brightly colored plastic disks on the school's broad green athletic fields his first weekend, he was captivated. "This must be something of the gods!" he exclaimed famously as his first disk came floating toward him. He did indeed master the skills of throwing and catching almost immediately, eventually earning the name "The Frisbee King," one that stuck with him, especially among those original younger boys, throughout his time at the school.

But the strange young man from California developed nothing else of distinction in those first months, and he would have been asked to leave by Christmas had he not been the only son of Dilly Burden, the greatest hero ever to attend the school, and had he not been befriended by the Haze, the beloved history master, who grabbed hold of Wheeler the moment he set foot on campus as if it had been a sacred assignment.

Shortly after Wheeler's arrival at St. Gregory's, one of the younger boys came to get him in his dormitory room. "The Haze wants to see you," the boy said cheerily. "He's Mr. Esterhazy and he's German or something and he's lived in the dorm forever, but everyone calls him the Haze, although never to his face." Then he paused with a quizzical look. "But I think he already knows you. He says he taught your father and that he knows your family and he is calling you the tabula rasa from California." Wheeler had no idea what the Latin meant, but he sought out the old man anyway.

Wheeler still did not know the Latin an hour or so later when the old man fixed his watery blue gaze on him at the end of their first visit and intoned, "So, Herr Burden, you are here at last, and we begin scratches on your persona, the tabula rasa."

Arnauld Esterhazy seemed to know everything about Wheeler, about the California provinces and small-town public education. Strangely, he also knew about the difficult transition to what his Brahmin grandmother was calling "the classical period" of his education. In fact, it was uncanny how the old man had picked him out and immediately knew all about his Boston grandmother, his hero father, his English mother, the rough details of his boyhood on the Sacramento Valley farm, even his prowess in throwing the baseball. From the moment the Haze sought him out on the first day and reached out his fine-boned hand, Wheeler felt an indefinable kinship and comfort with the old history master, something he had not felt before or later with anyone, regardless of age. It was, he realized much later, the feeling of complete understanding and unconditional acceptance.

The Haze's apartment—his "rooms," the old man called them—was a beautiful oak-paneled arrangement filled with knickknacks, small art treasures, and antiques, at the end of a dormitory corridor. "It's a museum," the boy who delivered Wheeler had said. "He's lived there since he came during the time of Paul Revere," all the boys said. It seemed foreordained that the Haze was taking the young Californian unquestioningly under his wing, and that was that.

"He's always in a tie or ascot, and you'll never see his bare arms," an old boy told Wheeler in his first week. Even though he was near eighty and supposedly retired, Wheeler got the impression that the way the Haze looked and smelled now was the way he had looked and smelled even when he himself was a schoolboy in Vienna.

The boys told scattered tales of his background, most of them filled with grand myths about his having been a spy during World War I, how he had never married because of a long and secret love affair with a prominent Bostonian married woman, about how one of his St. Gregory's boys years ago had actually been his son. But from the broad strokes, Wheeler pieced together the fine realities: how he came to St. Greg's from turn-of-the-century Vienna in the first decade of the century and left mysteriously during the Great War. It was never clear exactly what he did except that sometime after the war's end, he returned to the school, where he had to recuperate—from gassing, some said—for two years before taking on a full load again.

He had hit his stride during the late 1920s and never left, not returning to Europe, even in the summers, except for one ill-fated return in the midfifties, some years after Wheeler's father was killed in Nazi-occupied

France. He had never married and had never even been seen alone with a woman, it was said, although he was considered very social and invited to all the proper homes and parties. On rare occasions, over the years, it was said that he had told one group or another that he held the great Renaissance poet Dante as his model.

Dante had written his monumental *Divine Comedy* on the inspiration of a most beautiful Florentine woman named Beatrice, whom he had kept constantly before him as a vision but whom he had never married, never touched, even, and yet to whom he had remained indelibly faithful. "I am like Dante," the Haze said on those rare occasions. "I have my own Beatrice."

He rowed a single scull on the Charles River during the warm months and skated with the boys or alone in the winter. Through the school's long association with Harvard College, he had full use of Widener Library, where he did research for the writings in his "Random Notes." He was an honored member of the Boston Museum of Fine Arts, and he loved and knew intimately all the European masterpieces found there.

"Life is rich and good, if you study history," he told Wheeler, as he had been telling St. Gregory's boys for almost fifty years, fixing each of them in the affectionate blue fire of those legendary cobalt eyes—Klimt's blue, he himself pointed out. "You know history from your reading of Victor Hugo." Somehow, he knew before Wheeler's arrival that the young man had read all the novels of the great French writer, and *Ninety-Three* more than once. "I know history—" He paused for theatrical effect. "—because I *lived* it." And he parceled out his truth in staccato bursts. Litanies of historical detail as it had really been, history from the yellowed pages of the black binder he seemed to have with him always and that Wheeler, his most notorious pupil, would eventually have published. "My 'Random Notes,' it is called, although it was not really very random. I've worked on it over the years. The world according to Mr. Esterhazy, I've heard some boys call it."

Wheeler's father, Dilly Burden, like his own father before him, had attended St. Gregory's, he from 1926 until 1932, the period Arnauld Esterhazy called his Golden Years. The Haze never hid his admiration of Dilly, but with Wheeler he was purely and simply emotive. "So many people make much of your father's prowess on the athletic field—he taught me to skate, by the way—but it was the acuteness of his mind that we all should memorialize. He was a truly remarkable boy." He paused, obviously calling up images of time past. "A truly remarkable mind."

Also like his father before him and Wheeler after him, Dilly's given name had been Frank Standish Burden, the Standish inherited from the great Puritan leader. Where the Dilly came from no one fully remembered, except that "it's a dilly" was his favorite boyhood expression.

Dilly had sat through the word from the Haze's "Random Notes" as now Wheeler was sitting through it. At Arnauld Esterhazy's funeral in 1965, Dilly's famous maxim had been quoted liberally: "St. Greg's boys will carry the Haze inside forever."

And the sixteen-year-old Wheeler adapted to those classical lessons immediately, in a theoretical way at first, thinking they sounded to him like Victor Hugo plots. "Consider the empire," the Haze would say, and Wheeler became fascinated by its complexity. Once, he even memorized the names of the various Austria-Hungarian nationalities and could rattle them off rapid-fire: "Germans, Ruthenes, Italians, Slovaks, Rumanians, Czechs, Poles, Magyars, Slovenes, Croats, Transylvanian Saxons, Serbs, Bulgarians, and Slavs."

"That's capital, Standish," the old man said with glee, hearing the staccato recitation and laughing. "And the citizens of the multi-empire paraded through the city," the old man would say, "each conversing as he passed in languages and dialects as picturesque as the city itself. They couldn't fight worth a hoot, but they looked simply dashing." And the old man told Wheeler with moist eyes, becoming lost in the thought, "Oh my, how I wish you could see it all for yourself!" And then he would become quiet. "Some day, perhaps."

"I haven't traveled much," Wheeler would say.

"You will," he had said confidently. "It is part of your heritage. Your father traveled to Vienna during his college days. He wrote me wonderful letters. He saw how it was grand and dashing. He grasped the full sense of the old days, of the splendor. And that was it, wasn't it?" He would look at Wheeler as if looking at his own son, someone who understood all that he understood.

"You are the last Burden. We shall have to educate you as to what that means. I taught your father. It will be my job to get you through St. Greg's." His charge, the old man called it: to get this young naïf "up to speed." And quite a charge it was. Wheeler's mind was undisciplined and rangy, his study habits abysmal. "It would help if you could focus," the old man said once in near exasperation. And, to add to the problem, Wheeler seemed to care nothing about conventional success.

In a Boston prep school, one earned the right to be eccentric by coming up through the ranks. Few students joined the school as upperclassmen, and when they did they had to be careful about learning the ropes, and learning ropes had never been even remotely an instinct of Wheeler's. He had no interest in being broken in. To the seniors, St. Greg's first classmen, he was a constant irritant. Wheeler was unconventional and irreverent, with no respect for the time-honored pecking order, qualities hard enough to abide in an old timer let alone an upstart from California.

Wheeler's chief antagonist was a first classman named Prentice Olcott, the school's best athlete and head monitor. In spite of the exterior he showed to the majority of the world, Olcott was to Wheeler mean-spirited and cruel. Their first run-in came at the dinner table, where Olcott was presiding in place of one of the masters. After the first course, Olcott instructed a younger boy, a fourth classman, one of the Frisbee boys, to clear the soup dishes because he did not know the year the school was founded. "I'll help him," Wheeler said good-naturedly. "I didn't know either."

After the meal Olcott came up to him and pushed his index finger into Wheeler's chest. "Listen, pal. You stay out of my business. When I tell an underclassman to do something, it gets done."

"You were picking on the little kid."

Olcott looked furious. "I'm a first classman."

"You're a student here, like the rest of us," Wheeler said to the older boy. Olcott stared hard at him, incredulous that he had been spoken to in that tone.

"You don't get the picture, do you, pal?"

"What picture?" Wheeler said without even a modicum of the expected deference.

That was when the work details started. Whenever work assignments were made, Wheeler's name was on the list. His response to the persecution was simply not to show up. "It's that Prentice Olcott," he told the Haze.

"Don't let him bother you," the old man said, his eyes showing an understanding patience. "His father was imperious, and he is imperious. He's just trying to get your goat. But you had better start performing your assigned chores, and doing what the older boys say. It is just the way things work."

One day in the hall Olcott said, "I'm going to have you out of here by Easter." Then he laughed and snarled. "And your old Viennese faggot won't be able to save your ass. We'll have one less Jew at St. Greg's."

Wheeler eyed him coolly. "Is that it, Olcott? You don't like me because I'm Jewish?" The thought of being Jewish had never really occurred to Wheeler. His mother, whose parents had been Zionists and Marxist socialists in London, gone before Wheeler was born, rarely mentioned her heritage or her family, and they had certainly never practiced any religion together. Growing up in Feather River, Wheeler gave little thought to religion, one way or another. It was only around Boston, where people knew the Dilly Burden legend, that anyone knew or cared that Dilly had married a Jewish girl in London before the war. And it had never occurred to Wheeler that the Haze might be homosexual.

Olcott sneered. "I don't like you, Burden. Because you are an uncouth boor. And because you have no self-control. It doesn't matter to me if you're a hebe, or a spick or a ginni, or even another faggot. You don't belong in this school, and you won't be around for baseball season. That's a promise."

7

Emily James from Amherst

is first evening in Vienna, aware of his limited resources, Wheeler dined alone at a small rustic but clean restaurant off the Ring, near the center of the old city. The proprietor was a tall cadaverous man with a pockmarked face. He seemed polite but in no way inquisitive. Wheeler asked him for a stein of beer and the plate of beef cuts and sauerkraut he saw at the table beside his. He would wait until later for the delights the Haze had glorified for him and the other St. Gregory's boys, the veal schnitzel and fine wine, polished off with a rich Sacher torte and coffee, both *"mit Schlag,* always *mit Schlag,"* the obligatory and fabled sweet whipped cream. Finding himself in no rush, he ordered a second stein of beer and ate slowly, soaking up the juices with the thick brown bread.

After his meal, he took advantage of the light and the clean table and began writing in the journal he had found at a bookseller's stall that afternoon. It was bound in new red leather, with gilded edges, and would have cost a good deal had the first few pages not already been written in. As he paid for it, he asked the bookseller to remove the defiled pages with his penknife. Over the next few weeks he would wonder why he wrote with such care in this handsome book-size volume that he would carry everywhere. He concluded that in his state of disconnection the careful writing gave him a feeling of attachment, as if by detailing the events of his new life he was rooting himself to the place. Perhaps someone in a later time would pick up his journal and know what he had gone through. That thought made him feel not so alone and unhinged.

When he finished writing, he left the restaurant to find an inexpensive hotel even deeper within the old city, in an area where no well-dressed gentleman would venture except for sordid purposes and where no one saw anything out of the ordinary in his lack of identification or baggage. On the way, he wandered the crooked winding streets, some still surfaced in the medieval cobblestones. This was Vienna's shadowy underworld, but to a stranger very much out of place somehow it seemed more enveloping and protecting than the broad, grandly lighted Ringstrasse.

Vienna was and had long been, as the Haze described it, a community of contrasts in which the privations and squalor of the proletarian mass contradicted the splendors of an affluent minority. He understood the reasons for the contrast. In the expansive liberal period in the second half of the nineteenth century, Vienna, like other European cities, had accepted the bounty of industrialization without taking care of its lower classes. The housing situation, like all the living conditions for wageworkers, was intolerably bad. Fewer than one flat in ten boasted a bathroom, and only about one in five had an inside toilet. A quarter of the households sublet sections of their cramped apartments or rented beds only to lodgers, sometimes more than one to a bed. The city's progressive makeover brought on by Karl Lueger and his Christian Socialists had not yet begun. The gas supply for the inner city was still sporadic. The beginnings of a municipally owned electricity works had been erected, but the delivery was still located primarily in the outer Ring area. Costs of utilities to consumers were exorbitant, service intermittent, and the use of electricity in homes was pretty much restricted to the wealthy.

Wheeler's room was small and dark but clean, the bed short, but it did not matter. He fell into a deathlike sleep, wondering if he might emerge from it back in San Francisco, where he belonged. The day had passed and still Wheeler did not remember the event that had launched him on his journey.

He did not awaken until well into the morning. He lay in bed for a time, collecting himself, recalling his entry on the Ringstrasse the day before, adjusting once again to the peculiarity of his situation. At first, he had given little thought to how he had gotten to Vienna; his was not to question, he had figured. But now the questions began to inundate him, and he began wondering. Having no idea how he had arrived, he had no idea how long he was staying, nor when or how he might be yanked back. And most immediately, he had no idea how he was going to support himself in turn-of-the-century Vienna once his money ran out. A number of ideas came and went, some of them simple, some bizarre, but none seeming to have much practicality or appeal. None, save the Frisbee idea.

The previous day, he had passed a cabinetmaker's shop and stepped in and watched, fascinated, the man turning wood with great skill on a primitive foot-powered lathe, and the idea occurred to him. That second morning, Wheeler spent an hour or so on some rough drawings, re-creating as accurately as he could on paper the aerodynamic qualities of the plastic disk with which he had a more than passing familiarity. He took the drawings to a cabinetmaker in the center of the city and asked if the disk could be crafted out of some hard wood. If the wood could be finely enough lathed, then the strength built up with successive coats of lacquer, Wheeler explained, the Frisbee's lightness and aerodynamics could be replicated. The cabinetmaker seemed quite amused, but took the drawings and agreed to take a shot at the desired product. An agreement was struck that Wheeler would return over the next few days and view drafts of the object, until the thickness and shape were right. It was a very satisfying meeting.

It had been such a satisfying meeting, in fact, that as soon as Wheeler stepped back onto the Ringstrasse, his care seemed to vanish. Vienna, the Venerable Haze had told his students, was a city in which people loved to walk and watch people. It was after all an atmosphere that had gained a reputation for nearly half a century of abolishing concerns about hunger, cold, and impermanence.

Somewhat absentmindedly he entered one of the numerous small parks that adjoined the broad Ringstrasse and sat on a bench, content to watch the Viennese, continuing to make himself as inconspicuous as possible. He became fascinated by the faces of the people. What a broad spectrum of humanity they represented. What a rich collection of dialects and languages they spoke. What a simple and gracious elegance they carried with them. He sat by himself in the park for a time and then rose and walked slowly toward the Café Central.

Inside, he noticed that the *Jung Wien* table was empty, so he sat down and picked up the morning's *Neue Freie Presse* and began reading. "Ah, Herr Truman," he heard behind him. "I see you have returned to our men's club." He looked up to see Ernst Kleist smiling as he walked toward the table. They shook hands and Kleist joined him and ordered two coffees. "It seems the others are late to arrive."

Wheeler's attention drifted to the table across the marble floor where he saw the same well-dressed older man who had been the previous day's companion of the stern young man whose clothes Wheeler had stolen. "Who is that?" he said to Kleist. "He looks very important."

"Oh my, yes," said Kleist. "That is the most prominent man in Vienna, our mayor Karl Lueger. You have heard of him, no doubt."

"Some," said Wheeler, "but tell me."

"He is surely one of the most remarkable Viennese, the most popular mayor we have ever had. He's called 'Handsome Karl' because of his splendid presence and charisma. His forebears were peasants and artisans, his father a school custodian. He earned a doctorate in law and was elected to the city council as a Liberal twenty years ago, becoming from the start an outspoken foe of big, moneyed interests, uniting with the working classes to found the Christian Socialist party."

"He sounds like quite a force," Wheeler said.

"A force, yes," Kleist continued. "The only drawback is that he's using extreme anti-Semitism as a political force. A powerful and disruptive one."

Wheeler cringed. "I have heard that. It's not good."

"But it has been extremely effective. And it is a temporary phase, you know. It won't go anywhere. Viennese are extremely good-natured, and we know that things will settle down soon. There are just too many Jews in high places."

"I don't know," Wheeler said glumly. "It doesn't sound good to me. Maybe the mayor knows what he's doing, but someone is going to come along and take all this in a very bad direction." He repressed a shudder.

Even Wheeler did not understand the immediacy of his prediction. He had no way of knowing that the stern young American he had seen with Mayor Lueger had come to Vienna on a mission of which yesterday's meeting in this very café was the first step.

Wheeler left the Café Central in the early afternoon and had strolled back through one of the parks along the Ringstrasse. His focus drifted to a group of young people—wealthy young literati, he figured from their dress, in their early twenties, the kind who frequented coffeehouses and lived the now-legendary lives of sensitive artists. There were three men and four women in animated conversation, meeting in the park before launching some excursion.

One of them, a young woman, caught his attention immediately. She was standing with the group but closest to an artistic young man who seemed at first glance to be doting on her. She stood out from her effete peers as the epitome of the fabled Viennese beauty who had come to life in his Haze-inspired prep school dreams. She was not large framed and Germanically earthy, but full bosomed and small waisted and a touch more delicate than Wheeler's impression of Arnauld Esterhazy's ideal "sweet girl," a true Viennese beauty nonetheless, one worthy of the best gilded canvas of Gustav Klimt. Her skin was pale, and she wore just a trace of natural rouge on her cheeks and lips. There was something about her that struck Wheeler immediately, fatefully, something about the way her eyes sparkled as she spoke the gentle Viennese German that riveted his attention with the compulsion to eavesdrop on every euphonic syllable she spoke. An indescribable attraction radiated from her, something over-powering, the innocent and unattainable sexuality that the Haze's stories had given life in the adolescent fantasies of his oversexed prep school following.

Well-born Viennese women, said the Haze, were compelled to stay aloof and chaste until marriage, repressing whatever fires of passion flared up inside, either acknowledged or subliminal. No matter how libertine or free-thinking their artistic friends, there was a dimension they could neither express nor act upon until after the sanctification of marriage. This fabled repression, needless to say, gave the great Dr. Sigmund Freud and his colleagues most of their practice and the field for their remarkable insights. But it gave the young unmarried women of the Viennese bourgeoisie an irresistible appeal, the Haze told the boys, a subtle and unattainable sensuality.

Well-born Viennese men, on the other hand, compelled in an opposite direction, were encouraged to seek sexual exercise outside their class, despite the threat of dreaded venereal disease from the city's myriad prostitutes, or, more safely, as Arthur Schnitzler had made so public in his fiction, in the warm and easy embrace of a working-class "sweet girl," with whom he tallied up his plentiful sexual encounters, but whom he never considered marrying.

Wheeler had trouble keeping his eyes off her, and once she looked his way, she caught him in one of his enraptured stares. In the instant their eyes met, she did not look furtively away as one might expect from an innocent and pretty Viennese girl being ogled by a stranger in the park. In fact, that very moment when she might have looked away was the moment that she gave him the smile, one of the most remarkable Wheeler, even with all his experience, had ever had directed at him.

It was a Botticelli smile, gone almost before he could look away, at once filled with naïve openness and—far beneath the surface—an astute knowledge of how the world worked. It was the kind of smile that could stay etched on one's mind forever and the kind that made Wheeler know he would be compelled to approach this beautiful Viennese, with some hastily contrived introductory remark, before leaving the park.

"Can you direct me to the Imperial Hotel?" was what he chose, in his most elegant German.

She looked surprised and appraised him quickly with her startling blue eyes. "You sound like an American." Up close, her Viennese dialect sounded even more mellifluous and captivating than it had from the safe remove of the park bench.

"And I thought my German was so good," Wheeler said with the light charm that accounted for much of his comfort with women he had not formally met.

"Your German is perfectly sufficient," she said matter-of-factly, stepping away from her friends. "Your accent just gives you away as an American. That's all."

"I didn't realize Viennese women were trained at spotting Americans."

"I should not dare speak for Viennese women," she said, suddenly in perfect English, throwing her head back in a way that chided gently, *you silly goose*. "I too am an American, like you." She held her hand out forthrightly to Wheeler, who struggled to keep his composure. "I am Emily James, from Amherst, Massachusetts."

Normally, Wheeler would have retorted with something clever like *pleased to meet you, Emily James from Amherst, Massachusetts*, or *my, how like a character in a Jane Austen novel*, but in his embarrassed surprise he could only stammer, struggling awkwardly to imitate a nineteenth-century style he knew only from novels. "Truman," he said, taking her hand awkwardly. "Harry Truman, from San Francisco."

"Well, I am charmed to make your acquaintance, Mr. Truman from San Francisco." She shook his hand with a gentle firmness that may have conveyed an immediate attraction to him. She gave him the smile again before pulling back to join her friends who were walking toward a carriage. "How do you explain your good German?"

"I had an eccentric old Viennese as my teacher."

"Was that on the East Coast, Mr. Truman?" Her interest seemed immediately genuine.

Wheeler hesitated, discomforted by his own instinct to be deceptive in the presence of such disarming openness and beauty. "No, in San Francisco," he lied.

"What a shame that we New Englanders travel to Europe, but do not travel west."

"When you do, I hope you will add San Francisco to your itinerary. We are quite civilized there, you might not have heard." At this point, he was thinking this might be the most disarmingly attractive woman he had ever met in his life. He was trying desperately to keep her interest.

"I know that," she said with a twinkle, "from reading Mark Twain." She glanced back over her shoulder. "My friends and I have met here to ride out to Schonbrunn Palace. I am sure they would not mind if you joined us." She gestured toward the group she had left, at the edge of which was the young aesthete, who, Wheeler could see at close range, could not have been more than eighteen. He was handsome and refined, dressed neatly, with an unmistakable artistic flair, and very obviously intent on the young woman's every move.

Still stunned, Wheeler answered without thinking. "I'm afraid I'm busy for the afternoon," which, of course, was neither true nor anywhere near in accord with what he really desired.

"We shall, I hope, have further opportunity," she said with a new smile. "Are you in Vienna long?"

"Indefinitely," Wheeler said. "I seem to be between projects."

"Good reason to join us on our excursions. We as a group seem to be *between projects*," she said, with an obvious appreciation of the phrase and the idea.

The artistic young man moved back near them and hung on the edge obtrusively, obviously wanting to be introduced to Wheeler, not because of anything about a new man in the park, but because of his fascination, it seemed, with anything connected with her. The young woman disregarded him at first, then added as an afterthought, "I would enjoy introducing you to my friend."

The young man, caught in the act of fawning, looked sheepish, then approached Wheeler. "Arnauld, this is Mr. Truman," she said graciously. "From San Francisco." The young man held out his hand and looked up earnestly. His grip was more solid than Wheeler expected. "This is my Viennese friend," she said, "Arnauld Esterhazy."

8

A Strong-willed Child

e know from her own diary entries that exist from the time that Weezie Putnam had been taken by the older American immediately, in an alarming, and certainly a disarming, manner. There was something in his eyes, she wrote later, an intensity and kindness, that brought a flushed warmth to her face from almost the moment she had seen him walking toward her across the park. And when he approached and took her hand in formal salutation, she felt a rush of emotion that she could not explain. Perhaps that is why she came up so quickly with the invented name.

It was not new. She had used the fabrication Emily James a number of times over the past few years, whenever she felt the slightest bit daring and wild, or a need for anonymity. And she certainly could not use her other more public pseudonym, her nom de plume, her Smith College friends called it, her George Sand, her George Eliot. Nor did she wish to explain to this man she had hardly met how that assumed masculine identity was responsible for bringing her from Boston to Vienna in the first place.

Any such reflection as to why she was here brought her inevitably to the fateful meeting with Miss Hewens, her former headmistress at the Winsor School for Girls in Boston, who had invited her into her oak-paneled office during Easter time of her senior year in college and suggested rather pointedly that Weezie think of travel.

Miss Hewens knew her family well and knew Weezie well, knew many of the family secrets, and—we can conclude—had not made the suggestion lightly. "Weezie, dear, you really ought to think of going abroad after graduation. With your love of music, you must journey to the source. Perhaps we could find you a pension in Paris or Vienna." When Miss Hewens spoke, her girls listened. She was much more than a headmistress to each of them. She was their senior European history teacher, a mentor, a friend, a confidante, and in Weezie's case, a trusted advisor. For Weezie, Miss Hewens was a substitute for the mother who had died when she was eight, the wise and patient grandmother she had wished for, the close friend who could see beyond the superficial to the essence of being twenty-two, optimistic, and full of energy to do something special with life, even something radical. Miss Hewens eyed her carefully on that afternoon and as always chose her words with unmistakable care. "We would all like to see if perhaps a young woman using a certain pseudonym mightn't be able to write something of significance."

The sudden mention of the pseudonym made Weezie blush. Until that moment, she had thought, naïvely so, that no one at home in Boston—let alone her former headmistress and someone so close to her family—had known of his existence or, more importantly, his identity.

The idea of a masculine pseudonym had come to life one giddy evening in a Smith College sitting room. "I think it is stuffy rubbish," Weezie had declared. "With all the venturesome modern music being written, why do they insist on playing nothing but soupy old Schubert and Liszt?" She had just returned from an overnight train trip to New York City to hear the Philharmonic. She had not minded the program, actually, but she was feeling rebellious.

"Why don't you write a letter to *The New York Times?*" her friend Charlotte Simpson said. Charlotte had grown up in a brownstone in the Harlem section of Manhattan and played the viola in the chamber group to which Weezie was cello. She always seemed—as New York City women often did—so much better informed and more sophisticated than her friends from Boston. Weezie did write a letter, a detailed one, lambasting the hopelessly conservative tastes of the Philharmonic. She laced it with examples of modern music she had heard or read of, including that of Gustav Mahler, who had been in Budapest and had just moved to Vienna.

"They will never publish it," Charlotte had said when Weezie had perfected the broadside and read it to the group. "They only publish letters from men."

So, painstakingly, Weezie copied her diatribe over in her most masculine cursive, signed it with the man's name borrowed from the aged jani-

tor at the college's Hubbard House, gave the home address of her music
teacher in Amherst, and mailed it off. Within two weeks, the author had
been invited to submit a more lengthy review on the subject for the healthy
sum of fifteen dollars. All in all, the man from Amherst, Massachusetts,
had since written four musical reviews in *The New York Times*, all very
witty, insightful, progressive, and modern, and all—Weezie thought—
completely unbeknownst to people in Boston.

And now Weezie blushed in her former headmistress's office, but she
could see from Miss Hewens's expression as she held the collection of
newspaper clippings in front of her on the oak desk that she was not unmoved. "The man has great perspicacity and should not be discouraged,"
Miss Hewens said with a smile of obvious satisfaction that the all-girl Winsor School could have produced such a man of letters. "I wish we women
could write this well." She paused, smiling. "Fraulein Tatlock in Vienna
would serve as both your hostess and chaperone, if asked by certain associates in Boston. I hope you would consider it."

Miss Hewens had been the one person who had best understood what
it was like for Weezie at the family's Beacon Hill home. She had known
both Weezie's father and his stern sister, Aunt Prudence, almost from
birth. She had known Weezie's mother in school and had grieved at her
passing. She had been Weezie's guardian spirit, and probably her greatest
admirer. At Winsor graduation she had called Weezie "one of the finest
and most talented young women ever to have graced the halls of this
school."

And Miss Hewens had been the one who had suggested Smith College, in Northampton, a considerable distance from Boston, for Weezie's
college years. On the surface, the present suggestion from her former
headmistress appeared to be in the name of furthering her study of music,
and perhaps furthering the successful and very secret career of the clever
man from Amherst. But perhaps Miss Hewens's real motive could have
been better characterized as that of a kindly and wise old mentor stepping
in to further free her young protégée from the darkest of secrets.

Weezie suspected immediately that Miss Hewens knew she was giving Weezie her freedom, that Fraulein Tatlock's pension on Ebendorfer-
Strasse would indeed provide her with the respectable room, board,
and counsel that a young woman from Boston needed abroad. In fact,

Fraulein Tatlock herself, for all her cheerful goodwill and concern, would probably be described at best as inattentive, and at worst as permissive and libertine.

From the time of Weezie Putnam's arrival, Fraulein Tatlock had introduced her to what she would have called at home the music crowd. They were all in one way or another connected to music and musicians. Her principal gift to Weezie was to introduce her to Ernst Felsch, the handsome and progressive son of the director of the Burgtheater.

Through Ernst Felsch and his family, Weezie developed contacts whom the real journalists back in New York would have envied. She could attend any musical or dramatic events, always in the company of the most interesting and appreciative young enthusiasts, and she could retain her precious independence. Perhaps Miss Hewens had known the circumstance she was creating for Weezie. But, preordained or coincidental, it was unquestionably exactly what a young woman in Weezie's position needed. It was, she recorded in her own diary entries, a chance to explore the world, to find oneself, and to do a good deal of self-reflection in the process.

From these self-reflections we can read between the lines and discover much. Weezie's first eight years in Boston had been, she remembered, close to the perfect childhood. As he would remain for the rest of his life, her father was rector of small St. Andrew's parish, and was at the time of Weezie's childhood thought to become the next rector of huge Trinity Church, and eventually perhaps the Episcopal bishop of Massachusetts. Her mother was beautiful, scintillating, and warmly welcoming, from an old Boston family. She was a lover of books and ideas, with a flock of admirers who came to her living room, including William and Henry James. It was on her lap before the fire in the parlor of the Beacon Hill house that Weezie learned her appreciation of the poetry of Emily Dickinson and the romantic stories of Sir Walter Scott and Robert Louis Stevenson. Her mother's death had been sudden, and while not mysterious in cause to anyone in Boston, had for the young daughter always been cloaked in mystery. Without really telling anyone, Weezie had fixed on the idea that her mother had choked while eating.

In reality, Laura Putnam and her infant son had died of diphtheria. Immediately following the tragic death, the bereft Rev. Josiah Putnam had invited his respected but unmarried older sister Prudence into the home to administer household order and to assist in the raising of his young daughter.

Prudence was in her fifties, very proper and respectable, well read, polite, and an excellent hostess for Josiah's various social obligations as rector of a small parish. But Prudence Putnam was cold-hearted and held very certain opinions about how permissively young Weezie had been raised. She knew exactly how the damage could be rectified. "You are a strong-willed child," she said to Weezie shortly after her arrival, "as was your mother. While I admire strong will in young people, I shall not tolerate either wantonness or willfulness."

In spite of her strong views, Aunt Prudence had after all no actual experience with children, and if her treatment of Weezie had been unduly harsh from the start, only the Reverend Putnam could have known. But, of course, his not noticing could be excused on account of the ravaging effects of grief and later by the effects of the anesthetic alcohol. Weezie's father, unfortunately, was a man of weak will, a fact hidden by his extremely fortunate marriage. His generous and saintly wife gone, he was left with a desperate feeling of hopelessness from which he possessed insufficient imagination to remove himself.

Eventually, when Weezie was fourteen or fifteen, family and parishioners close to the family saw what was happening to the sprightly and positive young girl who so much favored her mother. They stepped in with what help and guidance they could. That was the time in her life when Miss Hewens appeared as a teacher, advisor, and friend. But when Weezie was between ages eight and fourteen, for six years, everyone assumed that all was upright, proper, and as God intended it on Beacon Hill.

Prudence Putnam was strict, granted, but she was certain about what a young Christian girl needed in the way of education and nurturing. Weezie would be up at six thirty each morning, with her bed made, her face washed, and down at the breakfast table for porridge. She would not return to her bedroom until nap time, if that was called for, and she would be in her night clothes by seven each evening, and in bed by seven thirty, unless the readings lasted longer. The readings were primarily from the

Bible, with occasional levity from passages in *Pilgrim's Progress*, which were repeated year in and year out for effect. Although Prudence believed firmly in the effects of family, Weezie was not allowed to visit with her young cousins except on holidays, as Prudence was firm in her belief that the young girl had not yet reached the age when children benefited from playmates. She attended a small school for girls near the parish, but she was instructed to come home early so that her times for prayer and contemplation could have their maximum effect.

Weezie was a good girl, and her willfulness, which Prudence claimed to admire, rarely presented a problem that could not be remedied by an evening alone in her room without eating.

One evening at dinner, a little more than a year after her mother's death, and long after a child should have adjusted, Prudence concluded, Weezie had made a scurrilous remark. Where it had come from neither the surprised father nor the ever-attentive aunt had any idea. Prudence, the concerned disciplinarian, had dealt with it well, and it had never come up again, for which the father was deeply and eternally grateful.

An event at her all-girls school led to her undoing. Weezie was nine. The other girls were older, probably twelve or so, and Weezie knew them to be naughty, but the kind of naughty that never was seen by the adults. They seemed harmless, and never intentionally mean to the younger girls. They were coming out of the lavatory on the second floor and stopped against the wall, continuing—once they had seen that the coast was clear—with their giggling. One of the girls held a small paper-covered volume, like a small magazine, to which she pointed. "She quenched his ardor," Weezie heard very distinctly, and both girls nearly fell on the floor, doubled up by laughing. "Maybe she swallowed his bone," the other said, and that brought such a convulsion of laughter that it looked as if both girls might expire right then and there. Neither saw Weezie approach.

"Why are you laughing?" Weezie asked matter-of-factly.

Both girls stopped immediately and pulled to attention, tight-lipped and straight-faced. "It was nothing," one said, but Weezie guessed that both girls were about to set off again. "Just some quenched ardor," said the other, and that did it. They were doubled up.

Weezie turned to walk away, and one of the girls grabbed her arm. She struggled to control herself. "Wait," she said, but then realized she was too far gone to talk.

"She'll find out soon enough," the other girl managed to say, and the two turned and staggered between convulsions down the hall.

Soon enough for Weezie was that night at dinner. They were eating shepherd's pie with cabbage. She took a big drink of milk and turned to the Reverend Josiah Putnam. "Father," she said very distinctly, "what is ardor?" The Reverend Putnam was in the middle of a sip of claret and swallowed loudly. He said nothing and looked over at his sister in what might have been interpreted as a state of panic.

The sister sat with her jaw tight until after her reverend brother had finished eating. Then without a word she rose, walked over to her niece's chair, took her by the hand, led her to the bathroom, and shut the door securely.

She poured water from the large china pitcher on the cabinet into the porcelain bowl and then took a bar of soap and dipped it into the water. "You will never use such words," she said, her voice harsh and tight.

At first Weezie did not know what her aunt intended with the soap, and then when the strong hands pulled at her jaw to open it, she knew and gave no resistance. The soap tasted awful, harsh and bitter. "Not at the dinner table," she heard her aunt say, and the soap went in and out. "Not in front of your father. Never." Weezie began to gag, but fought for control.

Her aunt put down the soap and grabbed her securely by the shoulders. Weezie fought to clear her mouth of the taste. She could feel the lather in the corners of her lips. "Willfulness and sinfulness are brethren," she said, pressing on Weezie's shoulders and rocking her slowly back and forth. "Your mother was willful, and you know what God brought her. Do you want to end up like your mother?" Her aunt looked down at her with piercing intensity. "Is that what you wish?"

"No," Weezie said weakly and began to cry.

"We will have no crying," her aunt said. "The sinful have no cause for tears."

That night Weezie had the dream for the first time. She was in the basement of the house on Beacon Hill and suddenly saw in the corner a woman with large breasts in a white summer dress sitting on a white blanket beside a picnic basket. At that point Weezie spoke. "What *is* ardor?"

The woman smiled wonderfully at Weezie and asked her to sit beside her. "Come, precious," she said, patting her hand in the folds of her dress at her side.

Only as Weezie approached did she realize that the woman was eating a chicken bone, which she took to her lips, and as she took a small bite of the flesh she began to cough. Suddenly, she was on her back, her hands across the chest of her white dress, and Weezie knew she was dead.

It was at that moment that she woke up, cold and frightened and alone, and with a bitter taste of soap in her mouth, on that night when she was nine, and on subsequent nights when the dream returned.

9

The Burden Project

 heeler struggled through his first year at St. Gregory's, where no one had ever heard the stories from the Sacramento Valley, earning failing grades in most of his courses. By baseball season, it was clear to most of the masters that Frank Standish Burden III, no matter whose son or grandson he was, would not be returning for a second year.

"Lackluster" had been the word for everything Wheeler tried, lackluster and erratic. "If only the boy would focus," one master said in exasperation in a faculty meeting, in such a way that it became a litany. *Focus*, that was it, the boy had no focus. From the beginning, for some mysterious reason, the Haze had been fully committed to the Burden Project, as the St. Greg's faculty came to call the introduction of the erratic, untrained California boy so late in the academic process. "Second class year is far too late to begin such a breathtaking enterprise" was how one old timer put it, as he saw the younger masters tearing their hair.

Only the venerable old Haze remained steadfast and patient, relentlessly cajoling and browbeating the young man, when the others could not get the boy to hand in papers on time, or prepare them with care, or when he did show care, write even remotely near the assigned topic. "Lackluster" was the word even for his effort in baseball, and he was immediately relegated to the second team. Nobody in Boston had ever heard of Wheeler Burden and his prongball, and nobody knew that he was holding back, let alone why.

Prentice Olcott was the main varsity pitcher and had been for three years. "Another Dilly Burden," a few optimistic alumni had called Olcott after seeing him pitch against Dover on Graduates' Day in his third class year. Another Dilly Burden. Over the years, a lot of St. Greg's students had said that hopefully about a lot of promising prep school athletes, but in their hearts they knew there was no comparison, as the old alumni who came back would remind them. "He's no Dilly Burden" would be the inevitable final result. And then the inevitable, "Who could be?"

Graduates' Day was always the Dover game, the big athletic event of the spring. On the annual calendar of nearly every St. Gregory's Bostonian were two fervent expectations: Harvard would trounce Yale in football and St. Greg's would do the same to Dover on Graduates' Day in baseball. Everyone was watching for Pren Olcott, now in his final year, to do something spectacular. Then two days before the Graduates' Day game, disaster struck. Olcott tore the ligaments in his ankle, sliding into third in a scrimmage. A group of alumni, hearing that Dilly Burden's son was a second teamer, a pitcher even, asked the headmaster if they might have a chance to look at the young man. "No chip off the old block," Headmaster Wiggins said sadly, announcing Coach Storer's decision not to play Burden against Dover. He would dress for the game, giving the old guard a chance at least to see the son of Dilly Burden in a St. Greg's uniform. "Fair enough," said the president of the Graduates Association, thinking privately that dressing was the first step toward playing.

Prentice Olcott's roommate, also a first classman, was the second line pitcher. And he did well for five innings or so, escaping with his scalp in the fifth, with St. Greg's still ahead, four to nothing. Then in the sixth he lost all semblance of control, walking the first two batters and delivering a home run ball to the third. So, with his pitcher shot, no outs, two innings from the finish line and a meager one-run lead, Coach Storer looked down his bench at his depleted pitching staff. The old grads held their breath, knowing not to intrude, but hoping against hope. There was simply no fresh arm to put in. A palpable hush fell over the St. Gregory's diamond. "Burden," Coach Storer said in little more than a whisper, and three generations of St. Greg's boys released a corporate sigh of joy and relief, not caring—at least for a moment—that the kid from California was no chip off the heroic block. Winning be damned, the son of Dilly Burden would pitch against Dover.

If Wheeler knew anything of the enormity that rode on Coach Storer's desperate decision, he showed nothing. He jumped up off the end of the bench and picked up his father's thirty-year-old glove, giving it a few hurried slaps with his fist. "Get us out of this damn mess" was Coach Storer's gravelly whisper to the untested second-teamer, his voice betraying suspicions of utter hopelessness. At least the boy could throw strikes, some of the time. "Focus, son," the old coach said.

Wheeler had made virtually no impression on the athletic program at his new school. He cared little for any sport but baseball, and he had not thrown the prongball since arriving. It was not that he had been unimpressed with the school and that he did not think them worthy of seeing it; it was just that as second-team pitcher he had never really thrown the ball very hard at all, coming up against few boys who could hit even his slow pitches, and it did not seem fair to the younger boys to throw anything they couldn't hit.

"How about strikeouts?" Wheeler said with a characteristic wildness in his eyes, popping his fist into his antique glove.

"Steady, lad," Coach Storer said without much enthusiasm. "Nothing fancy. Just get the thing over the plate." A few miraculous catches deep in the outfield, he was thinking, and we'll be out of this.

Wheeler was not sure if the umpire would watch the ball. Sacramento Valley teams had pretty much gotten wind of his doctorings and asked for new balls regularly. It was always disappointing to start on a new ball, especially with all eyes on his between-pitches moves. Of course, he could throw the pitch middling well, as Bucky said, without the goop on it, but it never felt as satisfying as with a ball he had had a chance to personalize. Wheeler had learned to wet his finger immediately *after* the pitch, when the whole world was watching the batter, not before, when all eyes were on the pitcher's mound.

Trip Thornton, the catcher, knew nothing of the prongball and gave Wheeler a queer look when he tried to warn him. "Ball's going to jump around a little," Wheeler said in a businesslike voice no one at St. Greg's had ever heard.

"You worry about pitching," Thornton said curtly, intending to put the upstart in his place. "I'll worry about catching." Thornton, a nine-letter man himself, but somewhat in the shadow of Prentice Olcott, knew only that—Dilly Burden's son or not—no one liked the brash Californian who certainly did not know his place. Thornton could not help wondering why Coach Storer had taken leave of his senses at such an important moment in St. Greg's history, with Dover men hitting the balls all over the place. But then again, who else was there?

"Just put it over the plate," Thornton, the catcher, growled, looking forlornly over to the bench as he slapped the ball into Wheeler's glove and walked back to his crouch behind home plate.

Wheeler blinked lizardlike at Thornton, as if to confirm his hopeless weirdness. During warm-ups he had laid some good wet ones on his finger and transferred them to the spot between the label and the stitching till it was slick, just the way he wanted it. The practice pitches snapped into Thornton's glove, giving little warning of what was about to follow.

Before the first pitch to a Dover batter, the first Burden varsity pitch at St. Greg's in twenty-five years, he took a deep breath and closed his eyes. He let his mind go, as he had done many, many times before. Back in the Feather River bottomland with his mother. He felt the smooth stone in his hand. He thought of his arm throwing the stone in the direction of the sparrow hawk. He felt the connectedness. He then opened his eyes and stared at Thornton's glove, pronging his fingers just so between the label and the stitch. He paused to hear Bucky Hannigan's litany: "How to chuck, wheeler-dealer. How to chuck-fire, wheeler-dealer kid."

The crowd seemed to wait through this ritual with a heavy expectant silence. Then slowly he raised his left leg, rocked backward with his upper body, swung forward, brought his arm over his head in a looping arch, and came down with everything he had. As his wrist snapped downward, the ball squirted out from between his fingers and sped toward Thornton's glove, right to the center of the strike zone. The batter, the Dover short-stop, a feisty little scholarship boy, a grocer's son from Swampscott, took a mighty rip. The ball, heading straight, took a two-foot drop about five feet from the plate and flew past the batter and Trip Thornton and clanked against the baseboard of the backstop. In one motion, the umpire, the catcher, and the grocer's son from Swampscott swung around and stared at the pitcher's mound where Wheeler was standing slapping his famous father's ancient glove. "Holy shit," the Dover kid said, shaking his head, looking back at Trip Thornton. "What in Jesus's name was that?"

The first classman catcher only stared back and said, "Beats hell out of me."

Whatever it was, it came back again and then again, both for strikes and then for two more batters. In Wheeler Burden's part of that next-to-last inning the Dover boys went three up and three down, leaving the bases empty and St. Greg's up by one run.

The baselines were now packed with teachers, students, and alumni. Almost as soon as Coach Storer had contemplated the pitching change, word had spread around the campus: Get over to the varsity diamond. Dilly Burden's boy is going in.

All eyes watched in awed silence as Wheeler slapped his fist into his glove one last time and headed back to the bench. The gravelly voice of an old grad came from over by third base. "Burden, rah—" it began, the way it had so many times before, a quarter of a century ago. "Burden, rah—" came the sound again, this time picking up ten or more other old voices. Then the pause, an entire school community searching into its mythic past, everyone—even those not born then—recalling memories of the great Dilly Burden, the school's one true and enduring hero. One voice rose this time, one voice from the throats of every St. Greg's boy past, present, and future. "Burden, rah," it boomed. "Burden, rah. Burden, rah, rah."

The seventh and last inning went quickly. There was no need to add anything to the ball. It was exactly the way Wheeler liked it. The prongball dipped and hopped and danced. Two Dover batsmen came up, took their swings, and went down. One, two—The third batter fared no better on the first two pitches, chasing two low outsiders. Strike two.

The last pitch. Wheeler thought of his Feather River bottomland walks with his mother. He saw the sparrow hawk, he felt the stone in his hand, he looked in at Thornton's target, and heard the "How to chuck-fire wheeler-dealer kid!" from his one true friend in the world. He thought of Buddy Holly, lost in the chords and the rhythm and the skip of the Tex-Mex voice he had first heard mimicked in the old Feather River Union High gym. For the first time since coming east, he was beginning to feel the "flow," as his mother called it, the connectedness of all things.

The crowd took a corporate breath, and Wheeler gripped the ball between the two fingers of his right hand, kicked up his left leg, brought it down, and fired. The ball did not dip or sink. It flew straight and true and snapped into Thornton's glove, past the last violent and hapless swing of the last Dover batter. It was a pure straight fastball, maybe the fastest, straightest, purest pitch anyone there that day had ever seen. "Steee-rike!" yelled the umpire. Strike three. The day was St. Gregory's.

The crowd exploded from the sidelines out to the raised pitcher's mound, where Wheeler's grandfather, Frank Burden, and his father,

Dilly, had stood, and Wheeler slapped his fist one last time into his thirty-year-old glove. They hoisted Wheeler onto their shoulders.

From his perch atop the swarm Wheeler looked back at the emptied bench. Only Prentice Olcott, the disabled captain, stared out at him with a mixture of joy and outrage. Wheeler blinked at him, his best lizard look, then he looked into the emptied stands. There stood the solitary remaining spectator, the Venerable Haze. Wheeler realized something in that moment, and he carried it with him for the next twenty-five years, for the rest of his life. It was love the old man held for his father, Dilly Burden, a love based on something more than his athletic heroics or his near-mythic turn as the Resistance hero Rouge Gorge. The Haze was now seeing two Burdens out on the St. Greg's mound, hoisted on the shoulders of the Dover game crowd, son and father, 1958 and 1932. Wheeler understood that in the tumultuous moment. Steadying himself on his rough ride, he looked the old man square in the eye and touched the bill of his cap, as if to doff it. It was then Wheeler noticed the tears soaking the old man's cheeks.

10

City of Music

heeler found himself wandering out on the Ringstrasse. Still shocked by the discovery earlier in the day that the Viennese in the park was his mentor, Arnauld Esterhazy, he needed time to sort things all out. He kept his appointment at the cabinetmaker's shop and viewed the near-finished version of the wooden Frisbee, making a few last corrections, then found his way back onto the boulevard. When he came to the Imperial Art History Museum he walked up the steps, paid his fifty kreuzer admission fee and began wandering through the high-ceilinged rooms, all the time preoccupied by the strangeness of his predicament. He was standing in front of a collection of sixteenth-century paintings, lost in a flood of thoughts, when a voice came from behind him.

"You have an interest in the finer arts, I see, Mr. Truman." He turned and looked into the bright smiling face of the captivating young American woman, Emily James. He pulled himself back from his reverie.

"Miss James, isn't it?" he said. "From Amherst, Massachusetts."

She looked pleased that he had remembered her name, and nodded. "You are good with names, I see," she said. "And places."

How could I not remember? he felt like saying. "I love the quiet of museums," he said. "They quiet the restless soul." He was quoting one of the Haze's favorite remarks.

"*Quiet the restless soul,*" she repeated with a smile. "That is Byron, I believe."

"Actually, I was quoting a beloved old mentor," Wheeler said, still not fully recovered from the surprise of running into her. He had nearly forgotten how disarming he found this young woman's manner of looking one straight in the eye, the way her blue eyes gained intensity as she spoke to him, and the flush that came to her cheeks. "But I don't know where he got it," he said, musing on the words. He paused. "I thought you were on your way to Schonbrunn Palace with your friends."

"Group indecision," she said quickly. "It was a short trip. We turned around almost as soon as we got there. And I decided to come here by myself, to have time for contemplation."

"I am sorry to disturb that."

"Oh no, Mr. Truman," she said enthusiastically. "It was I who broke into *your* contemplation." Wheeler noted that she was blushing.

"I am glad for it," he said. "Either way. Is this your first time in this museum?"

"I have come here a lot, alone," she said. "I too find museums very restful and a chance to collect myself. This one is very good. It was the emperors' and made public only in the middle of this century." She looked at the collection of watercolors in front of Wheeler. "I find these exquisite," she said. "They were a gift for the collection of watercolors and drawings by Austrian artists given to Rudolf and his bride, the Princess Stephanie, on their marriage sixteen years ago. You see the two of them pictured there—" She pointed. "And there." She pointed to one entitled *Defregger*, a charmingly colorful work of Rudolf and Stephanie in a rustic cabin. "I find it absolutely exhilarating that the arts abound so in this country."

"They really are quite exquisite," Wheeler said, leaning down to examine the watercolors more closely.

"They are," she said, seized by an involuntary frown. "But it reminds one of the awful tragedy of Mayerling. I suppose we will never know the full story."

The Haze told all of his boys the facts of the Mayerling tragedy each year, on January 30, the day in 1889, that in the grand bedroom of the royal hunting lodge, in the village of Mayerling, Crown Prince Rudolf, only son and male heir of the emperor, the hope of the future, took his own life and the life of a seventeen-year-old courtesan. "Rudolf shot the light-headed baroness first," Wheeler remembered his mentor intoning, "then he went downstairs for drink and companionship, then six or eight hours later returned to the upstairs room and shot himself in the head."

"I suppose not, Miss James," Wheeler said.

A look of great sadness came onto her face. "It was absolutely devastating for this lighthearted country. Just imagine the heir to the throne, the very future of the empire doing this—" She paused without being able to say the word. Then she shook her head. "I keep thinking of his mother, the great and beautiful empress. To lose a son this way—" She paused again, overcome by the gravity. "To lose a son any way at all. Simply awful."

A silence fell between them. "I suppose that is the reason for museums," Wheeler said lightly, to change the mood. "They allow us to relive poignant moments."

"Do you have museums out in California?" She smiled this time to restore levity.

Wheeler smiled back. "It's not the Wild West, you know." He gestured to the broad open room. "But nothing like this."

"I told you, my geography is terrible west of the Hudson River," she said.

"You're going to visit, remember?"

She looked genuinely pleased with the invitation. "I'm still absorbing Vienna. I don't know if I will ever leave here."

"What is it you find so compelling?"

"I'm really here for the music."

"Any music in particular? This city seems alive with it, reverberating in every nook and cranny," he said, quoting from the Haze's revered *City of Music*, the "Little Book" by Mr. Jonathan Trumpp that he always read from with such loving care. "Echoing, you might say, off every grand marble exterior."

"Oh my," she said, impressed. "You have a way with words, Mr. Truman."

"No," he said. "Not my words. I am just quoting again, this time from one of my favorite works, referred to often by the mentor I told you about."

She paused and assessed him for a moment. "Actually, I'm writing," she said. "But nothing as grand as your mentor's favorite work. Mine is just a humble series of articles on the new composers." She was amazed that she had said it. "But it's sort of confidential, and I wish no one to know. I am using a pseudonym."

"I have no one to tell," Wheeler said. "I'm in Vienna alone." If she only knew, he thought.

"Oh, I didn't mean to imply." She stopped. "I just saw you meeting Arnauld and his friends."

"Secret's good with me, ma'am," he said, and it made her laugh.

"You have a very different manner, Mr. Truman. I must say, I like it." Wheeler suspected that she was blushing again.

"Well, perhaps we can hear some Viennese music together."

"I would like that very much," she said with a sudden rush of candor. "Now, I must go. I'm expected back at my pension." She held out her hand, and Wheeler took it and felt its soft warmth, then she turned and walked away, but then turned back before she had left the room. "Mr. Truman," she said, framed against the baroque molding of the expansive doorway to the next room. "You have remarkably kind eyes."

Wheeler watched her turn again and disappear around the corner, his heart feeling an incredible lightness. *What a striking woman*, he thought.

⊰◉⊱

That evening in Vienna, distracted by the limits of his circumstance, Wheeler again ate modestly and moved even deeper into the old city to find an even cheaper room. His clothes were beginning to feel rumpled, and he longed for a shower. His money was nearly gone.

At the end of the second day, he began seeing in his new neighborhood a part of the Imperial City he would not have imagined. There was more of the poverty and wretchedness than he had seen before, the stench of crowded and abject conditions. As Wheeler walked deeper and deeper into the city he became even more aware of people asleep in the streets, uncared for, unwashed, crowded, and miserable, a homelessness and depression that had simply not come through in the Haze's stirring descriptions. There were prostitutes everywhere. Wherever he walked women of all ages, as old as sixty and as young as twelve, as comely and as haglike as one could imagine, approached and offered company and specific services. Some of the more aggressive actually took his arm and walked a few paces with him until it became clear he was not a prospect.

Later in the day, in the clean, well-lighted comfort of the Café Central, he would ask Kleist about the wretched conditions. He was sitting at the usual table with the usual *Jung Wien* group. "It is not a problem if one does not see it," the young Kleist said cheerfully. "There are not enough jobs and not enough homes. That is one reason coffeehouses like this one proliferate. People need a place for comfort. I know it might come as a surprise to you, but some of the gentlemen at these tables have no other warm place to sit and read." He gestured around at the marble-topped tables, nearly all filled with people reading quietly or engaged in animated discussions with groups of friends. "A surprising number of their families at home are hungry and cold."

"Is nothing being done about it?"

"You have found our vulnerable underbelly, Mr. Truman," von Tscharner, the architect, said.

"The conditions are deplorable." Wheeler raised his hands in frustration in the direction of the Danube Canal and the old city beyond. "There is filth and disease everywhere. And many of the prostitutes look no older than twelve or thirteen."

"It is not the Vienna of the Strausses father and son, is it?" Claus, the writer and cynic, said.

"There seem to be thousands of people living in storm drains and culverts out there." Wheeler could barely contain his exasperation. He stared across the marble tabletop at these well-educated young men with obvious liberal views who had become his hosts.

Kleist shrugged. "The famous liberalism of our fathers," he added. "It built the Ringstrasse, but it had no sense of responsibility for the underclasses, did it? If one of the major functions of culture is to shield its members from chaos, and to reassure them that they live at the center of the universe, then our fathers have failed."

"What's to be done?" von Tscharner chipped in. "It's a hopeless situation."

"You were expecting waltzes and gaiety, Herr Truman?" Claus said.

"Much is made of Vienna's splendor," Wheeler said. "It's only natural to expect—"

"Ah, yes, splendor," he said. "Splendor and *schlagg*." Claus lifted a spoonful of whipped cream from his cup. "Splendor before the fall." He dropped the dollop back into the cup. "It is is a false sense of well-being."

"A *sense of well-being*, oh no," Kleist said. "Look out, here comes Claus's false-sense-of-well-being speech."

"The death spasms of a culture," Claus said. "Dancing toward the Apocalypse."

"Look out," Kleist said. "Here comes the dancing speech."

"And that's where you see Vienna?" Wheeler asked.

"It's cultural hubris," Claus said. "It's an overweening presumption of aristocracy in a world basically insensitive to human needs, and it can only lead to a rude awakening."

"And what's that awakening?"

"I have no idea," Claus said gloomily. "But when people start believing that progress is inevitable and life easy, they abandon faith in the culture of their fathers and flounder." He paused and looked vacantly across the café.

Wheeler looked at him empathetically. "And that's where you and your friends are?"

"Exactly," Claus said. "We're watching the first signs of the unraveling of what our fathers still believe in—the rational rule of science and order—and we have no faith."

"The city can't take care of its own problems."

"In Vienna, we follow the imperial example and pretend they are not there," Claus said with an ironic little smile.

"How long can that go on?"

Claus kept his smile and gestured to a passing waiter for more coffee. He looked deep into Wheeler's eyes. "Till the Apocalypse," he said in both resignation and great wisdom. "And that may well be around the corner."

Back on the street, Wheeler was growing desperate. Alone, in the wretched quarter of the city, with the thoughts of his new Viennese friends' quips about poverty fresh in his mind, Wheeler had a practical problem. He needed to find a way of insuring himself room and board for the duration of his stay in this foreign city. The idea, wild and impulsive as it was, came in a flash and stayed with him through his humble dinner of sausage and cabbage in a grubby little café deep inside the old city where he had laid down his last marks for a room.

So in the morning of the third day, dispirited and drained of energy, nearly out of money and tired of his rumpled clothes, Wheeler Burden asked directions to the address he had learned from the Haze in his eleventh-grade year in prep school. "The modern age began at Berggasse

Nineteen," the Haze had said more than once, with that flair he had for pronouncement, and each of his boys was expected to know exactly what the pronouncement meant.

It was an unimpressive façade, the large front door opening onto a vaulted throughway large enough for a carriage. The stone stairs climbed to the second floor, where Wheeler stopped and waited a long apprehensive moment before knocking, driven to this monumental intrusion into destiny by practical necessity. Simply put, he needed support and a place to stay.

The sign on the door read, "Prof. Dr. Freud."

11

A St. Gregory's Boy

fter the Dover game things turned around for Wheeler at St. Greg's. In his solitary moment of athletic glory, an entire school seemed suddenly about to change its impression of the Burden Project. "In the eyes of the beholder," the Haze said. What had been beheld previously as the California boy's unregenerate reluctance to fit in now became charming eccentricity."Something we can work with," one of the faculty old-timers said. Teachers began to see in Wheeler a fascinating if peculiar mind. One day in English class his teacher asked loudly, "Good lord, Burden, have you read *all* of Victor Hugo?" He meant it facetiously.

"Only the seven novels," Wheeler answered matter-of-factly. "But *Ninety-Three* twice." The exchange became widely quoted among the students.

The headmaster, Mr. Wiggins, had been at St. Greg's since before the war. He had cut quite a heroic swath in football and hockey at Harvard himself, a little before Wheeler's father, and had known Dilly only obliquely. He taught French and then had been named headmaster in 1947. In many ways, Wiggins, whose craggy features looked as if they had been chiseled in granite, was the embodiment of the values of the school and the whole Bostonian way of life. It was largely because of his stirring talks before the boys twice each year, on the opening day of baseball season in the spring and on Armistice Day in the fall, that Dilly Burden's memory remained alive and current. He was formal and gruff on the outside, but displayed a soft inside on those special days as he explained what everyone already knew, that the words he was about to read had been composed by the legendary Dilly Burden as his graduation speech in 1932, the words that were inscribed on a plaque in the main corridor of the schoolhouse. Then he would call up Dilly's spirit with a kind of Barrymorian eloquence and always a tear in his eye. "I am a St. Gregory's boy," he would begin to the hushed all-school audience. "I win without bragging and can lose without whimpering; I am too brave to lie and too generous to cheat. Pride will not let me loaf and I will always insist on doing my share of the work in any capacity. I ask only to share equally with every boy, the sturdy or the weak, the talented or the humble, the wealthy or the poor, those blessings which God has showered upon all of us. All this because I am, above all else, today, tomorrow, and forever, a St. Gregory's boy." When he finished, there was rarely a dry eye in the auditorium, boy or man.

Even in the moments of darkest faculty despair over the Burden Project, the rough-hewn boy from California seemed to appeal to Mr. Wiggins's soft side, and in these moments the headmaster would often throw his head back and give an understanding laugh, the rare sign of endorsement that lent the project the little hope it held. Most everyone knew that taking the chance on the rough lad from California had been mostly Headmaster Wiggins's idea in the first place, out of reverence for the memory of his famous father and the widespread respect he and everyone else had for Wheeler's grandmother, one of the school's greatest benefactors, it turned out. "Your grandmother is quite a woman," Mr. Wiggins told Wheeler at their first meeting. "I think few people in this school—" Then he thought on it for a moment. "Few people in this *city* realize what a significant person she is."

Later, when Wheeler asked the Haze if the headmaster might not be exaggerating just a bit, the old man became a little teary himself. "Oh my, no," he said. "She *is* quite a remarkable woman." Then he too lost himself a moment in something like reverie. "Quite a remarkable woman."

So it was not incidental that Wheeler's coming to St. Gregory's, in this radical departure from tradition, had been suggested and perhaps engineered by his grandmother. And, considering that initial influence, it was not coincidental that Mr. Wiggins became the idea's dominant and enthusiastic proponent. An admitted admirer of the small bursts of informality that sprang up in the daily life of a school, especially from the younger boys, Mr. Wiggins had been from the start one of the keenest observers of Wheeler's eccentricities and one of their greatest supporters. It was he who took Mr. Esterhazy aside and assigned him mentorship of the project. It was said that privately the headmaster thought that the young man's eccentricities might be good for some of the stuffier and more staid elements

in the school. He seemed to take Wheeler's miserable academic performance in stride along with his unrestrained conversations. If Mr. Wiggins
found what he called *a special spark* in a boy, his security was insured.
And for certain, his reverence for the grandmother aside, Mr. Wiggins
found in Dilly Burden's son that *special spark*.

One of the few St. Gregory's supporters who had not been at the Dover
game was Wheeler's grandmother, Eleanor Burden, widow of the prominent Boston banker Frank Standish Burden Senior and mother of Frank
Standish Burden Junior, the famous Dilly Burden. Her heart was not
strong, so she no longer visited the school. But it was she who had engineered and financed the Burden Project. When she received the headmaster's phone call directly after The Game, as it was now being called,
she expressed immediate joy, not out of a love of baseball but for the effect
it would have on her grandson's success, something that had seemed unlikely a few months before. She loved her grandson unconditionally and
wanted the transplant to take hold, although she seemed always to have
an ironclad confidence that it would.

"Young Burden has quite a head on his shoulders," the headmaster
would observe in faculty meetings. He would then tell in a good-natured
manner how, on more than one occasion, Wheeler had called the headmaster's house and discussed with Mrs. Wiggins at some length the deeper
meaning of his address in morning chapel or an item he had read on the
Boston Globe editorial page, a practice the headmaster's wife and conse-
quently the headmaster chose to view as charming. "He seems to enjoy a
good dialogue" was the understatement Mr. Wiggins chose to describe the
boy's eccentricity.

In physics class, Wheeler recouped from a year of failing work by writing a final paper of some distinction. The editors of the school's literary
magazine chose to view the piece as "poetic" and published it in their final
issue. Mr. Warner, the physics teacher, known by even the young boys as
Zoof, submitted it to a high school writing contest sponsored by the *Scientific American*. The paper was an eloquent description of why the curveball
seemed to break. "In the world according to Burden," Zoof said without
warning one day in class, "he was able to strike out six Dover batters because
the speed of the ball for the first two-thirds of its flight overpowers the effect
of the spin on the ball. It's quite simple. When the ball slows down in the last
third of flight, the spin dominates and makes the ball arc suddenly." Anyone

who could understand that concept and explain it so eloquently and simply deserved to pass the course for the year, something that had seemed impossible in Wheeler's inauspicious beginnings as a physicist. It helped that Zoof had been a St. Greg's classmate of Dilly Burden, and as a huge Boston Red Sox fan had himself always wondered why a breaking curveball broke. When asked by the editor of the *Gregorian* how he came up with such an elegant explanation, Wheeler said simply, "Bucky Hannigan."

Things went well even with Prentice Olcott, or at least the older boy stayed away from Wheeler, knowing when he had been licked.

As unlikely as it had seemed at the outset of the Burden Project, Frank Standish Burden III, like his famous father and grandfather before him, was suddenly and triumphantly a St. Gregory's boy. He was invited back for his first class year. Wheeler, like his father and grandfather, would graduate from St. Greg's. That first class year would go by relatively uneventfully, with Wheeler becoming more conventional and Mr. Esterhazy continuing to fill in the empty portions of his slate.

If the pitching performance against Dover served to turn the St. Gregory's faculty, it also set in motion Wheeler Burden's acceptance to Harvard College. Mr. Wiggins, it was said, now gave his endorsement. Harvard, like St. Gregory's, was more than willing to accept the son of its legend Dilly Burden, Harvard Class of 1936—provided he was not going to be an embarrassment to the admissions process. By fortunate coincidence, the director of admissions was a St. Gregory's man and had been in attendance at the fateful Dover game. By winter of his second St. Gregory's year, his first class year, there was a groundswell to send the boy on to Harvard. Wheeler went along with the idea largely to please his grandmother, for whom he cared a great deal and of whom he had grown more admiring and more fond.

It was not until after Christmas of that first class year at St. Greg's that Wheeler went to New York to find Buddy Holly. Most of his weekends had been tied up with detentions and work details, and he had no idea how to find the man. He had written a handful of letters to Holly and had received nothing in return so decided to go to New York and see what he could do about meeting his idol.

He told the school he was going in to Boston to stay with his grand-mother, and he hitched a ride with a Boston University student who lived on the Lower East Side. He got a room at the YMCA, and the next morn-ing went to the office of Coral Records, where he asked everyone he saw who looked even remotely like a musician where Holly was living. Finally a man with a Cockney accent told him an address in Greenwich Village. Wheeler went to the apartment and got no answer at the door. It was a terrible Saturday night, raining and cold. He kept going away and coming back. Around one in the morning, miserable and shivering, he was stand-ing in the doorway when a cab pulled up and a man covered by a dark brown slicker got out and began struggling with two large equipment cases. Wheeler stepped out to help. "Thanks much," the man said and led him into the alcove of the apartment and opened the door with his key. "Perhaps you can help up the stairs," he said, as he turned to Wheeler. "You look wetter'n a muskrat. Better come up and have something warm." Wheeler was halfway up the stairway to the garret apartment before he realized that the man was Buddy Holly.

Holly was born Charles Hardin Holley, in Lubbock, Texas, in 1936, five years before Wheeler Burden was born in London. He grew up in a musical family and learned the violin and piano before developing a love for country music and beginning to play the guitar in elementary school. During his high school years, when he was in a rock band, he tried to take the songs he wrote to other musicians. In 1955 Elvis Presley came to Lub-bock, and that sealed Holly's fate. He and his band traveled to Nashville in an attempt to make records. But it was not until 1957, when he was out of school and playing music full-time, that he tied up with a music pro-moter named Norman Petty in Clovis, New Mexico. He recorded with his band, the Crickets, his song called "That'll Be the Day" and the phenom-enon that changed Wheeler's life was launched. A year later, restless to write and sing on his own, Holly split from his Texas colleagues and moved to New York City, where he was beginning to take his music in new directions. He was living in a Greenwich Village apartment with his new wife, Maria Elena, when totally by coincidence, he offered refuge from the wintry blast to a scrawny, misplaced prep-school kid from Boston, who probably reminded him very much of himself a few years earlier.

Wheeler sat in Buddy's apartment for five hours, until dawn. They talked and played guitars, and Wheeler watched while Holly recorded a song on his tape machine, asking his guest to join in. Then he walked over to his record player. "Listen to this," he said. "It's Haydn." The strains of a classical piece filled the room. "I'm working on something new," he said with a smile when he lifted the needle from the record, and then he picked up his guitar. "Listen," and he began a chord pattern and sang a first line. Wheeler listened, mesmerized, having no idea how important that moment would be in his life. "It's my new direction," Holly said.

"That's beautiful," came from Wheeler in little more than a whisper.

"Think it's got promise?" the rock-and-roll icon asked, and Wheeler only nodded. Then the mentor ran the pupil through the chord progressions until the two of them were playing together, and Holly began the uh-uh-ohs of the undeveloped chorus. "Here," he said. "You do the melody and I'll sing a third above you." And their two voices fell into that territory of flow so that Wheeler could not hear where his began and his great hero's ended. Holly beamed. "Whoooeee!" he said. "That's what I call *promise*." And thus began the seed of what two decades later would be called the definitive song for an entire age.

When they stopped it was nearly morning. "Better get some sleep on that couch," Buddy said.

At around ten, Wheeler awoke, embarrassed to discover how soundly he had slept, and found himself alone in the New York apartment. As he was leaving a note on the kitchen table, he discovered a package wrapped in plain white paper and rubber bands. It had "Kid" scrawled on it. "This is so you'll remember. Keep playing." He opened it and found the tape they had made, which he placed in his suitcase before he headed back to Boston. No one at St. Greg's ever knew about his trip to New York City or his early-morning music session with a legend.

About a week later, the morning of February 4, 1959, Wheeler was sitting sleepy-eyed at school breakfast when a younger boarder approached him with a sick look. "Sorry" was all he said and dropped the front section of the *Boston Globe* onto Wheeler's table. Wheeler stared down at the paper, at first in disbelief. The headline read: "Holly and two singers killed in Iowa Plane Crash."

The only black clothing Wheeler had was a dinner jacket that had belonged to his father. He wore it with a black shirt and black string tie the whole day.

12

The First Shomsky

n weekends while at Harvard, Wheeler would come into Boston and spend time with his grandmother at the family house on the narrow cobbled street where she had spent her childhood and had raised Wheeler's father. Eleanor Burden was in her eighties and in spite of her weak heart was sharp, alert, and witty. He had always loved visiting the house the few times when he and his mother traveled east. Now that he was on his own, and a man more or less, he and his grandmother had a growing friendship.

"You know, Standish," she said to him the first week of classes, "the men at Harvard are very restrained. They will think you a bit outgoing." *Outgoing* was the term she had used with him since his visits in his childhood. Wheeler figured it was her way of encouraging him to start cautiously. He had already survived the St. Gregory's campaign, so he knew a thing or two about Boston formality.

"I know, Grandmother. I think I already have a reputation as a wild bull on the pampas."

"They will ask you to join the Porcellian, your grandfather's and father's club. It's a pretty stuffy bunch, in fact probably the stuffiest of the stuffy bunches. But I hope you will consider their offer." As she finished, he saw her looking at him appraisingly. Wheeler knew she was crazy about him. "You will do them good," she said with a wry smile.

One visit in particular stood out in Wheeler's mind. One of his St. Gregory's classmates who had also come over to Harvard met him in the Yard one day and told him of an antique travel book he had found in Widener Library with what appeared to be his grandfather's name in it. Wheeler had gone to check it out and had found that, yes indeed, there was a travel guide, a Baedeker's Guide for Austria, 1896, with "F. S. Bur-

den, Jr." inscribed on the front page. Wheeler thought it peculiar because
he had not realized that his grandfather had been a junior. He took it to
his grandmother and expressed his puzzlement. "Wasn't Father the junior?" he asked. His grandmother held the small red book for a long time
without speaking.

"You are right. It was your father," she said softly, bringing the book to
her breast and holding it there for a long time, closing her eyes. When she
opened them, Wheeler could see that they were filled with tears. "He
loved old books," she said. "He must have bought this one and inscribed
it when he traveled to Europe in college with Brod Walker."

That first year at Harvard, Wheeler took a philosophy course from Professor Broderick Walker, "your father's dearest friend," his grandmother
said. She was touched and amused. "Standish, you in a philosophy course
will be a source of wonder. I hope they are ready for you." She had always
loved the way he roamed through ideas. She would sit in her Beacon Hill
living room and listen to him for hours, always encouraging him to digress
and embellish.

As his grandmother predicted, the philosophy course was the highlight
of the year, as was Joan Quigley. He learned far more than he expected
from the philosophy course and from a Radcliffe girl. His grandmother
had no way of predicting the Joan Quigley part.

As you have no doubt realized by now, my son, Wheeler, was something
of an obsessive, and while at Harvard College he became obsessive about
music. That is the only way to account for what was to follow. When he
first got to Harvard he had asked around about guitar players. He bought
a used Fender Stratocaster electric guitar to accompany his father's old
acoustic Martin and began daily practice, and was beginning to sound like
his rockabilly mentor. He wanted to learn more licks and maybe join a
band. A friend took him to Brattle Street, where he played a little and listened a lot. That was the part of the coffeehouses that compelled him,
the seemingly endless supply of musicians, most all of them guitar
players. Cambridge and the area around Harvard Square radiated an in-
fectious excitement in the early 1960s, and he found himself in the middle of it. Wheeler thought he was in Wonderland full of beatniks,
long-hairs, radical thinkers, unconventional poets, and even a few naïfs

like himself. It was a world that could not have been more different from the Sacramento Valley where he had come from. "One thing for sure," Wheeler observed later, "they were all people who had never heard of Dilly Burden. And that was a great relief."

He loved being around the coffeehouse scene; it drew him like a siren song. The Brattle Street cafés were filled with people reading papers, dressed in dark and simple clothes. But it wasn't just the new licks on the guitar that sent him back to his room to practice, it was also the wild ideas. There was always someone willing to sit and digress, always willing to listen and take seriously his ideas, and nothing stopping where he took them. There were always more to add, more references to pile on, more books to peruse after a late-night session. It was even better than conversing with the governor of California or Chet Huntley. "You're in heaven, pal," his friend Bucky Hannigan would say if he could see him now. Wheeler had never been around people who were willing to accept his wild questioning of things and to hear his views about politics and society, about the world as it should be.

The coffeehouse musicians were interested mostly in folk music, but as time passed it became clearer and clearer to him that it was rock and roll that fascinated him.

The Buddy Holly tape gained him a certain notoriety. He had shown it to no one at St. Gregory's, but when he played it for the coffeehouse group he soon became known as a kid who could play. A group of students from Boston University had formed a small band that specialized in imitations of top-forty rock bands. They called themselves The Shadow Self, and their leader was a guitarist named Hitzie, who could pick about as fast as anyone Wheeler had ever seen, lightning fast. He seemed to like Wheeler's hanging around and picking up guitar licks, but when the group heard the tape of the kid from California singing that song with the Buddy Holly soundalike, all of them took a different kind of notice.

"It's not a soundalike," Wheeler said, but no one believed him.

"What's on the rest of the tape?" Hitzie asked Wheeler one night in their practice room.

"I don't know," Wheeler said. He had rarely played the song after Holly's death, and he had never gone past the blank space at the end of the song.

"I think we'd better listen," another said, and they sat in stunned amazement as they discovered the remainder of the forty-five-minute reel. It was the master working of six new songs, never heard by the world, never recorded in any other form. Without knowing it, a few days before his death, Buddy Holly had given the young man in his apartment a gold mine.

"No one's ever heard any of these," Hitzie said, ecstatic. "Like King Tut's tomb." They all looked at one another in wonder, and instantly agreed in that moment that Wheeler Burden was now a full-fledged member of The Shadow Self.

In that same week, he sat near Joan Quigley at a group table on Brattle Street. "Who is that band you hang around with?" she asked.

Joan Quigley was just about the most beautiful girl Wheeler had ever seen. She was there a lot, one of the peripheral members of the scene, an actress more than a singer, who was willing to fill in when someone needed a female voice. "The ice princess," they called her. She was a year ahead of him at Radcliffe and had a football player as a steady boyfriend. Wheeler had kept his eye on her from the first time he saw her. She had been sitting by herself in a corner of a Harvard Square bookstore, dressed in a dark purple turtleneck, and smoking a cigarette. He had noticed her immediately, he figured, not just because she was about the most beautiful girl he had ever seen—a knockout, as Bucky Hannigan would say—but also because she was reading a copy of *Persephone Rising* by Flora Standish.

"The Shadow Self," Wheeler answered.

"That's Jung," Joan Quigley said.

"Who's Jung?" Wheeler asked.

"You know, Freud's disciple."

"Now, Freud I know. He is in my heritage."

That was when Joan Quigley first gave Wheeler significant notice. "You are something of an *idiot savant*, aren't you?" she said, using the French, which to Wheeler sounded like *eee-deee-oh savah*.

"What's that?" he said.

"Oh, brother," she said, taking a deep breath. She stared at him for a long moment, probably deciding then and there whether to drop him like a stone or make of him a project. Luckily or unluckily for Wheeler, the most beautiful girl he had ever seen chose the latter.

"I'm a refugee from Miss Porter's, and I thought I was protected." She took his hand. "Come on," she said calmly. "We're taking you to the Coop bookstore. If you're going to hang around anarchists, you might as well know what they are talking about," she said with no particular flourish. "And you'll need a guide."

Joan Quigley's family had been around Boston almost as long as the Burdens, and Wheeler's grandmother spoke of them with respect. "More than their share of bohemians," she said in a tone halfway between admiration and envy. Joan showed none of the Brahmin in her dress. As her coffeehouse self, she wore nothing but Levi's jeans and turtlenecks, "undoing the damage of four years of prep school," she said. Wheeler loved the crisp witty way she talked, and it wasn't long before he realized he had developed an enormous crush on her.

"Forget it," Hitzie said. "She'd freeze your balls if you ever got them anywhere near her passage."

But Joan kept coming back to him, watching over him, it seemed. "Fortunately for you," she said late one night at the coffeehouse, "I find innocence an aphrodisiac."

"What's an aphrodisiac?" Wheeler said, and Joan Quigley, who was a tough one to impress, only stared in amazement.

It was Joan's idea to embellish the Buddy Holly tapes. "Why not?" she said. "He's dead, and no one knows the songs exist. Besides, it's what he would have done." A friend of her father had a recording studio where they could work at two and three in the morning. After two months, The Shadow Self had added guitars, drums, and harmonies to six Holly songs, with the legend's voice in the lead. Wheeler had most of the ideas. "A vision," Joan Quigley observed. "You seem to have this picture of how it should turn out." They finalized them on a stereo tape with a collection of their own songs. "It's brilliant," Joan Quigley said as they were walking back to her dorm one night. "Of course you can't do anything with it, since it's all illegal." What happened was that the tapes got around and created an instant and huge black market hit. The band was nameless, faceless, and incredibly famous. In their appearances at the coffeehouses, when Shadow Self—"Drop the *The*," Joan Quigley had insisted—burst into one of their familiar songs, the packed house went wild.

It was still in his freshman year, after a session in the sound studio at two in the morning, when Joan had asked Wheeler to stay behind to help her close up. She had been paying closer attention to him than usual the last week of studio work, obviously impressed by the way Wheeler had learned to use the recording equipment. "You have legendary concentration," she said as he worked to fit a guitar track in with the voices. "That's the *savant* side."

Wheeler laughed. "I guess I sort of lose myself in things."

"Well, it's sort of your best quality," she said, leaning against his arm. Wheeler could smell fresh New England sea breezes in her hair and tried not to acknowledge the tingle up and down his back from her touch. They were standing by the piano in the main recording room, looking for the light switch. "I'm taken, you know," she said.

"I know," Wheeler said. "Your football hero."

"That's why nobody can know," she said and flipped him a smile and a small packet. "Ever seen one of these?" she said. He had seen a number of them before, but never at such close range. The most beautiful girl he had ever seen had just flipped Wheeler his first Trojan and, he judged from the smile, there was more. She took his hand and, lifting the bottom of her turtleneck, placed it on the warmth of her belly, holding it there. "I have a gift for you." She slid his hand under the band of her jeans. The Ice Princess looked up languidly into his eyes. "Men have conquered empires for this," she said, leaning forward, pressing his hand downward. "And you're getting it without even asking."

⚬

"I was afraid you might turn me down," she said, sitting up on the studio couch.

Are you kidding? he felt like saying to the girl of his dreams who was just now pulling on her turtleneck. "Because I was a prude?" he said.

"Because you wouldn't know what it was."

"Like the drugs?" he said. Wheeler turned down the psychedelic drugs that had begun to appear in the coffeehouses, through the influence of some Harvard professors. "He don't need to get any wilder," Bucky Hannigan would have said. "Wheeler doesn't need drugs" was Joan Quigley's famous quip to Hitzie. "He *is* drugs."

"That was really something," Wheeler said, sounding stupid as they found the light switch.

"I'm glad you think so," Joan Quigley said, leaning into him and pulling the door closed behind her. "We'll have to try it again sometime. But you'll have to earn it."

The trouble came about the same time, and it was Professor Walker, his father's old friend, who saved his fat from the fire. It all began with a paper Wheeler wrote for the freshman philosophy course. He called it "The Great Catch: The Highest Point in Civilization," in which he reasoned that Willie Mays's catch off Vic Wertz in the 1954 World Series was the highest point in civilization because of the preconditions. The ideas he had distilled from the lessons of the Haze. The nation needs to be at peace; the boundaries secure; people need leisure time and enough money to organize theater, sports, and the like; you need stadiums, uniforms, and a division race; and you need people with the aesthetic sense to know it is important. He put some time in on the outline, dashed it off longhand, and handed it in to his section leader, an intense young department youngster named Fielding Shomsky.

The following day Shomsky saw him going into the men's room in Widener Library and followed him in. From the neighboring stall, he delivered his diatribe to Wheeler. "This is damn good, Burden, but you show no pride. It could be a brilliant paper, and yet you hand it in like so much flotsam. Take it back, polish it, get it typed, and have it back to me by week's end." He shoved it in under the stall divider, and he was gone.

Wheeler did as Shomsky asked. He did polish it and think more about it. This time the typed manuscript was entitled "The Preconditions of a Cultural Apex." A few days later Shomsky told him he was submitting it to the department as a prize paper. Wheeler thought no more about it. The following week he was summoned to the dean's office. When he arrived, there sat the dean, Fielding Shomsky, and Professor Broderick Walker, head of the philosophy department and the foremost authority on Viennese philosopher Egon Wickstein.

The dean was an aristocratic-looking man who wore tweed jackets and had a long row of pipes on his desk. "We have a problem here, Mr. Burden. Your section leader Dr. Shomsky here—" He gestured to the young professor who glowered at Wheeler. "He has found a marked similarity between your philosophy paper and an original by Egon Wickstein." Wheeler could only stare in disbelief. The dean held up two papers, one by Wheeler, the other by Egon Wickstein. "Both bear remarkably similar titles involving the phrase 'Cultural Apex,' and each bears an uncanny resemblance to the other." Shomsky continued to glower, and Professor Walker looked concerned. The dean took a deep breath. "Do you understand the basic rules of plagiarism?"

Wheeler nodded dumbly. "I didn't copy that essay, sir," he said finally.

"This is a highly unusual situation. With Dr. Shomsky's consent, we will turn the whole situation over to Professor Walker for a judgment," the dean said, looking over to the young section leader, who gave a reluctant nod of agreement. "Fine," the dean finished and handed the evidence to his elder colleague.

In his meeting with Professor Walker that afternoon Wheeler explained that he had written the paper and had even submitted it in draft form. Professor Walker, a scholarly-looking man with kind dark eyes and huge black eyebrows, explained that Mr. Shomsky was furious and wanted blood. It was not until he submitted it as a prize paper that it was pointed out to him by a senior colleague how much it resembled an early and obscure work by Wickstein, a writer every department member should know completely and cold. "You, Standish, found a piece of writing Mr. Shomsky had never heard of. He thinks you duped him and that he looked bad in the department."

"I didn't find it," Wheeler said. "I've never seen anything by Egon Wickstein. I—"

Professor Walker interrupted and eyed Wheeler wistfully. "You are the last Burden, the last of your distinguished family to carry the name—as was your father, my good and dear friend, and as was his father before him. Much responsibility rests on the shoulders of the last member of a family. But Fielding is the first Shomsky, and he too feels certain responsibilities. You can understand, I am sure. He was not, shall we say, to the manner born."

"I didn't copy that essay," Wheeler tried again.

"Your father was my dearest friend. I don't know if you know that. My, he was a specimen. I was never much the athlete. Your father—" There was a longing in his eyes. "He was like an antelope. He had the grace of a dancer. And, oh my, he had a scholar's mind. In fact, it was he who first introduced me to Egon Wickstein. It was the summer we traveled to Europe together. Your father played his famous clarinet in the dance band on the ship, over and back, and I had plenty of time to read. Your father gave me his books. I was so taken by Wickstein's writing that when we got to England I looked him up at Cambridge University. Then years later, after he died in the concentration camp, I got hold of his papers and studied him in depth in London. That is how I ended up back here at Harvard." It was widely recognized that Professor Walker's great biography of Wickstein brought him to his position of preeminence in modern philosophy. "All because of this." Professor Walker held up an ancient manuscript. "A charming little essay I read on shipboard with your father entitled 'The Preconditions of Cultural Apex.'"

Wheeler shifted uncomfortably in his chair. "I don't know what happened," he said. "But I didn't see that paper. I didn't copy it."

Professor Walker, overcome with kindness, seemed totally uninterested in whether Wheeler had or had not seen the Wickstein piece. The rest of the session was spent talking about Dilly Burden.

After that the subject of the plagiarism never again came up, except from Fielding Shomsky, who continued to be furious. "You are from a famous family," he said, glaring at Wheeler with his dark eyes that seemed more menacing than the situation merited. "You plagiarized a paper and got away with it. You don't belong at Harvard. You have no sense of honor."

Wheeler stared back. "I did not plagiarize that paper, sir." His voice was calm and emphatic. "I don't know what happened, but I wrote that essay myself. You saw the draft." But Shomsky would have none of it. Reality to him was the reality he saw. There was no explanation other than his own.

He was worked up to a lather. "And your family isn't all it is said to be either. Read this—" He slapped a copy of *The Cambridge Voice* into Wheeler's hand. "This will settle a few things for you."

Wheeler read the article in the underground newspaper and kept it. It was an old copy of a 1954 edition, with a cover story about Dilly Burden, and it was obviously a negative one, and pretty nasty, debunking the legend. According to the story, Dilly Burden, with an abnormal need to be a hero, had been duped and betrayed by his own people and had not lived up to the *"ne chantait pas"* legend. He had talked; everyone tortured by the Gestapo talked. And Dilly's father, Frank Burden, the prominent Boston banker, had been a fierce anti-Semite and a heavy investor in Nazi Germany, and had actually killed a man, a Jew, in Europe, at the turn of the century, an event covered up by his family connections. In short, he was not the heroic character his appearance in the 1896 Olympics made him out to be. The article, which Joan Quigley told him to discount as sensationalist yellow journalism, was not at all a flattering portrait of the Boston Burdens.

After a week or so Shomsky had settled down. It was not until that May, when Wheeler was on the freshman baseball team as a reserve pitcher, that his arm came back into the spotlight, in two rather eccentric ways. The first was in a game in which he came in to throw just one pitch to end a tumultuous inning, and his teammates began calling him "One and Out." Then the second came when an MIT student was working on a radar device for measuring the speed of small objects, and he decided to test it on baseball pitchers. He had been to a Red Sox warm-up and then had come to Harvard, where a number of pitchers including Wheeler threw for him. That week there was an article in the *Boston Globe* about the device. The MIT student was quoted as saying: "There are a few bugs in it. I got a Harvard freshman substitute pitcher throwing as fast as half the Red Sox staff."

When Wheeler read the article he called the MIT student. "Your machine's not wrong," he said.

"What do you mean?" the MIT student said.

"I'm the one. Your machine does not lie." The student set the radar machine back up and, sure enough, same results. A writer for the university newspaper, the *Crimson*, did a feature on Wheeler.

"If you have that kind of speed," the *Crimson* reporter asked incredulously, "why don't you use it?," pointing out that Wheeler did not see much action even in freshman games.

"I've grown sort of bored with fastballs," Wheeler responded, without explaining his interest in giving batters pitches they had a chance of hitting.

The *Crimson* article was facetious, titled, "Kid with Major League Arm Bored with Fastballs." Shomsky read it. What Wheeler did not know about his former philosophy section man was that he was an incurable baseball fanatic, the kind who as a twelve-year-old kid had known the name and batting average of every left-hander in the majors. "You didn't tell me you had a no-hit game in prep school, Burden." For Shomsky, that changed everything.

"You said I have no honor."

"What'd it feel like?" Shomsky, it turned out, would trade honor for a no-hitter any day.

"Okay," Wheeler said flatly. The no-hit game had come in his last year at St. Gregory's, but it had meant little and added little to Wheeler's reputation because it was against Charles River Country Day, and everyone knew that Charles River boys were athletically hapless. And Shomsky's question came to him in the days when the life and music of the coffeehouses was filling his mind, and besides that he was having trouble concentrating on much other than his hand in Joan Quigley's pants. "It was a highlight," he said glibly. "For sure."

"I would have given anything for a no-hit game." Fielding Shomsky would have given anything to have thrown just one pitch in a real game. What Bucky Hannigan missed out on through an accident with a blasting cap, Shomsky missed out on by an accident of birth.

The next freshman game Wheeler was scheduled to start, and in the front row of the bleachers, big as life, was the first Shomsky.

That week also Wheeler received his invitation to join the Porcellian. "A bunch of stuffy pricks," Joan Quigley called them, but it meant a lot to his grandmother, so he joined.

By sophomore year Wheeler was playing guitar every day. Shadow Self had a standing engagement at a Brattle Street coffeehouse. And everyone seemed to know about the black market record.

He wrote home to his mother that his passions of the moment were music, philosophy, baseball, and a girl named Joan Quigley, in no particular order. He got so he could keep up with his courses, and he made the varsity baseball team by the skin of his teeth.

From time to time he would meet Joan Quigley secretly in someone or other's apartment because no one could know. That was the year she was absorbing Proust. "Tonight," she would say, "you are either getting into the honey jar or hearing five pages of *Swann's Way*." She paused. "Or both." Somehow it usually ended up as both.

Once, on one of the "both" nights, in the middle of wild and naked abandon, Joan Quigley stopped and sat up. "There's something I don't get," she said flatly. "Why's a guy with your talent wasting his time with college?"

13

Something of Significance

nce in Vienna, Weezie had experienced a rush of new vitality. The city itself was teeming with culture, energy, and life, and even though she had expected to find a richness of art and music, she was still overwhelmed by the abundance that the city offered. Every afternoon, in concert halls, cafés, parks, private salons, and sidewalks, music abounded. Choices for the evening included dance hall orchestras, operettas in large and small theaters, chamber music, and formal orchestras. From classical to popular to comic to the *schlagg* of waltzes, music poured from the city, most of it almost totally devoid of any seriousness. She had never seen such a joyous effluence, and at once it made Boston feel narrow, restrained, and puritanical. "How does one ever return home," she said to one of her new Viennese friends, "after such stimulation?"

Within the first two months, she had already mailed one exuberant article to *The New York Times* about the city's music in general, about her fascination with how Viennese children from the earliest years were given music lessons and encouraged to appreciate and play, and the phenomenon of whole Viennese families playing music in the home, though few were able to afford pianos. Orchestras for dancing and concerts in public parks were everywhere; folk tunes, waltzes, and marches were played by quartets of violinists, who were often joined by a guitar, clarinet, or an accordion. Even hurdy-gurdies in Vienna, she observed, ground out melodies of operas along with the ever-present folk songs that seemed to delight all classes.

And she had been collecting copious notes for a second article, a subject that seemed on the minds and in the gossip of every young music enthusiast she found herself traveling with: the bursting onto the scene of one indelible, charismatic personality, Gustav Mahler. That subject, she was beginning to realize, was also material for what her old headmistress Miss Hewens called "something of significance," a book perhaps on this fascinating character and the direction he seemed to be taking modern classical music. To Weezie, it seemed indeed a *significant* direction.

She had known about Gustav Mahler before coming to Vienna, of course. It was, after all, her excitement upon reading about his performance of his Second Symphony in Berlin two years before in 1895 that had inspired her original pseudonymous diatribe in the *Times*. Mahler too had just arrived in Vienna, in his case a return as the newly appointed director of the Vienna Opera, from Hamburg and Budapest, where he had already written three symphonies. But it was through his conducting and directing that he had developed a riveting popularity and a reputation for both inspiration and a fiery disposition. He had not yet received acceptance of his music or acquired the fascinating, beautiful wife who would outlive him by forty years and become the wife and consort to some of the most brilliant and artistic men in Europe.

Mahler was more than a musician—in a way a misfit—in this city that had spawned Mozart, Beethoven, Schubert, and many more but had also developed an obsessive passion for bubbly sweetness. Mahler was driven to speak of things to come and was not always accepted for that drive. He was a personality with flamboyant energy and passion, the son of a large and poor family some hundred miles from Vienna, halfway to Prague. His restlessness, complexity, and brilliance came from a number of influences, not the least of which was his awful experience with death. Of his twelve brothers and sisters, six died in childhood, and his beloved younger brother Otto committed suicide in 1895. Mahler himself was to die in 1911 of a heart ailment at fifty-one, only a few years after the death from scarlet fever of his young daughter, Maria. From its earliest, his music carried a profound emotional range. He had studied for many years in the conservatory in Vienna and knew well the music of lightness that made the city famous, but he also had immersed himself in Mozart, Brahms, and Beethoven. His early fame came from his songs, the cornerstones to his symphonies. But his years in Budapest as director of the opera allowed him to reinterpret Mozart and introduce Wagner, and he did it with such passion and zeal that his reputation was cemented in his late twenties. Now, at age thirty-seven, he had been invited to the pinnacle, to direct the

Vienna Opera. Anyone who met him for the first time commented on his magnetic intensity. Musicians who worked for him were at once offended by his rigorous demands and enthralled by his breathless talent and a charismatic appeal that had led, in gossip at least, to numerous affairs with famous singers he had worked with. For Weezie, meeting him was not only her secret goal in choosing to come to Vienna in the first place, over Paris, say, or Rome, but the experience of a lifetime.

She began to realize that the "something of significance" from her time in Vienna was going to be about this remarkable man, and she had already begun collecting stories about him that abounded within the music circle and throughout the city. In an attempt to avoid Vienna's growing anti-Semitism, he had converted to Christianity for the occasion of his triumphant return. He had been appointed through politics. One of Weezie's favorite stories was that toward the end of his time in Budapest in 1891, Johannes Brahms attended Mahler's conducting of Mozart's *Don Giovanni*, claiming famously beforehand, "Nobody can interpret *Don Giovanni* for me! That is music which I can enjoy only if I sit down and read the score." But afterward he was swept away. "That is just the way it ought to be done!" Brahms said to Mahler backstage, taking him by the shoulders and shaking him heartily. "That was the best *Don Giovanni* I've ever heard. Not even the Imperial Opera in Vienna can rival it."

Weezie wanted to know all she could about this remarkable man, to attend as many of his performances as possible, and she busied herself reading about his style and his influences, finding interviews where she could. Then out of the blue, Ernst Felsch said, almost in passing, one morning in the Café Central, "Well, Papa will have you meet Mahler in his studio in his home."

Immediately, her heart fluttered. "That would be thrilling," she said, anticipating a meeting that would become one of the inspirations and one of the great embarrassments of her brief time in Vienna.

She was surprised in being met at the door by a very plain-looking maid, a girl of no more than eighteen. She had imagined the great center of so much of her attention being surrounded by people of exotic and exquisite beauty. "Herr Mahler will see you in his studio," she said and led the way.

The room was high ceilinged and spacious, with large windows and a good deal of daylight spilling in from the garden outside. Beside the piano was a disorderly array of boxes, in various stages of being unpacked. "Fraulein Putnam," she heard and turned to find Gustav Mahler, of average height, in a plain dark suit, vest, and bow tie, with wire-rimmed glasses. His receding hairline and high forehead gave his eyes added prominence. He was beside her with outstretched hand before she could catch her breath. "You will have to excuse the unpacking. It is the sad plight of the eternal homeless musician," he said, taking her hand and pulling gently. "I am sure you will want a seat."

She was in the high-backed wooden chair beside the piano before she had taken her first full breath. "Thank you for seeing me," she got out. "I know you are a very busy—"

"These visits," he interrupted, stepping quickly toward the piano, "they add the *piment* to my life." He looked over the top of his glasses. "You know *piment*, Fraulein Putnam? It is French. I believe *spice* is the English word." We can surmise purely from his reputation that the great musician had already surveyed his guest thoroughly and decided, on account of her disarming and totally unself-conscious attractiveness, that he would enjoy spending some time with this interview. "Herr Felsch has told me that you write musical *feuilletons* for the Boston newspaper."

She did not know exactly what Herr Felsch had said, and she did not know how much Ernst had told his father in order to obtain this extraordinary audience with the master. "It is a New York paper, actually," she heard her voice saying. "I live in Boston, but I send the articles to *The New York Times*."

"All the better," he said and stepped closer to her, allowing little space between them. "Even in the far outposts of Europe, we have heard of *The New York Times*," he said enthusiastically. "It is quite well respected."

Her face felt flushed, and she had little control over her words. "I write with the pseudonym of a man," she blurted out. Immediately, she wished she had not been so forthcoming.

Mahler looked at her curiously. "Ah," he said with a smile. "You can say as a man what would never be accepted from a woman." Obviously, he liked the presumptuousness of a woman speaking out.

She was regretting already that she had revealed so much. "It just happened," she said, sounding little-girlish. "I wrote one article and it was published." She was surprised that he seemed interested.

"You write about modern music, I gather."

"That is how it started. I observed that the New York Philharmonic seemed to be avoiding modern music. Actually, I suggested they perform one of your symphonies."

The great musician paused and looked her over. "Heresy," he said, with a flair. He nodded as if immediately seeing the whole fabric of her dilemma. "In New York City and Boston, I am sure, people are very conservative and cautious. It would be hard to espouse successfully the music of a European renegade such as I." He paused and eyed her again with a smile. "And be a woman at the same time."

"Precisely." She was further surprised with how quickly he understood.

"It is not unlike being a Jew," he said. "You must learn to intrude yourself, if you expect to get anywhere. One cannot always be concerned with being polite and proper, if one is going to achieve anything." He was arranging a group of papers on the top of the piano. "Come, let me show you my work in Vienna." She rose and joined him, feeling both stimulated and light-headed.

"You have heard my symphonies?"

"I have not," she said too quickly. "That was my point. I have not, nor has anyone else in America. But I have read the scores."

The great musician looked surprised. "I am impressed."

"But I must admit that I read incompletely. I hear music imperfectly through the cello, the strings."

"And what would be better?"

"For your music, Herr Mahler?"

"For my music, yes."

She looked at him appraisingly for an instant, to see if he was perhaps belittling her. "Are you testing me?"

He suddenly looked concerned. "No, no," he protested quickly. "Far from it, Fraulein Putnam. I am deeply interested."

"Why, the horns," she burst out. "It is the horns, Herr Mahler, that distinguish your second symphony. That is what I want to hear in full symphony."

"An excellent point," he said with a wry smile. "I am impressed. And
that is what you wrote in your *feuilletons*?"

"Yes," she said, looking a little sheepish. "I am afraid I came off a little
pretentious."

"And the prestigious *New York Times* published it."

"That," she said apologetically, "and others."

"I am flattered that you came to my defense."

"How could I not?" she said.

Perhaps she was too agitated to perceive that Mahler was liking her
conversation very much.

He guided her attention to the sheets of music spread out on the piano
top. "These are the songs, my 'Lieder eines fahrended Gesellen,' the
songs of a traveling journeyman, I think you would say. They have made
quite a splash." He ran his hands over the manuscripts of musical nota-
tions.

"We have not had the honor of hearing these either," she said
quickly.

"My time in America has not yet come, I think you would have to admit. But with your help, it sounds as if it might come sooner, rather than
later."

"That is my hope," she said, and he could not have helped hearing her
earnestness.

He looked into her eyes with a vibrancy she found both attractive and
disquieting. "They are really my most original work. The symphonies are
more conventional, but the songs express—" He closed his eyes and
placed his fingertips on his forehead. "Express my true—" He closed his
eyes again, tapping something even deeper. "My deep inner feelings." His
eyes were on hers again. They had a hypnotic appeal, pulling her toward
him. "Take one," he said and handed her a number of the sheets. As he
did, his hand brushed hers. He had picked up a baton from the piano and
used it as a pointer. "These passages in here, written for voices, have become without tone, almost disharmonious." The baton brushed against
her hand. She saw the point of the baton gliding across the ink scribblings.
The images began to swim in her head. He had moved closer and she
could feel the touch of his lapel against her shoulder. "Always I need to
restrain myself, always I need to remember what an audience is willing to
tolerate. Always—"

She was aware of his hands moving and suddenly his voice began to fade away and her vision blurred. Later she recalled the room spinning and the feeling of falling. Then blackness.

"You dropped like a sack of turnips, Fraulein Putnam," Herr Mahler said to her after she had come back to earth, lying on the couch beside the piano. He had been gracious and stayed with her until she had fully awakened. Before the maid showed her to the door he asked that she come back, "sometime when you have had a full meal," he said with a charming smile, supplying a reason for her collapse. But she had not returned. She had been to see him direct at the opera, and she had written much of the article.

But she had been too embarrassed to return.

14

Berggasse 19

erggasse 19, where Sigmund Freud lived for nearly half a century, was an unpretentious apartment house on a respectable residential street. When he moved there in the summer of 1891, Freud was a promising but unknown young neurologist with unorthodox ideas and an uncertain future; when he left the house and Nazi-occupied Austria for London in June 1938, "to die in freedom," he was a world-famous old man, "an explorer as significant as Copernicus or Columbus or Charles Darwin," the Haze used to say.

As Wheeler Burden climbed the narrow stairs to Dr. Freud's second-floor apartment on his third morning in Vienna, he was more than a little familiar with the building and its soon-to-be-famous occupant. As he knocked on the door, we know from his journal, he was filled with both awe and relief. The awe came because from his earliest days he had heard stories of the great man from his mother, who as a young woman had been a devoted disciple, then later, because of her *Persephone Rising*, a famous antagonist. And he felt the relief because this bold move on his part promised to lead to some kind of support for his desperate condition. Recently, in preparing the Haze's book *Fin de Siècle*, in which a whole chapter was devoted to Freud, Wheeler had devoured many descriptions of the man and the apartment, including many photographs. So Wheeler felt well prepared for what he was about to see and the delicate intrusion into the great man's history he was about to engineer.

Also, from his journal, we know something of his purpose in concocting the plan, his thinking that if he could interest Dr. Freud in his plight, he could perhaps prevail on him for room and board, at least until the Frisbee was ready, or until he found some other means. But we know also that Wheeler was fully aware that he would be walking a fine line between interesting the doctor and interfering with the great man's future, something he very decidedly wished not to do. A fine line indeed, but he was confident that he was up to the challenge.

The maid answered and led him into a small waiting room, where he sat for some time before the door to the inner sanctum opened and Wheeler found himself staring into the face of one of the most famous men of the twentieth century. Freud was surprisingly short, five six or so, and meticulously groomed. His manner was immediately cordial, curious perhaps, but definitely guarded. "How may I help you?" he said.

Wheeler reached out his hand. "My name is Harry Truman," he said as he entered the study. "I was wondering if I could have a moment of your time." Caught off guard perhaps or simply wishing to be polite, Freud took the hand and invited his guest in without much second thought. There is, of course, the possibility that from the very first glance the doctor recognized in this visitor the potential of a conversation, and even more importantly, fellowship.

What might have had something to do with his willingness was that at this moment in 1897, Sigmund Freud was at a transition point, waiting for an inspiration. He was still two years away from his monumental *Interpretation of Dreams* and over ten years away from the fame and recognition he gained in 1909, when, seemingly out of the blue, the great Viennese doctor would receive a rather remarkable invitation to travel to America and deliver a series of lectures at Clark University, near Boston, "his breakout event," Wheeler called it. And, of course, the great doctor, laboring in near obscurity in 1897 Vienna, had no way of knowing that the arrival of this strange visitor was setting in motion a series of events that would lead to that all-important invitation.

But the storyteller is getting ahead of herself. Here in 1897, the great doctor was at a pivotal point in his career, just formulating his first historic connection with mythology, catalyzed by his recent attendance at a production of Sophocles' tragedy *Oedipus Rex*. In a letter to a friend, he had recently written, "I have discovered in the human condition a great similarity with the Greek myth of Oedipus, who murdered his father and married his mother." This shift to the "Oedipus complex" meant that he had moved away from his broader child-abuse theories and was now seeing as the cause of devastating sexual hysteria a primal drive he would describe and would fervently continue to believe in for the rest of his life. In short, he would conjecture, little children wanted to murder and sleep with their parents.

For the past decade Freud had been on the trail of the unconscious mind and the connection between mental state and physical disorder, and proof positive that the causes of physical ailments were often mental. Alone with his patients in his office, he had begun to realize the power of what he called "the talking cure." Patients with debilitations could find relief by simply engaging in free-form exposition.

Like Darwin's new science, where clues to the mysteries of evolution rested on the surface of the earth in fossils, the clues to the mysteries of the unconscious lay in surface gestures and words. Freud, an astute observer anyway, had over the past few years become obsessive in his observations of mannerisms and how they presented clues to the unconscious mind. The clues, of course, led slowly to discoveries that the brilliant doctor hoped would eventually bring him notoriety, wealth, and fame, and in that stubborn and solitary quest had isolated himself. At this moment in Sigmund Freud's life, for anyone such as Wheeler Burden who sought his attention there was one huge advantage. In 1897, in his early forties, Sigmund Freud was a deeply lonely man, desperate for companionship.

⚭

We can only speculate about Sigmund Freud's reaction to his visitor. He must have been intrigued from the beginning, watching his strange guest with more than usual interest and care, searching for clues as he and the visitor exchanged introductory conversation.

He must have found himself uneasy and indefinably fascinated. This total stranger had shown up without introduction and without an appointment, entering the room confident, clear-eyed, and offering his hand as if meeting an old acquaintance. At first Freud might have suspected a prank, concocted perhaps by university students or Mayor Karl Lueger's anti-Semitic nastiness, but those suspicions were put to rest by the obvious sincerity of his visitor.

From the doctor's point of view, the new intruder, Harry Truman, he called himself, appeared to be in his late forties, about Freud's age. He was tall and slender, and he wore a rumpled suit that looked as if it had been tailored for another man, and might have been slept in. His tanned skin suggested that he came from a clime sunnier than Vienna's. Although he spoke intelligently and articulately in both German and English, he preferred the latter, obviously his native tongue, with an accent that suggested the western United States, with a touch of the British, although Freud admitted to not being proficient with American accents. His German, although perfectly understandable, was academic rather than colloquial. His hands were soft, suggesting a bourgeois lifestyle, his fingers long and delicate, like those of a musician.

Clearly, the man was less than fully familiar with Vienna and the Viennese, a fact that came out in a number of points of conversation. He seemed unusually open and forthright about most aspects of life, but he had spoken his name hesitantly: the thought that the name Harry Truman was a pseudonym occurred to Freud.

For certain, there was something he was hiding. Perhaps overly sensitive to the threat of being duped by the con man, Freud had trained himself to see duplicity in the eyes, the windows to the soul, and now with this stranger he watched for it vigilantly.

From the start Freud sensed that the man held him in a certain reverence and possessed more than a passing knowledge of his theories.

"You know my work then, Mr. Truman?"

"A bit," the man said without hesitation, looking away for an instant, obviously hiding something while at the same time appearing almost too open and naïve. He was, after all, an American, and from his bearing Freud gathered that he had not traveled in Europe. How would he have known? A puzzlement.

Sigmund Freud usually knew the truth when he was being told it, at least truth as the patient saw it. Patients rarely lied for any other reason than to suppress painful thoughts and to avoid embarrassment. Even on the conscious level, some facts were simply too painful or confusing or even shocking to admit, although in time patients usually found they could discuss most details of their lives openly. Sometimes they lied for another purpose.

He often retold with amusement a story from his student days about a patient in the state mental hospital incarcerated because he was certain he was Napoleon Bonaparte. This particular patient was famous among the hospital staff for having an eye that twitched violently whenever he was in the middle of lying. One day, the patient was on his best behavior during a psychological examination because he wanted very much to be released from the ward. He had been doing well in the interview, and when as a final question the doctors asked him if he was Napoleon, the man answered an emphatic no, and his eye began to twitch.

Now in his study with the surprise visitor, Freud bore in. "You are here then because of amnesia, Herr Truman?"

Wheeler nodded. "I have absolutely no idea how I got to Vienna."

"What are your last memories?"

"I was in San Francisco," Wheeler said, now genuinely troubled, struggling with his memory. "Then I drifted away. And I came to my senses slowly, walking along the Ringstrasse." Up to this point he was telling the truth. His answers were clear and direct.

"San Francisco is very far from Vienna." There was a calm neutrality to the doctor's tone, nothing judgmental or accusing. "How long ago were you there?"

But now Wheeler's eyes shifted focus, imperceptibly perhaps, unnoticeable to the untrained observer. "It was not long ago—" he began, clearing his throat. "A month ago."

Freud would have sensed a change in his guest's composure.

"What is it you want from me?" Sigmund Freud asked the intruder.

Wheeler thought for a long moment. "Perhaps we could trade. I need food, clothing, and a place to stay."

Freud was unimpressed. "And what do I need?"

"Good male patients are hard to find, Herr Doktor."

Freud smirked at the pretension that struck a little too close to home. "And what makes you think you would be for me a good patient?"

"I have a classic dilemma."

"And what, pray tell, is this classic dilemma that would be of such great interest to me?"

Wheeler looked stunned and said nothing, his confidence evaporating. "I wouldn't be believed," he stammered.

Still waiting for some sign of the truth, the doctor said nothing, allowing his dark probing eyes to do their work. He rose slowly. "I am a busy man, Herr Truman—or whatever your name is. I see no reason for us to continue. I am not fond of being manipulated, and certainly not by someone who possesses all the mental faculties to know better." He walked toward the door and spoke without looking back. "You will let yourself out, I assume."

Wheeler was now in full panic, seeing his last hope of rescue slipping away. He stopped his reluctant host before he reached the door. "Wait!" he blurted out. Freud turned. The guest's confident exterior had evaporated. Suddenly, an appearance of desperation had taken its place. He looked hungry, lost, and out of place in his ill-fitting suit. "I need your help, Dr. Freud."

The doctor maintained his silence. He only stared at the pathetic visitor. Sigmund Freud was basically a kind man and did not wish to state the obvious: "And just why is your needing help of any interest to me?"

"My name is not Truman," Wheeler said quickly, searching desperately for a change in the great doctor's face, but seeing none offered more, words coming out in a stream, memories returning in a flood. "That is the name of a twentieth-century American president. My name is Wheeler Burden. The last thing I remember was San Francisco, just a few days ago." He paused, and Freud would have seen that he was about to drop his bomb. "A few days ago, only it was 1988, at the end of next century."

Freud had turned and taken a few steps back into the room, his interest now slightly piqued. "I was coming home from a bookstore," Wheeler continued falteringly, "where I had gone for a signing. My new book—" He appeared now to be completely in the grip of returning memories that surprised even him. "My own book," he said decisively. "And I was confronted by a man on my front steps. He had a gun. I knew this man, someone I hadn't seen in years—" Wheeler was lost now in the trance of recall, suddenly not caring about the listener or the fine line he had planned to walk. "I just stared at him and began to slip away, at first terrified. I drifted and many thoughts and images came to me and then more and more of them involved scenes from the Ringstrasse, until I realized that was exactly where I was."

He paused for a deep breath. Suddenly, he was looking at the doctor again, with an expression Freud would have characterized as both authentic and quizzical, one not even the most experienced con man could have counterfeited. "I came back a century to be here, Herr Doktor. I've been in Vienna now a couple of days."

The great doctor stood near the doorway for a long moment, his eyes piercing the distance between them, taking in all that his guest's unconscious was allowing to surface, aware that he was suddenly getting the truth.

"And there's more," Wheeler continued. He paused, trying to collect his thoughts, now desperate to keep the doctor's attention, all hope of restraint now evaporated. "I think I am here for a purpose."

"Yes?"

"I am here to tell you something." Wheeler now looked uncomfortable, but no longer seeking approval.

"Well, Herr Burden," said Dr. Freud, pausing then and taking a tentative step back into the room, his face betraying genuine empathetic concern. "We are making progress."

Wheeler cleared his throat and looked away. Then his eyes drifted back to the surprisingly short man, surprisingly neat and precise, across from him in the fin-de-siècle Viennese study. "I am here to tell you—You will have to pardon me for saying this." He spoke distinctly, all restraint and caution abandoned. "You will be known as one of the great minds of the twentieth century, some say the greatest mind. Your theories are taken as great cultural and psychological truths. You would be very pleased—" Wheeler paused and looked at Freud, who seemed remarkably calm, engaged, and waiting. "On some of it, sir, you are way off the mark."

"So that is why you have come to see me now?"

"I have come to tell you, sir, that you are dead wrong."

The great doctor stood for a moment, watching the face of his strange visitor, then he stepped back into the room. "It seems, Herr Burden, that we have much to talk about." And the relationship between my son and the great doctor had begun.

15

Last Waltz

t was shortly after his grandmother's funeral, in the Yale game, that Wheeler threw his legendary last pitch, "The Pitch," as it became known.

He had been with his grandmother the last night. She had turned eighty-seven that winter, and her heart was not good. He spent time with her whenever he could, often arriving with stories of his adventures in school, in which she took unusual delight. He could not explain it, but somehow Wheeler felt completely comfortable and at home in his visits, able to sit with his grandmother and talk for hours or sit with her quietly and read. Sometimes he brought his guitar, once even bringing Joan Quigley.

That last night, Mrs. Spurgeon, the woman who had been with the Burden family for more than fifty years, cooked lamb with mint sauce and apple strudel for dessert. Wheeler and his grandmother dined together and moved to the living room after dinner. She was feeling very warm and nostalgic.

"These four years have been wonderful for me," she said, looking across the couch at Wheeler. She seemed very tired. "I have felt very close to you and have seen you grow." She paused and looked serious. "I know you will probably not stay at Harvard." It sometimes astonished him that from the start she could intuit so much about him. "St. Gregory's and Harvard have been good for you. Helped round off the edges. You have handled the assignment admirably," she said with a warm smile.

"I have been a little too eccentric, Grandmother," Wheeler said, in something of an understatement.

"You get eccentricity from your mother," she said without apology. "That is a good thing. I have never told you this, but I always admired your mother. She was Jewish and a communist or a pacifist or whatever she was." Wheeler had never heard his grandmother speak of his mother. "But I have admired her most for her life force. And she gave your father something he needed so very much." She seemed to be floating back over time, and her eyes moistened. "They would have had a deeply fulfilling life together." She paused and collected herself. "Your father was such a good man, so full of talent and purpose. But too stiff and Bostonian, I always knew. She had something he needed. One could see a miraculous change in him. Under her influence, he was less staunch, more in touch with things, but also more vulnerable, as if he had just begun to feel. It was quite miraculous, actually." Then she seemed to drift even further away, into a resigned sadness. She released a small controlled sigh that came from the depth of her being. "What a shame he could not have lived past the war. You would have enjoyed his company." Then she smiled in total enjoyment. "And he yours."

"I would have loved that," Wheeler said. "Just to get to know him and see what he was really like."

"You and your mother were greatly deprived."

"Mother suffered, I know." The thought stopped him. "You know Mother is different," Wheeler said. His grandmother picked up on the tinge of apology in his voice.

"Do not undersell your mother. She is better than the whole pack of us Burdens." There was a genuine warm sincerity to her words that surprised Wheeler. He had always thought his mother something of an embarrassment to the Burden family. "And, oh, how your father loved her. She had—" His grandmother paused, and Wheeler waited. "She had ardor." Years later Wheeler still remembered how she pronounced that word and her devilish little smile. She repeated the word. "Ardor. That is what your straitlaced Brahmin father needed."

"He could do so much," Wheeler said. "He seemed to be a Renaissance man."

"Yes," she said, "but he was missing life force. That is what she gave him. Life force." She closed her eyes and breathed deeply, as if trying to withdraw the very essence of this living room that held so much of her history: her own childhood, her early years of marriage, raising two daughters, her life with her only son, and even her brief memory of Wheeler's mother, the Jewish girl from war-ravaged London.

Suddenly the memory turned painful. "How I loved!" she clasped her hand to her chest. "No one should love that much." Then as if by will, she drifted past the pain, even further back, and for a moment Wheeler thought she might fall away completely. "The waltz," she whispered dreamily, and slowly opened her eyes. He was completely with her in that moment. What a beautiful woman she was. Then she snapped back.

"I would like to waltz," she said with her famous resolve, and she rose from the couch, suddenly the tiredness giving way to a kind of affectionate formality. "I feel like dancing with my favorite grandson."

She was twenty again, with a twinkle in her eye, and a burst of almost reckless energy. She walked over to the hi-fi and put on a record, then walked back toward him holding out her hands. "Shall we?"

"I don't know how, Grandmother."

"Nonsense. Everyone knows how to waltz. It's in your fiber, waiting to be released." She pulled him after her as she took little steps around the carpet. "One, two, three . . . One, two, three," she whispered a few times, then let the gentle rhythm of the steps take over. Within no time they were dancing. "Isn't it divine? When I was young, people would waltz until they dropped. It was absolutely wicked."

The music seemed louder than usual for his grandmother's house, and for an instant he found himself lost in it, forgetting he was dancing with his eighty-seven-year-old grandmother. She was lithe in his arms, and she seemed to pull him toward her. It was at once sensual and delicious. Her eyes were closed and she smiled as if in a fabulous reverie.

Wheeler had lost track of time. He felt for another moment in his life that he was in that state of flow, connected to all things in the universe. It felt absolutely wonderful.

Suddenly he thought of her heart. "We had better stop, Grandmother. Your—"

He paused and looked down at her beauty. He had no idea where it came from, but he had a sudden impulse to kiss her. He stood frozen and looked into her face for an interminable instant before her eyes fluttered open and she became aware of his rapture. "I hoped—" she said and guided them gracefully over to the couch. She took his hand in both of hers. "Thank you, my dear grandson. I hoped just for a moment that I would be taken away right then. Is that awful?"

"You have many more years," Wheeler said bravely, as if suddenly he was the elder.

She squeezed his hand tightly. "Dear Wheeler—" She had never before called him by that name. "You will have to remember this for later. You will have to *know* this later." The words were puzzling to him, but he did remember them for use later. Then the evening was over. "Thank you," she said, "for giving your old grandmother an evening to hold forever." He looked into her face again and saw pure beauty. They parted, and he went to his room.

Mrs. Spurgeon came to get him at one thirty in the morning, wringing her hands. "You must come, Master Standish."

His grandmother had expired in the night. She had been propped up on pillows, her reading light still on, and then had tried to rise from the bed apparently and had fallen awkwardly, as if trying to get somewhere suddenly. The book she was reading had fallen out ahead of her, and her hand reached toward it protectively. The book, which Wheeler barely noticed in that moment of great trauma, was an old leather-bound volume, a diary or journal of some sort. It would be picked up by Mrs. Spurgeon afterward and placed in a box of special things, out of circulation. Wheeler walked over to his grandmother and lifted her back onto the bed, and closed her eyes. Then he sat down beside her and he wept with a ferocity that surprised him and that he had never experienced before. He sat there, guarding her, until the men from the funeral home came and took her away from the house where she had spent her childhood, in the dead of night.

At her funeral at Trinity Church, one of the saddest events in Wheeler's life, there was a huge collection of people. He sat in the front pew with his two aunts and his four girl cousins. Among the mourners was Arnauld Esterhazy, the Venerable Haze. The main eulogy was delivered by the Trinity rector, an old family friend, and an eminent churchman and orator. Wheeler was too much in the fog of grief to hear all the details, but he absorbed the main points: Eleanor Burden's childhood surrounded by intellectual luminaries, her distinguished college career, her accomplishments in the arts, her role as mother of two distinguished daughters and, of course, the legendary Dilly Burden, and finally her largely unknown prominence in the eleemosynary life of Boston. "Eleanor Burden," he said, "was a far greater force for good than any of us know. She was always one to hide her light and allow others to bask in glory. She wist not that her face shone." Wheeler did remember one detail among the flood of tributes and accolades when a small scholarly man from Clark University in Worcester, Massachusetts, the president, it turned out, described her as "a significant force" and said that it had been a substantial gift originated and engineered by his grandmother's family that had brought Sigmund Freud to the university in 1909. Freud's famous "Clark Lectures" introduced psychoanalysis to this country and launched the modern psychological revolution. "The little-known fact," the president said, "is that the idea had been entirely Eleanor Burden's."

At one point in the service Wheeler looked back at his old mentor and found that noble, dignified, and reserved Viennese aristocrat, like Wheeler, dissolved in tears, sobbing with great heaves of intolerable grief.

Wheeler's mind raced, and then as if his grandmother's frail hand reached back to him one more time, he remembered her last words at the conclusion of the waltz a few days before, as they sat on the couch. "You need to know—" she had said, catching her breath in short little gasps, then recapturing her composure. "My life was very different from others. But—" She paused and looked down, as if distracted by a thought too complicated for words. "Because of what I knew." Then she looked up squarely into his eyes, as if trying to penetrate across time to the deepest recesses of collective history. "You must know—" He remembered something in those strong eyes of hers. What she might have called ardor. She took his hands in hers and held them tightly. "You must know this and remember this." Wheeler felt something indescribable in her eyes and held them with his. "That I was happy."

16

Dilly Burden's Kid

fter the funeral, Wheeler's attitude toward Harvard changed and a lot of his enthusiasm for baseball had gone out of him. He still went to practice every afternoon, as he had for nearly ten years, but much of the spontaneity was gone. The coach, a former Red Sock from South Boston named Eddie Donovan, took the unproven but promising sophomore aside after practice and explained that, as everybody knew, his team was in a slump, and he was looking for some change of momentum against Yale. "I like the way you put the ball over the plate, son," the coach said, putting a good face on his despair. He then announced with a shrug to the Harvard *Crimson* reporter that "Burden'll go a few innings and we'll see what happens."

"One and Out's going to shut down the Yalies," his teammates kidded, and the *Crimson* ran the headline, "Son of Legend to Start against Yale." The article pointed out the rich baseball tradition in the Burden family, how Burden Gate, the entrance to the varsity field, was named after Wheeler's grandfather—a member of the first American Olympic team of 1896—and how the great Dilly himself had made his great catch in deep center field off a Yale batsman, while also lettering in track the same season. The article pointed out that everyone knew that, although the sophomore had pitched a legendary game at his prep school and could pitch strikes, he was being carried on the team for sentimental reasons. Wheeler was pretty much an unproven entity and a flake—although the writer never actually said it—who cared more about coffeehouse folk singers than baseball. He did have—it was conceded—quite a fastball, when he could control it. Wheeler felt like telling them what his pal Bucky Hannigan had known years ago: "Controlling the ball's not the problem," Bucky had said. "Controlling yourself's the problem."

The *Crimson* article also pointed out that a fellow St. Gregory's alum-nus, Prentice Olcott, a junior, was the Yale captain and a candidate for the All-American team. There seemed to be a great confidence on Yale's part because Harvard's weakened pitching staff meant that it was having to start the unseasoned Burden. Just about everyone picked the visiting team from New Haven to win.

Wheeler admitted to Joan Quigley that he had had a hard time con-centrating since his grandmother's death. "It's a great honor to start a Yale game," she said, although she had never actually been to one, and she was generally pretty much unsentimental. "It would mean a lot to your grand-mother." Joan's family was old Boston, and she knew well how much Wheeler's coming to St. Greg's and Harvard had been his grandmother Burden's idea and how much she had enjoyed thinking of him there. She paused, as if he might not accept her as a sports authority. "Because of your father." Wheeler pointed out that because of her heart his grand-mother had never come to see him at Harvard, which now made him sad.

"I guess I'll sort of be pitching for her," he said, suddenly overcome by the sense of loss.

"For her," Joan said, "*and* your father, I think."

On the afternoon of the game, Wheeler was pulling things together in his room, getting ready to head over to the field house when there was a knock on his door. Joan Quigley was standing in front of him, looking more beautiful than ever, wearing a low-cut cashmere sweater and an in-viting smile. "Nervous?" she said.

"A bit," Wheeler said. "That's an understatement, actually. It's sort of a big deal."

"Well, I've got something to settle you down," she said and pushed her way past him and into his room. "It'll only take a few minutes."

"Is that what you give your football captain before games?" Wheeler said, when they were finished and she was pulling on her cashmere sweater, which he had discovered had had nothing underneath it, and he was once again putting things together to head over to the field house.

"Are you kidding?" she said. "He's much too focused for that."

Wheeler was standing in the middle of his dormitory room, almost naked, the light from the curtained window casting him in dramatic chiar-oscuro. Joan Quigley looked up at him and seemed awed for a moment, then she smiled. "My god, look at you," she said. "Michelangelo's David in a jockstrap."

At the field, not long after, Wheeler was operating on pure adrenalin. He began almost by instinct working on the ball in warm-ups, finding that spot by the seam, loading it up with Bucky Hannigan wet ones until it was good and slippery. People came up and patted him on the back to wish him luck. He kept looking over to the Yale bench and seeing the arrogant Prentice Olcott, who didn't seem to acknowledge him.

He gave the first couple of Yale batters his straight fastball, and it sizzled in there, as Bucky would say, just about exactly where Wheeler wanted it, high, low, inside, outside. He was onto his game.

Prentice Olcott batted in the third spot. When he first walked up to the plate, poised and cool, everyone from here to Worcester knew what was at stake. Wheeler eyed him squarely, tugging at his cap. Olcott's Aryan blue eyes didn't flutter; he looked back with warm indifference, tapping his spikes with the handle of his bat. The ill will of the past now, for Olcott at least, seemed a vague and distant memory. Wheeler touched his cap in salute. Olcott seemed not to notice.

Wheeler threw his leg high and fired toward the plate a fastball that would have sent the MIT machine back to the shop for repairs. It zinged into the center of the Yalie's strike zone, and coolly he fouled it off. Strike one. Again, Wheeler threw his leg high, and again Olcott fouled it back. Strike two. Another high kick by Wheeler, and another foul ball. Still strike two. This could go on all afternoon.

Wheeler slapped the ball into his glove enough times to get the memories rolling in his elephantine sense of recall. This young man in the Yale uniform had dealt him measures of humiliation at St. Gregory's School, had tormented the younger boys. Olcott was Wheeler's first run-in with an anti-Semite. A sudden fury grabbed at his gut. "Asshole," he found his lips whispering. Almost without thinking he sneaked a last gob of saliva onto his middle finger and onto the spot by the seam and rubbed it in. "Good and ripe," Bucky would call it. He threw up his leg, the same as for the fastball. Down came the arm, and the ball snapped out of his fingers like a watermelon seed.

About halfway to Prentice Olcott it was headed right for the eyebrow hairs between his bigoted all-American blue eyes. He began to lean back, nothing hurried, but pulling his weight away from the plate. The ball dropped down and in, into the pay dirt of his strike zone, and slapped into the catcher's glove. Olcott was away from the plate catching his balance when the umpire's right arm shot up. Strike three. Prentice Olcott glared back at Wheeler Burden, as if noticing him for the first time. Inning over.

Wheeler strode from the mound, popping his fist into his glove. His eye caught the face of Fielding Shomsky in the bleachers. He was staring even more in awe than the rest of the crowd, his mouth wide agape, and for just an instant as he sat down in the no-man's-land beside the old Red Sox coach, Wheeler wondered if the young professor had gotten over his resentment. "I'm in this," the young pitcher said to the veteran coach, popping his fist into his ancient glove. "I want to go all the way."

The middle innings went about the same. Wheeler's control was good. He was in the groove, as Bucky Hannigan used to say. One of his Harvard tutors, a Hungarian graduate student with an unpronounceable name, called it "the state of optimal experience." Wheeler had written in his notes, "A sense that one's skills are adequate for the challenge. Concentration is intense. No attention left over for anything else. An activity so gratifying that people are willing to do it for its own sake, with no sense of time." That is where Wheeler now found himself. He was in the flow.

The good thing about the prongball was that it saved his arm. No one said anything to him after about the fourth hitless, runnerless inning, not wanting to be the one to break the spell. He continued to sit beside Coach Donovan, but there was a good four feet on the bench on his other side. Wheeler knew exactly what he was doing, even if no one else did. He had been here before. It's just that they hadn't. After inning five, he plopped himself down and slapped his glove furiously. Donovan put his hand on his knee. "Easy, son" was all he said, but didn't look at him.

For the second time in his life word of Wheeler's feat spread through the campus. "Dilly Burden's kid's got a perfect game through five" passed across campus. At Harvard, even important baseball games were pretty sparsely attended, but now, with the news spreading, an unusually large crowd began to form. Midway through the seventh inning Wheeler noticed that Professor Walker came up to the back of the stands. Wheeler looked up at him. He was smiling proudly and had brought with him a distinguished gray-haired man: the president of Harvard University. That was when he faced again his old nemesis Prentice Olcott, the last batter in the inning, who now carried his team's hopes on his broad shoulders. Olcott's eyes had changed. They now burned with an old Germanic fire, the deep-seated meanness Wheeler remembered from school. Wheeler saved the prongball. First, he let the Yale captain have an inside fastball that he fouled away, then another one inside that missed the zone by inches. Then Olcott took a ferocious rip and missed everything. It did not matter what each of them had done with old injuries and resentments. It did not matter that Yale's All-American was a bigot and an anti-Semite. There was simply no way Prentice Olcott was going to hit Wheeler's next pitch, and it was coming right down his strike zone. Wheeler glared into his catcher for the sign and saw in the batter's Aryan blue eyes something worth a lifetime of waiting. The pitch blew past Olcott. But before the delivery Wheeler had seen what he had come for: in the eyes of his old adversary Prentice Olcott he had seen raw fear.

The eighth inning came and went, and as Wheeler stood to take the mound for the ninth and last inning, a palpable silence filled the air around Varsity Diamond. Everything seemed to stop. Even traffic out on Massachusetts Avenue, one could imagine. It was as if the eyes of an entire civilization were riveted on this young skinny kid from the Feather River bottomlands of California. He rose and inhaled deeply. Coach Donovan reached out and touched his knee again. Wheeler looked at him. The old major leaguer spat on the ground. "Burden—" he said. Wheeler turned and blinked at him, lizardlike. "You've showed a lot of sand today." If it doesn't last, he was saying, you've done nobly, and a helluva lot better than anyone had expected. Wheeler nodded as he rose and strode out to his place on the mound.

The first batter struck out on four pitches, next batter grounded to the first baseman on two. To the third batter, only the twenty-seventh he had faced, he threw a no-nonsense fastball for a strike on the first pitch. "The horse smells the barn," Bucky Hannigan would have said. He was two pitches away from a perfect game, no hits, no runs, no errors, no runners on base.

It was the next, the penultimate pitch that everyone talked about, "The Pitch" it was called years later. Wheeler was pumped up, for sure. The ball was just the way he liked it. He was feeling in flow as much as he ever had in his life, and everything seemed present with him on that mound of earth in Cambridge, Massachusetts, where both his grandfather and father had stood. He reared back and threw the ball and it left with his greatest velocity and his fingers slid off the seams to virtually stop the spin. The ball flew toward the plate, then dropped a foot or two in a way that no one could hit it. The Yale batter swung at air, a good twelve inches above the ball. The umpire yelled, "Strike two." Later, Wheeler thought that was the best he could do, the moment when the whole world stopped, with no need to go any further. The perfect pitch, the penultimate act in the perfect game.

His grandmother was gone. Back home, in Feather River, California, his mother was reading Jane Austen or haggling with a bank representative over a row of prune receipts, oblivious to this moment. But in the world that really mattered, what Frank Standish Burden III did with a small cowhide sphere in the next forty-five seconds was of monumental importance.

It was the Harvard-Yale game. No Yale batsmen had reached base. Wheeler slapped the ball into his father's glove. He looked at the Yale batter, he looked over at Coach Donovan, he looked over at the president and Professor Broderick Walker, renowned authority on philosopher Egon Wickstein, and Dilly Burden's best friend in prep school and college, then at the First Shomsky, who cared more about baseball than honor. He looked for Joan Quigley, but he knew she did not attend baseball games. The world that mattered waited, denying itself breath until Wheeler released the ball. One pitch away from athletic and kinesthetic perfection and from legend.

Wheeler breathed for them, a deep inhalation and loud release. Then he stood for a moment, lost in time.

He bent down and placed the ball on the rubber part of the mound. He removed his crimson cap with the white *H* and placed it with his glove beside the ball. He removed his shirt, with *Harvard* emblazoned on the front, dropped it neatly beside the cap. He pulled the cotton undershirt with the red sleeves up over his head and dropped that. He kicked off his cleats, then unbuckled his belt and removed his pants. Then he picked up the glove.

The world that mattered stared in disbelief. Wheeler stood for a moment on the mound. Michelangelo's David in a jockstrap and a thirty-year-old baseball glove. Then he walked calmly off the diamond, out through Burden Gate, away from baseball and Harvard College forever.

17

An Unexpected Meeting

 heeler was now very comfortable in Vienna. Dr. Freud had arranged everything. He had known a kindly older woman in the neighborhood of Berggasse 19, Frau Bauer, who had recently lost both her husband and her son and who had an extra room, a supply of clothing, and the desire for company. Questions of his mysterious appearance without identifying papers or a means of supporting himself seemed no issue. And Dr. Freud agreed to meet with him further every few days or so.

One gray and rainy Sunday shortly after moving in with the widow, Wheeler was walking toward the Café Central when he looked up to find Ernst Kleist hustling toward him, his eyes wild with excitement. "You've got to come see," he said, barely stopping and pulling on Wheeler's arm. Low dirty clouds hung over the Danube plateau, adding a kind of melancholic heavy mood. "The setting for revolution," Kleist said as they sped along the damp curbside.

The Haze's orations had drilled into Wheeler the explosive political situation in Vienna at the time, so he was prepared. "It's about the Language Ordinances," Kleist said, as they walked. "The German Austrians are furious. They don't want the lowly Czech language forced on them, and the Slavs want their language respected. The tense politics exploded all over Austria, and now it is happening right here in capital city."

Kleist looked terrified and exuberant. "Look at this," he said, pulling Wheeler along with his exuberation. "The whole thing is about to erupt. Meetings have been scheduled all over the city, and now they are all rallying and marching to the Parliament and demanding the minister's dismissal. Look, there're thousands of them!"

They hustled together toward the Parliament building, and as they approached Wheeler could see the beginnings of a crowd forming, and he could hear the sounds of shouting. "The workers," Kleist said. "They're pan-Germanic." A large group of workers, some thousands strong, had formed a few blocks away and was now marching toward Parliament. They were dressed in formal clothes, a mixture of laborers and white-collared ladies and gentlemen. They were singing their "Song of Labor."

Then Kleist pointed down the wide boulevard. "Students from the university. They're pro-Slav, of course. They got wind of the workers' march and are forming a countermovement." Off to their right, a second group approached, and the students met them marching from the opposite direction, obviously looking for a confrontation, singing a song of their own, "Watch on the Rhine."

"Where else but Vienna," he could hear the Haze saying, "would street rioters be singing?"

Thousands of spectators surrounded them; some joined in the riotous chorus. They all milled aimlessly around, many not knowing why they were there or what they were supposed to accomplish. Everybody was cold and wet.

Just as the two masses approached each other, a small group of students, the loudest and most belligerent, made a run at the workers. They exchanged angry words, then one of the students swung out at one of the workers and grabbed his wool cap and threw it on the ground. A burly worker stepped out of the group and cuffed the student on the ear, and one of his fellow students took a swing at the worker with a stick. Both groups stepped back, realizing for just an instant the volatility of what they were doing, and then they began yelling insults at one another. It's just like Berkeley, Wheeler would have said, if he thought his friend would have had any idea what he was talking about. "It's hard to hear them," Wheeler yelled, close to Kleist's ear.

"This has been boiling for weeks," Kleist yelled back, pausing. "Look over there," he said, pointing over to a line of soldiers on horseback who had cordoned off the Parliament building. "Same with the Hoffburg," he said. "They're sealing off the entrances. Police and soldiers blocking everything. No one can get in or out."

Police were walking and riding horseback among the crowd, trying to encourage order, asking people to disperse and go home, but they seemed to be generally ignored. "They'll keep order. Nothing bad will happen," Kleist yelled above the noise.

Just then, segments of both crowds seethed toward the other, and what had been two clear sides melded together in a melee of flying fists and shrieks of vituperation. The scattered mounted police tried to pull together and form a phalanx, using their horses to intimidate and control the seething mass, but there were too many protesters, and the police were too spread out. One policeman on foot yelled at a group that was flailing at one another, and then he raised his stick to try to strike one, and he was set upon by a group of students, who disarmed him and shoved him to the ground, where he had to jump up quickly before being trampled. He yelled to his fellow officers for help, and suddenly, at what must have been high noon, a loud command sounded through the rain. The soldiers stationed in front of the Parliament building formed a disciplined line, drew their sabers, and began galloping straight forward.

The parts of the crowd that saw the soldiers charging lurched backward into those who were still oblivious and milling about, some still singing. Those too far in the middle of the pack could only sense the escalation in violence and began moving off to the side. "Let's get out of here," Wheeler said, but he could see that there was no dissuading Kleist, who was itching to be in the middle of things.

Wheeler and Kleist had worked themselves over to the side of the crowd closest to the Parliament building and the soldiers. "If anything happens," Wheeler said, "this is the side we want to be on." He had been in the middle of enough unruly crowds to know that you didn't want to place yourself in the path of the potential stampede. Now, in full view of the whole spectacle, they stood transfixed, able to see the line of mounted soldiers charging forward, their swords drawn and flashing. "Surely they are not going to use those," Wheeler yelled at Kleist.

"They'll just control things," Kleist said with a look of calm confidence. But then the first sword came down, and a spurt of blood came from the neck of one of the multitude before he dropped to the ground. The young man looked at Wheeler with a kind of desperation in his eyes. Then another sword came crashing down, then another. "It has gone beyond control," Kleist yelled in alarm. "Chaos has come."

The soldiers, their brightly colored uniforms flashing, their swords drawn and held high in the air, charged their horses straight into the crowd, with no regard for safety or compromise, intent on mayhem and no-quarter rout. Wheeler thought suddenly of the Kent State debacle in 1969, when National Guard troops opened fire on students, and how the whole unfortunate event had gone against everyone's intentions. "American youth didn't want to fire on American youth," one observer said. "Some National Guard kid just panicked." Not so with the hussars of the emperor's Fifteenth Cavalry Regiment, it appeared. They rode into the unarmed crowd the way they would into an enemy infantry, with every intention to use their swords.

An immense panic ensued. The soldiers began hacking right and left. Blood was flowing everywhere. "This is awful," shouted Kleist. And the scene in front of them was pure bedlam. Men fell in the mud cursing, women screamed, young boys were bleeding, as many injured by the stampeding crowd as by the mercilessness of the swords and horses. Later, there would be reports that the panic lasted all afternoon and spread through the city.

Seeing the swords flashing in the gloomy light, Kleist was finally making his exit. "This is no place to be," he yelled and stepped away from Wheeler, disappearing into the crowd of students.

But Wheeler held his ground, pushing forward even, for a better view. Seeing that the line of soldiers was not going to pass the point where he was standing, he felt that advancing or retreating would attract more attention than just standing in one place. He stood transfixed and watched the soldiers wade into the crowd. People were trying their best to avoid the sweeping arcs of the swords, stepping on one another. The soldiers were riding forward, taking full swings with their swords, seemingly without regard to age or gender or whether or not the victims were trying to stay or flee. Many were dropping, and wounded citizens lay everywhere. Since there was no way for the people on the street to protect themselves or fight back, the soldiers were unscathed. Now fallen bodies were in the path of fleeing feet and horses. People were screaming and tripping, and blood began to spot the ground.

Later, in accounting for his hasty retreat, Kleist remarked how calm Wheeler was. "You must be very brave," he said. "Or very foolish."

But Wheeler knew it was neither. It was more of a sense of being above it somehow. Having been dislocated in time, he felt invulnerable, as if knowing that he had not been transported to this foreign time and place to be a casualty of such a scene of incoherence and riot. He stood his ground as an unassailable and detached observer.

As the scene diminished and the crowd dispersed in panic, Wheeler became aware of one other observer, a man in his late twenties, it seemed, whose eyes had a steely calm about them, as if he, like Wheeler, knew he was simply an observer at the scene. Distracted by the dwindling pageant, by the sweaty horses and the bloody bodies on the ground, he did not notice Wheeler's eyes fixed on him.

Almost instantly recognizing the young man—how could he not?—Wheeler approached and gave him a thorough, close-up examination. The man looked at him now, surprised by his attention. "Can I help you?" he said, a challenge, not really a cordiality.

Wheeler gave him one more long appraisal, looking him up and down. "You are from Boston, aren't you?"

At first, the man looked totally stunned but quickly seemed to understand. "Why, yes, I am."

"From Harvard."

The young man's look shifted quickly to one of puzzlement, aware that he might be being mistaken for someone else. "How would you know that?"

"You look very familiar," Wheeler said.

The young man knew too much to do anything but accept it. He spoke slowly, forming the words cautiously, almost afraid of their results, then regained his confidence. "You're from Boston?" he said.

"Enough to know who you are," Wheeler said, helping him out.

"I'm sorry. You have mistaken me for someone else." Understandably, the young man was incredulous, feeling quite sure there was no way he could be recognized.

Wheeler held firm. "No, I'm quite sure."

The man stuck out his hand. "Let me introduce myself," he said vigorously. "The name's Herbert Hoover."

Wheeler took the hand and shook it, looking the man square in the eye. "Pleased to meet you, Mr. Hoover," Wheeler said, pausing for only an instant's calculation without offering his own name. Instead, "That isn't your true name, is it?" was what he said.

"How could you possibly know that?" said the man with a look of total bewilderment.

"I know who you are," Wheeler said definitively. "You are Dilly Burden."

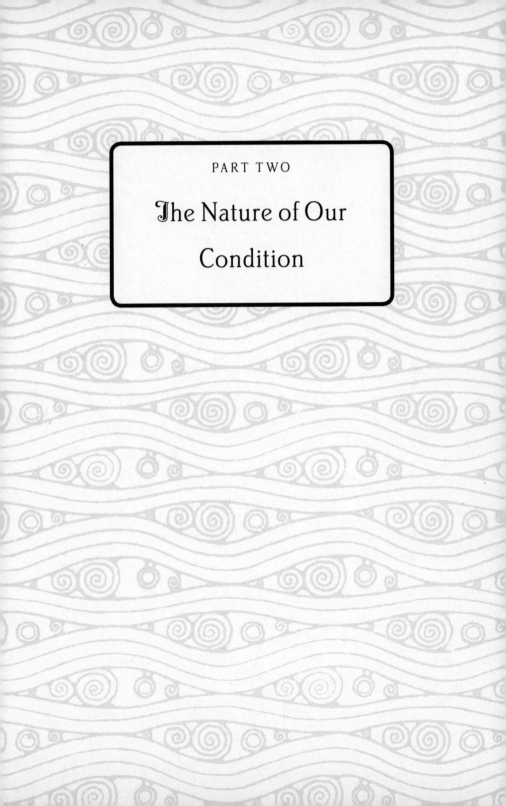

PART TWO

The Nature of Our Condition

18

Famous for Being Famous

 xactly how Shadow Self became national icons and Wheeler became one of America's Most Recognizable is documented in two major *Rolling Stone* articles, the most memorable being the first, shortly after the Woodstock festival in the fall of 1969.

When Wheeler dropped out of Harvard College, he had enrolled almost immediately in the Berklee School of Music in Boston, studying guitar formally. During that time, Shadow Self moved away from the Brattle Street scene, where they had become very popular, and began playing at a roadhouse on Cape Cod, striking out on their own, you might say. They were still singing the Buddy Holly songs, but they had also begun writing songs of their own and perfecting their three- and four-part harmonies. Word of their musicianship spread, and famous musicians from all categories began stopping in to listen. Wheeler by that time was lead guitarist and had developed quite a name among the folk groups and hot new rock bands.

Among those who came to see them from time to time was a young Yale Law School graduate from New York named Joel Rosenman. Rosenman, a singer and guitar player himself, had with a wealthy partner hatched a dream of creating an annual rock music festival in artistic Woodstock, New York, something to rival the Newport jazz and folk festivals. No one really took them seriously, but Wheeler and his band had said yes, they would be there, if the festival ever got going. This was in 1967. Rosenman came to see them a year later and said he had lost the rights to the Woodstock site because things had gotten too big, but he had contracted with a farmer named Max Yasgur in nearby Bethel, Sullivan County, New York, to use his open field. Their grandiose scheme was becoming even more grandiose. They were in the process of contracting about every famous band and personality they could think of and still wanted Shadow Self to be in that number.

The rest of the story is well documented in many sources, but Shadow Self performed before some four hundred thousand people, their album sold over a million copies, and they were suddenly a name. Wheeler was sporting his Wild Bill Hickok look by then, "so he wouldn't look like Harvard," Joan Quigley said. His image began appearing in newspapers and magazines as, more than any of the other musicians, Wheeler Burden became a symbol of the times.

In the euphoria following Woodstock, a San Francisco promoter organized a festival to be staged in Golden Gate Park a few months later. The show was to feature the Jefferson Airplane and a number of famous California bands, with rumors including the Rolling Stones. Shadow Self was among the invitees, and when permits with the city fell through, the remote location of the Altamont Speedway in Livermore, California, was chosen for December 6, 1969. Plans were finalized less than twenty-four hours before the event was to take place, and the result was disaster.

Things began to get out of control even before word leaked that the Rolling Stones were in fact planning to perform there, and that the event would be free, a "thank-you concert." Someone made the disastrous decision to hire the Oakland chapter of the Hell's Angels motorcycle gang as security—for five hundred dollars in free beer, it was said—a shocking bit of naïveté on the part of the organizers. The crowd swelled to three hundred thousand, and it became obvious that the Angels intended to use sawn-off pool cues for control. "After one of the Angel's bikes got knocked over," a reporter told Wheeler afterward, "nobody was safe anymore, not even you band guys. Somebody thought that keeping the bands playing would quiet things down, and you saw where that went." Actually, Wheeler remembered very little, having been knocked pretty much silly by one of the supposed peacekeepers.

Trouble reached its climax during the Stones' appearance, after Shadow Self had finished playing. From the beginning, the performers had bad feelings about the staging and the audience. What had blossomed at Woodstock, the charm and spontaneity of the free, limitless conditions, had ripened and rotted at Altamont into dangerous recklessness. "I have a bad feeling about this," Hitzie had said, as Shadow Self finished their last number. The crowd, many of them hallucinating on one drug or another, bleary-eyed and for some reason angry, not peaceful, pushing up toward the stage, was filled with disorderliness and hallucination. "Someone's going to get hurt."

He and Wheeler were standing side stage watching when a confused naked man rose from the seething audience and rushed the stage. A burly Angel saw him coming and felled him with a blow from his pool cue and then continued to beat him on the ground. Wheeler stepped forward, and Hitzie grabbed his arm. "Watch it, man!" he yelled, but it was too late. As Wheeler lunged in to try to shield the fallen naked man, the Angel took a mighty swing at the top of his head, doubling him forward, and then drove the butt of the cue into his gut. In the mayhem, no one realized how hurt both the naked man and Wheeler were, and they both almost bled to death before an ambulance could be directed to the stage area to carry them off. Again to try to keep the crowd under control, the show went on until an eighteen-year-old African-American man with a gun came flying up toward the stage and hit the wall of Angels, one of whom pulled out a switchblade and stabbed him to death right in front of Mick Jagger, the famous Rolling Stones lead singer. The awfulness of that culminating incident fixed the disaster at Altamont as the end of the innocence imagined by Woodstock. Oddly enough, the near-death disaster was the final event that propelled Wheeler Burden and his Wild Bill appearance into national symbology as one of *People* magazine's Most Recognizable.

"It's not your music," said Joan Quigley, who was married to her football captain, now a lawyer in Pittsburgh, and would meet Wheeler clandestinely on the road when she could. "Which has gotten very good, by the way. You are famous for being famous." That was the public part.

What no one knew, the deep secret part, was that shortly after he left Harvard, an attorney from Boston had tracked Wheeler down at music school and broke the news to him of the family trust. It seems that his grandmother had been an extremely active investor and had invested her own family money with extraordinary shrewdness over the years. "Beginning at the turn of the century, she picked start-up investments in the most prosperous American corporations," the family attorney said. "Her choices were uncanny."

The highly secret result was the Hyperion Fund, which she had controlled totally from behind the scenes it seemed, making contributions to civic causes and Harvard University. Her will had made Wheeler Burden along with his two aunts her heirs and directors.

"Mr. Burden," the attorney said, "you are an extremely wealthy man."

Wheeler paused for only a moment. "Who knows this?" he said to the lawyer.

"No one," he said. "That is how Mrs. Burden ran it. She was one of the wealthiest and most secretive investors in Boston. No one knew. Not even her husband, your grandfather, I am told. Our firm held her secret for over sixty years. We are not going to change that now."

"We'll keep it that way," Wheeler said. "Top secret."

"Absolutely," the banker from Boston said.

"Fine," said Wheeler and continued with his study of the guitar.

It was not until some time later that Wheeler noticed a most unusual detail about the Hyperion Fund. Aside from the fact that his grandmother had made a number of uncanny investments over the course of more than fifty years, in the summer of 1929 when stock prices were soaring and investors were speculating and buying wildly with huge margins of credit, Eleanor Burden had withdrawn all the funds from the stock market a few months before the Black Monday crash of October 28, 1929.

19

A Great Weight

illy Burden's discovery of his son had come in two stages. The first was the shocking realization that this man, who approached him in the midst of the chaos of the Language Ordinances riots now wildly running to escape the mounted soldiers charging into their number, was someone who knew him. That could mean only one thing, of course: that this man had experienced the same dislocation in time as Dilly himself. "You must have traveled here in the same manner as I," Dilly said above the tumult around them.

"I have," Wheeler said.

"And you knew me at Harvard?" Dilly said.

"I knew *of* you," Wheeler said. "Dilly Burden was a hard person not to be aware of." Wheeler held out his hand. "The name is Harry Truman," he said.

"Like the senator from Missouri."

"Exactly," Wheeler said, "but no relation. And actually, I am from San Francisco, but I have spent a good deal of time in Boston."

Dilly shook his head. "And you went to Harvard?"

"Actually, I did," Wheeler said.

"What class?" he said, then realized before Wheeler had to answer that both of them had for the moment disregarded the surging crowd and the melee of rioters running to avoid the sword-wielding horsemen. He looked up to see one of the mounted soldiers, sword raised above his head, charging straight for them. "Look sharp," he yelled and gave Wheeler a shove and the two of them nearly fell backward into the fray. "We've got to get ourselves out of here."

And both Dilly and Wheeler abandoned their preoccupations with each other and concentrated on weaving through the crowd and off to a side street. "I suggest we find a nice secluded café somewhere far from here," Dilly said.

Wheeler nodded and followed. "That would seem a good idea."

⊰⊙⊱

After they had retreated for a few blocks, the sound of the melee fading behind them, Wheeler found his new friend and himself in a neighborhood he knew and a workman's bar where he had eaten once before. "Could you use a meal?" he said, and just for a moment Dilly closed his eyes and said without words that, yes, he could sure use a square meal.

"So you recognized me?"

"You were in the papers. And we attended a few events together."

"You knew my parents then?" the thirty-year-old Dilly said, once they were seated, acknowledging their difference in age.

"Only indirectly," Wheeler said, trying to mask his discomfort, then changed the subject. "I believe you played with Benny Goodman's orchestra."

"Only one summer. How did you know that?"

"I ran into a teacher of yours. We met on the train to New York. He was a very dignified Austrian gentleman, and he seemed quite proud of you."

"Oh my," Dilly said. "That would be the Haze, Arnauld Esterhazy. I am sure you heard quite a trip's worth. We were very close."

"So now you see how I know so much about you," Wheeler said, comfortable that he had come up with an acceptable explanation.

"While I was in school, through law school actually, I dabbled in music. I played the clarinet and always wanted to play with John Philip Sousa."

"Don't you have to be in the Marine Corps for that?"

Dilly smiled for the first time. "A minor obstacle."

After lunch they walked out on the Ringstrasse toward the Danube Canal. "How did this happen?" Dilly said suddenly, gesturing out toward the whole city. "I mean, how did we get here? What have you figured out?"

Wheeler shook his head. "I have no idea. I was hoping you would know something."

Dilly shook his head. "It baffles me. I just woke up here. I was sitting at a table in the Prater. No idea how I got there."

"Me, I was walking right along here by the canal. I just sort of came to and found myself walking, sort of out of a fog."

"Mystifying," Dilly said. "I find myself a little out of touch with Vienna. I suppose it is my weakened condition. I am rehabilitating, I think you would say."

Wheeler nodded. "Part of it is just traveling, I think. It has taken me a long time to adjust to being here."

Suddenly Dilly stopped and stared ahead. He pulled on Wheeler's arm. "Would you mind stepping into this shop?" he said, and pulled Wheeler out of the sidewalk. Once inside, looking out the shop window, Dilly continued. "There is a man I am trying to avoid, and he was heading right toward us. I thought it best if we ducked in here for a moment." As he finished, a young man, walking briskly, appeared in their view out the store window. Wheeler watched for a moment before recognizing him as the young man in the Hotel Imperial from whom he had stolen the clothes he had on his back.

"Who is he?" Wheeler said.

Dilly looked grim. "Someone with whom I have had some dealings, and whom it would be better to avoid." Almost without wanting to, Wheeler's eyes scanned Dilly's clothes, wondering if perhaps he too had encountered the same problems Wheeler had faced upon entry to Vienna and had victimized the same poor man.

"You didn't steal from him," Wheeler said, thinking of the remarkable coincidence he was proposing.

"Oh, goodness no," Dilly said quickly. "I just don't want him to see me."

"Well, he doesn't look very friendly," Wheeler said.

"I would just as soon avoid him all together."

After the man had passed, they continued walking and came to the stone bridge over the Danube Canal. They walked out onto it and stood at the stone railing and looked out to where the river wound around through the city out to the main river.

"You have been by yourself a good deal, I gather."

Dilly sighed. "Yes. I thought it better as I was recovering. When I first arrived I needed time to myself."

"How have you been supporting yourself?"

"Not very well, I fear. I found that I could do some translating at the university. I found an assignment the first day."

"You seem to be—" Wheeler paused, wondering if it would be appropriate to bring it up. But holding back had never been one of his fortes. "You seem to be carrying something heavy."

The remark caught Dilly off guard. He stood up straight and looked at Wheeler, considering walking away at the same time sizing him up as you would an unknown sparring opponent. "What do you mean?"

Wheeler pressed on. "It's just that you look like someone who is carrying a great weight."

For just an instant Dilly looked as if he might let down, but then he pulled back. "I have come from a terrible experience."

Wheeler looked out at the city, as if he was not particularly interested in the conversation, then he looked back into the tortured face beside him. When he spoke, his voice was full of compassion. "This time travel is rough stuff, isn't it?"

Dilly closed his eyes and leaned back onto the stone railing. He took a deep breath of the canal air. "Yes," he said finally. "The last thing I remember it was 1944. I was—" Then he stopped.

"You were with the Gestapo?"

Dilly eyed his companion suspiciously. "You know about that?"

"Yes," Wheeler said. "After the war, we all heard."

Dilly looked too tired to resist. "Oh my," he said. "You come from *after* the war then?"

Wheeler nodded. "Quite a while after."

"It is all very confusing." He released this time a huge sigh, then he became reflective for a long moment. "I kept thinking about Vienna. My mother had filled my head with stories about all this, as had the teacher you met on the train."

"Your Mr. Esterhazy. The Haze, I think you called him."

"Exactly, he knew all about this." Dilly raised his hands out toward the city. "And I tried to fill my head so full of what it must have been like that I didn't think of what was happening. I guess as I got weaker and weaker and the thoughts got stronger and stronger something broke loose. However it was, I woke up in a chair in a café in the Prater, listening to waltz music. How I got there, I have no idea, but I much preferred it to where I had been."

"They were torturing you, weren't they?" Although he had not dwelled on it, the thought of his father's torture at SS headquarters in Paris had occupied some of his thinking about what his death must have been like.

"They certainly know how to do *that*," Dilly said, repressing a shiver. Then he stopped, with his hands spread out on the stones, pulling himself back to the present. Slowly, he turned his head and eyed Wheeler, an idea beginning to grow in his mind. "How do you know about the Gestapo?"

"It became pretty well-known," he said, giving his father a shrug and a conciliatory smile. "Dilly Burden worked with the French Resistance."

"You seem to know an awful lot about me."

Wheeler looked away for a long moment, deciding. "Look, Dilly," he said abruptly. "There's something I've got to tell you." Dilly was silent, waiting, and Wheeler looked over at him. Their eyes met, and Wheeler knew he was going to have to go all the way. "My name isn't Truman," he said quickly. "It's Burden, like you." Then he paused and let it soak in. "Stan Burden."

Dilly paused now for a long while, examining Wheeler's face. "How could that be?" he said curiously, without much clarity, still trying to grasp what he had just been told.

"Because I'm your son," Wheeler said. "I'm Stan Burden, your son."

Dilly could only stare. "Stan, my son?" he said in something like a mumble. Then he shook his head, poised between disbelief and acceptance. "Well, I'll be switched," he said slowly, letting his eyes run over the man across from him. "Well, I'll be." Suddenly, he looked as if he might cry. "You'll have to pardon me," he said. "I have been having a hard time with my emotions lately." He looked at Wheeler and both men's eyes filled with tears.

"That's what I kept hoping for," he said after a long moment, wiping his eyes. "This is an awful lot to absorb." He shook his head again to clear the cobwebs. "I kept thinking about Vienna and your mother and you." Then he smiled and gave Wheeler a long appraising look. "Only when I saw you last it was just a few weeks ago." He stopped and gave Wheeler a long satisfied once-over. "And you were three years old."

20

Handsome Karl

t should come as no surprise that Dilly had taken to the café scene in Vienna with relish, as if he had been born to it. He and Wheeler had found themselves alone at a table and they were talking together quietly, going over the details of their miraculous arrivals here in this mythical city, comparing notes and becoming acquainted. Dilly, adjusting with remarkable alacrity to the presence of his son twenty years his elder, was clearly stimulated by the environment of the famous Café Central. "Isn't this capital," he said with the broadest and most satisfied of grins, looking around at the marbled floors, the partially filled tables, the attentive waiters, and the racks of newspapers. "Absolutely capital." He took in a deep pleasurable breath, savoring the unique aroma of baked goods and coffee, recalling as Wheeler had the elaborate descriptions of their great mentor, the Venerable Haze. They sat and talked.

Soon the *Jung Wien* table began to form, and inevitably the two Americans were invited to join. "I am Herbert Hoover," Dilly said with gusto to the group, without even a twinge of hesitation or self-consciousness.

"We are happy to meet you, Mr. Hoover," Kleist said, with the patented good-natured acceptance Wheeler had come to expect. "A few days ago we knew no Americans except your famous Mark Twain. Now we know three. I hope you will join us in our discussion."

"Splendid," Dilly exuded. "We will do our best to keep up. I hear there is a robustness to these conversations."

Karl Claus, the writer, let out a burst of laughter. "I don't know that the word *robustness* has ever been used on us before."

"How then would you describe our deliberations?" said Schluessler, the scientist.

"Candid and honest," added von Tscharner, the architect. "We simply express our opinions in a candid and honest fashion."

"And the results," Kleist said, completing the circle, "just happen to be *robustness.*"

"So there you have it," Claus said. "We have now been categorized, and we must live up to it. Does anyone have anything especially robust to begin with?"

"The Language Ordinance riots," Dilly said quickly. "Let's start there. My friend and I were just in the middle of them and nearly got our skulls bashed in. What are we to make of these?"

"Oh my," Claus said acerbically. "Now you are asking us to notice the current political realities of our little empire. Don't you know that the first lesson of denial is to stay in the café here, head in the sand, and not notice anything in the street outside?"

Von Tscharner, the pragmatist, jumped in. "Mr. Hoover is asking for an interpretation, Karl, not your gloomy message that we are all dancing on the edge of the precipice. This is an interesting time to be in Vienna, but it deserves thoughtful interpreting observation and not raw cynicism."

"All right," Claus said, too quickly to register any offense. "I'll give our guests something thoughtful. We are living in the capital city of an empire that is looking very much like one on its last legs. Our emperor is a tired old man, an anachronism. Our Parliament is cacophonous and disruptive beyond repair. Our army, in spite of its grandly colorful uniforms, has not won a battle, let alone a war, in this century. Our borders keep shrinking. We have built a splendid boulevard of gaudy marble façades, but we cannot house or care for our lower classes. We have huge uncontrolled debt, and no one with a clue how to reduce it. All the nationalities, our dear Slavic countrymen, are dangerously restive, clamoring for attention and independence. And all we Viennese want to do is drink our coffee *mit Schlag*, listen to operettas, meet our sweet girls, and waltz ourselves silly to the strains of Strauss the younger. Let us not call it 'dancing on the precipice,' heavens no, that would be cynical. Let us look at the rosy hues only."

"There is much to be done. I grant you that," von Tscharner cut in.

"And we are the group to do it, or haven't you been noticing that either, Karl? We are Secessionists."

"Ah, the Secession," said Claus. "That is going to quiet the political chaos and right the ship of state."

"The Secession is the movement we are all part of," Kleist said, looking at Dilly and Wheeler, as if they needed explanation, but Dilly nodded to let him know he was following. Truth be told, Dilly knew exactly what they were talking about, and was loving this. "It is a group of artists who are fighting against the establishment and blazing a new trail. Very exciting." And again Dilly nodded his understanding, the Secession and the creation of the modernist movement in fin-de-siècle Vienna being one of the Haze's favorite subjects.

"We have the power to do something, to redesign politics, art, and the buildings of the city," von Tscharner said.

"You and our mayor Handsome Karl," Schluessler said. "There is a brighter tomorrow."

"Mayor Lueger, he means," Kleist interrupted again, helping his American guests, and again Dilly nodded.

"Handsome Karl is fine," Claus chipped in, his lip curling his contempt as he spoke. "If you don't happen to be Jewish."

"I think you Jews can take care of yourselves," Schluessler said. "Last time I looked you were running everything. Jews dominate Vienna's public life, the banks, the press, theater, literature, social events. Everything is in the hands of the Jews."

"I will have to agree with Herr Schluessler there. Just look around," said Kleist good-naturedly. "In the famous Viennese arts, it is the Jews who are the real audience. Without them we'd all perish: they fill the theaters and concerts, they buy the books and pictures, visit the exhibitions. Being newcomers to aesthetics, they have a more flexible way of looking at things, less burdened by tradition. That is why they have become everywhere the champions and sponsors of everything that is new."

"And that is also why the anti-Semitism," Schluessler said.

"You are saying the anti-Semitism is justified?" Kleist said.

"Not justified," Schluessler said matter-of-factly. "But not harmful either. Handsome Karl knows what he is doing. He is using certain anxieties and resentments among the working people to solidify his supporters. He's a natural leader."

"Certain resentments?" Claus snarled. "And those certain resentments just happen to be virulent anti-Semitism."

"It is a popular cause," said Schluessler. "Lueger is a demagogue. He knows the one issue that brings the working classes together."

"And that is denigration of the Jews?" said Claus.

"That is how he has gotten himself elected all these times," added von Tscharner, ever the pragmatist. "And all in all the unity is a good thing for the city, and for the empire. The method is unfortunate, but it works. It has its limits as a useful tool, for sure, but it will go no further. He can rein it in anytime. I honestly don't think your Jews are going to stop owning the banks or controlling the industries."

"So it is because of us Jews that there were riots in the street and people killed?" said Claus. "That is how we began this conversation."

"No, the riots were because of the pan-Germans," Schluessler added. "Those noble Austrians who love Bismarck and that cretin Kaiser Wilhelm. They think of themselves as Germans, they would love to be part of Germany, and they don't like the Czechs."

"And the Czechs don't like the Hungarians," Claus quipped.

"Or the Jews," von Tscharner said.

"Nobody likes the Jews," Schluessler said.

"Nobody likes anybody," Kleist said.

"My point exactly," said Claus, looking triumphant. "The whole thing is coming unraveled. The whole thing is teetering on the abyss. We are indeed dancing on the precipice."

"Bravo," Dilly exploded. The whole time he had been sitting on the edge of his chair, looking absolutely ebullient. "Now that is what I would call a robust discussion," he said.

21

A Highly Complex Delusion

rom the frequency and content of their meetings, all re-corded in detail in Wheeler's journal, and from what we already know about Sigmund Freud, we can arrive at a few conclusions. First, the great doctor would have been fasci-nated by his strange visitor, and second, he would have been absolutely certain that the man's story of time dislocation was a delusion, a highly complex, intriguing, and unusual one, but definitely a delusion. And third, that delusion was about to command the doctor's full attention. It was, as with so many of his intriguing cases, shrouded in mystery. And it was that mystery, more than anything else, that would intrigue the young doctor and keep him in conversation with his brash American visitor much longer than would have been his usual practice. In short, Sigmund Freud was hooked.

Ever the clinician, Freud would have believed emphatically from the very outset that a grand delusion, such as the fascinating Herr Burden's, occurred because of hysteria. It was really quite simple: some traumatic experiences of the past—most likely from childhood—had their normal outlet blocked, and these "strangulated" effects were causing abnormal symptoms. These symptoms could be stiffened limbs, chronic pain, de-bilitating nightmares, or even—as in this case—imagined realities, an elaborate time-dislocation fantasy. Not unlike the sense of being Napo-leon, in which the patient immersed himself totally in the life and identity of a famous historical figure, this illusion remained as a permanent bur-den (hence the invented name). *Intriguing*, the great Sigmund Freud must have said to himself.

And this we know about Wheeler Burden: no matter how he tried, no matter how he knew that he must be careful with what he said or how he interacted with people in this world of his past, he was not good at self-control. If for this difficult assignment the requirements were to be extremely careful with what one said and did, the process had selected the wrong person. But, of course, in the beginning Wheeler would be trying, maybe even successfully, to control himself.

Freud, of course, would have noticed that effort from the outset. This man was trying hard. He really believed that he was from the next century, and like so many of the delusional patients Freud had seen, his unconscious processes had constructed a highly specific bundle of imagined details, a complex and elaborate alternate reality. And the doctor could see the dilemma. The visitor had to remain very protective of specific information, wishing not to influence in even the slightest way anyone's present decisions, lest they disrupt the future he would need to be born into. And yet, the built-in excitations made such withholding difficult or nearly impossible. *Fascinating*.

Realizing the delicate situation, the ever-patient doctor would have been highly respectful, never pushing for specific information that was not forthcoming, as tempting as that might be. He was always confident that the patient's unconscious mind would eventually divulge the pathway to the original precipitating causes, those painful experiences of the remote past that triggered the condition. Thus with this man who called himself Truman, then Burden, both highly symbolic names, the great doctor would have been certain that the creation of an elaborate future world, and hence the sensation of having traveled backward from it, allowed an elaborate escape from some deeply hidden, repressed memories. And if what was repressed was brought back again into the conscious mind, through talking, the patient would eventually become cured.

Freud could see that the man wanted to talk, and that is why he dispensed with the usual use of the couch, and encouraged what appeared to be the normal upright intellectual conversations of two very intelligent men. The doctor would listen and wait, following his own rules, letting the patient's associations drift, and eventually the invented details would reveal the all-important origins of the illness. It was a process of converging, getting closer and closer with each talking session to the traumatic causal events in the patient's deep unconscious memory. But what it would not have taken Freud long to realize in this case with Herr Burden was that things were not converging, but diverging, and dangerously so. But we shall get to that.

You must know how much Wheeler's mother would have enjoyed listening in on this conversation. She had first become enamored of Sigmund Freud's ideas while a medical student in London, and the discovery of his writing led her to realize very quickly that she was more interested in where those writings led than in the biology and anatomy of conventional medicine. By the time she learned that the great doctor would be moving to London she was a full-fledged disciple and insinuated herself into the group that was arranging for his move.

Freud could see early on that Herr Burden walked a tightrope, trying valiantly to withhold information yet, through his compulsive nature, very much accustomed to expressing everything that popped into his head. Eventually, the doctor was confident, if they went at it long enough, all would be revealed. And it would not have taken the great doctor long to conclude that in the patient's invented reality Freud himself was a very important player, something of a highly influential celebrity, in the league with, dare he say, Copernicus or Newton or Charles Darwin. This part of the reality explained that Herr Burden's arrival at Berggasse 19 was not accidental. And the conversations flowed voluminously. Without divulging the specific details of the doctor's own future world, this Herr Burden was willing to, or unable not to, construct his arguments based on those details, leaving a trail for the perceptive scientist to follow. And from those arguments, the ever-patient doctor of the mind could piece together at least part of the world the man inhabited, probably constructing notes between visits. At the same time, Dr. Freud would have had to acknowledge that he genuinely liked this man.

Basically, you see, Sigmund Freud had no reason not to play along. Somewhere in the process, this giant of a thinker—a total devotee of science and empirical evidence—must have wondered about the possibility that eventually he would come upon a patient whose unconscious ramblings would concoct an accurate, or at least more or less accurate, version of the real future: vehicles powered by the new internal combustion engine, telephones everywhere, wireless communication through voice and picture, mass global wars, weapons of huge destructive ability: evolutions on a gigantic scale, all predicted from existing technologies taken to logical outcomes. If an infinite number of monkeys, pecking away at an infinite number of typewriters, could eventually produce *Hamlet*, then eventually an individual unconscious, in delusions, could create a real future. At first, Freud would have listened intently from an objective distance. But eventually even the most objective scientist ran the risk of being seduced. Somewhere along the line, we know from the journal entries, the great scientist suspended the rules of therapy and began conversing.

"Aren't we all subjective, Dr. Freud?" Wheeler said. "Haven't you just like the rest of us been swayed by your own subjectivities?"

"Subjectivities?" Freud would have said, nonplussed.

"Your own relationship with your father."

Freud moved in his chair ever so slightly but basically he took the blow, having trained himself well to have no reaction to the projections of even the most hostile patients. "And what of my own father?"

Wheeler paused in one of those moments when he was not sure how much knowledge to divulge. "Haven't you let your feelings of aggression toward him as a boy shape your generalizations about all little boys?"

Freud gave his visitor a suspicious look. "You have read my writing, I take it."

The visitor was on thin ice here obviously, careful to divulge nothing that Freud did not already know. "I am familiar with your ideas about fathers and sons," he said, as noncommittally as possible.

"You seem to know a great deal about my newest thinking."

"You may conclude that," Wheeler said cautiously, now the one shifting uncomfortably in his chair. "But I need to be careful here."

Freud's eyes bored in for a long moment, considering perhaps just how deeply he could indulge the man's delusion. "You can be frank with me, Herr Burden. I understand that you are in a difficult position. But you do not need to worry that you will affect my thinking. I am going to be what I am going to be and think what I am going to think without any slips of yours ruining things."

"Thank you," Wheeler said, giving the comment just a moment's thought. "You have been operating in a pristine world," he continued.

"Meaning?"

"I mean that your patients are completely untouched and uncontaminated by psychology."

"Meaning?"

The words now came pouring out. "They have never been asked about deep inner emotions. In school they were not asked to write about feelings. Parents do not read books about child rearing. Women with premenstrual tensions are not given leeway. No one has suggested to them for years that their ailments might be psychosomatic. In fact, no one in Vienna in 1897 even knows what that word means."

"I see," said the great listener.

"You have seen many people overcome by symptoms that you suspect are psychological in nature and not derived from physical causes. You discover that they seem cured by hypnosis."

"You know of my work with Dr. Charcot in Paris?"

Wheeler nodded. "I know that the use of hypnosis proved to you that hysterical illnesses exist, and you made them go away with hypnosis. But those cures didn't last. So you abandon hypnosis, but your practice with it has led you to your great yearning: what is the true source of hysteria, its *etiology*, as you call it?"

Freud nodded. "Go on," he encouraged. "I am impressed."

"You realize that the great majority of your patients, mostly women, report some sort of sexual assault by a father, an uncle, a brother, and you conclude that the early sexual trauma, incomprehensible to the child, is the cause of the hysteria. You reported that in a well-publicized lecture. You have launched the idea. It will come to be known as your 'seduction theory.' You have offended most of your colleagues in the medical establishment of this city, but you have staked out your turf. You have begun to make a name for yourself. You have brought into the daylight the incredible power of sex."

Wheeler had hardly stopped for a breath. Freud sat watching him, transfixed, now uncertain whether to join in the discussion. "And hypnosis," Freud said cautiously. "Where does that leave hypnosis?"

"Hypnosis," Wheeler continued, "is the door through which you entered, but it was not enough, and easy as it is to get dramatic results, and to draw patients in this pristine city where hysterics abound, it was not good enough for you. You devised a new technique."

"And that would be?"

"Talking," Wheeler said confidently. "You discovered that merely by getting the patient to talk, you could bring about much of the spectacular cessation of symptoms that you had arrived at by hypnosis, and it seemed to last."

"And that tells us?"

"The cause of the hysteria is something that has not been talked about before. It has been suppressed for some reason. Talking about it somehow frees it and brings it forward into the light of day where the mind can work on it."

"The original precipitating trauma."

"Exactly," Wheeler said enthusiastically.

"It's miraculous, is it not?"

"Yes. And in this city at this time the idea of cure by such a simple means is surprising, almost unbelievable. And yet you can prove it. You have encountered great success. It all comes from that fact that people have not talked before."

"And that is why you say it is a pristine world, Herr Burden?"

"You are in new territory. It's Eden."

"And things are different, I take it, in the world you come from?"

"I'll say." Wheeler shook his head. "Where to begin? Imagine a world—" Wheeler paused, trying to find the words. "Imagine a world in which conception, infection, detection, and guilt have been neutralized. A world in which sex is freely practiced openly outside marriage—beginning with teenagers—in which women are admitted as equals in number and status in universities, medical and law schools, in which children are raised without corporal punishment, with an abundance of lessons and activities, in which schoolteachers really care about how children are feeling, where adolescents have sex education, where married couples are given counseling on conflict resolution and methods of intercourse. A world in which a seemingly endless variety of drugs and chemicals have been developed to counteract negative psychological conditions and to produce ecstasy." Wheeler paused again for breath. "And, imagine most of all, Dr. Freud, a world in which your ideas have been accepted as a religion and you are considered the most influential thinker in the century, sainted, revered, condemned, scrutinized, and critiqued, and in minute detail."

The great doctor was now shaking his head in disbelief.

"Imagine a world," Wheeler continued, "in which you are so famous that you will become an adjective."

"You mean I would be Freudian?" the doctor said, smiling.

"Exactly," Wheeler said, dead serious. "And how would you be right now, if you knew such a world was coming?"

The great man gave the idea some thought. "I would have no choice but to be what I am right now, would I?"

"Perhaps not."

"Why *perhaps*?"

"Well," Wheeler said, drawing in a deep breath. "It seems that much of what you have come up with so far is defensive, against the fact that you know the medical establishment is offended by what you have discovered and by the fact of your Jewishness. You rocked them back on their heels by saying sexual abuse was at the bottom of everything."

"I thought you would add that I have accused them of molesting their own children."

"So that is what the talking has led you to. Your patients talk and talk and suddenly their images and memories come back to trauma associated with sexual assaults, and that is what you have brought forward to the elders of the medical establishment. Hysteria is caused by sexual abuse at an early age."

"I thought that, and I exposed that. But—"

"Enter your new theory."

"And what is that?"

"Oedipus."

Freud at this point would have looked surprised, shocked suddenly, and Wheeler would realize in an instant that he had made a great error, that he had gone too far. Freud had followed him patiently, even enjoying his diatribe describing the great doctor's evolution over a decade's work. Wheeler realized in a moment his new dilemma. He could refer to any of Freud's public statements up until this moment; they would be common knowledge, talked about by any Viennese academic or medical student. He could mention any of Freud's theories in the future—interpretation of dreams, the pleasure principle, totem and taboo—because the great man had not thought those up yet, and they would be unknown and foreign to him. But what he could not do—how he had touched a raw nerve—was mention those ideas on which Freud was currently ruminating, as he had just done with Oedipus, a theory that has not yet been made public. Wheeler had stumbled onto the very moment when the great doctor was formulating his monumental discovery, the one his critics said abandoned the plight of abused children, and the one his devotees said set him free to become the most influential thinker of the next century.

"How do you know about my Oedipus thinking?" Freud said, suddenly turning serious, sensing a threat. "Just this morning I wrote to my friend in Berlin about it. It is highly private."

Wheeler froze for a moment, realizing his error, for the first time feeling the cold sweat of the risk he was taking. The two men stared at each other. "I saw the book when I came in," Wheeler said suddenly, taking a wild stab.

"Oh, that," Freud said, motioning over to his desk, where Wheeler saw for the first time a volume of plays by Sophocles. "You are very observant, Herr Burden."

"I have a high interest in Greek mythology," Wheeler backpedaled.

Freud's eyes searched his guest's face, looking for some sign that he might be being manipulated. "Myths are the dreams of cultures," he said finally. "They tell much about the human unconscious, don't they?"

"So enter Oedipus."

"Exactly," Freud repeated, as if suddenly enjoying the conversation.

If we are watching for the moment when the relationship turned, we will notice it happening here. Now it was the great doctor who felt compelled to speak. "It has occurred to me that we are subject to the same dilemma as Oedipus. It means that the stories that my hysterical patients tell are metaphoric and imagined and *do not* stem from real sexual assault by their fathers." The doctor's fierce dark eyes looked into his guest's. "That will come as a great relief to thousands of adults in Vienna. Don't you agree, Herr Burden?"

"I agree, Herr Doctor. But maybe you oughtn't to let them off the hook so fast. Perhaps you abandon too quickly the possibility of real seduction. Perhaps you are pulling away too quickly from the controversial."

"And you think I desire to avoid controversy?"

"No, I know you are not afraid of controversy. In fact, there will be those perhaps who think you invite it."

"That I prefer controversy? That I enjoy this self-flagellation?"

"I didn't mean to imply—"

Freud stopped him. "No, no, Herr Burden. You do not offend me. I have heard that over the years. I appear masochistic to some."

"You are after truth," Wheeler said, returning his intense gaze. He could see that the doctor was touched by the empathy. "That means you step on many toes, sometimes even your own." That brought back the doctor's smile. "Now, I want to hear more about your Oedipus idea."

A new warmth had come into Freud's eyes, as if he was actually enjoying himself. "I am beginning to believe," he said slowly, "that falling in love with the mother and jealousy of the father are the universal events of early childhood, and if that is so, we can understand the riveting power of *Oedipus Rex*, in spite of all the objections raised by reason against its presupposition of destiny."

"Very interesting," Wheeler said.

A break came in their conversation. Freud fixed his guest in his gaze for a long hard moment, a look of true concern now on his face. "So *this*, Herr Burden, is where you think me dead wrong?"

"No," Wheeler Burden said. "We will come to that."

22

Duty and Purpose

t was late fall of 1939 before Dilly Burden got to London, a navy lieutenant fresh out of Harvard Law School. The British and French had declared war on Germany in September, after the invasion of Poland, but no hostilities had broken out across the Rhine, and the English waited. Dilly, who had received his commission as a naval officer a few months after law school graduation, was assigned by the War Department to work informally and secretly with the British Admiralty on a program of arms and munitions sharing that would eventually become Lend-Lease. Dilly was attractive to the War Department because Americans who spoke both French and German were a rare commodity. It didn't hurt that President Roosevelt, a proud Harvard man, called him "someone admired by all," and wrote him a personal letter of introduction to his old friend Winston Churchill, who had just been appointed lord of the Admiralty. And England was attractive to Dilly because he could continue his studies of medieval cathedrals, which had been a lifelong fascination.

There was an uneasy calm about the city when he arrived and settled into the apartment the Admiralty office had arranged for him near Piccadilly Circus. It was not until a few months later that he arranged a day off and took the train out to Coventry to see the cathedral. Not giving much thought to it one way or the other, he wore his military uniform because the train fare was free.

Gothic cathedrals were one of his specialties, and he had been to most of them in Britain and Europe, but for some reason Coventry had always been his favorite.

"You just like the thought of the Lady's bare bosom," his old friend

Brod Walker had accused when they visited the summer during their Harvard College days. It was through the streets of Coventry in the eleventh century that Lady Godiva rode naked on a white horse, to protest her husband's cruel taxation of the peasants. Although not indifferent to the subject of bare bosoms, it was one in which Dilly had had, in spite of his other rather remarkable accomplishments, very little practical experience. In poking around old cathedrals he was a master, and he had poked around extensively in the one at Coventry—that college summer and then more extensively the year he spent at Oxford, his second year of law school.

Dilly was down in the crypt, reading the inscriptions on the stones when he saw a rather pretty English woman on her knees making a charcoal rubbing on a large sheet of butcher paper. Actually, "stunning" was the word he used later, obviously a bit carried away, seeing her in the Gothic half light of the vaulted underground chamber. She had dark hair, pale skin, and "something of an eye-catching bosom" herself, he would tell her later. Her hands were small and deft with the stick of charcoal. She was so immersed in her work that he watched her for a long while before she looked up and he saw her intense dark eyes. "Oh," she said with a start, giving him and his uniform a quick once-over, trying to ignore the absolutely smashing presence it gave him. "An American warrior."

"Hardly," Dilly said. "Just another tourist."

She went back to her rubbing. Dilly Burden was used to a lot of attention. It was nothing he coveted or sought, just something he had gotten used to, and a pretty woman showing absolutely no interest proved suddenly unsettling, not to mention challenging.

"You don't usually see people down here," he said, pretending to be reading an inscription in Latin. She gave no response, but kept working on her rubbing. "I guess it is too cold and dark. Most people associate the crypt with death. They prefer the lighter stuff up with the stained glass." Still no response. "A lot of people don't realize that the crypt was the first part built and often served as the church in the early years of construction."

She had both palms flat on the stone floor when she looked up at him finally. "You might not have realized that I am ignoring you."

"Oh," he said, surprised. "My heavens, you are." She was back at her rubbing. "Looks as if you have about twenty minutes left, and then"—he looked at his watch—"it will be tea time." There was an old oak bench against the wall. He sat and crossed his legs. "I'll wait."

"Don't bother," she said without looking up.

They had tea in a sunny courtyard across from the cathedral. "You might think I don't like Americans," she said, savoring a last bit of scone. "Actually I like Americans. I don't like warriors."

"I'm not really a warrior," Dilly said. "I just graduated from law school and needed something to do."

She gave him a look that registered somewhere between total scorn and pity. "That is the worst kind. At least warmongers are honest about it."

"I've never fired a gun in anger or swung a sword."

"And what will you do, sit in a war room and push little models of human life around a map?" She was looking down into the tea leaves in her cup.

Dilly paused. He loved snappy dialogue, but suddenly he did not want to be trivial. He stared into the young woman's face until she looked up. "My name is Dilly Burden, by the way."

"Dilly." She mused on it, her hostility arrested for a moment. "What a lighthearted name."

"It's from grammar school."

"Somehow I don't see it going with all the killing." It had been a false armistice. "I would think Taras or Vultan would be better suited." She opened her purse and searched for money.

"Someone named Vultan would probably insist on paying for your tea and scone."

"Someone named Betty or Sue would probably let him." She withdrew a coin from her purse and dropped it on the table. He looked at his watch.

"I suppose if we rode back to London together on the five-forty train, you might tell me your name."

"You are only interested in me because you have never seen an English Jewish pacifist doing an Anglican brass rubbing."

Dilly appraised her for a long moment. "I caught the English part immediately," he said with a look of concern. "I'm good at that, but the pacifist Jewish part escaped me."

"Well, then, now you have it all."

"It must be hard."

"What? Being a Jewish pacifist?" She was keeping it light.

"No. Being a pacifist with all this horrible violence going on. I'd like to hear more about that."

She was a good five paces from the table when she turned back to him. "Please don't count on it," she said before seeing the look of earnest concern on his face.

The outskirts of the industrial Coventry passed by the window of the London train. "Do you think he would approve of all the factories ruining his countryside?" he said.

She had been doing her best to look unencouraging. It was clear from the start that he might follow her all afternoon and onto the train, something she admitted later to hoping for, along with hoping against hope that no one she knew would see her sitting beside a military man, and a handsome American one at that. One of the main reasons for war, she once conjectured, is that ordinary-looking men look handsome in uniforms, and handsome men ravishing.

"Who?" she said, trying to look preoccupied by the crossword in the *Times*.

"Lord Godiva."

That brought an involuntary smile. "That's clever," she said without a hint of sarcasm, and then allowed a pause. All right, if she was going to smile she might as well be cordial. "My name is Flora Zimmerman," she said. "I am single—obviously—I have a medical degree, I am Jewish, and—" She wrote a word in the squares. "I am a pacifist."

"I picked that up," Dilly said with that disarming earnestness he had. "I want to hear about the pacifist part."

"I thought you were teasing." She stopped writing and looked up. "You are serious."

"Dead serious. I don't know many pacifists, just Bertrand Russell and George Bernard Shaw."

"Well, there are more of us than you think."

"It must be very hard right now."

"That's very disarming, you know."

"What is?"

"Wearing that very attractive uniform and saying you are really and truly interested in hearing about pacifism."

"Well, I am, really and truly. Tell you what," he said, looking at his watch. "I won't wear my uniform at dinner."

"It'd take away half your charm. And besides—" She had gone back to her crossword puzzle. "I'm busy for dinner."

The restaurant was near the British Museum, only ten tables and a French menu. "I realize war is atrocity," he said. "But what do we do about what is going on right now in Poland?"

"There are better ways of dealing with the situation than fighting," she said. She was just beginning to realize that Dilly—now dressed in a blue blazer and crimson tie, which looked even more dashing than the uniform—had retained his look of concern. She realized she was having trouble concentrating. "All I'm saying is that if everyone understood from the start that there would be no violence, if it were absolutely forbidden, like incest or drinking strychnine, we would find the better way."

"Do you think that 'better way' would stop Herr Hitler?"

"How did we get into this mess in the first place? By thinking war was the solution. Now, how do we think we can get out of it? Have another war."

"But suppose," Dilly said, his tone calm and reasoning, "suppose war comes to you. And there is no way you can avoid it. What then?"

She could not remember being with a man who reasoned with her, especially on this subject. In her past, the men who met her on trains or had dinner with her—or more—either agreed with her from the start—admittedly, very few—or argued, usually the latter. And she could hold her own with both types. With this new type she was beginning to have a very difficult time.

"I do suppose," she said softly. "I suppose every day now. I know what you think. You think we are starry-eyed utopians who need a straight dose of reality, and you see that reality arming itself right now on the other side of the Rhine. Well, we are as heartsick about it as anyone in London." She took a sip of wine. "You've noticed this city. People are walking around mesmerized by apprehension. We fear just as much as they."

"I wish we had all listened to you ten years ago."

Flora Zimmerman looked into his blue American eyes. "Thank you," she said softly. She had been waiting for a man to say that to her for a long time, a lifetime to be precise. Whatever it was he wanted from her, she realized right then, looking into her wineglass instead of into his eyes, he had it.

He looked at his watch. "Tell you what. On our way to the theater, we won't mention war."

"I'm busy after dinner," she said, but there was no more snap left in her voice.

It was a Noel Coward play, and at intermission they shared a whisky. "I want you to know before you ask," she said, looking a little cautious. "In case you ask." Another weighty pause. "If we go back to your apartment—" She looked down into the ice in the empty glass. "It wouldn't be my first time."

"It *will be* mine," Dilly said.

"I am in love, the head-over-heels kind," he wrote his friend Brod Walker back at Harvard. He had never met anyone who swept him off his feet with the vitality of this Flora Zimmerman, he said. "She is witty, quick of mind, and what you would call 'an absolutely stunning girl.' She has delivered a devastating left hook to my chin."

Work at the Admiralty heated up. The unrealistic calm of the winter, in which Hitler had merely revived his war machine, gave way to a hellishly tense spring as the next move became clearer and clearer to anyone with ears and an even halfway decent sense of military intelligence.

He saw her whenever he could, which ended up being two or three nights a week, and day trips by train to cathedral cities. For the most part, their relationship—in spite of its hasty beginning—was sitting around or lying around talking.

"I cannot believe you have never picked up a girl before," she said after they had seen more of each other. "You did it so well, all smashing-looking in your warrior's uniform."

"I guess I have always been a little proper."

"I am doing my very best to be an antidote to that," she said, after they had been to each other's apartments a few times.

As well as he knew her and as love-struck as he was, it took him a good while to shore up his own strength to ask about York. He did at the end of March.

"I'd like to go up to York, in two weeks," he said. "To look at the cathedral and the manuscripts." She noticed the look on his face, but at first could not trace it. She wasn't sure, but he seemed to be blushing. She had already gotten the idea that he was an American football hero. It never occurred to her he would be nervous about something as simple as asking a girl to a hotel room. "We'd be spending the night."

She burst out laughing. "You *are* blushing," she said. "That's it. You *are* blushing. My military hero, veteran of a hundred campaigns in football and hockey and that baseball."

"I'm just not used to asking young ladies to go off with me on a weekend."

"What were you doing all that time in Boston?"

"I guess I was awfully—" He paused for the word. "Reserved about that sort of thing."

"You know what Dr. Freud would call it?" she said, trying to control an urge to laugh. Dilly winced, expecting something unflattering. Sigmund Freud had moved from Vienna in 1938 and had spent the last year of his life in London. Flora had become a latter-day disciple and had been part of the team that had prepared his entry and his London quarters. "*Repressed*," she said very distinctly, without waiting to be asked. "You have been very repressed."

"Well, right now I am feeling very unrepressed." Dilly still sat very straight. "Does that mean you will come with me to York?"

Flora looked at him and suddenly became quite serious. "The way I am feeling right now, it could be Borneo or Antarctica. You just have to ask."

"York it is, then, April eighth." He looked determined to say it as if reading a baseball score. "Overnight."

※

He could not keep his eyes off her during the whole train ride and at dinner. He could not keep from looking at her during the night in the hotel room as she undressed or as she lay beside him without clothes. "There is such vitality to you," he said, "such a lack of anything contrived, and it was what drew me to you in the first place and that now has me addicted." She pursued sex the way she pursued most everything in her life, with intensity and total commitment. "You seem to be without any sense of guilt, so uninhibited," he said.

"What's to *hibit*? It is something you want and that I want, and we have gotten it. In this case, I want it very, very, very much." A seriousness came into her eyes suddenly. "Too much, I fear."

They had a late breakfast outside within view of the cathedral's lofty Gothic towers. His face felt flush with deliciousness.

"Don't you ever feel—" He couldn't finish.

She was sipping coffee and switched to spread marmalade on her toast. "Guilt?" she said between bites.

"Right."

"I have tried hard in my life never to hurt anyone." She paused. "Is this hurting anyone?" At that moment she seemed nearly overcome by how much she loved him, a dangerous feeling for her.

"I've got to warn you," he said. "I think I am something of an eagle. I mate for life."

She smiled and shook her head. "Are you sure you have never taken a girl to a hotel before? You are awfully good at it."

And at that moment a waiter found him with the telegram. He took it, read it, and looked into her eyes, grim faced. "Sweet Jesus," he said. "We've got to head back to London. Hitler's invaded Denmark."

The proposal for his trip to France came at the end of October, after the terrible spring and summer. The Germans kept going after Denmark and swept into France in May, cornering 300,000 British troops at Dunkirk from the end of May till June fourth, when the miraculous evacuation was completed. The bombings started in August, by which time Dilly was working day and night on the defense agreement that would lend the British Navy destroyers to fight the German submarines, in return for ninety-nine-year leases of military bases in places like Newfoundland, Bermuda, and the Bahamas.

By the fall of 1940 the air war over London and the southern cities was ferocious.

The top-secret proposal to Dilly was simple. In his role as a Canadian French scholar, an expert on stained glass, he would gain access through Marseilles and would pass north, then set himself up at Chartres. From there, using French papers, he would travel through northern France for two months. The trip was dangerous, but it was not on the surface military. He would do nothing but observe, then come back to London. He was not certain that this was the turn he wanted for his military service even before he told Flora.

She was incensed, filled with worry and rage. "I thought you were not a warrior," she said, following him back to his apartment. "I thought you were just a lawyer working out agreements."

"They have a need, or they wouldn't have asked."

"And if you get caught?"

"I would be seen as a spy."

"You *would be* a spy. The Germans torture and kill spies."

"I wouldn't have any information. It's designed that way. I wouldn't know anything. They just want to know what it is like in France—"

Frustration now filled her eyes with tears. "You know what they are doing, don't you? They are trying you out. If you survive it, you pass the test. If you survive it, you also will know your way around northern France." She struggled to get through to him. "They are trying to recruit you, and you are an excellent candidate—so staunch, so full of duty and purpose."

"What does that mean?"

"They are looking for someone they can use for the war machine."

"Flora, you don't have to be so cynical."

"They are looking for a war hero."

"There is a need."

Flora had a look of desperation. "I very, very majorly do not believe in war, and now I am making the biggest sacrifice of my life for what I don't believe in."

It was not just Flora's desperate reaction that decided him. He really did want to make his contribution in a more academic way, as a negotiator and an international lawmaker. There, he told himself, his parents, and

Flora, was the chance to work toward securing something hopeful. He did not want to stray too far from the olive branch.

He told the Admiralty no.

It was the night of November fourteenth that the Luftwaffe pounded away at Coventry. Military analysts were as weary and bone-tired as everyone in those first awful months of the bombings, but they were able to see the patterns. The German high command was using the bombings indiscriminately, attempting to break civilian morale, going after the industrial cities, but not just the industrial targets.

On the evening of the fifteenth he got the first report that the Coventry Cathedral had received a direct hit. Two days later he borrowed a car and drove with Flora into the gutted parts of the city.

They stood together at the entrance to the great nave and looked out at the enormous pile of smoldering rubble, each stone hand-carved by medieval masons. The lofty vaulted ceiling was gone completely. Only the short apse side walls stood upright. The stained glass was gone. It gave the appearance of a vast rubble-strewn marketplace.

Dilly was trembling, the tears streaming down his face when he turned to Flora, who was pale with shock. He tried to speak, but the words would not form in his throat.

"I must go," he said finally.

23

Something Like an Eagle

 illy had a friend in the Admiralty office named Rory Stuart, whom he had known at Oxford, and with whom he and Flora had spent many evenings. She was sure that young Captain Stuart wished Dilly had not told her as much as he did, and wondered in his darkest moments where her pacifist leanings would take her with the information. Out of friendship to Dilly, he had a pint with her from time to time.

"I am not asking you where he is or what he is doing, Rory. You know that," she whispered at him across the table in the crowded pub. "I just want to know when he is expected out."

"Flora, you push too damn hard. Why can't you just do your patriotic duty and wait patiently?"

"Because—" she said, giving the rhetorical question some thought. "Because, first, I am simply not the kind who can wait. And, second, I am very much in love and I am very, very worried."

Rory had dropped his intense national-security look, and smiled. "You're a piece of work, Flora. If we could get your kind of intensity working on the war effort, the whole bloody thing'd be over by Easter."

"Will you tell me, then?"

He reached out and touched her cheek. "I'll let you know, dear girl." His tired eyes looked into hers. "And don't worry. The Yank can look after himself."

She felt absolutely awful about the way they had parted. She just had not been able to think about how he felt in those few days. They had one last evening together in SoHo. He had looked very wistful as he raised his glass of claret toward her.

"You will take care of yourself," he said, trying to get her out of her pout.

"Of course I will take care of myself. It's you we need to worry about."

"I'll be okay. I'm good under pressure."

She felt like telling him that this was not some American college game, but resisted. Something had been eating at him all night, and he looked as if he might be about to say it. "Flora—" He stopped and looked uncomfortable. "When I get back, would you consider marrying me?"

It was probably because she had been completely unprepared. How she wished she had taken some time to think. He needed something to take with him, to help him through tight spots and sleepless nights, something good to come home to, something that might increase—even slightly—the chances of his coming home safely.

But taking time to think had never been one of her strengths. She shook her head. "I can't marry you, Dilly."

He looked stunned. "Why?"

"There are lots of reasons. We've only known each other six months. I am a pacifist, and you are a warrior—"

He interrupted, "I love you, Flora."

"I'm Jewish. I'm English. I'm radical, for god's sake, maybe even a communist."

This was not the conversation he wished to have on the brink of his departure into the war zone. "Whatever happened to love conquering all?" He sounded dispirited and deflated.

"I'm serious." Things were turning south fast. "Well, there just are some things it can't conquer, and we have between us enough for a roomful of people. You have sex for the first time, and now—"

"I can't accept this, Flo," Dilly interrupted. "We've had so much—" He stopped, his eyes filled with tears, frustration, and sadness.

She wasn't backing off. "Here's what it is, Dilly. It's your bloody sense of duty again. You've slept with the lady, and now you have to marry her. That's just not what I want."

"That's very much *not* what it is. Not anywhere near." But there was

no conviction in his voice, absolutely none of his famous bravado. Dilly
had looked tired coming into the evening; now he looked sad and tired.
And now in January, two months after the awful evening, she realized it
was not just sad, not just tired, but heartbroken. She had caused it, she
who had always tried not to hurt another person.

She didn't go with him to the airstrip, and she didn't think of him with
his head down, heading out into the dark of the Channel. That night she
went out with old friends and drank too much and did something absolutely stupid with an American officer, an ambassador's son from Boston
who had been after her for a long time. She woke up the next morning,
feeling desperately guilty, with a deathly headache and an aching in her
heart and soul. That only got stronger as the time of Dilly's unmentionable stay in France dragged on interminably, with no word whatsoever,
even when she called and pleaded with Rory Stuart for just a crumb of
information. Twenty-four hours after Dilly Burden boarded the plane for
his entry into France, her one night's awful mistake totally behind her,
Flora had known in the deepest recesses of her English Jewish pacifist and
maybe even communist heart that he was indelibly, profoundly, and totally the love of her life.

Rory called her in late January. "He's out" was all he said. "He'll have a
few days of debriefing, you know. Ghastly lot. And sorry about the no
news, old girl. The nature of the business, you know."

She waited in the freezing rain outside the officers' club at an airfield
outside London for what seemed like hours. Pilots kept passing by offering
her an escort inside. She smiled them off and waited with her arms folded.
Finally, she took one offer, moved inside, and accepted a cup of coffee.
Then a large burly Scotsman came in a side door and tapped her on the
shoulder. "This one's it, missy," he said, motioning to the small transport
plane that had just taxied to a spot of runway nearby. "Come along, dea-
rie," he said, and she followed him, heart in throat, to where the folding
steps descended from the airplane fuselage. Suddenly a man in a dry raincoat was standing in front of her. She could see his face in the dim runway
lights. She knew he did not know she would be there. He looked into her
face, speechless, then held out his arms and she fell into them.

"I will," she said, before he could speak and let her know if the offer was still on or not, and then repeated it over and over. "I will. I will. I will," she blurted out.

In the backseat of the car going back to London he asked if she wasn't soaked through to the bone. "I would have stood for *thirty* hours," she whispered. "In sleet and gales."

In the light from the passing headlights his face looked drawn, but he smiled. "Why the sudden change of heart?"

"It's not sudden. I changed about thirty seconds after you left," fudging a bit on the timing. "But I couldn't telephone, or write, or Morse code, or anything. I couldn't get through to you in any way. 'Nature of the business,' your friend Rory said. I realized this after I had made a total ass out of myself and after I hurt you, I'm afraid, very, very much. And besides—" She had opened her raincoat and laid her hand on her belly. "We wouldn't want the little bastard to be a little bastard."

The spark came into Dilly's eyes slowly. At first, he didn't say anything, but just nodded and smiled that wonderful world-winning smile of his. "What is this?" he said. "A guy gets you pregnant, so you think you have to marry him?"

She turned in the seat to pull away and face Dilly. "That's very much *not* what it is. Not anywhere near," she said with all her famous conviction, recognizing his ironic humor but considering the moment too serious for sport. "I am marrying the guy because I love him very, very, very much." It was her eyes that were now filled with tears of relief and joy. "But I've got to warn you. I'm something like an eagle."

24

A Good and Fine Man

heeler would have known that there were no limits on what was appropriate to reveal about his own past. With Sigmund Freud there were no inappropriate or irrelevant details and no coincidences. "I need to tell you about my father," Wheeler said. Anyone knowing anything about Dr. Freud in 1897, the year after his own father's death, would know one could not sustain his interest for long without talking about one's own father. And Wheeler knew his own absent war-hero father's story would serve to keep that interest alive. In Wheeler's case it was also convenient that he was not one to exhibit much self-control; once stirred up, the memories would come pouring out in a stream of consciousness. And they did.

Freud would have been amused that this patient saw Freud himself as a hero, and one of considerable proportion. The doctor found it flattering that his patient saw psychoanalysis itself becoming accepted worldwide. Much as in Freud's observation that young female patients transfer their strong emotions and sexual urges to their therapist, this patient had transferred to Freud the necessity of seeing his own father as a global hero.

This fascinated Freud. So too did the unusually complex historical epic the patient had created in order to give his father sufficient weight as a hero, a man who quite literally had been given the responsibility of saving the world. Perhaps it was not interest in the patient or his father that fascinated the great doctor, but the epic tale. It was an absorbing and fantastic view of the future.

According to the patient's structuring of the future there would be a great war shortly after the dawn of the twentieth century, a first world war, the man called it. Following this would come a worldwide financial depression that had as its consequence, as well as the collapse of the Hapsburg empire (which happened almost in passing), two significant consequences: a worldwide military-industrial build-up and the rise of Germany under an evil dictator.

Another great world war was to ensue, with Germany taking over and occupying virtually all of central Europe (Austria and Vienna, again almost in passing). The first half of the 1940s would be consumed by the epic struggle that pitted America and Britain, with their heroic leader Winston Churchill, against the evil German empire. At one point it would even be called the Crusade in Europe.

Freud noted from the beginning the immensity of the struggle the patient needed to fashion in order to provide a sufficiently heroic stage for his father.

To a degree it was a fantasy with which Freud himself had some familiarity. As a boy he had identified closely with a hero of no smaller proportions than the great Carthagenian Hannibal in his own gallant struggle against the Romans. He had seen his own father as Hamilcar, a Semite general who had defended Sicily against the Romans in the First Punic War. It was a fitting heroic example for a son as well as for a father. Of course Freud was a boy at the time and not a forty-seven-year-old man.

Wheeler's father had been a legendary schoolboy and college athlete, a ranking scholar in medieval history, and a superb musician, talented enough to play with a famous American band Freud would have equated with Johann Strauss. He studied law and became a navy officer who played a major role in the great war of the time, falling in love with the beautiful Jewish girl who became Wheeler's mother. He served his nation gallantly as a spy, bringing great notoriety to himself posthumously because of accounts of his extreme bravery in the hands of the evil enemy. And the fact that his wife, after hearing reports of his capture by the enemy, entered the newly liberated war zone in search of him, dragging her young son along with her, only added to his legend. His death was mourned and his heroism celebrated by three nations.

Wheeler did not remember his father in more than photographs and family stories, but in 1952, at age eleven, he traveled with his mother to Paris where a plaque to his father's memory was dedicated in a square in the heart of the city. By this time Wheeler and his mother had been living on the farm in California. She did not like war heroics in general, and the heroics of her husband in particular. She thought the former helped perpetuate the folly of war, and that the latter had deprived unnecessarily the world, and her, of a great and decent man.

Freud would have noted that Wheeler spoke with no resentment of his father, in fact he seemed to hold him in great affection and recounted a number of stories from his time growing up with his mother in which the memory of his absent father was an issue. And the doctor would have found most significant an incident when the patient found a trunk full of his father's possessions in the attic of the California house.

That was when Wheeler found his father's old baseball glove. He was ten.

His mother had asked him to stay out of the attic. She had always said it was dusty, there was no light, and it was filled with black widow spiders. Although all that gave the place a certain mysterious appeal, the black widow part kept him away.

One afternoon when Wheeler thought he was alone in the house and when his sense of adventure seemed high, he climbed the stairs to the attic and let himself in with the key from the old cookie tin in the pantry.

The spacious attic was lighted only from the small windows at either end. It was indeed dusty and there were cobwebs in the corners. He found the old rocking horse he had given up at age six, his mother's dress mannequin, a number of cloth-draped chairs, a stack of large-framed paintings, and an old guitar case. In the center of an assortment of book boxes was an old steamer trunk, which creaked loudly when Wheeler opened it.

Packed inside was a clean, pressed navy uniform and officer's cap. Sitting on top of them was a collection of medals, some of them inscribed in foreign languages, and a photograph of Dilly in the uniform, and a packet of letters, tied with a ribbon. In the next layer Wheeler found a clarinet, a crimson track jersey with a white *H* on it, and a college yearbook. It was in this layer that he found the baseball glove. It was the flat kind of five-fingered glove that Wheeler associated with the olden days, with shiny worn leather. He slipped his fingers into the holes. At first it felt stiff and cold, but as he opened and closed his hand and struck it with his fist, it seemed to warm to his hand. He lifted it over his head and caught a high pop-up, then, still on his knees, popped an imaginary ball in it and chucked it toward the bright afternoon light streaming in through the window.

He had not heard his mother climb up the stairs. "What are you doing?" she said. Her voice was stern.

"I found this glove."

"You were told not to come up here." Wheeler could see his mother standing above him. In the dim light of the attic her look was cold and disoriented. He was filled with the most horrible feeling. He knew he was seeing something forbidden.

"I was looking at the black widows." It was a stupid thing to say. He had come up with the sole purpose of exploring and had found exactly what he was looking for. How he wished in that moment that he had never come up to the attic.

His mother looked down at the opened trunk and the scattered contents. "You have made a mess." There was an unfamiliar brittleness to her voice. Her eyes were fixed on the uniform on the floor beside Wheeler. "You know better—" she began, but her voice cracked and she stopped, letting out a soft moan. Slowly, she dropped to her knees beside him. He could feel the folds of her dress and her leg. She said nothing, but reached out and fingered one of the medals. Then her hand moved to the dark navy uniform jacket, and slowly she opened her fingers and ran them along the cloth beneath the lapel. Slowly, her head moved from side to side, and breath came out as a soft sigh.

Wheeler watched her face. It carried an expression unlike anything he had seen there before, one of terrible longing. "Such a fine man," she whispered, but clearly not to him. "Such a good and fine man."

Perhaps it was a moment. Perhaps it was an hour. Wheeler scarcely dared breathe. He just could only watch his mother's gentle fingers stroking the material of the navy jacket, fingering the edge of the lapel.

When she rose, she did it slowly, the folds of her dress touching Wheeler lightly. Then she stood and looked down at the contents of the trunk. "You will put everything back as you found it? Carefully?" Wheeler nodded, relieved that she no longer sounded angry with him.

She walked back toward the attic stairs, where she paused and turned. She appeared in silhouette with the light from the far window surrounding her in such a way that he could not see her eyes. "Why don't you keep the baseball thing," she said, her voice having taken on a mystical softness.

She was in her bedroom with the door closed for the rest of the afternoon. This is how Wheeler acquired his trademark ancient glove, and in so doing, long before he realized the fact, picked up the heroic mantle of Dilly Burden.

25

No Ordinary Situation

n obligation to keep to oneself," Dilly said with a staunch certitude for which he was famous, assuming as he often did that everyone with even a modest sense of propriety would be in agreement. "That is what the situation requires, and that is what we shall follow." Dilly and Wheeler, father and son, were finishing their morning coffee at a café near the Imperial Art History Museum. "That is the most difficult challenge in this whole business. We must not intervene in any way. Even the slightest conversation could have a disastrous effect on—" He paused, weighing the gravity of his own words. "One slip could ruin everything. One errant word could do irreparable ruin to *the future* we need to be born into." He buttered his bread and added a small portion of strawberry preserve.

"It's a little staggering," Wheeler said, obviously deciding to withhold information about the conversations he had already participated in, with a variety of people, Sigmund Freud being the most significant.

"We can say nothing to anyone." He savored again a bite of croissant.

"Between ourselves, of course, the pressure's off," Wheeler said jovially. "We cannot change each other's history."

And even that dimension Dilly gave a moment's pause. "Indeed," he said finally. "That is a relief."

"It is a relief to have someone to talk to."

Dilly nodded. "And you still don't remember how you got here?"

"Something traumatic, I'm pretty sure of that. Some sinister images have come back, but it is pretty much total amnesia, I am embarrassed to say. I just can't remember."

"Well, I can," Dilly said, repressing a shudder. "I was lying on a cold cement floor, hoping and praying that it would end. I had been trying to reconstruct Vienna; it was a mental game. I'd been here in college, you know. I drifted." He looked deadly serious for a moment, then shuddered again. "That's how it works, I'm pretty sure. As you are going out of one world, you drift. In my case, I drifted here. And you—"

"I just can't remember. I remember the drifting in, the morning I arrived here. I just don't remember from where."

"You had just finished the Haze's book. Your head was full of Vienna. That's it."

"My head was full of Vienna, for sure. I was giving book talks all over the country. I just don't remember the last few hours." He paused. "Except for the man in my doorway—"

"It will come to you."

"What caused yours?" Wheeler said. "You must have really wanted to be here."

Dilly looked away, as if he might be hiding something. "I just picked a place," he said a little too quickly. "Something I could reconstruct in my mind. That's what you need to do in those torture situations; I studied up on it. You know, preparing for the adventure and all that. Have a vivid picture, you know. When you are in the position I was in, you grab at anything. I grabbed Vienna."

Wheeler could have pressed: Why Vienna? Why 1897? But he let it drop. In a way both men were adjusting to the shock of being together in this strange and wonderful city, getting to know each other, adjusting to the enormity of it all.

"But I am still in something of a shocked state. When I left your mother, it was 1944, and she was thirty. When you left her, it was 1988, and she was seventy-four. When I last saw you, just a few weeks ago, you were three. Now you are old enough to be my father."

"It is sort of hard to fathom," Wheeler said, looking away, then bringing his focus back to Dilly's eyes. "This has been more than I ever could have hoped for."

Dilly did not look away and for a moment remained speechless, his famous staunchness falling away for just an instant. "Other than meeting your mother," he said, tears coming to his eyes, "I simply cannot imagine—" Then he caught himself. "It is just bully," he said, dropping coins on the table beside his coffee, leaping to his feet. "We'd better get out there into the morning." They had decided earlier to do the one thing they both wished for, spending the day as ordinary tourists. Dilly had bought a Baedeker's guidebook in English for the purpose and was prepared. He wrote his name boldly on the inside cover: *Frank Standish Burden, Jr.* "Remember," he said, "I'm still not in tip-top shape, thanks to our friends the Gestapo." He shuddered again. "You might have to wait for me from time to time."

But it turned out to be quite the opposite. And Dilly, probably not ordinary at anything, was certainly not an ordinary tourist. Wheeler found that he was the one struggling to keep up, and that his father was not a walking history lesson as much as a cultural experience, one who appeared to be of boundless energy.

After lightning attacks on three museums, they found themselves at the cathedral of St. Stephen's, looking up at the tower. "Just look at the majesty," he said, pointing up. "This one is not among the finest examples of Gothic magnificence, but still one of the marvels of medieval Europe." The serrated silhouette of the slender Gothic spire rose out of a bundle of light buttresses and pointed arches. "It was in its day a modern-day Tower of Babel, bringing together a mass of cultural influences. This cathedral has been vandalized and restored so many times since the 1100s that it's like an architectural history lesson. Look—" He pointed to various places on the cathedral edifice. "There is Romanesque, Gothic, Renaissance, Baroque, not to mention some nineteenth-century tampering thrown in."

Dilly paid the twenty-kreuzer admission charge for both of them at the sacristan's office and led the way up the more than five hundred steps to the top, which he seemed to reach without stopping. "That's some climb," Wheeler said, catching his breath. Dilly seemed unaffected, exhilarated rather by the brisk climb.

Dilly was standing at the stone railing, his eyes closed, breathing in the Viennese morning air. "Isn't it thrilling," he said, looking out over the countryside. "In the fourteenth century people came from all around just to climb those steps and see this view." They were facing west, out toward the foothills, where the Vienna Woods rose in a gentle slope off into the mountains. He pointed out beyond the Ringstrasse. "It makes you realize why this was such a valuable piece of landscape. A flat plane between two worlds—Europe out there beyond the Alps and"—he turned and swung his hand behind them—"the east with all its riches out there beyond the

Hungarian steppes. In the thirties, people who rode the Orient Express from Paris to Istanbul called it the last Western city before the plunge into the Balkans. It is such a beautiful combination of mountains, river, and the plain. And it has been fiercely fought over. Out there, just outside where the great wall used to be is where the fierce Turks camped during their devastating siege that was raised in 1683, driving the infidels back home for the last time, leaving their coffee behind. There, on that plane, are the great battlefields of Essling—where Napoleon in 1809 was driven back across the Danube—and Wagram, in which he united with the Italians at the Lobau and drove back, to become master of Vienna. For ten thousand years people have fought for control of this lovely fortress city on the bend of the Danube. Metternich said that Asia began just east of his palace. Incredible wealth and treasure passed through here when this cathedral was being built." He gave the railing in front of him a hearty slap.

Back at ground level, in the nave of the great cathedral, Dilly took care to point out each exquisite detail. "A Gothic cathedral is like a book, and the stained glass the pages. The people of the time couldn't read, so they built themselves the stories, instead of writing them. They intended them to last forever. The stories taught how to live good lives and how to ensure entry into the kingdom of God." He pointed across the great vaulted space. "You see, over there on the sunless northern wall are Old Testament stories and biblical characters depicting the world before the Messiah. And here, on the south wall, where the sun shines, we have the New Testament stories of Christ and the saints. Very clever and very geometrical." He paused and looked squarely at Wheeler. "That's what I love about the Middle Ages. Everything is so rational and logical. I would have loved to live then."

"Don't you find it a little confining?" Wheeler asked. "Rules had a pretty tight grip on things."

"No, don't you see? It was the inner life that mattered." He touched his temple. "The life of the mind. It was so pure and clean. The material world was transitory. Look around. Do you realize how many man-hours it took to design, carve out, and place each one of these stones?" He reached out and touched the rough wall in front of him, drawing its history into his fingers. "Whole villages devoted their entire working lives to the projects. And the masons who worked on this level knew they wouldn't finish in their lifetimes. Imagine being comfortable with that thought. They took hundreds of years to complete. For us in our rushed lives that is unfathomable."

Dilly paused and furrowed his brow. Wheeler was familiar enough with his father's history to know what was coming next. "And your mother and I saw firsthand how quickly it can all be destroyed." He cringed. "We walked through the rubble of Coventry Cathedral the day after the bombing. Timbers, stones, shards of glass everywhere. The work of centuries destroyed in an instant by a couple of maliciously placed two-hundred-pound bombs. The people who destroyed that shrine in a moment had no idea what they were doing, had no idea what an irreplaceable treasure they were obliterating forever. What if—" He stopped and closed his eyes, shaking his head slowly. "What if the people of fourteenth-century Coventry had known to what end their work would come? Would they have labored painstakingly to hew each beam, lay in each piece of glass, carve so precisely each stone?" He repressed an involuntary shiver. "It was the most horrifying thing I have ever seen."

"I know. Mother told me."

Dilly paused for a moment and reached inside to regain his exuberance. "A cathedral is a stupendous technological achievement." Dilly closed his eyes again, this time to breathe the rich and musty air of centuries. "They are the highest point in civilization."

"Better than the great catch?" Wheeler said, out of nowhere.

Dilly looked surprised and then eyed Wheeler for a moment. "You have your mother's sense of humor," he said. Then he turned silent and fell for a moment into deep, troubling thought. "How is she?" he asked, as if finally mustering the strength to get the question out.

"She did fine. You would be proud of her. You know, your family gave her the Feather River ranch in 1946, and she became a farmer. A good one. She never went back to England."

"A farmer," Dilly said, shaking his head. "That woman—" A flood of memories showed on Dilly's face, and he smiled savoring them. "A farmer. How was she with the books?"

"Ferocious like a tiger. She had a legendary style," Wheeler said with the same sort of smile. "And great with the workers. She has a reputation as a great bargainer."

"Last time I saw her she was quite the pacifist." Dilly smiled even more warmly. "You know, that isn't easy when there is war raging all around you . . . and your husband goes off to sacrifice himself to the cause."

"Mother never seemed to do anything that was easy."

Dilly looked down at his feet. "Including teaming up with me."

"Are you kidding? She always said it was the best thing that ever happened to her. She said you were repressed and an incredible overachiever, and it gave her a whole new way of looking at the world."

Dilly laughed soulfully. "She had a hard time with my sense of duty," he said. "I'm pretty singleminded on that score, I guess."

"She said it was your father in you."

Dilly grew serious. "My father was a stern man, the consummate banker, very forthright and prominent. He had been an athletic star, you know. Three sports at St. Greg's, football and baseball at Harvard, the first modern Olympic games."

"That was true, then?"

"Oh yes. In 1896, when the Olympics were formed in Greece, he and some athletes from Princeton and Yale formed a team and paid their own way. Father went to the Boston Museum of Fine Arts and built a discus from the sculpture. It was quite a project, and he won the event. I think he did it to prove the superiority of Anglo-Saxon bloodlines. I suppose he was an influence." Dilly paused and fell into thought, then wished to change the subject. "So your mother thought I was too duty bound?"

"She used to say you had an overdeveloped superego."

Dilly laughed again. "Your mother had a wonderful way of taking a few hundred years of excellent New England Puritan heritage and making it sound like a nervous disorder." There was deep affection in his voice, but he stopped and looked up again at the Old Testament stained glass across the nave. His eyes filled with tears. "My goodness, I loved that woman."

They had an elegant lunch at the Hotel Imperial. "If this is going to be a grand tour," Dilly said, "we will not short-change the *grandesse*. That is the word a favorite teacher of mine at St. Gregory's School used to describe this hotel."

Wheeler smiled. "You wouldn't be referring to our Venerable Haze, would you?"

Dilly returned the delighted smile. "I would indeed," he said with a flair. "Our great Arnauld Esterhazy. I forgot for a moment that you too were one of his boys."

"I was indeed," Wheeler said proudly.

"What a joy we both shared him."

"Me, for only two years, unfortunately."

"His world must have been quite a change from a California farm."

"You might say."

Dilly looked wistful. "And Esterhazy was still in form?"

"Still around, and probably even a greater character."

"He was like a father to me."

"I know. He used to tell us how great you were. Sort of worshipped what you were, they said."

"Did he still call his select gathering of students *Jung Wien?*"

"He did indeed."

"And their essays *feuilletons?*"

"Still did. Right to the end."

"Oh my," Dilly said, swept away by a feeling of nostalgia. "What a force he was! And what a luxury to have those Hazings in our schoolings."

"That's how we know about all this." Wheeler's hand swept out as if from the cathedral railing to the magnificent city below.

"To the Haze, then," Dilly said, tearing up, raising his glass of young white wine.

"To the Haze." Wheeler tasted the wine and gave a satisfactory smile. Then he paused and looked square into Dilly's eyes. "He's here, you know."

Dilly looked puzzled. "The Haze is here?"

"Of course. He's in Vienna right now, and he should be about eighteen years old, if I figure right."

The new thought stunned Dilly. Dilly who thought of everything had not thought of that. "You know, you are right." An impish smile came onto his lips. "We could go pay him a call."

"I wonder what he is like," Wheeler said, not letting on that he had actually seen him. "Probably a prissy little guy."

"You don't suppose it would interfere with his history if we just took a little peek at him. I mean, we wouldn't want him to end up at Dover." He frowned as if having bitten into a sour fruit.

"Maybe we could borrow some money from his father," Wheeler said, looking into his wineglass. "I was beginning to wonder how we were going to pay for all this *grandesse?*"

"We'll just have to invent the airplane, and sell the patent," Dilly said, lifting his wineglass toward his son and his elder.

"Too late. It's already been invented, I think."

"Well then, the automobile."

"That too."

"Then something."

"The Frisbee," Wheeler said quickly.

"The what?"

Wheeler gave Dilly a long look. "Right. You wouldn't know about that," he said, not bothering to explain that he had already had a beautiful prototype lathed by a Viennese cabinetmaker.

"How about the ball-point pen."

Wheeler lifted his wineglass and returned the toast. "To the ball-point pen." As Wheeler looked at Dilly, the younger man's face blanched.

"Oh lord," he said, suddenly, aghast, his eyes darting as if looking around for an escape route. "Here he comes."

Wheeler turned around behind him and to his horror saw walking toward them across the dining room the stern young man from whom he had stolen the clothes. He turned back quickly and buried his head. "Let's not let him see us. He's walking right this way," Dilly said. Then with great relief: "He is turning." Dilly's eyes followed the man as he left the ornate and spacious dining room, then looked at Wheeler.

"You look pale," Wheeler said, regaining his own composure.

"I didn't mean to alarm you, but I very much do not want to run into that young man."

"You've made that very clear." Wheeler did not dare look up.

"Well, it is not what you would call an ordinary situation," Dilly said, collecting himself. "That young man is Frank Burden, my father."

26

The Nature of the Condition

or some reason Wheeler had not told Dilly that the stern young American both of them were now assiduously avoiding was the very man he had robbed in his first hours in Vienna. "It is Frank Burden?" Wheeler asked uneasily. "He's from Boston, the 1896 Olympics and everything. You're absolutely positive?"

"Absolutely positive," Dilly said. "I ought to know my own father, even if he is younger than I am. But I wanted to make very sure, so I followed him into the hotel and asked the clerk at the desk, and sure enough, he said it was Mr. Burden from Boston, and he was in Vienna for 'an indefinite stay.'"

"What's he doing in Vienna?" Wheeler said abruptly.

"That, I don't know. I realize he was in Germany after the Olympics, a year at the university in Berlin, studying international banking. He became quite the expert. But I'm not sure about Vienna. Some position with the department of state, studying the Austrian currency exchange, I think."

"Well, he doesn't look any too friendly," Wheeler said.

"Friendly?" Dilly repeated, reflecting. "No, not friendly." He paused again and looked up at Wheeler. "There are some things I want to tell you about my father. He was a serious and stern man. Mother was bright and cheery, the one who brought culture and warmth, and Father provided the discipline." Dilly stopped again and smiled. "I get confused with tenses. I don't know whether to say *is, was,* or *will be.*"

Wheeler laughed. "It's the nature of our condition," he said.

Dilly returned to seriousness. "Father *was* something of an autocrat, a

black-and-white kind of fellow. One thing I can guarantee you: he is always absolutely certain that the way he sees things is the right way."

"You can sort of see it in his face."

"Well, don't get in his way when he wants something. I know that."
Dilly's voice was cold and had lost its enthusiasm.

"That sounds a bit harsh." Wheeler was fishing for more information.
"And what of the rumor?"

"What rumor?"

"When I was at Harvard, I read an article in an underground newspaper. It was pretty hard on the Burden legend, you included, and it
said that Frank Burden had killed a man in Europe, a Jew, and it got covered up."

Dilly frowned. "I did hear something like that a couple of times, I'll
admit. But I didn't take much stock in it. There was that and—" Dilly suppressed a shudder and fell silent. "There are things I don't wish to talk
about. Maybe later."

"I don't know much about him," Wheeler said. "I knew Grandmother
pretty well. We spent time together when I was at St. Greg's and Harvard,
but he was gone by the time I got there. I knew Mother didn't like him,
but I never really knew why."

"He never accepted her," Dilly said coldly.

"There is a part you don't know," Wheeler said suddenly. "He took
your death the hardest of all. People said in Boston that he never got over
it. He was terribly proud of your accomplishments, and he had great plans
for you after the war, 'the hope for a new world,' he called you."

Dilly shuddered again. "I find that very hard to believe."

"It is true. Mother said that when you died, the life went out of him.
You were his pride and joy, his main reason for creating the life he created, but I guess he didn't express it very well."

"You could say that," Dilly said with a rare cynicism.

Wheeler shook his head. "I didn't know him at all."

"I can tell you about him," Dilly said, the color returning to his face.

Frank Burden's roots went back to colonial days, back to Miles Standish,
and he was a well-educated man. He had gone to St. Gregory's, a fine new
Episcopalian day and boarding school outside Boston, and to Harvard, the

oldest and finest college in the country. He had studied European economics and politics with the finest of academic minds. He had traveled to
the continent a number of times, the most recent as a victorious member
of the first American Olympic team.

Then he stayed in Europe for the academic year, studying international economics at the university in Berlin. Now, in 1897, he had been
sent by a consortium of Northeastern bankers to Vienna, to coincide with
a personal mission. He formed a perspective that the greatness of his country was being eroded by immigration, a perspective that was perhaps not
unique among his American peers, but one that gave him the feeling of
being a prophet for his times. He saw his own country on the brink of disaster and decline. He spent a good deal of his time in Europe searching
for answers.

While in Berlin, he heard stories about Vienna and its charismatic
mayor, Karl Lueger, and he began to see a possible solution there, so he
planned a visit to the Hapsburg capital to meet the man he had studied
and admired. Lueger, a longtime member of Parliament, and a former
liberal, had created the Christian Social Party and had been elected mayor
by a popular majority. So controversial had been his election that the emperor, who despised what the man stood for, had waited a year and a half
to ratify the election. Now, in full triumph, Lueger and his policies were
firmly entrenched in the seat of power for Vienna and for much of the
empire, no matter what forces raged against him.

It was unusual for a young man from Boston, a young man in the heroic mold himself, to find as one of his own heroes a little-known leader
well out of the first tier of European powers. Part of what attracted young
Frank Burden to Lueger was his dapper good looks—*"der schöne* Karl,"
he was called popularly, Handsome Karl—and his political acumen, but
at a distance of five thousand miles those qualities made little difference.
What Frank Burden liked about Lueger was his simple use of one issue to
gain political power. In 1897, after nearly a full century of falling away
from aristocratic power and the rise of an industry-based bourgeoisie, Karl
Lueger was the first major figure in European politics to rise based on
anti-Semitism.

The enemy philosophically was liberalism and reform, of which the
northeastern United States had had its share, although not as much—nor
had it needed as much—as England and France. Social reforms of all

kinds had swept in to protect the lower classes from exploitation by those in financial and social power. Frank Burden found no fault with many of those reforms. Certainly child labor laws, uniform health regulations, and minimum wage considerations were justified and effective. Even the extension of voting rights made a certain practical sense. In fact, the rise of a powerful and wealthy middle class was all in all a good thing for capitalism.

What Frank Burden could not understand or abide was the way many of his St. Gregory's and Harvard classmates—especially those preparing for teaching and the ministry—seemed bound and determined to undermine and give up their advantage. These classmates, by supporting sweeping reforms and the lower classes, seemed to be using their inherited social and economic power to erode the very foundations of their own class. He thought of these people not so much as traitors but as fools. It was important to keep financial and political control in the hands of those best equipped to handle them judiciously, and that meant the real Americans, those like himself. If Frank Burden learned one thing from the Olympic games in Athens in 1896, it was the superiority of the Anglo-Saxon American boys. Not only were they stronger and more athletic, they were also mentally more agile. It was their northern European heritage that made them so. In the early days of American settlement, the hardy and strong-willed chose the long ship ride across the Atlantic to the new world. That trip was a far cry from that of the poor eastern Europeans who now, cowed and huddled in the holds of steamers, made their way to Ellis Island.

It was through the almost pathetic attitudes and performances of the athletes from those eastern European countries that Frank Burden first realized his superiority. And it was in Athens that he first realized the threat of the Jews. As the natural values of America became more and more watered down by liberalism and reform from the top and by the huge influx of low-quality immigrants from the bottom, the Jews would only gain leverage.

Jews, he reasoned, had an unhealthy advantage in capitalism. They were cohesive, well focused, and good at manipulating profits. They were not held back by some of the principles that restrained Christians, and they were vastly more talented than other European immigrant minorities. There were, for instance, in Boston, enough Irish to form a serious economic and political force, but the natural Irish ineptitude in business eliminated them as any kind of threat. The same could be said for immigrants from Poland and the Slavic countries. There were actually few immigrants of any kind in financial power in Boston and New York, but Frank Burden looked to Europe for trends, and he did not like what he saw. Jews, who were very good with money, flourished and rose to control of the banks. That was just what happened.

In turn-of-the-century Vienna, 80 percent of the money and 80 percent of the banks were controlled by Jews. Liberalizing of social and political rules had allowed them to rise unfettered. Vienna, because of the extreme cultural diversity of the empire, was a melting pot, and in that way was very much like the northeastern United States. And Jews did very well in melting pots.

Frank Burden saw in Karl Lueger's vastly successful strategies a new and successful style of politics. The ingredients were essentially these: appeal to the masses, heavy use of propaganda and slogans, and—perhaps most important—a strong emphasis on personality. For the first time in modern politics, the followers of Mayor Lueger were overtly encouraged to act on their prejudices. Lueger was a genius at exploiting the discontent, weaknesses, and desires of his fellow citizens. It was as if he had stripped away the illusions, and after pulling off layer after layer had seen the kernel at the center. It seemed that Karl Lueger had found what really mattered.

To Frank Burden, Karl Lueger was a leader ahead of his time. A shrewd young man could learn a great deal from him and, in recognizing all this, Frank Burden thought himself, by association, ahead of his own time.

He had been in Vienna only a few days, and he was beginning to feel comfortable. He had attended a few political meetings and had made an appointment to meet with Mayor Lueger himself. He had also been collecting as much political literature as he could. And he was getting over the terribly unsettling incident at his arrival. He had just moved into his room at the Hotel Imperial when he found himself victimized by a common thief, a man who entered his room blatantly and stole money and a suit of his clothes.

He caught the thief in the act and was so startled that he allowed the man to escape untouched. Frank Burden had always thought of himself as able to defend himself in any circumstance, and the memory of his allowing the man to leave unapprehended was the source of great embarrassment. For one of the only times in his life Frank had been bested by a man who was now somewhere in Vienna causing him daily humiliation by wearing his clothes. That ate at him and became an extreme embarrassment that Frank could not get out of his head. It would have been bad enough to be bested by a peer, in open competition, but this was an act of deceit and treachery.

And Frank Burden strongly suspected that the man was a Jew.

27

A Private Matter
Between Two Gentlemen

our mother did not want me to go back to France," Dilly said, his face grim. "I promised her I wouldn't." Wheeler and Dilly had finished their tour of the old city close enough to five o'clock to arrive at Gerstner's in time for *jause*, the afternoon ritual the Haze brought alive to all his students. Anyone lucky enough to have been in his thrall knew exactly what to order: coffee with sweet whipped cream and a pastry.

"She was opposed to my going with all the facets of her being. And we are speaking of a woman with many facets. She was, you know, a committed pacifist and thought badly of all activities of war, she thought it horribly dangerous—which it was—and she did not see any merit in national defense, let alone espionage. Men playing men's games, she called it. But above all, I think, she thought I was grandstanding." He had scooped most of the whipped cream onto a side dish and was drinking the coffee in small sips. "Oh, I don't mean showing off, but doing the whole thing because I wanted to do my wartime duty in the grandest possible way. She said I was incapable of sitting out the war in the Admiralty office. And, in a way I guess she was right.

"I had been in occupied France two times in all. The first was when you were on the way." He cleared his throat. "Before we were married. The second time I was flown in to a drop spot in the north. I did have a few weeks of training, courtesy of the British, in Scotland. I learned to parachute and to fend for myself, to look for escape routes, to handle a pistol, and to think of the hands as lethal weapons—a sharp blow to the Adam's apple, you know. But all that was pretty silly. The secret was to avoid getting caught. Once you were caught, the only recourse was the pill, and we learned to have that with us, on the ready, all the time. That was the grim part, the part I never told your mother. Of course, I was most assuredly *not* going to get caught. I knew my way around." He paused and took a sip of his sweet coffee. "It was those times that we used the code name 'Rouge Gorge.' The first two visits went without incident, pretty much, with a couple of close calls. I had good papers, and I could speak French well enough. There was a Resistance network that helped me with what I needed and usually it was just information collecting. Pretty routine. But this last time was very different. It seemed doomed from the start."

When Dilly came out for the second time, in September of 1943, Flora had been beside herself with worry the whole time. She tried to be a good sport about his trips behind the enemy lines, but since she did not believe in it in the first place, and since it was obviously so terribly dangerous, her good intentions wore away to practically nothing. "Think of Stan," she said. "He's already out-of-wedlock. Let's not make him fatherless."

Their friend Rory Stuart, now up close to the admirals, had seen the strain on Flora during Dilly's last trip and saw how it continued after his return. "You ought to leave London for a while," he said to Dilly. "You can be home for Christmas for a month or two and there will still be plenty of war when you get back. We'll muddle through without you." Dilly said he could not do it, that he had to be with the ship as long as the war was going on. "I must stay and do my part," Dilly said.

But Rory insisted. "Listen, old man, you're still exhausted from your last stint abroad. Go home to Boston and get some rest." He even got some of the admirals to back up his point. Dilly was no good to anybody burned out.

The idea cheered Flora up so that he agreed to accept passage on the *Queen Mary*, returning to New York for new troops. And even though it was winter and a little "roughish," as he called it, the crossing was one of the most wonderful times of their marriage. Nothing to do but read and talk and play with Stan.

The two-week stay on Beacon Hill, including Christmas, was a joy that ended badly. Flora, aware that she was the English Jewish girl who had stolen away the favorite son, was at her absolute most charming, never mentioning politics or liberal ideas, and letting Dilly's mother take her to museums and shops and luncheons with old family friends. And to all the places she knew from Dilly's stories. Since Dilly had not been home for more than three years it was a time for visits and the refueling of memories. And for long sessions in the living room with his mother. Being separated from him for the war years had been hard on her, and she and Dilly sat for hours and talked and read aloud, and sometimes just looked at each other.

Diametrically opposite in temperament, Dilly and his father, Frank Burden, had always kept a distance between them. Dilly had performed as a son in a way that made his father proud, and Dilly had excelled at St. Gregory's and Harvard, Frank's old schools, which was very satisfying. But there was no close bond between the two. Dilly was aware that his father had not approved of Flora from the start, but there seemed to be no more coldness in his greeting of her than there had been when he had brought any young woman into the house. "Your father doesn't show much emotion," his mother said. "But he is glad to see you."

When the trouble came, it was a private matter, between two gentlemen. Neither talked about it. It was in the father's study, with the thick oak door closed, so no one heard anything. They only saw Dilly's face as he left the room. His lips were drawn together tightly and his brow furled. He went for a long walk by himself. His father did not come out until suppertime. Nothing was said, to Dilly's mother or his wife.

That evening after dinner Dilly announced that they would be leaving a few days early, because there was a plane going from Washington they could catch. Dilly's father did not take them to the train station, and his mother stood on the platform, her eyes filled with tears, as if she knew she would not see her son alive again. He gave her a long tight hug. "Don't worry so, Mother," he said. "The invasion is in sight. And then it's just mopping up."

She had trouble forming the words. "Standish, a mother does not have many rights in moments like this—" She held him out where she could look into his eyes. "I want you to carry with you this one thing." Her eyes burned with a deep intensity through the tears. She had a look of classical tragedy on her face. "You carry my heart with you." She hugged him again, then watched him join his wife and son on the train. "Always," she repeated after him. "Always, always, and always."

On the trip back Dilly was pensive and serious, and Flora knew whatever it was, three hundred years of New England Puritan heritage was going to seal it inside where a crowbar couldn't pry it out. She just hoped against hope it did not mean he would go back to France.

It was late winter of 1944 when Dilly returned to the Admiralty. Everyone noticed that he was rested and fit-looking, but that he seemed to be sullen and brooding about something, grimly resolved. It was the beginning of his most secret work of the war. Flora knew the subject was invasion—everyone in England knew that—but that was all she knew.

❦

It was shortly after Easter when Dilly reported the surprise. "How would you like to have tea with the king?" he said. They were lying in bed on a Sunday morning, in that delicious hiatus when Stan was still asleep.

"Dressed like this? He'd be daft for it," she said frivolously. She was wearing his pajama top, unbuttoned.

"Well, you'd better find something."

She sat up and looked at him. "You're serious."

"No," he said, laughing. "It's worse. The prime minister."

"Good lord, when?"

"This afternoon."

❦

In the Admiralty car on the way to 10 Downing Street, Flora was trying to hide her nervousness by remembering all the times in her life when she had imagined teaing with the prime minister. "I always made up the room full of people who were there to greet me," she said. "Oh lord, Dilly. Who *will* be there?"

"Don't worry," Dilly said, leaning over to kiss her, remembering how she looked in his pajama top. "He knows your views." He was wearing his navy dress uniform and of course looking purposeful and smashing.

"Oh lord, you didn't tell him I was one of those peace maniacs, did you?"

"He already knew. One of his sisters is one. Don't worry."

It was not until they had been admitted and were in the prime minister's living room that she realized that it was just a threesome for tea—they and the prime minister—and that she had all the reason in the world to worry.

"My dear," Mr. Churchill began. Flora was amazed at how much like a parody of himself the bulldog of a man appeared. "Standish has told me of his promise to you not to return to France . . ." He drew out the word *France* with his patented elegance.

Flora sat on the edge of the sofa, her back straight, her legs together and pulled in beneath her knees, her teacup poised on its saucer a perfect eleven inches from her mouth. She was frozen in terror.

Suddenly, Dilly looked more like a war hero than ever. He was standing beside the couch where she sat. He was looking awfully handsome and awfully filled with purpose. It was then, in catching a good look at him out of the corner of her eye, that she realized the prime minister did not invite people for tea unless it was *very* important. What was *very* important in this case was the life of her fellow eagle.

"Standish has told me of your deep concerns for your country and for his role as father of the little fellow." Mr. Churchill took in a wheezy breath. "Your friends at the Admiralty have told me"—he snorted, bulldog-like— "of your deep belief in the cause of peace, and that you are indeed a pacifist in the finest British tradition. They have for you the highest admiration," and he pronounced the word as only he could, with an elegance that took generations to develop. There was a centuries-old ring of sincerity to his voice. And it was then that she realized that although she believed in peace as a general thing, it was really a very specific thing. Wars were folly, vain, and senseless, but they were awful and sinful because they killed individual people. The death of a million men is a statistic, the old saying went; the death of one is a tragedy.

"The highest admiration," the prime minister repeated, his voice now parodying its own rich sonorousness. "Now, one's country is asking for great sacrifices." Flora's head began to spin. She felt as if she might faint dead away, but she held her position, and stared back at the prime minister. "We are asking Standish to return to France on a mission so important and secret that even our meeting here today must never be known outside this room. We are asking that he return to France—" He snorted again and looked over at Dilly, whose eyes were on hers, hoping that she could understand, and now something immeasurably sad and tired came into his voice, the full weight of responsibility and war, Flora thought later. "We will ask him to stay until the invasion is successful," the great prime minister said.

A million images seemed to rush into her mind as she struggled to stay conscious and vertical, but like a giant roulette wheel, spinning and spinning, it finally settled on one image: the look on Dilly's mother's face as she let him slip from her grasp on the Boston train platform. How like Cassandra she looked, she who knew her son so well, seeing the future but being powerless to stop it.

"Prime Minister" were the words that came out. "Might one have something stronger than tea?"

⚬⚬⚬

Only a handful of months later, a few days after the liberation of Paris, in August 1944, she sat in Rory Stuart's office. They had learned that Dilly had been captured a week or so before the invasion, back in June, and disappeared, held in Paris somewhere, probably at Gestapo headquarters, or worse, a lot worse. The not knowing was killing her. "I want to go," she said for the fifth time, after his objections.

"You aren't Wonder Woman, Flora, you can't just go across the Channel with the troops." Rory looked at the set of her jaw. "You tell me. How?"

"Make me your assistant, and you take me."

"You can't be my assistant. You aren't in the Royal Navy. You're a woman and a bloody pacifist for god's sake."

"Get me a nurse's position." There was no reaction from Rory. "I could drive an ambulance." Still nothing. "Ernest Hemingway is over there. Get me a press pass."

Rory's eyes lit up and he grabbed for the phone. Within hours he had a position for her as assistant to the official Admiralty photographer, accompanying the troops. "Who's going to take care of young Standish?"

"I'm taking him with me," she said, and Rory only shook his head in disbelief.

⚬⚬⚬

The rest was legendary. The wife of Rouge Gorge traveled across the Channel on a supply ship, then rode a British army caravan into Paris, her three-year-old son in tow. She traveled across war-torn France, like the heroine in Victor Hugo's *Ninety-Three*, all the time running into French citizens who had heard of her husband, Rouge Gorge, and wished her and her son Godspeed. She found room in a small hotel in the fifth *ar-*

rondissement and talked to everyone she could find who had ever heard of
the Resistance, let alone Rouge Gorge and what went on in the gruesome
Gestapo headquarters on Rue Hubert Simone. She was willing to follow
the campaign across the Rhine and into the concentration camps until
she found out. Resistance prisoners, it turned out, were held in Fresnes
Prison, south of Paris, but were taken to Gestapo headquarters for inter-
rogation, which entailed the most brutal torture, usually proportionate to
the prisoner's significance as an enemy. What was left of the prisoner after
the last bit of information had been squeezed out was either executed immediately or sent by cattle car to Buchenwald or Dachau, most times
never seen again.

Flora talked to a number of former prisoners who described lying on
straw sacks on the cold stone floor of Fresnes, listening for the sound of
the coffee cart that usually meant that prisoners were going to be given a
last cup of awful ersatz coffee before being shipped out. But no one had
news of Dilly. They had all heard of Rouge Gorge, of course, but no one
had particular information. One former prisoner handed her a handwritten sheet in an envelope, which she did not open until later. It was written
in French and had a title on the top, "The Last Shave," like a schoolboy's
creative writing paper. It read: "A German guard told me to follow him
and bring my razor. He led me to the north court, between the front gate
of the prison and the entry to the main building. On a bench a man was
stretched out, immobile. 'Shave him,' the guard told me, gesturing at the
man lying on the bench. I took a closer look and recognized Rouge Gorge.
He was unconscious and his eyes were sunken. Through his swollen lips
he was barely breathing. There was no doubt that he had been tortured.
The Germans urged me to begin. How ridiculous, I thought. I was trying
to shave a man who was barely alive. I was able to get really close to Rouge
Gorge, touch his clothing, his freezing-cold hand, but he showed no reaction. Suddenly he opened his eyes and looked at me. He murmured something I couldn't understand, something Italian like *Ringstrazza*. He took
a few gulps of water, then lapsed back into unconsciousness. I left him
there and never saw him again."

Finally, in her second week, with little sleep and horrible apprehension, Flora was led by a Resistance man to a cell in a Paris jail where she
met an Alsatian who had been caught during the liberation of Paris trying
to leave the city disguised as a priest. The man had been a guard at

Gestapo headquarters. The Resistance man accompanied her into the small cell. "This man will tell you the truth." He looked as if he had already been well roughed up.

The Alsatian man had seen the body of Rouge Gorge being taken out for cremation, he said. "Are you sure it was Rouge Gorge?" the Resistance man said sternly.

"Everybody knew *him*," the man said. "There was no doubt. He had serious bruises on his face and one leg was broken at the shin, and an arm also, I think," the man said, looking away from Flora, whose eyes were closed tightly. "Just above the wrist." The young man now looked at Flora and for the first time perhaps realized who she was. His eyes filled with the closest he could come to sadness and compassion. *"Il ne chantait pas, madame,"* he said in consolation. "All that, and Rouge Gorge did not sing."

Having fulfilled her tragic mission, Flora Zimmerman Burden and her son caught a military ferry from Cherbourg, and were soon in London where they waited out the end stages of the war. Later, in 1946, with the war finally over and England and all of Europe recovering from the shock and beginning the slow process of rebuilding, Flora Burden, like her country, emotionally ravaged, left home forever and headed first to Boston and then to a small farm in the Sacramento Valley of California, to a piece of land given to her by Dilly's family, where she could raise her son away from the awful remembrance of duty and war, a solitary eagle.

28

An Awfully Modern Invitation

heeler had gotten in the habit of walking along the Danube Canal each morning before his first visit to the Café Central, so that when he began his journal writing he was fresh and alert.

Shortly after he had taken his seat at his usual table, he looked up to see Emily James from Amherst, Massachusetts, entering the café with a group of her friends. He watched for a moment before she noticed him. Her friends all looked to be in their early twenties, an attractive group. They looked a little less bohemian than Kleist and the group Wheeler had begun to associate with. She saw him and made her way over to his table.

"Good morning, Miss James," Wheeler said, rising, noticing that he was not just a little ruffled.

She flushed slightly. "This is the second time I have seen you this morning, Mr. Truman. The first was down by the canal."

"You were spying on me."

"I saw you from the window of my pension. You were too far away to greet."

"I've started taking that walk every morning. It helps settle out some of the rich experiences of the day before."

"We shall have to walk together some mornings," she said. "I think early-morning exercise is very good for one's constitution, and for one's outlook on the day. Unfortunately"—she pointed over to where her friends had seated themselves—"my friends are not a very good influence. They would rather congregate in a stuffy old café."

"Will you join me?" He pointed to an empty chair.

"You are kind," she said. "But I have to rejoin them, and I don't want to disturb your work."

Wheeler looked down at his journal, open on the table. "It is a compulsive habit, I guess. I've been writing regularly since the start of my stay in Vienna."

"What do you write?"

"Just the details. Thoughts and reflections, mostly." He didn't mention that his work on the Haze's book had given him the habit of daily observations.

"You could be a good influence there too, I suspect. I came to Vienna to write something of significance. I do wish I did more. There are so many distractions." She gestured back toward her friends' table.

"I am planning a trip out to the Prater this morning. I've never been. Would you like to join me?" Wheeler had no plans for the morning, but the return of the fluttering feeling provoked him.

She looked nonplussed for an instant. "Oh, I'm sorry," she said quickly. "I've an appointment at the university."

Wheeler watched her walk back to her table and felt he had unknowingly breached the rules with his bold invitation, a breach that he hoped was not irrevocable. It was something of a relief that she had turned down his bold move. Dilly's admonition against contact with anyone still rattled him. How could he explain in the face of Dilly's anxious worry that he had actually attempted an assignation?

He struggled not to look up in the direction of her table as he wrote but was aware when her group rose to leave. "Mr. Truman," she said, no more than two feet away. He had not heard her approach. "I have rethought your offer and have made other plans for the university. If the offer is still good, it seems a perfect morning for a ride to the Prater."

He arranged to meet her in front of her pension on Ebendorfer-Strasse. He had a carriage waiting. "I must be honest with you, Mr. Truman," she said once they were under way, sitting pertly on the edge of the carriage seat. "I did not have an appointment at the university this morning. I just thought it awfully modern to accept an invitation, unaccompanied. My very proper aunt would never approve."

"I hope it was not inappropriate for me to ask."

She could not suppress a sudden and complete smile. "I am glad you did."

"Well, I am *delighted* you changed your mind."

"I have been trying to be more venturesome. Young women back home are raised to be very cautious and proper, at least on the East Coast. I don't think it is good for either men or women to conceive of themselves too narrowly."

"Now *that* seems very modern."

"Certainly not for San Francisco, I am sure. In San Francisco women probably smoke cigars and ride bicycles."

Wheeler laughed. "And carry six-guns strapped to their bustles."

"I know you are teasing, but I am serious. I think it would be far healthier for everyone if women were less cautious and more willing to express themselves."

"Just between you and me," Wheeler said, "I think women should vote."

She gave him a suspicious sideways look. "Are you teasing again, Mr. Truman?" And she could see from his face that he was not. "Now, that *is* very modern. But not completely radical. I think women could make excellent choices about certain matters in politics, and perhaps we would not get into the problems we do in government with better choices being made all around. A married woman can always express her opinion through her husband's vote. But what about all those women who do not intend to marry?"

"Are you among them, Miss James?"

"Oh heavens no," she said quickly. "I am probably sounding very unconventional. I am not really. In fact, I am pathetically circumspect. It is just that this time in Vienna has done something to my natural reserve. It has been—" She paused, searching for the word. "—liberating." Then she looked a little embarrassed for having chosen that particular one. "That is not too forward, is it?"

Wheeler laughed again. "I come from the Wild West, remember. Besides, it is very appropriate," he said. "*Liberating* is a perfect word."

As the carriage moved along the Franz-Joseph-Kai, beside the Danube Canal, she said suddenly, "There is the Hotel Metropole. We could stop in on the Clemenses some time. Wouldn't you like to meet Mark Twain?"

The huge, fashionable Hotel Metropole, Mark Twain's home for most of his time in Vienna, came into view. Wheeler watched it closely as it passed. The Hotel Metropole was not only the home of Mark Twain while he was in Vienna, but it would also become infamous. In 1938, when the Nazis took over Austria in the Anschluss, it became the headquarters of the Gestapo, and hence the most despised building in the city. In 1945, during the Allied bombing, the hated Nazi landmark received a couple of direct hits, and the site was later demolished.

"Do you know the Clemenses?" Wheeler asked.

"They are from Hartford, you know, which is not far from Amherst. They are here so that their daughter Clara, who is just my age, can study piano with Theodor Leschetizky. He's quite famous, you know. Once I gave a speech in Hartford for the Daughters of the American Revolution, and Mr. Clemens was present."

"That is very impressive," Wheeler said. "You entertained the great entertainer."

"Hardly that," she said. "And I have played cello with Clara back home on a number of occasions, so we know each other, but I have yet to see her in Vienna. I have been thinking I must contact her."

They fell silent for a moment, watching the hotel pass, and Wheeler smiled at the thought of paying an informal social call on Mark Twain.

They crossed the canal and came to the entrance of the famous park.

The Prater, one of the spectacles of Vienna, was the spacious 4,300-acre public park to the east of the old city, adjoining the Leopoldstadt. Once the private hunting estate for the imperial family, during the time of Mozart, the Emperor Joseph II donated it to the public trust. Its numerous outdoor and indoor restaurants, cafés, and gathering places were the scenes of celebrations and merriment during the full calendar year.

They had lunch at one of the many cafés and then went to the Giant Wheel. "This is quite the new thing to do," Wheeler said. "We must go up."

"Or see it at least," she said. "It was built after an American design, you know. An English engineering firm, but after the design of the original Ferris wheel, made for the Chicago World's Fair five years ago. It's quite a feat."

"You seem to know a good deal about it," Wheeler said.

"I wanted to study engineering in college. But the ladies back home in

Boston wouldn't have approved. That, and a small problem," she said, trying to look up at the imposing structure.

"And what would that be?"

"Fear of heights," she said timidly. "It's hard to be an engineer with that hindrance, so I studied literature and music."

They stood in line for a time, and he bought tickets. She was looking up now at the top of the two-hundred-foot circular structure. "I suppose it is safe."

"Well, Miss James," he said, ushering her toward the wheel's small stairway. "You have come to Vienna to be venturesome."

She looked up again, then stopped frozen as they stepped toward the open door of the cabin. "Perhaps not this venturesome," she said meekly. "It gives me a peculiar feeling in my stomach."

"It should," Wheeler teased. "If woman was intended to fly, God would have given her wings."

"You are teasing," she said and laid her hand ever so gently on his arm, for support. "You are far more worldly than I." Wheeler looked at her face and could see that she had turned quite ashen. "I think I might faint," she said in little more than a whisper.

"It is completely safe," he said in the most reassuring tone he could muster, but he stood still and did not move forward until she was ready. "Midwestern American engineering. Thousands of trips up and down without a mishap."

"I think it is not for all people."

"We don't have to, you know." He took a beginning step away from the carriage door and felt a sudden pull from her hand.

"No," she said abruptly. "I want to do it. I want you to take me." It came out like a command.

Wheeler moved them both toward the open door. "All right, then. Just don't look up."

"No," she said emphatically again. "I do not want to be controlled by my own silly fear. I shall look up, and you will guide me."

"Very well," Wheeler said, and she matched his step forward. The only residue of her terror was the hand on his arm that had changed from the most delicate grip to a viselike one.

"I do not wish to be fearful. It is a silly consequence of my upbringing."

"Then take small steps," Wheeler said with a patient voice. "Take small steps." As they entered the carriage, Wheeler thought of the scene in the 1949 movie *The Third Man* when Joseph Cotten meets Orson Welles in this very wheel, a movie Miss James might see near the end of her life. As the Giant Wheel set into motion, there was an almost minuscule lurching. "What was that?" she said, jerking his arm.

"We just started up. It is very normal. I will let you know if anything untoward happens."

After one half revolution, the cabin came to rest near the top of the wheel, rocking slightly. "What is it doing?" she said, her eyes wide with something very close to terror. Her hand had not relinquished its command of his arm.

"They are letting people on at the bottom side of the wheel," he said, now patting the clutching hand. "It is still within the normal range."

The cabin rocked gently and all of imperial Vienna lay out before them. "Is it meant to be this way then?"

"It is meant to be this way." For a moment, he felt the soft warmth of her covering hand. She had calmed a bit.

"My heart has stopped racing."

"Don't forget to breathe," he said calmly. "And don't forget to look." From the top of the Giant Wheel one could get a beautiful view of the old city just to the south. They were standing back from the window. As Wheeler leaned forward, he could feel her stiffen, then she looked up at him and smiled almost pathetically.

"One should not be afraid to approach the window, should one?"

"One should not," Wheeler said. "Remember, small steps forward." And together as in the first tentative step of a dance, they moved forward, until their faces were nearly pressed to the glass.

"You are very courageous," Wheeler said.

"You have initiated me well." Her grip on his arm loosened.

"Nothing to fear," she said, obviously trying to be convincing. "This is nothing I have ever done before, but there is nothing to fear."

"It would be a shame to allow such fears to interfere with the splendor of this view." Wheeler gestured with his hand out toward the vista before them. The day was remarkably crisp and clear.

"One can see all the way to the Alps," she said, her left hand now relaxed on his arm, and from it Wheeler could feel her warmth and an incredible softness. It saturated his arm and gave a warm tingling at the base of his neck.

For a moment, he was overcome by the sudden memory of the descriptions of this very scene that came from the Haze's beloved Little Book. "City of music," he said in a reverential whisper, as if to invoke the spirit of his great mentor.

She looked up at him, struck immediately by his tone. "That's it, isn't it?" she said softly. "City of music," she said, matching his reverence. Then she paused and looked back at the vista. "You have such a power with summary, Mr. Truman. I must admit that I find it totally enchanting."

"Most of the words you like I've borrowed."

"Well, borrowed or not, they are enchanting nonetheless."

The carriage lurch again was minuscule, and they began their downward movement. "What was that?" she said suddenly, her grip tightening on his arm.

"Normal range," Wheeler said. "We're descending." He looked over at her, taking a hard look at her beautiful profile as she gazed out at nothing in particular through the large thick glass of the cabin. He was suddenly feeling guilty about having come this far and the thrill it brought.

"There is something I wish to tell you," she said slowly, the words seeming to give Wheeler time. She paused, bolstering again, but her warm hand stayed unmoved and steady on his arm. "I have a second identity," she said, and Wheeler had an almost uncontrollable urge to tell her to stop, but she went on. "It is a secret and a deceit that might shock you." Wheeler held his breath, but said nothing. "I am here in Vienna on an assignment to write about music for a famous American newspaper."

"Please tell me about it," Wheeler said, and out poured the story of how a pseudonym was created in a college parlor and became a successful and controversial music critic for *The New York Times*.

"His modern ideas raised quite a stir," she concluded.

Wheeler showed the trace of a smile, but he did not move. He closed his eyes for a moment and then looked over at her beautiful, elegant profile and noticed how this new wrinkle in her circumstance enhanced his feeling of affection for this independent young woman. "So you have

gained some notoriety and are here to write, under an assumed name?"
he said.

"Yes. I have already mailed two reviews and I am working on the third.
But I have"—her free hand swept out over the broad vista out the carriage
window—"distractions."

"These articles you have written in a man's voice are well known?" he
asked.

"I fear they are," she said, and Wheeler shook his head and remained
silent for a moment, the news carrying with it a surprising and unexplainable weight.

"Are you shocked that a young lady would represent herself as a man?"
she said.

"No," Wheeler said quickly, grasping for equilibrium. "I am impressed."

"You aren't shocked that a proper young lady would do such a
thing?"

"No," Wheeler repeated. "Not in the least. I am just concerned all of
a sudden that I might be getting in the way of such a noble enterprise. A
distraction."

Relieved, she said, "Oh my, no. You are serving as my muse, if a man
can serve in such a role." And she laid her hand on his arm now in a way
that brought to Wheeler a warm smile.

"If a woman can write as a man, I'm sure a man can serve as a muse. It
seems only fair."

She turned and her eyes said how much she did not want him to take
offense. "You are not shocked then?" she said.

"Not in the least," he said, working to make it come out lightly. "And
besides, I have a great fondness for pen names." He could see the enormous relief in her eyes as the cabin began moving again, toward earth,
and her hand stayed, giving its warmth to his arm.

"You don't think it too progressive?"

His smile broadened. "I do not," he said. "In fact, I think it quite remarkable and impressive. Courageous even."

"Oh," she said with a great release of tension. "I am so glad." She
paused. "Now I need the courage to get it done. I fear I have run out of
my small supply."

Wheeler stopped and took a deep breath, trying his best to hide his concern for Dilly's admonition. She seemed to sense nothing.

"I thank you," she said as they exited the cabin of the Giant Wheel, her hand now back to resting delicately on his arm, "for guiding me past my fear of heights."

"You are one who tries to do things all at once, I suspect," Wheeler said, smiling.

"You are very observant," she said. "That is my great flaw. I am too impulsive. I want things all at once. I need to remember—" She paused and thought for a moment, then returned Wheeler's smile. "You have taught me to take small steps."

"It is my greatest accomplishment since arriving in Vienna, I think. A great pleasure."

"Will you still walk with me mornings by the canal then?" she said.

He stared into her beautiful smiling face and noticed once again the slight blush. "Starting tomorrow," Wheeler said, quickly realizing that he was in too deep.

29

The Enormous Weight of History

t first, just as she had not told her new friend Mr. Truman about her male pseudonym, she had also not elaborated on her embarrassing meeting with Gustav Mahler. She felt that the information was private and perhaps pretentious, scandalous even. She had been thrilled to meet Herr Mahler, and regretted deeply the negative light her humiliating frailty cast on the incident, how it turned out to be an embarrassment far too complicated to explain to anyone. But now on her morning walk beside the Danube Canal with this strange man from San Francisco, now that the part about her *New York Times* notoriety was out of the bag, she began to feel that she might reveal the whole bundle.

She had looked forward to the next time she would be with him more than she admitted to herself, a fact she was forced to confront when, up and dressed, she noticed in herself a distinct apprehension that perhaps he might not appear, that he had been leading her on for some reason and had no intention of meeting her for the morning walk. Why had this feeling developed as quickly as it had? He seemed so deeply sensitive, so aware of what she felt. He said that he had had a love of his life many years before and that he had loved her very much, maybe he had even been married, but she had died. Perhaps that was the reason.

She felt such a surge of relief when he called for her at the pension that it took a good deal of time before she realized he was slightly reserved this morning. As they walked and she told him more and more about herself and about the Mahler incident, she began to attribute his subtle distance to the fact that, as an older man and not one of her circle of friends, he felt with her something of an outsider, and that perhaps he found her immature and silly. One of her tasks for the morning was to convey to him how very much she preferred his company to any of the young Viennese she had come to know, and how she found him unusually kind. Of course, what one was going to say before the event is markedly different from what comes out of one's mouth in the immediacy of the situation. "Mr. Truman," she began as they walked along the canal. She had placed her hand on his arm, as she had done in the cabin of the Giant Wheel, when she had found in him such warm reassurance. "For the remainder of your stay in Vienna, I would enjoy spending the majority of my time—" She paused. It was not exactly as she had planned to say it, but it was close enough. She pressed on. "I would enjoy spending time in your company."

She had not realized until that moment how vulnerable she had made herself, how for the second time in Vienna she was about to appear terribly foolish in front of an older man. She watched in something akin to horror as he hung his head and looked down at his feet. She could tell from the way he held himself that he was preparing to deliver in the most tactful and considerate manner possible—in the name of pity and sensitivity to her innocence—what would be the most stinging rebuke of her young life.

Wheeler had spent the evening mulling over his conversation with Dilly about minimal contact and the dilemma it brought with it. Dilly's reproaches about interfering with Frank Burden's time in Vienna in even the slightest way sat heavily on him. His candid conversations with Sigmund Freud were already a violation, and now to begin a liaison of the heart? He would simply have to go out of his way to avoid this young Emily James from Amherst, Massachusetts. It did not matter that he found her independent spirit irresistible and compelling and that he felt a warm glow from her cheery company, an antidote to the loneliness of being in a strange land. He would simply have to avoid her, and the way to do that in the most effective manner was to walk with her along the canal the next morning, be cordial but distant, and then simply not arrange any more meetings with her, making the necessary excuses so as to cause her the least discomfort. He needed to establish clearly that he was an older man with older tastes in both art and company. Without hurting her feelings— he did not wish to interfere even the slightest with her emotions—he would gently arrange not to see her again.

He called for her at the pension. Fraulein Tatlock was exceedingly friendly and offered him a seat in the front room as she went to the stairs and called for Miss James. She entered the room with a burst of good cheer, as if she might have thought he was not going to show up.

Outside it was a glorious morning, clear and with a fresh chill in the air. She placed her hand gently on his arm as she had done on the Giant Wheel the day before, an act he interpreted then and now as one of polite but innocuous convention. They walked along Karntner-Strasse, past St. Stephen's Cathedral, to the canal. He had been powerfully impressed the day before with the story of her publication of music articles in *The New York Times*, under the pseudonym of a man. Now, with a remarkable calmness she told him of her meeting with Gustav Mahler, the director of the Vienna Opera, and of her embarrassment of fainting.

As he was taking his last walk with her, just as they passed the cathedral, where Rotenturm-Strasse began, the enormity landed on him suddenly. What if they walked headlong into Dilly or Sigmund Freud, or, for that matter, Frank Burden?

"I so much prefer seeing Vienna," she broke into his thought, "through new eyes such as yours than through the jaded vision of the young Viennese."

When they reached the canal, she had begun telling him how much she enjoyed this time in Europe by herself and how greatly she appreciated the kind, inattentive sponsorship of Fraulein Tatlock. "I will not stay in Vienna forever," she said with purpose, "and I will certainly return to a conventional life back home eventually. But for the time being—" She looked out beyond the canal to the Praterstrasse and the Danube beyond, and sighed with conviction. "—I am enjoying myself greatly."

She stopped and took a deep breath, as if to cinch up her courage. And, at the very moment that Wheeler was thinking how lovely she looked with the rosy glow of a morning walk on her cheeks and her eyes so clear and full of life and future, she spoke her mind.

Wheeler could not remember ever seeing another human so completely devoid of guile saying something to him so completely captivating and appealing. He looked away for a long moment, recapturing the steely resolve of the previous evening, knowing full well what he was obligated, by fateful circumstance and Dilly's admonition, to do. Wheeler himself took a deep breath and began. "Miss James, I think that is the nicest offer anyone has ever made to me. However, I must tell you—" He stopped, feeling the enormous weight of history on his head, catching for a briefest instant the look of apprehension on her face. *Oh, to hell with it!*

"I too would enjoy—" he began again. "I would enjoy very much spending the majority of my time with *you*."

30

The Illusion of Flight

 n 1897, during Wheeler Burden's time there, Vienna sat at the center of the vast and richly diverse Hapsburg empire that had once controlled half of Europe and now included a collection of important satellite cities, Prague, Cracow, Sarajevo, and Budapest among them. Twenty years later, by the end of World War I, the empire would be dissolved, the ruling family exiled, and the great imperial city reduced to a small insignificant position governing little more than itself. During the time of Wheeler's visit, Vienna was a city in turmoil, although few people living within the confined perspective of the time—listening to operetta music, eating Sacher torte *mit Schlag*, waltzing till exhaustion—wanted to notice it or admit it. The pro-Germans wanted alliance with Germany; the Slavs and Hungarians wanted independence, their own separate states and their own language; the working classes wanted better public services and housing; the artists wanted freedom from the old order; the sons in general wanted out from under the oppressive thumbs of their fathers. Just below the surface of the gaiety of the city there was such a powerful turmoil, in fact, that to an astute and pessimistic critic of the Café Central crowd or a historian with the benefit of hindsight who searched for the kernel by peeling away the layers nearly a century later, the whole culture appeared a whirling mass, headed for apocalypse. And if there was any one unifying and precipitating event that symbolized and perhaps played a major role in causing the unraveling, it was the tragedy at Mayerling nine years before.

At the time of Wheeler's visit, the tragedy surrounding Crown Prince Rudolf was still on everyone's mind, and still cloaked in mystery. The royal family's efforts at covering up the facts had been successful, or one would say later, had been as successful as anything the royal family had tried to do. Within weeks of the awful tragedy, German newspapers, freed from the yoke of imperial censorship, were beginning to uncover the details, real and imagined. But even nine years after the fateful night in the imperial hunting lodge, fact and romance blended together into a version that the national psyche could accept and endure. The suicide of the heir to the throne seemed to be a metonymy, a part that represented the whole, an event that symbolized what lay deep in the great heart of Vienna and the empire itself: intrigue, enigma, and doom.

The Haze would tell the whole story, filling in all the details. The tragedy at Mayerling, after all, was a central part of his gospel, the gospel according to the Haze. The crown prince was despondent for a number of reasons. He had contracted a painful, and then incurable, case of venereal disease, the same disease that had driven his mother's cousin Ludwig of Bavaria to lunacy and suicide only a few years before. He hated the thought of Germany, and perhaps all of Europe, being dominated by his crude bully cousin Wilhelm II. He feared—and justifiably so—that Austria would lose the Balkans to Russia. He had become addicted to opium and alcohol. And he was unhappily married. More than all these, however, the most significant contributor, probably, was the crown prince's relationship with his father, who had thwarted him at every move and had systematically and cruelly excluded him from all decisions of state.

For a city and an empire that so associated itself with optimism and gaiety to accept that the heir to the Hapsburg future had killed himself in a fit of temporary derangement was difficult enough; accepting that he was a murderer was nearly impossible.

In his refusal to let out the truth about Mayerling, it would be said later, the emperor displayed the same hardness of heart that had made him a disaster as a father. The son who had embarrassed him in life shamed him in death. And yet Franz Joseph was unable to share authority with his son, unable to bear the spark of independence the young man possessed, could not bear sharing authority with his offspring and eventual successor.

The crown prince's mother, the aloof and beautiful Empress Elisabeth, a concerned and loving mother perhaps but caught in the cold distancing of a patriarchal military society, powerless to intercede between frustrated son and harsh rule-oriented father, could only watch and hope. After that awful night she never again appeared in public except in mourning. Rudolf, her beautiful son, wrote her a good-bye note saying he had not been worthy of her. "In the dawn of the modern age of psychology, born in Vienna," the Haze would intone, "when mental anguish would be pinned on the doorstep of parents, Franz Joseph and Elisabeth's was exposed by implication as the prototypical destructive family." Then he closed the notebook, the storyteller at the end of his story. "Mayerling," the Haze would say in barely more than a whisper, "dashed hopes and ended the era of optimistic liberalism in Vienna."

Wheeler's personal involvement with the tragedy came about in a peculiar way. On his way back from one of his meetings with Freud one morning, he set his mind on the Imperial Academy of Art and the "Crown Prince's Album" he had been so impressed with when Emily James showed it to him. It was, by coincidence, the morning he had stopped at the cabinetmaker's shop and picked up the finished Frisbee. "An object of true elegance," the cabinetmaker had said to him with a broad satisfied smile, "no matter its function."

"Beautifully turned," Wheeler said, giving the disk an upward flip and catching it. "Light, just as we designed it, and stained and finished like a fine violin." He had thanked the cabinetmaker, paid him, and told him he would report back after a trial flight in the Prater. "It will do magic. I'll invite you to come see," Wheeler said as he left the shop.

When he entered the museum and climbed the huge marble stairway to the second floor, he ran into a sign that announced that the section was closed. Never one to allow signs and rules to stand in his way, Wheeler looked around to see that he was in the clear of guards and stepped nimbly around the sign and found himself all alone in the collection of watercolors and drawings. Out of the corner of his eye, he noticed a dark shadow and turned. Standing alone beside him, having appeared from around a corner, stood a woman in black, wearing over her head a thin black veil. She possessed an arresting beauty, ivory skin, dark eyebrows, and deep sad eyes. She took no notice of Wheeler, yet had slid up beside him with quiet grace. "Hello," he said with a nervous extroversion that belonged neither with this setting nor with this century.

The woman showed no alarm, but looked over to him with an ethereal calm, her eyes showing first a sad indifference, then seeming to catch something in his face that brought the traces of a distant smile to her lips. "Good day," she said.

"These watercolors are exquisite," Wheeler said, as if he needed to explain why he had intruded in the closed wing. "I've come from the American west, from San Francisco, to see them." For an instant it occurred to Wheeler that perhaps he could pass as some special visitor with privileges and not just the crass interloper that he actually was.

"I hope they meet your satisfaction." Her voice was soft and genuine, intended to put him at ease. There was in it nothing to suggest her being impressed or offended by what Wheeler had tried to imply. At that moment a man in elaborate military dress appeared around the corner and, seeing Wheeler, seemed startled. His sudden move toward him was stopped by an almost imperceptible sign from the woman in black. The officer frowned, eyed Wheeler haughtily, then moved to the far end of the room. "They were made lovingly," she said.

It was only then that Wheeler realized why the floor had been closed and the profound pretension of his being there. "I am sorry to have intruded," he said, stepping back.

"No, no," the woman said, raising her hand gently. "I enjoy the company. These works are to be enjoyed. And we would not want to discourage someone who had come from as far as San Francisco."

"He was very handsome," Wheeler said, looking at the watercolor and wanting to acknowledge that he understood the extraordinary circumstance chance had laid before him.

Again, her sad eyes took him in slowly, showing for just a moment a deep satisfaction. "You share some of his traits," she said. The words had a timeless ring to them; they came out of a place in the soul many layers below joy or sadness, where distinctions between monarchy and peasantry no longer mattered. Her eyes shifted to the wooden disk in his hand, and Wheeler noticed it.

"It is a saucer," Wheeler said tentatively, lifting the disk as if to show that it was not some sort of harmful device. "It is designed from a pie plate."

The woman looked amused. "And its purpose?"

"Recreation. It's for throwing," Wheeler said to fill the silence. He flipped it a few inches out of his hand and caught it. The woman watched it and smiled. "I brought the idea with me, but it was crafted in Vienna." She nodded. "It is thrown across open space, thirty meters sometimes, and it soars and floats, lighter than the wind. People in my country like it because it gives them, regardless of station, the illusion of flight."

The woman in black was charmed. The thought occurred to Wheeler that maybe for the first time in years she had felt in her heart something at least in the proximity of joy. "If we weren't inside," he said, "I would show you." He looked around the room of watercolors and down toward the officer, who still frowned and still pretended to be examining the drawings in front of him. He would have made a terrible Frisbee partner.

The woman smiled, full and open, and in that moment Wheeler saw what no mortal had seen for almost a decade and none would be likely to see again, the most beautiful face of the nineteenth century in a full and warm smile. "You have a captivating manner," she said. If the remark and the look had come from across wineglasses in a dark corner of a café, its recipient would have inferred rich connotations.

"Only to match an extraordinary presence." Wheeler bowed slightly and lifted the wooden object with both hands. "I would like you to have this." He offered it to her. Her two pale hands came forward away from the black silk in which they had shrouded themselves, and it was only then that Wheeler could see their extraordinary beauty. They lifted the object from him ever so gently and held it out for a moment. "Always imagine it soaring."

"I shall," she said in little more than a whisper. "I shall picture it soaring."

"Good day," Wheeler said, this time bowing deeply and moving to leave, and then pausing a moment before walking toward the giant stairway to the Ringstrasse. "And thank you for sharing with me this brief moment honoring your beautiful son."

31

A Mesmerizing Spectacle

is friend Kleist took such a keen interest in Wheeler's first trip to the opera that one might have thought it was to be his own. He arranged to borrow a formal suit of clothes from a young medical student who was Wheeler's exact size, then he told Wheeler how to hire for modest expense the most elegant cab, and finally he showed his American guest how to carry himself like a Viennese gentleman. "The arts in Vienna are the common ground of the classes," Kleist told him. "Your intention here is to make all stations think you are one of them. Harry von Truman," he said with a flourish. "Or Truman the scrivener."

Wheeler called at Pension Tatlock at six o'clock precisely. Fraulein Tatlock greeted him with her usual enthusiasm. "My," she said, "how like young nobility you are looking tonight, Herr Truman."

"I have come to take my new friend to the opera," Wheeler said, bowing.

They both turned to watch her come down the stairs. She was wearing an evening dress of coral-colored lace with a low neckline and a white shawl around her shoulders. She seemed to float down the stairs with a joyful glow. "Isn't she radiant, Herr Truman?" said Fraulein Tatlock in her best broken English. "Does she not light up the room?"

For a moment Wheeler found himself unable to speak. She had pulled her hair up and fastened it with a jeweled brooch, and her cheeks seemed redder, her eyes a darker blue, her lips almost crimson. She was in that moment a woman of stunning beauty.

"I am so excited to be showing you the opera," she said in the cab, leaning toward him in the leather-upholstered seat. "It is one of the spectacles of the modern world. My Viennese friends have grown up with this city.

They do not realize how splendid it is. And—" She leaned into his ear. "You are looking very handsome. All the young men who have been watching me for the past few months will be insanely jealous and will want to know immediately the identity of my dashing escort."

"I think more than likely their eyes will be fixed on you."

The Opern-Ring teemed with people, all heading toward the broad steps before the magnificent Renaissance façade of the Hofoper, the imperial opera house, the jewel of the Ringstrasse. They joined the elegantly dressed company and passed through the huge archways into the building. The vast interior was a riot of interconnected arches, gilded details, sculpture, and bright frescoes. The floors were marble tiled, the doorway arches decorated with ornate columns, and up in the parapets stood huge Greek statues. The foyer was richly embellished with scenes from operas and busts of famous composers.

Inside, the auditorium space felt cavernous, all richly gilded and painted, holding easily two thousand seats, on the main floor and in the balcony and boxes. Wheeler, who had played in Carnegie Hall and Symphony Hall in Boston with Shadow Self, had been in more than his share of renowned music halls but had never seen anything to match this. "It is absolutely astounding," he said, as they moved toward their seats.

"This is an apex," she said. "There are even two curtains. This one, a scene showing Orpheus descending into Hades, is for tragedy. There is another one they use when they are playing a comedy." Her eyes shown with an excitement Wheeler had never seen before.

"This is a musician's dream."

"I have been dreaming of it for months now," she said, looking over at him, her face glowing with the delight of having someone to share this spectacle with. "The people in Vienna take this for granted. They think this is all part of the normal flow of life. You have to come from another country to appreciate it." She scrunched her shoulders in a gesture of delight. "I am so happy you are here to see it."

The opera itself, Wagner's *Tristan and Isolde*, was exactly what Wheeler imagined as fitting for the setting. It was long, serious, and beautifully melodic. The staging was spectacular, with magnificent, colorful sets that took the breath away with each opening of the giant curtains. And, of course, Mahler's dramatic entry was riveting. He swept in and rose to the podium with an energy that was breathtaking.

"I can see why he mesmerizes people," Wheeler whispered, himself the perpetrator of grand entrances in another time. "If he is that magnetic in a space this size, I can only imagine what he would be like alone in a small room."

"*Overwhelming* would be an adequate word for it," she said.

At the first intermission, she took hold of Wheeler's arm and nudged him toward one of the exits. "This part is almost as good as the music," she said. "We get to mix with the Viennese, except those—" They were passing under the overhanging boxes of the first tier. She gestured upward. "They are the patrons—titled families and the very rich—who own boxes. They do not have to move for their refreshment. It is brought to them." They passed through the door into the vestibule. "But they miss out on all the spectacle down here."

The crowd had begun to form. Elegantly dressed military officers and mustached gentlemen stood in groups, talking with beautiful ladies in richly laced dresses. The room buzzed with animated conversation as they drifted through toward the champagne, where Wheeler found his friend Kleist.

"This is Miss Emily James," he said with a flair, and Kleist took her hand and kissed it dramatically.

"I am impressed by your elegant taste in women," Kleist—with a reputation for dalliances with a "sweet girl" or two—said, loudly enough for her to hear.

"Kleist is a painter, a friend of Klimt," Wheeler said. "One of the regulars at the Café Central."

"Where at this very moment," she said with a touch of irony and a charming smile, "the problems of the world are being solved."

"If not being solved," Kleist retorted, his champagne glass at his lips, "they are certainly being flogged to death. You are also an American, Fraulein James?"

"I am from Massachusetts," she said.

"And you are living in Vienna?"

"I am in Vienna studying music."

"Ah," said Kleist. "You are a musician?"

"A music theorist," she said. "My playing is not up to the standards of this city. I have been sent to write something of significance."

"You should meet Schoenberg then. He is one of our crew at the Café

Central. He could introduce you to Herr Mahler and a host of other of our luminaries."

"I have already had the honor of meeting Herr Mahler," she said, looking down at her hands. "I was introduced by Herr Felsch and went to his studio for an interview—"

Kleist was caught by surprise. "You met Herr Mahler in his studio?" he said, obviously impressed.

"Alone in his studio," she said forthrightly. "And I fainted dead away, I am afraid to say."

Kleist was eager for the details. "Most of us would die to talk music with Herr Mahler," Kleist had said after listening intently to her story, "and you have already fainted in his arms."

"It was hardly that romantic. I dropped like a stone onto the hardwood floor beside his piano. He summoned his maid to revive me. It was terribly embarrassing, and I did not go back to complete my interview."

The chime sounded, calling them back to their seats. She moved forward and Kleist stayed behind. "What an absolutely charming young woman," he said to Wheeler when she was safely beyond hearing. "She has such an unusual combination of savoir-faire and—" He paused, not wanting to appear either catty or disrespectful. "Openness. I would find her quite disarming." He watched her walking away. "Quite disarming indeed."

Back in their seats, she turned to him. "You speak German excellently, Mr. Truman."

"Not as well as you, Miss James." It was true. He loved listening to the gentle tones she drew from the language from which he seemed to extract nothing but harsh edges. As the lights dimmed, Wheeler leaned toward her bare neck. "Kleist was quite smitten," he said into her ear. "That does not happen easily."

"Viennese gentlemen," she snapped back matter-of-factly, "are hopeless flirts."

One thing you could say for Wagner, on either continent and in either century, was that he did not believe in brevity. It was late at night, and the drowsiness that had swept over the opera crowd after the last intermission had dropped heavily onto Wheeler. "We are dressed for Demel's," she said as he lowered himself beside her in the cab they had found in the dense pack of carriages outside the opera house. "There is much to discuss."

As the cab began moving, she slid to the edge of the leather seat. "I became confused," she said brightly. "Were we listening to Herr Wagner or Herr Mahler?"

"A scintillating blend of geniuses," Wheeler said, quoting from the Haze, who had been quoting from the "Little Book."

She smiled. "Once again, you have arrived at the perfect articulation. It is Herr Wagner and his brilliance that makes the event so thoroughly moving. And yet his music is very—" She waited a moment for the right words. "His music is predictable somehow, almost formulaic, a tribute to the past. And one gets the impression that Herr Mahler with all his energy wishes to break loose, to take the music to new places, to set it free." She paused again, and Wheeler allowed the silence. A dreamy look came into her eyes. "I do so wish that I could hear one of Herr Mahler's symphonies."

"They are superb," Wheeler said all too quickly, forgetting for an instant where he was. How would he ever tell this beautiful nineteenth-century woman that upon his grandmother's death he had inherited her complete set of stereo recordings of all nine of Mahler's symphonies, by the famous Bruno Walter, and that during his time at music school in the early 1960s they had been his constant companions?

"You have heard his symphonies?" she asked suddenly, swinging around toward him in surprise.

"In San Francisco," Wheeler said curtly, backpedaling.

"I didn't know that he had ever been performed in America."

"Someone brought his Second from Hungary. It was a trial, and I was lucky enough to attend."

"Oh my," she said, clasping her hands in front of her. "How I envy you! What was it like?"

"Superb, as I said. Absolutely superb. But I fear it was too much for the traditionalists, and it was quickly dropped."

"I would give anything to hear just one of his three. I have been hoping for that while I have been here."

"You will hear them," Wheeler said, as the carriage stopped in front of Demel's. "And you will like what you hear."

Inside the famous Demel's, the atmosphere was warm and inviting. Many of the clientele had come from the opera, so the dress was perhaps more formal than usual. "The confectioner for the aristocracy is none too good for us tonight," Wheeler said, after they had been seated at a center table. "I hear that the chocolate and raspberry torte, *mit Schlag,* is an obligation." She smiled broadly as Wheeler placed the order.

She took her first bite of the rich whipped cream with absolute relish, then closed her eyes as if holding on to a dream. "I think this is probably not very good for one's health." Her eyes flashed. "But isn't it absolute divinity?"

Wheeler watched her, amused. "You've thrown yourself at this city," he said. "You've done it with a passion."

She looked into his face for an instant to find any trace of disapproval. "It has such a powerful effect on me. Perhaps I've gone too far."

"Not at all. It's fine. In fact it is admirable. It's just that people are more reserved, I guess." What he meant, of course, was *people of your century.*

"It wards off the chaos," she said, holding up a fork full of the thick whipped cream and torte.

"What an interesting observation," Wheeler said.

"It is from a teacher of mine in college. He said that the principal function of music was to organize the details into harmonies that were intended to make us forget that there was randomness all around us. The same, he said, could be said for great books."

"What a fascinating idea," Wheeler said. "You will have to include it in your work of significance."

She frowned. "Oh no," she said with a sigh. "I fear my alter ego has written his last. This morning I wrote to the editor at *The New York Times* and resigned. I explained that the muse has abandoned the project. There will be no more penetrating observations from Vienna."

Wheeler did his best to hide his surprise. "I am sorry to hear it. It sounds as if the pseudonymous fellow was making a contribution."

"Well, all that is gone now," she said. "Poof. The inspiration has left the author. She is too distracted by all this—" She waved her fork, now empty, at the room. "His time has passed. But I will tell you one thing." She looked into his eyes. "If ever he did return, it would be my conversations with you, which I go home and write down in detail and almost verbatim, that provide the inspiration."

"They have been very special to me too," Wheeler said.

She looked off for a moment, silent. "You know, my stay in Vienna has given me a lot of time to think. I came here really quite by chance, at the suggestion of my former headmistress, looking for new trends in music. But I am finding much in myself. Back home, even away at college to a degree, I was always afraid to move about too vigorously, afraid always what the elegant ladies of the parish would think, or what the founders of the cotillion would say if I wore my hat at a rakish angle or talked to one of their sons too passionately about suffrage rights. And here no one knows me, and there seem to be fewer rules, perhaps *no* rules for foreigners."

A seriousness fell onto her brow. "Sometimes I think there is a lot more to us than we know. I mean deep beneath the surface. For years I have felt a desire to uncover something buried inside. There is no one at home interested in talking about it, but parts of me—some deep inside—would never come out in the place I was raised. I am pulled in two directions by life. I know something of what the two directions look like: my mother's side, a side filled with joy and light, and my stern and severe aunt's, filled with darkness, repression, and judgment. Sometimes, it is as if I am both those people. The forces are stronger than I can understand, and the directions, both a part of me, sometimes make me feel a house divided."

"I understand," Wheeler said, not losing her eyes as she spoke. She continued without hesitation.

"Somehow, here in all this gaiety and rich life and whirling music, my division seems closer to the surface. I feel as if I might be coming close to knowing what it is that pulls me in two directions." Having said that, her brow lifted and she eyed the dessert in front of her. Wheeler sat enthralled, barely able to stir.

"It is funny. Fraulein Tatlock is my chaperone, and she does not seem to mind where I go or what I do. She writes home to my former headmistress that she is watching over me with care, and my former headmistress, I am sure, passes the word along to the fine ladies. The situation is really quite—" She took a spoonful of whipped cream and torte. "—licentious."

Wheeler was captivated. Her openness, somehow accentuated by her unabashed attack on the torte, gave her a guilelessness that Wheeler had loved in her from the start, but that now drew him to her like a siren's call.

"That is a long-winded explanation," she said.

"But very much to the point, I would say."

"It is difficult for me to explain, Mr. Truman. I have told you how being in this foreign land has affected me. 'Poised between the rich cultures of central Europe and the riches of the Orient,' as my guidebook says. But you are not part of this. You are from America, from the Wild West. Yet, you have only accentuated the effect of Vienna. At first I found that disquieting, and then I grew to like it very much. In your presence and with this city as a backdrop, I feel like a flower opening." Suddenly, it was Wheeler who was beginning to feel disquieted.

"I have grown fond of your company," she continued, "and your influence on my thinking. You seem to guide me without being paternal or directive." She looked down, as if building courage for the conclusion.

"And I have enjoyed being with you."

"My fear of the Giant Wheel was an embarrassment." Her eyes widened for an instant. "But real nonetheless. You pulled me beyond it."

Wheeler smiled. "It would have been a shame to miss that view," he said.

She looked at him for a moment. "Even at home, I have a habit of embarrassing myself with directness." Up until this point Wheeler must have felt in control, on the brink perhaps, but still within the bounds of his own interpretation of Dilly's no-contact admonition. He was definitely skating close to the thin ice with this captivating Emily James from Amherst, Massachusetts, but still safe, influencing things in a minuscule way, causing nothing major in the way of a shift. Then her eyes came up to his.

"Mr. Truman," she said with the perfect, gentle elocution she found even with her own language, "I would like very much for our strong mutual attraction to become physical."

32

Caught Off Balance

heeler knew he had to stop thinking about her, and to stop his heart from racing. The *Tristan and Isolde* evening had been one of the most delightful and most sensually captivating of his life. There was something about the opera that defied even his old teacher's words of description. Mahler's magnificent Wagner had filled the air in a way he had before only imagined. And to have shared it with her, to look over at her face and see the rapture, to see the way the low cut of her dress accentuated her most lovely neck and smooth alabaster skin and the swelling of her breasts, the way she looked over at him in the poignant moments of the fated love story, all had defied anyone's words of description. He was most sure that she had no idea what she was radiating in the way of a persona, how stunningly beautiful she was in the obscured light of the opera house, how mature and worldly she looked in the midst of all that Viennese splendor, how she held her own, as Kleist had pointed out so vigorously, amongst the most beautiful women in the city. What was her allure for him? Why was he drawn to her so part of him was now calling out through her for completion?

And then her words at the evening's end at Demel's, and how they had caught him so completely off guard. Such candor was unusual for a woman in her century, he reflected, even more unusual for a girl raised in nineteenth-century New England. The feelings of the past few days, the richness of the evening's sounds, the *grandesse* of the scene, the indulgence of the chocolate and raspberry torte *mit Schlag*, all that coupled with her startling revelation that she was intending to write articles under a masculine pseudonym, and now that she had abandoned the project.

And he had pulled away, as he said in his journal. It all turned what he thought would be an innocuous evening into potential disaster. He took her home without discussing her request, without allowing himself any form of closeness at the end of the evening in spite of the allure of the dress and the way she leaned into him in the carriage. He did not allow himself to consider *her* feelings, that she had asked for this at extreme risk to herself. He held himself at a distance, something very new for the impulsive Wheeler Burden.

"I will avoid seeing her again," he had written in his journal. "It's that simple!" He had to stop playing with fire. He had let things get out of hand, rushed forward without heeding Dilly's warnings, and should never have allowed the feelings that were now raging inside him to begin. He thought, of course, that he could go along just enjoying her company, just looking at her beautiful face, just skating on the edge of the thin ice. He skated there in spite of Dilly's warnings because he knew he could handle the consequences. And now he had lost control. There was still time to get out before there was real damage. "Get the toothpaste back in the tube," he wrote. He imagined telling Freud about the proposal and his reaction to it.

"Why do you think *she* initiated such things?" the great doctor would have asked dispassionately. He could hear his voice.

"She is very attracted to me," Wheeler would say. "I am older and quite different from men she has known."

"Old enough to be her father," Freud would reply too quickly.

"You know what I've been feeling," he would continue. "And she has eyes. I'm sure she could see it too. We had a very romantic evening at the opera and at Demel's and she got that feeling. She's young and inexperienced. I'm probably the one who started it all. I mean, I am the one who kept agreeing to meet with her, even when I knew the situation—"

"And now her request for something physical makes you uncomfortable?"

He knew well Freud's view that everyone in civilized society is repressed. "Is it not highly unusual for a twenty-two-year-old American woman to say something like that to a man?" the doctor would ask.

"Very unusual," Wheeler would say, becoming annoyed by Freud's clinical attitude. "I don't think that a man in my position can afford to get involved in something like this," he would say emphatically. "I have made a big mistake."

"I see," the doctor would say with that annoying abstracted distance of his. "What are you thinking?"

"What was I thinking? I am thinking that what I have here is a real flesh and blood dilemma."

Fraulein Tatlock answered the door and did not seem to notice Wheeler's sheepishness as she ushered him into the sitting room. "I was wondering if my friend is in," Wheeler had said.

"Your friend is right here," Weezie said from inside the sitting room. "Thank you for an absolutely delicious evening." She gestured to a place on the couch from which she had just risen.

"We both enjoyed ourselves," he said. She had an air of caution about her, he thought. "I have come to apologize for not being very polite last night."

"You were the perfect escort," she said, but her voice was flat and without enthusiasm. "The opera was beautiful, the dessert was delicious, your company was scintillating, and the conversation was, as always, worth coming home and writing about."

"I mean at the end. I was not very considerate of your feelings," he said.

She looked down. "I don't know what you are talking about. It was a delightful evening."

Wheeler kept his eyes on her until she looked up. Her eyes met his, then she looked down again. "I came to apologize. I wish I had been more considerate," he repeated.

There was a long silence in which she was obviously deciding how to proceed. Finally she broke it, but without looking up. "I feel terribly ashamed," she said finally. "I do not know why I said what I said. You have been a gentleman and even a friend to me, and I intruded on that by following some shameful dark impulse."

Wheeler moved to speak, but she stopped him. "No," she said, "let me continue. I thought you would not come back, which would have meant my not having to tell you this, but now I will. There is something about you, Mr. Truman, that has disarmed me from the start. You are the most curious and probing and yet caring person I have ever met. You seem to bring emotions to the surface in a way that I find magnetic and at the same time disturbing. It is not good for me, and my reaction is not good for you. I am sorry for what I did." She looked more compelling than ever as she spoke. It was all Wheeler could do to resist reaching out to her and pulling her toward him.

"And I came to tell you how very flattered I was by what you said. It was perhaps the nicest thing anyone has ever said to me."

"Please." She shook her head softly, looking down. "I am ashamed."

"No, listen," he said again and waited until she looked at him. "I wanted so to respond to you." He could see that this whole conversation, in the light of Fraulein Tatlock's parlor, without the wine and the Demel's was making her very uncomfortable.

"I wish I had not said certain things."

"Certain things," Wheeler said, "are what I am here to talk to you about."

"Oh, I know. I was terribly inappropriate."

"Quite the contrary."

She interrupted him by raising her hand. "You don't need to soften your reaction, Mr. Truman. I understand."

"What you perhaps do not understand. What I am here to tell you is—"

She put her hands to her ears, not wanting to hear the stern rejection. For a moment Wheeler teetered dangerously between his two strong desires, first to adhere to Dilly's admonition with all its wisdom, and then, second, to leap at the inexplicable siren call of this woman's total being. For a moment, he sat paralyzed, gazing into her beautiful, apprehensive face.

"Miss James," he said suddenly, "what I am here to tell you is that I too want very much to allow our strong mutual attraction to become physical."

Nothing more was said of it. The next morning, they met as usual, walking along the Danube Canal, she with her hand resting gently on his arm, telling him stories of her attractions to music and her ideas about modern trends. They made arrangements to dine together and afterward Wheeler arranged for a carriage to take them around the Ring and then home. The air inside the cab was warm and lightly scented by her perfume. In spite of the pact they had made, then not mentioned again, their mood was relaxed and happy. As she sat beside him in the carriage, he felt her arm gently against his. "I feel very comfortable beside you," Wheeler said as the cab approached Fraulein Tatlock's. "I feel we could stay this way forever, talking."

"I too feel that." She looked into his eyes. "I feel the ultimate trust right here, right now." She leaned toward him. "I suppose this is how it begins," she whispered.

"Are you comfortable with this?" he said.

She had closed her eyes and did not move. "Completely," she said, and he lifted his arm and surrounded her with it. "Completely," she repeated.

"Don't look up," he said.

"I want to look up," she said, her lips now close to him, a convulsive tremor taking over her body. She let go a deep moan. "I want to see it all."

"Small steps, remember."

"Small steps," she whispered, and she seemed to dissolve into him, and their kiss became intense, their bodies pressed against each other, first gently, then with the ardor that had been for her such a mystery. She let go a deep sigh and moved her hand to the back of his neck and pulled him to her, and he responded in kind. There was a moment of wild explosive release, and she let go a small almost helpless whimper. Wheeler was about to signal to the driver to drive on.

Suddenly, she was struggling free and gave him a push with a strength that caught him completely by surprise, and with a stifled moan she pulled herself across the leather seat of the cab and threw open the door. Before Wheeler could collect himself she had fled the cab. He rose and saw from the window her white skirt disappearing into the front door of the Pension Tatlock, too far ahead to follow. "Please," he called after her, which in retrospect seemed a silly thing to say.

As the cab circled on Ebendorfer-Strasse and headed for his room at Frau Bauer's, he collapsed back into the leather seat shocked and amazed by the remarkable and ironic turn in this forbidden relationship.

33

A Feeling of Desperation

heeler called for her at the Pension Tatlock a little later than his usual nine o'clock. It was not that he wanted to make her wait; in fact this morning he had been sensitive to the fact that she might worry if he was not on time. But he needed time to think. He had been up early and had taken a long walk alone along the Ringstrasse.

He turned Dilly's warning and the consequences of disregarding it over and over in his mind. Dilly was a rules man, and Wheeler was for spontaneity. Dilly decided what was right to do and stuck with it. Wheeler was more of an adaptor. Dilly was an oak, Wheeler a bamboo. He certainly never intended for things to have taken this turn, but actions on both their parts had brought about this consequence, and now he needed to be with her, to guide her past the torment she must be feeling. His thoughts were with Emily James as Fraulein Tatlock greeted him, wringing her hands. "Something urgent has come up," she said fretfully. "She packed in the night. She has left for home. I did not know about it until this morning, and there was no stopping her."

Wheeler's heart sank. "Did she mention the cause?"

"She said nothing, but she looked as if she had not had much sleep." Fraulein Tatlock walked into the sitting room, to the fireplace mantel and retrieved an envelope. "She left this letter for you." Her hand shook as she handed Wheeler the envelope. He didn't open it because he could guess its content.

"How long ago did she leave for the train station?" he asked Fraulein Tatlock suddenly.

"An hour ago, sir. She asked me to take care of the shipping of her trunk."

Wheeler ran out into the street and down to the corner, where he found a cab. He told the man to hurry. Jumping from the cab at the Nord-bahnhof, he asked about the Paris train and ran to the platform. "There it goes," the platform attendant said and pointed down the tracks to the departing observation car, now a quarter of a mile distant. "There is another one at eleven."

Wheeler stood watching as the train disappeared down the complexity of tracks, a feeling of desperation growing within him.

Weezie had an abundance of time to think on the train ride to Paris. As the countryside of the Danube basin rolled by outside the window of her private compartment, she tried to sort through her complex anguish.

Shame had descended on her once again like the shroud of night. She had felt it first from the cabby's eyes burning into her back after she had struggled free from the cab and hurried toward the door of the pension. How many times had he witnessed similar scenes of fallen women slinking away? She felt it in Fraulein Tatlock's sharp eyes as she must have seen the ruddy glow of passion still burning on her boarder's cheeks. She felt it closing in on her as she lay sobbing into the counterpane so as not to spread the news to the neighboring rooms.

She tried to recall how the embarrassment had happened, but the painful memories came only in fragments, enveloped in haze like the events leading up to a head injury.

Leaving Vienna was precipitous, but the only way out. All her life people had tended to find her impulsive, jumping this way or that because of a moment's fancy. It was a criticism she never much cared for nor one she found particularly accurate or fair. Certainly now she was not acting impulsively. Her useful time in Vienna had run out anyway, she reasoned. She had abundant notes for future writings about the new music, and now she simply could not stay there. She would return home to lick her wounds and restore her self-control. That was it, get herself back under control. And come to terms with the great loss of love that even now had begun to tear at her. And yet she could not shake the feeling that somehow she had fallen from grace.

She had given in to the heat of illicit passion, she who had always very privately thought of herself as someone special and elevated. What man would want to marry her now? What gentleman would be fascinated by her and would travel across the globe for her hand, as it had been rumored back in Boston? Was that sort of romantic tale now lost to her forever, gone with her lost innocence and purity?

She had joined the world of the women of easy virtue who seemed ubiquitous in Vienna. She had lost access to the world of light and had inherited one of darkness, her integrity and essence stolen by urges she seemed to have no control over. Again, she felt her aunt Prudence's judgment upon her.

How had she succumbed to it? Why now, in the feverish hallucinations of the past few hours, in her fitful flashes of memory and dreams did the incident with Herr Mahler keep coming back to her? How was that embarrassing incident now tied at least symbolically to what had happened the night before with Mr. Truman? Who was the man who had caused her to feel reckless and daring in his presence and who had ever so subtly, without ever asking, gotten her to join forces with the dark evil world Aunt Prudence had depicted so vividly in her evening readings?

"Enough!" she said out loud, to stop the downward slide of her self-reproach.

She could not stop thinking about Mr. Truman. She remembered how she had been drawn to him that first day she had seen him in the park, and had given the name Emily James. How like Svengali he had been for her, luring her into his world, rendering himself irresistible with the way he defied formality. That was definitely it: He was not the stuffed shirt Weezie was so accustomed to in Boston, and he seemed relaxed and without pretension. What a powerful drug that was.

How like an alien he seemed, as if from another planet, with a different set of values. He had guided her so effortlessly toward a physical release, all the time giving her the illusion that it had been her instigation, paying little heed to the strict moral code that bound those of her upbringing. Perhaps he was some Mephistopheles. Faust had, after all, lived for a time in Vienna. That was it. He did not believe in duty and honor and righteousness, the forces that drove Aunt Prudence in her stern and holy life. In rejecting the cruelty of her aunt's view of the world had she not thrown out the good of social rules and moral codes?

At the bottom of it Weezie had sinned, had slid into wantonness, and now in the loneliness of her private cabin on the Paris train she felt the desperate consequences of that sin. She felt hopelessly alone and wretched. In that last week in Vienna with Mr. Truman she had felt so vibrant and fully alive to experiences, as if she was about to open up, to look down into her soul and finally understand the conflicting forces pulling at her. She felt on the brink of the most exciting of discoveries. But somehow the same forces that drew her toward self-discovery also drew her to the desire for consummation that welled up in her with such force and for which she was now paying such a dear price. Her head whirled and she fell into a troubled sleep.

She awoke with her head resting against the glass window of her private compartment. She rose and opened her door. "What is the next station?" she asked a passing conductor.

"We will be in Nuremburg"—he pulled his gold watch out to the end of its chain—"in forty-five minutes, Fraulein."

"Thank you," she said, and went back to her seat by the window where the German countryside rolled by.

On the ride back to Frau Bauer's in the cab he opened the envelope. The letter was written on pale blue stationery with a fine steady hand.

> *My Dear Mr. Truman,*
>
> *I am so terribly ashamed about what happened last night. I had considered you such a close friend, and neither of us was watchful enough. I do not blame you, but I do blame myself. In the interest of finding out more about myself in this foreign city I ventured too far from the conventional path, and now I must suffer the consequences. My only choice open now is to return home and try slowly to reconcile in my own way what has transpired, as I know you will in your own way.*
>
> *I have not been honest with you, and I did not know how to set things straight. I do not know why I kept up the deception, when you were being so open and honest with me. My name is not Emily James. That is an amalgam of my two great literary heroes. And I am not from Amherst, Massachusetts. I am from Boston.*
>
> *Please do not try to follow or contact me, it would only worsen*

an already deplorable situation. I am sorry for any hurt my actions have caused you.

   Yours penitently,
   Eleanor Louise Putnam, called Weezie

He stared at the letter and at the name that he knew so well. Slowly, distractedly, Wheeler folded the letter carefully and replaced it in its envelope, then removed it again. He sat without moving for a long time, staring at empty space in front of him. Had we been able to see him in that moment, we would have described his appearance as ashen. Wheeler's hand shook as he stared down at the handwritten note from his young grandmother.

PART THREE

The Last Burden

34

Keeping No Secrets

e can assume that Dr. Freud remained fascinated, addicted even, and that he held doggedly to his assertion that, like all of his hysteric patients, this patient Herr Burden was making up his elaborate time-dislocation story. As engaging as he was, the man who called himself Wheeler Burden was delusional and deranged. And therefore the patient's intense relationship with this beautifully innocent and yet highly sexualized young American woman—whom in a remarkable turn he now had fashioned into his own grandmother—must be serving some useful function in his complex and highly compelling fantasy.

We know some things about Sigmund Freud in that pivotal year of 1897. We know, for instance, that this brilliant, relentlessly logical, and scientific thinker, depressed by the isolated path where his steel-trap logic had placed him, alienated from his colleagues at the university, found himself lonely for conversation and company.

And so Dr. Freud had come to enjoy more than he was willing to admit his conversations with his extroverted American visitor, setting aside time every few days. He encouraged Herr Burden to tell his story, and he listened with great interest. As soon as he learned of the journal's existence and guessed at the wealth of evidence it contained, he encouraged readings from its full contents at each session.

Wheeler reacted quickly. "I cannot," he said.

"And why is that?"

"Because it is uncensored and unvarnished."

"And you still believe that your honesty can somehow compromise me, that you might somehow alter history? That history cannot bear it?" There was nothing sarcastic or deriding in his tone.

"I know things you shouldn't know."

"I am my own man, my friend. I think I can cope with that which I should and should not know. You are not going to turn me to stone."

And so Wheeler, the compulsive conversationalist, in order to keep up the interest of the great doctor who had become his material and financial support in this strange land, began reading from the journal, at first bit by bit, with summaries and editings, then slowly evolving to every word, every day, unabridged, and unexpurgated.

One can see in reading the journal entries that eventually Wheeler held back nothing. Dr. Freud would hear the whole story. Wheeler must have reassessed and decided it would do no harm, probably because he knew that the doctor viewed him as one of his hysterical patients—compelling, but hysterical. "Dr. Freud thinks I am delusional," he wrote and subsequently shared on the day following the decision. "And as such my truths will always seem to him my separate reality. Fascinating, for sure, but a separate reality always. But the die is cast now. He will know all the details of my strange visit to Vienna. I will be keeping no secrets."

The deal was struck. Freud would sit attentive to every word, weighing every detail and allusion, giving this visitor—"my American visitor," he called him—an intensity of concentration he gave to no other person in his family or his professional life. As Wheeler read, the great doctor would focus his steely gray eyes on him, smoke his cigar, and listen, always searching for that golden path that would lead him and his patient back to the causal traumatic event, to the mother lode of a complex and fascinating hysterical state. As we have the journal in front of us, we know what the doctor knew, and we can surmise how he interpreted it. To crack the code of the offending amnesia, Freud wanted all the information he could get, and having a patient keep a meticulous daily journal and then be willing to share it was, in short, a gold mine.

We know that the great doctor formed strong attachments to great men around him, some say with a kind of filial adoration. First, in his medical student days there was Ernst Brucke, one of Europe's finest and best-known physiologists, who influenced him to insist that every last detail be confirmed by empirical scientific evidence, an attentiveness to which he became a stickler throughout his professional life. Then in 1885 he went to Paris and studied under Jean Martin Charcot, the greatest neurologist of the time, who introduced him to hypnosis. Then returning to Vienna he studied with Josef Breuer, twenty years his senior but the colleague who helped him focus his attention on sex as the root cause of hysteria, and who through the compelling case of Bertha Pappenheim, called Anna O, gave him his most significant and most famous study and the development of "the talking cure." And recently, he had formed an affectionate alliance with Wilhelm Fleiss, the Berlin nose and throat specialist, and an unlikely subject of his respect. Fleiss was unlikely because of his mediocre researches and his devotion to the idea that hysteria originated in the nose.

In spite of these intense friendships, the young Freud had developed a style that no one would consider collegial, isolating himself with an independent bearing and controversial subject matter. In 1896, at forty, he had delivered a speech to the Viennese Academy that had painted him in a corner. "All your life," Wheeler reflected back to the doctor in his journal writings, from what he knew of the doctor's personal history, "you have shown a remarkable ability to choose a direction and stick with it. You grab hold of a subject with a bulldog grip and don't let go. You are always searching for the universal truths beneath the surface few others can see.

"In that 1896 speech," Wheeler wrote, "Dr. Freud had announced to the academy, and to any of the rest of the world willing to listen, that the cause of hysteria was childhood sexual trauma, most likely perpetrated by the father. It was a brilliant conclusion based on the evidence of his patients, but one that brought him derision and isolation. The formal and traditional all-male establishment was simply unwilling to accept the fact that the parents of hysteric patients, mostly women, were child abusers and that the abuse had been sexual. The derision and isolation did not shake Freud's resolve; in fact, they strengthened it."

The great doctor would have listened intently to the journal entry, then responded. "You make it sound as if my ideas are shaped by controversy."

"Isn't it true that your famous resolve has been shaken with regard to your seduction theory," Wheeler said, "by troubling conclusions about your own father?" It was true. Through self-analysis Freud had concluded that he too was obsessive and neurotic, a hysteric, and since both he and his brother were hysterics, the cause had to be their own father. So in early 1897, shortly after that father's death, the great doctor concluded that

Jacob Freud must have molested his children. Jacob Freud had been a decent but somewhat hapless man, unable to find a job, unable to stand up for himself. Considering him a child molester required a stretch of the imagination too great for his son. Sigmund Freud moved to another conclusion. And in the fall of that same year, the very moment Wheeler Burden entered his Berggasse 19 apartment, Freud was on the brink of a stunning new discovery.

Along with the complete details of his daily life in Vienna, Wheeler always added a paragraph or two about his personal background and his sessions at Berggasse 19, his *feuilletons* of insight, which Freud particularly enjoyed. We can imagine the scene as Wheeler read a journal entry that included this: "I imagine Dr. Freud the hero of an ancient Greek classic, Odysseus in search of home, Jason after the golden fleece, Perseus tracking down Medusa, indelibly positive, certain of his goal, searching for the truth, unflinching in his pursuit of universal truth."

"How are you so certain that I am on the right track?" Freud said. "Perhaps I am Don Quixote, tilting with imaginary giants."

"Perhaps. It is your determination that sets you apart. I just know you are not going to relent in your quest."

"But at the same time you believe that the sexual abuses are real?"

"Caustic child rearing abounds in Vienna," Wheeler said. "That is a known fact. Children are raised with religious austerity and harshness at best, and actual physical abuse at worst. You know this, and you are willing to overlook it." Wheeler became animated, gesturing with his hands. "When you addressed your medical colleagues with your observation that hysteria came from actual incidents, you had justification. Your new Oedipus theory discounts the evidence of real abuse and blames the child."

"But surely not every hysteric could possibly be the child of sexual trauma. That would make incestuous monsters of half the men in Vienna." For a moment, Freud would stop treating Wheeler as a patient and view him as a colleague of astonishing if delusional insights.

"But some cases are legitimate abuse. You must account for those."

Freud looked troubled. "In some cases, yes," he said. "But it cannot be the universal I once thought."

"And for you it is no good if it is not the universal, the absolute? Can't it be both?"

Freud thought for a long painful moment, knocking the ash off the stubby end of his cigar. "If it is not universal, how can it be of any use?"

Aha, wrote Wheeler in his journal, *if it is not universal, it is of no use. That is the problem: all-or-nothing black-and-white thinking.*

"It is a matter of degrees, Dr. Freud," Wheeler said. "In the Anna O case, you argued that Bertha Pappenheim's neurosis came from the actual fact that she had been sexually abused as a child, and you attributed that to all victims of hysteria. That assertion is what brought to you so much attention and disdain of your 1896 speech. P. T. Barnum, by the way, said that there is no bad publicity. For almost two years you pursued doggedly the notion that sexual abuse, 'seduction,' you called it, was the root cause of all hysteria, a brilliant piece of deductive science."

"You are being facetious, Herr Burden."

"No, not at all. You examined the evidence in ways no one else was willing to do. Brilliant. Then you went to the next logical step in analyzing yourself, and you concluded that you had hysteric symptoms and that your own father must have abused his children. Science led you there. Logic. But then the absurdity of that logic hit you. If not carefully checked, pure science can lead to ridiculous and harmful conclusions, you deduced. Suddenly the story of Oedipus caught your attention, and the literal cause of abuse evolved into the metaphoric one. Children secretly wish sex and violence, you concluded. Again brilliant, but again the stuff of castigation and controversy."

"It is not an easy message for the average Viennese to hear."

"And so here you are now," Wheeler continued, "upending all that you deduced before: the conclusion that the sexual assault actually happened gave way to the symbolic or metaphoric act—the assault happened only in the patient's mind. That is going to be even harder for the proper bourgeoisie to accept."

"It *has* to be symbolic," Freud said, protesting too much. "The imagined assaults cannot be real. I am now certain of that. It has to be a sexual impulse in the child, what I have found in the Oedipus myth, not the real act of father on child."

"But your Oedipus theory says that every child wants to have sex and commit murder. It lays the blame on the child."

"It is metaphoric," Freud said, now purely defensive. "And accurate. The guilt felt by the child over wanting no rival for the parent's attentions, and the fear of being punished for it are powerful forces, long into adulthood."

Wheeler looked at him with a wildness in his eyes. "That is your flaw," he said, pulling back from his exasperation, then going quiet for a moment, looking into the great doctor's eyes. "That is the brilliance of your next move," he said. "Seeing in a few patients the general human condition, moving from the local and finding the universal. But this new Oedipus view is too extreme. It is just too narrow."

"My conclusions are already dismissible, preposterous to the medical establishment of this city."

"You got their attention," Wheeler said.

"And you think that I seek attention?"

"That's a starting point. You need notoriety to get where you wish to go."

"And you think I will now shift the focus to the Oedipus myth to get that notoriety."

"Your express train is heading down that track," Wheeler said coolly. "I don't think you have any choice."

35

Rouge Gorge Ne Chantait Pas

heeler did not share with Dilly any of his great devastation: the double blow of losing the woman to whom he had become viscerally attached and the discovery that Emily James was in fact his own grandmother. His own grandmother! He kept it to himself and suffered in silence, convincing himself after the initial shock that no grave harm had been done and that Eleanor Putnam's return to Boston was how it was supposed to be. He had just sped the eventuality along, or perhaps even supplied the catalyst for what was inevitable. *This too will pass,* he had learned to say about debilitating loss. But how, how? How had he not seen what was happening? How had he missed the clues? He knew that his grandmother had been the one who brought Arnauld Esterhazy to St. Gregory's in the first place. Of course, she had met him in Vienna: how else? She should have been the first person he looked for when he arrived. How could he not have recognized her? Had she changed so very much in sixty years? However it was, he had dodged a disaster, and she was gone from Vienna now and headed home. No damage done. The unspeakable averted. And yet, he had this awful aching in his heart.

He knew Dilly was working up to something of his own and would surely not notice any despondency in someone else. But Dilly had little practice at beating around the bush. "You look awful," Dilly said to him when they met.

"A sense of loss," Wheeler said. "Sometimes it creeps up."

"It is difficult to adjust to the fact that our former life seems to be over," Dilly said, reflective for a moment.

"That's it. You alone can understand."

But Dilly's mind was elsewhere. "There are certain nagging questions," he said finally. He needed to take advantage of Wheeler's knowledge of what was for him the future. He was hiding something.

"Go ahead and ask," Wheeler said openly, aware that telling what happened between 1944 and 1988 to Dilly, who had life behind him, was a whole different matter than telling Sigmund Freud, who still had life out in front of him.

"My run-in with the Gestapo was, I gather—" He paused awkwardly, searching for the word: "—decisive," he said.

"It was terminal," Wheeler said sadly, adding the word his father was stumbling over. Wheeler had forgotten that his father would not know about his own heroic end. "You died just about the time of the invasion."

Dilly did not seem shocked by the news, but Wheeler could see disappointment in his eyes. "I gathered," he said. "Things weren't going too well. I guess anyone could see that. Still—" He paused again and looked up at Wheeler. "One always hopes."

"They wanted your information," Wheeler took over. "And they were people with powerful means. I guess they pulled out all the stops, tried to wear you down till you talked, but you never did, and that's what made Rouge Gorge such a big hero to the French, and for a couple of generations of St. Gregory's boys. When I was a boy I went back to Paris with Mother to the dedication of the plaque on Rue des Americains. It has your name on it and then it says *'Rouge Gorge ne chantait pas,'* which I guess became sort of a code phrase, sort of a rallying cry in the last days of the Resistance."

Dilly shifted his weight uncomfortably in his chair. "You know about the last days," he said.

"The war with Germany ended in May of 1945, after the invasion in June 1944."

"That's 'present time' for me, you forget."

"Right. I did forget. The Allies pushed into Germany from the west, General Patton leading the charge, and the Russians came in from the east. Hitler shot himself in his bunker with his girlfriend, Eva Braun, and that was that, except it took a long time to rebuild the mess. Berlin and all of Germany were pretty much devastated. Democratic Germany grew up from the ashes to be one of the modern industrial powers, along with Japan. Sort of ironic."

Dilly was still fishing for more. "How about the invasion? How did things work out?"

"It wasn't easy, I guess, but it worked. It started in early June and the Allies had captured Paris by August, although I guess it was pretty hard fought. There were lots of deaths."

Still Dilly circled around for something more specific. "Did the Germans know?" he said painfully. "I mean did they seem to know?" Then he came right out with it. "With the invasion, I mean. Did they know where and when?"

Wheeler gave it some thought. "I'm not much of a military historian. I'm not the greatest authority. It was a long time ago." Then he added, "I'm sure they could guess. I mean there was only so much coastline, and the Allies weren't going to wait forever to make their move. But I think the Germans were caught pretty much by surprise."

Dilly looked off in the distance, struggling to dig down into painful memories. "I did know time and place," he said seriously. "When I met with Winston Churchill just before I went back into occupied France that last time, the Admiralty high command briefed me on the whole plan, Operation Overlord they called it. It was sort of a huge deal. I was one of only a few men who was to know the details. It was my job to coordinate the Resistance in the northern area, to take out some key communications installations, destroy railroads, stymie troop movements and the like. I had worked over there behind the lines before. Churchill knew I would handle the information properly, and that—"

"You wouldn't talk."

Dilly nodded sadly. "If caught. Exactly. I had the cyanide pill. I just never thought I'd be caught. I'd been in France before, you know, and operated with ease. I had a lot of confidence in my ability to blend in, to make myself inconspicuous. I could look, and sound, very French, they said. It had worked so well before." He shook his head in disbelief. "Your mother had a premonition, I guess. She didn't want me to go back, and I had promised I wouldn't. But this was a unique situation. The prime minister himself recruited me for it. He showed me the huge army of invasion preparing in England and told me details of how it would come. Thousands gave their lives. It was that important. It just seemed bigger than my promise to your mother. Mr. Churchill himself met with your mother to explain, you know."

"I know. She told me."

"Do you think I was foolhardy? Did I have an overblown sense of duty?"

"Those were monumental times," Wheeler said. "Everyone knew that."

"Did she forgive me?"

Wheeler smiled. "I think she just missed you. Sort of desperately. Mother figured you were as much a slave to your sense of duty as she was to her own convictions."

The thought brought a brief smile to Dilly. "I hope so. I felt terrible about betraying her trust. She was such a committed pacifist. But it seemed so very important," he said, serious again. "We had so much at stake, and there was an obvious need for someone to coordinate things from the inside. I knew the territory."

He shook his head, slowly and painfully. "Then they caught me. I hadn't been in France for more than a few days, and they picked me up outside of Lille. It was fast and certain. They seemed to know exactly whom they had. It was as if—" He stopped and shook his head. "I had a pill, and I broke it open and swallowed it, but it didn't work. It made me pretty much violently ill, which was not the best way to go into what they had in mind for me."

He paused for a breath. "Then they started in on me. Those people really know how to work someone over. I'll spare you the details, but it is pretty grim stuff. I had a lot of things to sustain me and to counteract what they were doing. I thought a lot of your mother." A gentle smile came to his lips. "I just closed my eyes and thought of her beautiful face and the way she used to tease me about my propriety. And then when the pain got so terribly grinding, and I needed something even stronger, I developed the Vienna plot. It was like creating a three-dimensional novel in my head, filled with all this—" He gestured around him. "Music and coffee-houses and your grandmother and ... you. I didn't know about you being here: that's a bonus. I created it all in my head, gave it all texture and life. Painstakingly, I worked out each detail, creating colors and words and shapes.

"I convinced myself that if I created it in enough vivid detail, I would travel there. So I worked and worked and shut out more and more of the awful Gestapo headquarters and the awful grinding pain—" He paused again. "The pain. The nausea, the sleep deprivation, and the repetition and the pain. It was a science for them. I never understood how it would wear one down. I really thought I could withstand it, you know, persever-ance, stiff upper lip, mind over matter, and all the rest." He stopped and looked into Wheeler's eyes, his own filling with tears. "I had never before in my whole life — ever! — come up against a challenge I couldn't meet."

He continued looking intently at Wheeler, wanting very much to make him understand. "I think I was a challenge to them. So much had been said about Rouge Gorge and about how he would not talk. The Nazis with their tremendous respect for Aryan willpower wanted to see how far they could push. They put their best men on it, convinced that they could make Rouge Gorge sing, and knowing somehow that I had deep inside me the most valuable information of the war. Not just the names of key Resistance workers, but the actual kernel of information: under all the layers, I knew the exact time and place of the invasion. I should have died with the secret inside me." He stopped, now looking physically ill.

"They set out to break me. And I dug in to thwart them. Pretty much a battle of wills, you know. Only thing was, it was no contest. This wasn't Dover or Yale; it was the major leagues. I was a bush leaguer in Yankee Stadium. They searched for the way to get me, and finally — after hours and hours — they found it: drowning!" His eyes were piercing now. "I have this awful uncontrollable fear of drowning. And that was it!"

He had to stop. His head was down, moving slowly from side to side, recalling the grueling struggle and all the horrible pain it brought with it. "I got away. My Vienna strategy worked. I created such a believable place in my mind that I slipped away from them into it. Here I am, with you. But before I went, when the pain was at its worst and the terror began. I was so very tired — " He paused for a long moment. "That's what you don't count on," he said wearily. "Being so worn down it gets to the point where all you want is for it to be over. Head held down in the tub of water. And you know there is only one way to get there." When he looked up finally, his eyes were filled now with tears. He shook his head.

"I have always succeeded in everything all my life," he said. "I have never failed. I have never let anyone down." There was now a wild des-peration in his eyes, and he was struggling with words and a long dark pause, the darkest. "I talked, Stan," he said finally. He closed his eyes and continued to shake his head, holding back things that had weighed on his soul for so long. And then for the first time in his life Dilly Burden began to sob. "The great legendary Rouge Gorge *chantait*," he cried out between sobs. "I sang. I spilled my guts and told them everything I knew."

Wheeler just looked at his father, shocked and speechless. This just never occurred to him, not to him or to hundreds of other St. Gregory's boys.

"Not possible," Wheeler stammered involuntarily.

"I'm afraid so," Dilly gasped. And he just kept shaking his head, spewing out the agony. "And then they just left me lying there. Alone with my shame for hours and hours, waiting for death, the only thing I wanted then. That's when it started," he said. "That's when the plan kicked in and started to actually work." Then he stopped abruptly.

"What plan?" Wheeler said.

Dilly went silent, shaking his head. "Escaping to Vienna," he said finally, but Wheeler had a feeling there was more to the story.

Wheeler looked at his father. "Why Vienna?" he said. "Why here?"

"It is such a relief to know that the invasion was successful. I have been feeling that I caused the failure single-handedly. Imagine knowing something that important."

"You think they believed you?" Wheeler said.

"They knew they had the truth. They kept going out and checking. They knew they had the plan all right." Dilly's quick mind was working now. "That's why they started the rumor that I didn't talk. They didn't want anyone to know they knew. All the names I mentioned were safe, I'll bet you'll find. They didn't want anyone to know that I'd told everything. They didn't want anyone to know what they *knew*. All because of me."

"As I said, I'm not a historian, but as far as I know the Germans were caught by surprise, as if they were expecting the invasion somewhere else," Wheeler said in his most reassuring voice. "Whatever you are afraid of didn't make much difference."

"You are just trying to console me, and I appreciate that. It was a terrible betrayal. I'm just glad it didn't ruin the whole thing," he said soberly. "What I spilled to them was too specific. And I knew when I said it, it was going to cost thousands and thousands of lives, and cause the invasion to fail, but I was just too run-down—afraid of more drowning, don't you know? They won, and they knew it. And it would wipe out the advantage of the Normandy Feint. I knew it all, but I just couldn't hold back any more." He shook his head slowly; his face looked drained, all the famous Dilly Burden spunk gone. "You get so tired, too tired, and don't want any more. You just want to die in peace." He looked up, struggling with the memory. "You don't know what it is like," he closed his eyes again and said slowly.

Wheeler was still back on something his father had said. "Normandy Feint," he repeated, slowly recalling the article he had been forced to read in his Harvard days in *The Cambridge Voice*. "What is the Normandy Feint?"

"You know, that the invasion on the Normandy beaches was going to look like the big one. Hitler would move all his forces to Normandy. Then Patton would hit with the real big one: one million men storming in at Calais."

Slowly it was all coming back to Wheeler. "A bigger one was coming a few days later somewhere else, right?"

"Of course. You know, Calais, where it happened," Dilly said matter-of-factly, looking at his son as if to say, *boy, you really aren't much of a historian*. "Patton's army, waiting for the killer blow. Across from Dover Beach, the logical and obvious place where the Channel is the narrowest. And the Krauts knew it because of me." He stopped again and looked away. "Damn!"

Wheeler shook his head, suddenly aware of the powerful new information. "I don't know how to break this to you, Dilly Burden, but you were snookered."

Dilly looked at him uncomprehendingly, and a little miffed. "You are going to have to explain." But from the look on his face, Wheeler could see that Dilly was figuring it out for himself.

"There was no Normandy Feint; it was a ruse. Normandy was the whole invasion. Utah Beach, Omaha Beach, they called them. The whole Allied force landed there and fought its way across France and into Germany. There was no second invasion in Calais."

Dilly looked even more confused. "No," he said, trying to get a grip on what he was hearing. "You just don't remember. It was Patton's army. They were built up in East Anglia, across from Calais. A million strong—"

"There was no army there," Wheeler interrupted. "It was an elaborate hoax. It was blow-up rubber tanks and trucks and equipment under fake nets, created to look like an army in waiting. They are writing spy thrillers about it now—in the 1980s. The Allies wanted to create the illusion that a second invasion was coming after Normandy, so that Hitler would not move his Panzer divisions, his real tank power, out of Calais until *after* the invading forces had a chance to build up their strength."

"No," Dilly said again emphatically.

"It's true," Wheeler said with a shrug. "It all happened at Normandy."

"It's not possible."

"It is how it happened."

Dilly sat shaking his head. "I just can't believe it," he said. "There is just too much information. Too many details. All that Winston Churchill and the admirals' men showed me."

"That was part of what they called the bodyguard of lies."

"I still don't believe it," he said, but his voice had lost its conviction. Dilly Burden was running enormous changes through his head.

"There's more," Wheeler said. "If it's true, it made convincing you as important as convincing the Nazis. And I'm just going to tell it to you straight." He pulled his chair closer and leaned both elbows on the table, closer to his father. "The whole world after the war—or at least most of it—thinks that you died heroically with your information about the time and place of the invasion sealed inside that legendary strong will of yours. But a story came out in an underground newspaper back when I was at Harvard. It claimed to have come from information from a former aide of Churchill's and it said this—"

Wheeler told his father how, according to the exposé, the British had wanted to convince the Nazi high command that a huge invasion force, under the direction of the infamous General George Patton, was being readied for a secondary assault on France. In order to do this effectively they had engineered the famous "bodyguard of lies," which included various intentional plants of inaccurate intelligence information in the hands of the Germans. One of the most effective means, according to this underground article, was to send the Gestapo an impeccable source, someone whose dying testimony would be absolutely believable for two reasons. First, because of his already established reputation as Rouge Gorge—who would never talk—and second because he himself would really believe the information to be accurate, thinking as he was broken to the point of talking that he was actually divulging monumentally important information. "There is a no more convincing liar," Wheeler said in concluding, "than one certain he is telling the truth." Wheeler let his message sink in. "You saved thousands and thousands of lives," the son said, himself adjusting to the new twist of the Dilly Burden story he was only now absorbing. "Because of you those dreaded Panzer divisions never arrived. Because of you—" He paused, stunned by what he himself was realizing. "Because of you, the whole thing was won, the invasion, the war, everything."

Dilly remained sitting, in stunned silence, struggling not to believe, but at the same time grabbing at the ironic fact that his giving the Gestapo information had *saved*, not destroyed, thousands of lives. "You are saying that I was plied with false information, then purposely turned over to the Gestapo for torture."

"That must be what happened. The cyanide pill was fake. You were sacrificed. The British had been working on the plan for three years. You were their trump card. The legend of Rouge Gorge carried the final bluff."

"And all because I was 'so damned bloody heroic.'"

"I didn't tell you this, but Mr. Churchill had a second meeting with Mother. It was after the invasion, after she had returned from France and knew what had happened to you. She was preparing to leave with me forever, to go start her life over again in California. He called her in to tell her how sorry he was about what had happened to you. He told her that he couldn't give details but that your mission in France had been the most important single sacrifice in the whole enormous business. He gave Mother a medal, something very big. Winston Churchill was not one to show his emotions, you know, but Mother said that he cried with her when he told her that he thought of you as his own son, that you were his Isaac. It wasn't much consolation to Mother at the time, because she wanted you alive and with her."

It was falling into place for the incredulous Dilly. "Mr. Churchill knew it."

"It was a strategy not even the Nazis thought possible. No civilized people would purposely betray one of their greatest heroes."

"And it worked?"

Wheeler nodded slowly. "Those Panzer divisions, all those fabled tanks that were supposed to drive away the invaders, they were never sent to Normandy, not on the day, not for weeks later. No one knows why. Hitler ordered them to sit tight at Calais. It made the whole invasion success-ful."

Dilly looked exhausted. He exhaled loudly. "Waiting for General Pat-ton's imaginary army."

"And the world never knew," Wheeler said. "They didn't know about the deception, and they didn't know you talked. The world thought you were the stoic hero who foiled the Gestapo. That's what I grew up with. That's what I had for a father."

Now Wheeler was pausing and doing the thinking. "I have an image of this man who could withstand anything and never give in. That was what I thought my bloodline consisted of." He laughed gently. "I can't for the moment think of what it would be like without that image, that I had *that* blood in my veins. What if I had known? My father was this great iron-willed hero—"

Dilly stopped him with a raised hand, looking pained again. "As long as we are being honest here," Dilly said, "there is more I need to tell you." He was about to rid himself of a second great weight. "This has been quite a lot for me to take in, and for you." Wheeler nodded. "There is one more detail. It involves the circumstances of your beginnings. You know that I love your mother very much, 'very, very much' as she would say, to distrac-tion. And I loved you from the time before you were born, and I have considered you my son and heir, in every way. But—" He paused for breath. "That first time I went into occupied France, on a mission your mother thought foolhardy for a war she did not approve of, she expressed her exasperation and worry with a folly of her own. The night I left—she told me very honestly and candidly—she got roaring drunk and gave in to a randy ambassador's son who had been pursuing her for some time. Your mother was a knockout, remember, a very good-looking girl. Quite a con-quest. It was an event of one night's duration, she admitted, and she never saw the man again. He was killed in the war. It was a mistake made in one moment of weakness, and one I cannot blame her for. The sequence of events, which I had plenty of time to contemplate in my recent incarcera-tion, and—" Dilly looked down at his feet uncomfortably. "And what I know of myself. It all suggests strongly—confirms actually—that mine was not the sperm that made the ultimate contribution."

Wheeler stared at him in silent disbelief. "You think that you are not my father?" He paused, just staring.

"Certain."

"I can't believe this," Wheeler said.

"You are my son," Dilly said in a burst, his confidence back. "I made your mother promise never, never to tell of any such doubt, and it sounds as if she kept that promise. You are my son, my one dear son, in the most wonderful of ways," he said, looking into Wheeler's eyes for signs that what he was expressing was understood. "It is just not in the biological one."

Wheeler looked stunned. "Then that means—" He stopped himself short of expressing the thoughts of Weezie that raced into his mind, allowing Dilly to interpret in his own way.

"Sorry, old boy. But I had to tell you."

Wheeler rolled his eyes and saw with his mouth open. "That's all right," he said calmly, his mind spinning. "It is just sort of a shock."

"Well," said Dilly, looking totally spent. "That is enough for one day, wouldn't you say?"

"I'd say," Wheeler said, his mind still spinning.

36

The Preconditions of Cultural Apex

here are considerable differences in Wheeler's journal entries between before he began his sharing with Sigmund Freud and after. Some are subtle and some not very. The entries become more concise and probably more accurate, a little more self-conscious, and definitely more introspective after he began sharing them with the greatest mind of the twentieth century. One way or another, knowing that the great doctor was now hearing every word certainly quickens the pace and adds to the intensity of Wheeler Burden's story.

The morning after his long talk with Dilly, after a night's thinking and thrashing, Wheeler was up early, as was his wont, alone at the *Jung Wien* table in the Café Central, enjoying the time by himself and the chance to collect his thoughts in his journal. He was glad now that Weezie's sudden departure had yanked him out of circulation and that in spite of his considerable heartache he was now no longer in the center of the story. The discovery of Emily James's identity and its fateful implications, the painful loss of her, Dilly's revelation of his betrayal by the Admiralty, the story of his conception, all rolled and rolled around in his mind in a jumbled mass, and he needed to stop and pull his thoughts together, take a deep breath, and to write.

"For you, talking is discovery," Wheeler had been told by his old prep school mentor, and writing was not far behind. As he admitted in his journal entries, he did not know what was going to come out as he first laid pen to paper. And this particular morning he had much to discover. This morning he began conjecture about his father. Had he known from the start what he had just learned about his beginnings, the fact might have affected his life in very significant ways. All his life he felt special, with heroic, even mythic, blood flowing through his veins. His father was larger than life and had always risen to occasions and, in the end, had even withstood the worst tortures of the Gestapo. Wheeler knew that he, the Last Burden, would have done the same. Now, he had learned that his father was not his father and that the great Dilly Burden had been duped and betrayed by his own people, a victim of his own narrow sense of duty. This non-father had, like everyone else, given in to the horror of Nazi brutality and stumbled into giving them perhaps the most important false intelligence in the whole campaign. Wheeler felt both shock and relief. Why had his mother never told him about the ambassador's son who was killed in the war? Was it really because of a promise made to her dead husband? Had his grandmother known that he was not his father's son?

And what now of Eleanor Putnam? Wheeler admitted to a relief knowing that he was not really a Burden, that she was not really his grandmother, at least not technically, and that his aborted liaison with her was not incest. She was now safely on her way back to Boston, and he no longer needed to carry the weight of knowing how much they had fallen into each other's auras and wondering constantly how he was affecting her and her future. He felt enormous intellectual relief that she was now gone and out of harm's way. But that did little to assuage the gnawing sense of grief.

Rationally, Wheeler had concluded that there was nothing he could do about Weezie's leaving. He would soon, he hoped, get over the gnawing feelings of longing and loss, and she would recover from whatever hurt she carried away. And he hoped that back in Boston she would proceed with life in such a way as to attract Frank Burden, a not-altogether-pleasant thought. He did not know, after all, what date in 1897 or 1898 she was supposed to have returned from her visit to Vienna. Perhaps Wheeler had indeed inadvertently become the catalyst for getting Weezie back to Boston, where she was supposed to be. He had no reason to believe that he had altered anything that was going to happen anyway or caused to happen anything that would not have. And yet irrationally, as he sat alone in the Café Central this morning, he felt total and irreparable despair. Now, with Weezie gone, with Dilly's secrets revealed, he thought back on something Dilly observed in one of their first conversations. "We know how all of this turned out," he had said, perplexed by the confusions of living life backward. "It's pretty confusing, but anything we do here must conform to the causes and effects that have already happened in our own pasts."

From the beginning of their time together in Vienna, he and Dilly had discussed the effects their presence would have on the future. Dilly had put forward Einstein's theory that each moment of a time traveler's presence in the past would create a separate reality and spin these separate realities off into an infinite array into the future. Or, they considered, perhaps nothing would change, that the future would unfold exactly as it was meant to, no matter what they did with their time. Whatever it was, Dilly had concluded that their role was to stay out of the way, to have as little impact as possible.

"You're at your station early this morning," he heard and looked up from his deep contemplations to find the youthful smiling face of Egon Wickstein.

"I like my inspirations early," Wheeler said. "Usually I take a morning walk."

"With a young lady, I have noticed."

"No longer," Wheeler said, trying to mask his great disappointment. "She returned home."

"So that is why you look so forlorn."

"We all recover from such affairs of the heart, don't we?"

"Ah, you are philosophical," he said. "That is good. I like philosophers." Wheeler suppressed a laugh. Egon Wickstein at nineteen would have had no appreciation of how a visitor from the late twentieth century might look with amusement at the remark.

"What brings you out so early?" Wheeler asked.

"I'm looking for inspiration." The young philosopher held up a pile of loose sheets of paper. "A *Neue Freie Presse* deadline. The editor is impressed by my work and says he will consider my *feuilleton*, if I submit it this afternoon. I am full of hope, but devoid of ideas."

"What have you so far?"

"Chaotic thoughts. I am arguing the twelfth century was the pinnacle of civilization."

"Interesting," Wheeler said. "Let me hear more." And the young man handed him the small pile, which he read through quickly. "These are

good," he said. "They just need a little library paste to bind them together."
The remark was straight from the Haze.

Wheeler motioned for the young student to sit down beside him as
Wheeler wrote in his journal. "How is this?" the young man said after
scribbling for a while.

"Much better," Wheeler said, amused. "Except I would move this to
here—" He pointed to one paragraph and found a spot on another page.
"And change this around to come after the list." He was sounding like the
Haze, the drill sergeant of *feuilleton* style, barking out orders to the re-
cruits. Then he thought. "And the list—have you thought of these reasons?" He wrote down three items in the margin of one of the sheets.
Wickstein looked at them and smiled. "They're beautiful," he said, looking admiringly at Wheeler. "May I use them?"

"Of course," Wheeler said. "Why not?"

"They are your thoughts. If the *feuilleton* is published people will credit
me for the insights, when they are in fact yours."

Wheeler smiled at the young student. "You can say you stood on the
shoulders of giants."

Wickstein recognized the quote. He raised his index finger and waited
for a thought. "Sir Isaac Newton," he said.

"Precisely," said Wheeler and watched Wickstein scribbling out the
final draft of his *feuilleton*. As he finished, he held it up to read.

"Listen to this," he extracted from Wheeler's scribbled notes. "'The
Preconditions of Cultural Apex.'" Then he paused. "It isn't too pretentious?"

Wheeler, too deep in mournful thoughts of his lost Emily James to
notice what just transpired, smiled absently. Why had she affected him so
deeply and her leaving torn at his heart so devastatingly? Her very presence had changed him, him the compulsive conversationalist. With her
he did not need to speak, only observe and watch her develop. With her
he felt, maybe for the first time, a total sense of belonging and acceptance.
With her he felt total and passionate and peaceful love. How was that possible? How did it work? "That will be just fine," he said absently to the
departing philosophy student.

After Wickstein had rushed off to finish his last revisions and take his essay to the *Neue Freie Presse* office, Wheeler remained by himself, writing, lost in reverie. At one point, in the middle of a thought, he looked up, out toward the doorway to the street. A vision in a white high-necked dress slid into his field of view and glided toward him, past the sparsely peopled tables. Her smile was beatific, Botticelli-like, as she approached, first as an apparition, then as reality.

"Oh, I so desperately hoped to find you here," she said, looking both distraught and relieved. "I was so afraid you would be gone." Wheeler was looking into the beautiful, expectant face of Weezie Putnam.

37

The Child in Lambach

 got as far as Nuremberg," she said, looking into the blank stare that expressed at least part of the turmoil in Wheeler's mind. Her cheeks had a rosy glow and her eyes shone. "So much for my famous decisiveness." She looked around at the scattered patrons of the café. "Do you think we could walk?"

Her hand was again gently on his arm as they walked along the Ringstrasse, from the Burgring to the Franzensring. "I feel so ashamed of myself," she said for the third time, the words now bursting from her. "I have been overcome by a dichotomy of feeling, one telling me that I have done something unpardonable and need to flee, the other saying that I have just begun to open like a flower. I have chosen to honor the second." She paused as they walked, and Wheeler said nothing. "The more I thought and worried," she continued, "and the more I felt terrible and wretched, the more you were central in all my thoughts. The reason I came back—" She pulled him to a stop and looked up into his eyes. Everything came out in a rush. "I have never known anyone who was as kind and sensitive and who had deeper and kinder insights or deeper and kinder feelings for me. I return to you and face the fears and erase the shame once and for all. I come back to something I cannot describe, something distractingly and debilitating and passionate. And so I found another train from Nuremburg, a desperately slow train, I might add. After what I have done I would not be surprised if you would want no more to do with me." She stopped for breath.

"I could not—" Wheeler began.

"Oh, you do not need to speak," she kept going.

Wheeler realized he wasn't going to be called on for much of a response; all he could do was look into her beautiful, innocent face. "I think—"

She stopped him with the slightest movement of her hand. "Let me finish," she said. "I have had too much time to think, and now I need to tell it." They began walking again. "I do not want to be a dry, shriveled spinster like my aunt Prudence. I want to drink fully from the cup. If what has happened so far is sinful, then it is a sinfulness I want to embrace openly. You and your spirit have become an opiate to me. And I return for it willingly and willfully, like a moth to a flame."

"And Fraulein Tatlock?" Wheeler said with a smile letting show his immense relief.

"Fraulein Tatlock was overjoyed," she said. "She somehow had neglected to get my trunk to the station."

They stopped again, and he looked at her in amazement. "I was devastated by your leaving," he said, then caught himself, saying more with his eyes than any outburst of words could. "You fill my head so that I'm even beginning to talk like you."

"You are not shocked then by my return?"

"I'm like Fraulein Tatlock. I am overjoyed," he said, and they continued walking. "I could keep walking with you forever."

"That would fill my time well," she said with a warm smile.

"But unfortunately, I have an appointment at the university."

"You keep many appointments in Vienna, Mr. Truman." She pulled good-naturedly on his arm. "You are quite the man of mystery."

"Hardly that," he said lightly. "I just have made certain acquaintances, all very masculine, I assure you."

"Well, I will admit to being jealous of time lost." The determination had returned to her brow, and she pulled them to a stop again. "Now that I have returned to Vienna, I want very much to be alone with you."

⁂

When he met Dilly in his small office in the university, as they had planned, his mind was so full of Weezie Putnam that he could barely concentrate on what on earth he was going to tell Dilly now.

"Look," Dilly said, gesturing to a stack of papers on the desk.

Wheeler assessed the stack of translation work. "Looks like enough to keep us out of the bread lines for a long time."

"I'm so glad you came," Dilly said cheerily. "There is more than enough work here for both of us. Take a stack." He pointed to a group of paper stacks on the table in front of him. Wheeler reached out and picked up one. "Oh, not that one," Dilly said quickly, and Wheeler looked down at it.

"What is this?" Wheeler said, his eyes scanning the papers in his hands.

"Oh, nothing," Dilly said, reaching to retrieve the papers. "Just some hasty notes."

Wheeler pulled them back and continued to examine what he had in front of him, his eyes darting across the surface of what looked like a collection of scribblings in Dilly's hand.

"That is nothing," Dilly said, reddening. "Here, give those to me."

"Hold on a minute," Wheeler said. "What is this?"

Suddenly, Dilly looked a little sheepish, as if he had been caught shoplifting. "Doing some research in public records," Dilly said.

"You're trying to find *him.*" Dilly's face reddened just enough to arouse suspicion. "Aren't you?" Dilly said nothing, and Wheeler began reading aloud from the notes. "Father's name: Alois. Civil service pension. Linz, moved to Lambach. That's the name of the town, isn't it?" It started to sound familiar. Dilly said nothing. "Oh my god," Wheeler said slowly. "I don't believe it." Dilly only looked sheepish, wanting to change the subject. "You're hunting down Adolf Hitler." The idea had not sunk in until that moment. "And what are you going to do if you find him?"

Here Wheeler was feeling guilty about pursuing Dilly's mother, and all the time Dilly was preparing an intrusion of far greater impact. "I thought you wanted to walk softly so you wouldn't change any history."

"I'm just going to go look at him," Dilly said quickly.

"He's a ten-year-old boy, for god's sake."

"Eight, actually. I just want to see him," Dilly said. But he didn't sound at all convincing.

It was dawning on Wheeler. "That's why you came here, isn't it?" The thought was just beginning to form in his head.

Dilly looked relieved more than anything else. "I'd better tell you the last detail of the story," he said. "I'm not exactly objective on this subject." He paused and collected himself. "The torture—" He paused again, closing his eyes. "It was the most terrible— It wore me down. I was supposed to die, but the magic pill contained no magic, and after it went on and on and I kept holding out, they finally got me to the breaking point and I broke. I gave them the names of the Resistance contacts and the details of the invasion as I knew them. I spilled it all. Then they left me alone for what seemed like days in my cell. I was a wreck. I could barely move, but at least they didn't come back and drag me to that awful room. They were checking facts, I guess, and as soon as they confirmed my story, they had no more use for me and left me alone to die. I guess in case there might be more information to squeeze out. They wouldn't spare me my terrible guilt."

His easy demeanor had hardened now, like a man possessed. "That's when my hatred of Hitler began to totally take over; it became all I could focus on. It was not hard to blame the whole thing on him, and so I started thinking of him as a child and thinking of coming to Vienna to find him. I thought and thought and reconstructed every detail of the city I knew from my college days and Mother's stories, and slowly I drifted away from that hard bench in the cold cell and found myself here, transported by hatred, sent to kill the child. I began asking around, then took a trip to Linz, where I remembered him coming from and found out what you just read. His father, Alois, is a retired civil servant with a pension, and the family has moved to Lambach. We can travel there, and we can find them."

"All this because of the torture?" Wheeler said.

"That, and what I found out about my father."

38

First Waltz

ou see so much beneath the surface," Weezie said as they walked along the Franz-Joseph-Kai. "It is as if you come from a different world. You seem to have none of the . . ." She paused, searching.

"None of the repressions?" he supplied.

"That is the phenomenon we do not even have a word for. You seem to have words for ideas my friends and I have never thought of. Where do you get it all? Are you a sorcerer?"

Wheeler laughed. "No, just from San Francisco," he said quickly.

"And my fear is," she said, looking up at him, "that to someone from San Francisco, someone from Boston appears a horrible bore."

He stopped for a moment for emphasis. "Do I look like someone who is bored?"

That brought to her the Botticelli smile that melted his heart. "No, I guess you do not. But I do fear that I enjoy our conversations too much. In fact, they have gone beyond enjoyment, so far as to be counted along with food and rest among my daily necessities. It is as if my soul were a deep rich basement into which you, for some natural or supernatural reasons, have a window." She spoke with the same innocent freshness that had long since captivated Wheeler so that he too now counted their morning walk along the canal among his own daily necessities. "I do not want to go back home and become a boring old slug," she said seriously. "But then again, I cannot very well afford to become a gypsy."

"What about a gypsy slug?" Wheeler said quickly, and she lifted her head toward him and gave a small laugh.

"Is there such a thing?"

"Not really, not even in San Francisco. I made it up for the occasion."

"You see," she said, tugging on his arm. "You tease me out of my seriousness in such a compelling way. You are always seeing the light side of what I say. The elders in my father's church think me progressive, and my friends roll their eyes and call me perverse when I talk like this. It's not that they are empty-headed, but they just don't seem to look very deeply into what they call ordinary things."

"You are very introspective, that's all."

She paused. "*Introspective.* What an interesting word." She tilted her head and thought about it a moment. "Looking within. I *am* introspective. That is what my mother's great friend Dr. James calls me."

"Would that be William James?" Wheeler asked, dipping into his secret source of knowledge about her.

"You have heard of him?"

"Even in San Francisco we have heard of William James, and his brother Henry."

"They were both dear friends of my mother's, and Dr. James took a great interest in my education after Mother died. He is a dear man."

"And he calls you introspective?"

"He does. That is not such a bad thing, is it?"

"On the contrary. It's very good. Very modern. Introspection is the fashionable thing these days in Europe, the rage with the café crowd, and at the university with Dr. Freud and his colleagues." Then he smiled. "It is very good, that is, unless overused. I am famous for overusing things."

"I too am famous for that, I fear. My aunt Prudence would say introspection was self-indulgent, that it was—" Involuntarily her face took on a stern frown that she turned playfully on Wheeler, shaking an accusing finger at him. "It is not Christian."

"I don't mean to cast stones," Wheeler said, "but your aunt Prudence doesn't sound very Christian."

"Oh, she has good intentions. She's just a little rigid, I guess you'd say."

"What would she think of all this?" Wheeler gestured to the life of the inner city that had begun to unfold around them.

"Oh goodness, she would never approve of Vienna. She would call it *careless* and *wanton*, or some such word. She has never traveled away from Boston."

When they came to the end of the Franz-Joseph-Kai, at the point when they usually turned and headed back to Fraulein Tatlock's, Wheeler had an urge to extend the morning meeting. He began walking toward an outdoor café. "Could we sit awhile?"

It was a gloriously sunny morning, and the number of strollers was beginning to increase. "Do you ever wonder," she said as the waiter brought the trays of coffee and milk, "why there are so many people walking by in this city? Don't people have places to go or obligations or occupations?" In Weezie's charming purposefulness the smitten Wheeler saw the soft side of Puritanism.

"Couldn't you learn to adapt to it?"

She brought her index finger to the side of her cheek, and thought for a moment. "I would need to be doing something. Playing the cello, or writing, or—"

"Or working in a bank?"

She wrinkled her nose. "I don't think I could ever be shut up inside for hours and hours." Then she looked at him, assessing. "You know," she said, "I want to ask you something."

"Ask."

"Your openness is very disarming and different. But I want to know if there is not anything that you would not say."

"Like what?"

"Certain unmentionable subjects. Would you not hold back on anything?"

"Let's try one," he said.

Suddenly, she looked uncomfortable. "I didn't mean to demonstrate. It was a theoretical—"

"Try one," he insisted. "Tell me what you were feeling the night in the cab when you fled."

"Oh, I could never—" She stopped and looked down. Wheeler allowed the silence to remain until it became intolerable for her. "I felt a surging," she whispered, and looked up. Wheeler remained silent, encouraging her with a motion of his hand. "I felt overtaken by something animal. I had to stop it."

Wheeler shrugged. "That was unmentionable, and you said it. Did anyone die?"

She gave him a resigned smile. "I thought I was being taken over by my baser nature and was heading for something terrible. There, I said it."

"And where was it headed?" Wheeler was not letting her off the hook.

"It was headed for wildness, and—" She stopped.

"And?"

"And release."

"And is that so bad?"

Weezie had closed her eyes and an expression of calm had come to her face. She opened her eyes and looked at him with a slight tilt of her head. "No, it is not," she said finally. "It might be a blessed release."

On the walk back, she had her hand on his arm again. "I keep fearing we will run into Frank Burden." From what we can tell from the journals, it was the first time she had ever mentioned him and must have near stopped Wheeler in his tracks.

"Who is that?" Wheeler said, trying to appear nonchalant.

"Oh, Frank is from Boston. He was a football hero at Harvard College, and he went to the Olympic games in Greece last year. He asked me to marry him. I told him I needed time to find myself. But he is very single-minded about it and wants me to say yes to him. I think he is impressed by my family." She laughed. "Frank Burden is a banker. He is not the sort of man to care much for finding oneself. He is not very introspective, as you would say. He is actually quite possessive. He would not enjoy seeing me on the arm of another handsome man." She readjusted her hand on his arm. "He has come to Vienna to study international monetary structure." She wrinkled her nose again. "That, and to ask me again, I think, although we seem so far to have avoided each other."

"Well, do you want to marry him?"

"Eventually, I suppose, it would be fine to marry someone as respected and proper as Frank. He is very handsome and well educated. He comes from an old Boston family—of which he is the last male—and he is decent and well read. And he will probably be the father of a good line of children."

"Then why haven't you jumped at his offer?"

"For the moment I need to try to figure out a few things about myself, and Frank has very set ideas about what life should be and about what role women should play in it. Before I settle down to that, I'd like to know a little more of the ways of the world."

"Don't you fear that if you know more about the world, you will not want to settle down to a sedate way of life?"

"You mean if I uncover the gypsy in my heart, I may choose to wander forever?"

He gave a little laugh at her expression. "Something like that."

She thought for five or six steps and then said, "I don't think the gypsy is a very large part of me, nor is the wild and evil side. But I at least want to get it out and look at it, before it is retired forever."

As they walked on, she began talking about her visit to Gustav Mahler. "It was terribly embarrassing. I really do not know what happened. He was standing beside me, pointing at the sheet of music in front of me with his baton, and I felt everything rushing around in my head."

"Was he—" Wheeler paused awkwardly.

"Was he forward with me?" Weezie said quickly, anticipating the question. "Oh heavens, no. I just became very dizzy and the next thing I knew, I was lying on the couch looking up into the concerned faces of Herr Mahler and the maid. I felt like a silly little girl."

"What did Mahler do?"

"Oh, he was very nice. I am sure he was very embarrassed for me. He was extremely solicitous. But still I was so humiliated I did not wish to go back."

They reached the Pension Tatlock, and Weezie pulled Wheeler to a stop. "Wait here," she said. "I am expecting some news from Herr Felsch that I think will interest you," and ran up the steps. In just a moment's time she reappeared, carrying an opened envelope. "This is quite exquisite," she said excitedly. "Mr. Clemens is speaking tonight at the Concordia, the grand press club, and we have two tickets. They are only for the gallery, as it is what they call a *Festkneipe*, a stag event. Absolutely everyone will be there."

The event was indeed one of the grandest the city had to offer. It was held in the great hall of the Merchants' Association, one of the most spacious of Vienna's many ballrooms. "This place is resplendent," Wheeler said, looking around as they entered. The room was garlanded with red, white, and blue bunting, and on the far wall hung a large portrait of Mark Twain, accompanied by a grand American flag. The speakers platform was covered with an abundance of plants and flowers.

Also in the gallery with them were the Clemens women, the author's wife, Olivia, and his two daughters, Clara and Jean, and Weezie brought Wheeler over to introduce him. Wheeler was deeply impressed as he shook hands with the family of the legendary writer. Clara Clemens was pleased to see Weezie. "I didn't realize you were in Vienna," she said. "Father will be pleased to hear of it. You greatly impressed him with your DAR speech last year. In fact, he couldn't stop talking about you."

They took their seats, and the festivities began. Weezie leaned in to Wheeler and began pointing out the famous Viennese she recognized: musicians, actors, singers, and dignitaries, including the American minister Mr. Tower. "There is Herr Mahler," she said, pointing to the left of the speaker. "And look," she said, pointing to the seats on the floor. "There is my friend Arnauld Esterhazy." As she pointed, Arnauld turned around and waved. "I think everyone in Vienna is here," she said jubilantly.

Mark Twain's speech lasted only ten minutes. The famous guest cut quite an impression with his characteristic bushy hair and mustache and his formal black cutaway jacket and white tie, as he read what sounded to Americans like elegant German from written remarks he pulled from his coat pocket. When he finished, there was wild applause. "They say in Vienna that Mark Twain is the most famous American in the world," Weezie said. "That is far more acclaim than he is granted back in Hartford." There followed a number of musical pieces, then more applause, and the crowd began swarming toward the famous American guest to congratulate him.

Clara approached them. "Come," she said to Weezie. "Father will want to see you."

They made their way through the crowd and waited their turn, then Clara pulled Weezie forward. "Father," she called out, "you remember Miss Putnam from Smith College." The famous American raised his hand and gave a broad open smile, gesturing for the crowd to stand back and let his daughter and her guests through.

"Miss Putnam," he said, "I remember indeed. You were eloquent and persuasive."

"Father was very impressed with you," Clara said loudly as the author took Weezie's hand. "He has called you quite striking, a sterling example why women should be given the vote. I think Father is sweet on you."

Mark Twain looked down, surprised by his daughter's candor, and Wheeler noted that the famous raconteur was blushing.

"Our children betray our deepest secrets," he said, making light of his daughter's frankness.

And Weezie, oblivious to anything discomforting, said, "It is my honor to see you again, Mr. Clemens." Then she turned to Wheeler. "This is Mr. Truman," she said, "from San Francisco."

Mark Twain took Wheeler's extended hand and shook it vigorously, both men looking each other square in the eye in a way that suggested they both knew a thing or two about fame. However it was, suddenly Wheeler found himself in the grip of the most famous writer of the nineteenth century. "Charmed," Clemens said, regaining his old form. "I have a great fondness for San Francisco," he said. "I found much naturalness there, to which I was accustomed, unlike some environs that are rich and grand"—he gestured to the room around them—"but lacking in naturalness." There was an immediate warmth in his eyes carried over from his welcoming of Weezie. "And how are you adjusting to being in this city of grandness?"

"It has been something of a shock, I must admit," Wheeler said a little too quickly, responding to the great writer's genuineness. "I will admit to feeling a bit like your Hank Morgan."

The reference brought an immediate smile. "Don't we all," Mark Twain said. "Out of place in a strange land, I know the feeling. But we must not forget that we have certain gifts to bring these people, Mr. Truman." He laughed. "Perhaps you are feeling that they are not quite ready for what you have to offer."

"I find myself cautious that I might share too much," Wheeler said. "I sense that you know about that yourself."

"I have known that caution for a long time now, and I am comfortable with the role."

"Well, I am greatly honored to meet you, sir."

"As we are both honored by this remarkable associate you have found." He looked at Weezie, and Wheeler could have sworn that he was blushing again. "I hope you will honor us again, Miss Putnam," he said. "Perhaps you and Clara can play music together."

On the way home in the cab, Weezie was in a euphoric mood. "It is odd to see so much fuss made over Mr. Clemens." She shrugged and closed her eyes. "I fear that at Smith College we never took him very seriously as a writer. He writes those boys' books." Wheeler had no way of commenting that in her lifetime Eleanor Putnam would see Mark Twain become considered, at Smith College and elsewhere, one of the most significant of American writers, and one of those "boys' books" come to be considered the great American novel.

"Well, he seems to have taken *you* quite seriously," Wheeler said. "I think his daughter is right. I think he *is* sweet on you."

She opened her eyes and looked at him fiercely. "Oh, that is fiddlesticks," she said with passion. "She was hyperbolizing."

"He was blushing," Wheeler said.

"Oh my," Weezie said. "I seriously doubt that."

"William James calls you *introspective*, and Mark Twain blushes in your presence. I don't think you know the effect you have," he said cautiously.

"Now, I think *you* hyperbolize."

But Wheeler would not let the observation drop. "You seem to have two highly developed natures. A rational one that is good with reading and numbers and analyzing things. But you also have an earthy side, one attracted to music and painting. That side is very appealing, much more than you are aware of, I think."

She looked at him seriously for a moment, about to quip something, but she paused. "You know," she said, "that is exactly what it feels like. All my life as a girl I was being told to sit up at the dinner table, learn my handwriting, memorize from the Bible. And all the time I felt there was more, but I couldn't put my finger on it. And you just have."

"The Chinese would call it your dual nature, your masculine and your feminine sides. Do you know the symbols of yin and yang?" He formed an inwardly-facing C with either hand and brought them together to form a circle, remembering the Haze's lectures from his beloved "Little Book." "They are equal and congruent, dark and light, rational and spiritual. They are a duality at the core of life. That is from Taoism, an ancient religion. Whenever the world is being too much one way for you, just think of the other half of the yin-yang."

She reached over and put her hand on his arm. "I love it so when you tell of such things and when you quote me passages from inspired writing. I just want to go right home and write them down."

"That would mean leaving here, and I do not wish you to do that."

She laughed. "There is so much I must thank you for. You have opened so many doors for me in the past few days. It is as if you have known me for a long, long time."

Suddenly, he became serious. "We need to match the exhilaration of meeting the most famous American," he said. "It is not too late to go waltzing."

For just an instant her Boston reserve brought a frown of disapproval, but she caught herself. "You see, I have this voice inside me that says 'do not do that.'" She stopped and leaned into him. "I would love to go waltzing, to escape into the wild magic of a fast triple-meter."

"The rhythm of the wildly cathartic waltz," he could still hear the Haze expounding, "overwhelmed the careful and reasoned measures of the minuet the way your modern rock and roll has demolished the fox trot. It became the mania of the bored middle class, a whirling intoxication that engulfed the staid quadrille and became an obsession for a whole city." He loved quoting from a nineteenth-century German visitor who had seen in the waltz an escape into the demonic. "African and hot-blooded, crazy with life, restless, unbeautiful, passionate, it exorcises wicked devils from our bodies, capturing our senses in sweet trance. A dangerous power has been given to the waltz. It stimulates our emotions directly, not through the channel of thought. Bacchantically, it is lust let loose, with none of God's inhibitions."

"It is merely dancing," Weezie said innocently, after Wheeler's rendition of the Haze's diatribe in the carriage on the way to the Sperl in Leopoldstadt.

Once in the great hall, they were shown to their table by a waiter who brought them white wine in a pitcher. "I guess we should get our feet wet," Wheeler said, leading Weezie on his arm through the crowd of smiling happy people, out to the dance floor. "Usually the Viennese are overly polite," Weezie said. "Here they seem to bump and jostle without a word of apology."

"So it is at a bacchanal," Wheeler said, readying himself, with his arm around Weezie's slim waist. The conductor, the successor of both Strausses, father and son, lifted his baton and smiled out at the expectant crowd. Down came the baton, and the music began to swell.

"Shall we," Wheeler said gallantly.

"I don't know how," she said.

"Nonsense. Everyone knows how to waltz. It's in your fiber, waiting to be released." Wheeler's words came directly from an evening long ago. He took her right hand in his left and lifted it, then placed his other hand on her waist and pulled her toward him, holding her for a moment close enough to feel her warmth against his chest, then pulled her after him as he took little steps around the floor. "One, two, three ... one, two, three," he heard her whisper a few times, then let the gentle rhythm of the steps take over, and they dipped down into the opening motions, at first self-conscious and hesitant, then pulled along by their neighbors into the smiling, joyous whirl.

"I absolutely love it," Weezie said, beaming. "It is, I think, the opposite of repression."

"How many does one do in a row?" Wheeler said after they had stayed on the floor for at least three.

"I don't know," Weezie said, pulling him off toward their table. "I need something to cool me off before I start up again." They made their way to their table. "I think the Viennese change partners—" She held tight to his hand. "But I am not sharing you with anyone."

"You see," he said, helping with her chair. "Already you are losing your inhibitions. Take care."

"I wish to lose all of my inhibitions. Simply all." Then she looked serious, a fullness had come into her cheeks, absolutely compelling. "Do you think that is absolutely wicked?"

"I think it is quite natural."

"You know? I feel as if I am three people, and they are at war with each other. I am my aunt Prudence, sitting in severe judgment, and I am an impulsive child always selfishly and impulsively pushing at the edges."

"And the third?"

"I am my mother, the wise and sane adult, trying to find the reasonable and kind way." Wheeler just looked at her, amazed, as she took a breath. "And I feel you have been sent as my protector," she said, throwing her head back. "You will protect me from my warring personages, to bring me to—" She didn't know the word.

"To wholeness?" Wheeler said, bringing the Cs of his two hands together, and she looked at him in gentle amazement.

"To wholeness," she repeated.

They danced for what seemed to be hours, with no thought of leaving, swept up in the gaiety. "Have you noticed the young women?" Weezie said at a break in the music.

"I haven't taken my eyes off you."

"No, I mean their lack of decorum," Weezie said, patting his arm. "They walk through the crowd unchaperoned and don't mind pushing people out of the way. It is very liberated, I'd say."

"Next thing you know, they'll want the vote."

The music started again, and the crowd whirled. "This is what my venerable teacher called Gay Apocalypse," Wheeler said, looking around in awe.

"It is wonderful," she said with a broad, delighted smile. They danced away in the center of the vortex, until the orchestra played its last strains and the crowd began filing out of the great hall. "I feel wild and liberated too." Her face positively glowed, and he acknowledged in that moment how very much he wanted her.

Out in the cool night air, they found a cab in a long waiting line. "That was absolutely enthralling," Weezie said once inside. Her eyes flashed with a new light, and her face was still flush from the exhilaration. "I think this has been the most thrilling night of my life."

"I've told the driver to take the long way back," Wheeler said as they left the gaiety of the Sperl. "I hope you don't mind." He looked over at her in the dim light from passing streetlamps. Outside he could hear the *clip-clop* of the horse's shoes on the cobblestone streets and feel the gentle swaying of the carriage. Her eyes looked back at him with a depth that went beyond gratitude or even respect. The press of her arm against his seemed to transfer a warmth that filled the interior of the cab.

"You know, I did think you a sorcerer in that awful moment when I fled. I felt you pulling me down to a dark world."

"And how do you think of me now?"

"No change," she said with a lascivious smile. "But I think that I am meant to be here with you, that you have been sent as my guide."

He took both her hands in his and looked deep into her eyes. "I will not guide you where you do not wish to go." Then he paused, still looking into her eyes. "I need to tell you something directly," he said.

She did not budge from his gaze. "You are the most direct person I have ever met."

"Well, in that spirit of directness, I must tell you that when you left, I was devastated. I had pushed too far and driven you away, and I found the results devastating." She began to offer an explanation, and he stopped her. "I have been deeply touched in this glorious city where we have found ourselves, this city of music." She took in the words and released a gentle sigh. "And I must tell you that I have found in your presence a peace and comfort that I have waited for a lifetime. I have wanted to be your guide, and yet you have guided me. I do not want to go too far or too fast, but I am the one totally enthralled, and I wish—"

"We both wish," she said, now stopping *him*, meeting his gaze and leaning forward ever so slightly.

Without taking his eyes from hers, he matched her forward movement, as if to examine more closely the glow that the evening bacchanal of music had placed within them. And then his lips met hers and he felt their welcoming softness, and he lost track of time or space, being drawn to her by a strange and powerful force that began to surge within her, matching his own. "This time, we will go very slowly," he whispered. "Slowly and surely."

"Remember, small steps," she said once again, this time as a full commitment.

Together they rose with the strains from the imagined music, and suddenly, almost without knowing it consciously he was with her, again driven forward by the inviting vitality and warmth, riding the wave of mutual passion to the crest, then together crashing in each other's arms. "Slowly," Wheeler repeated.

This time no one ran away.

39

Coming Together

heeler had gone back to the cabinetmaker in the heart of the inner city, this time to replace the wooden Frisbee he had given the woman in black. "Let's go out to the woods," he said to Dilly, holding up the wooden disk. "This is our meal ticket. I want to show you how it works."

They took the train out of the city and found an open spot in the trees in the fabled Vienna Woods, the *Wienerwald*, and Wheeler gave his father his first lesson in the fine art of Frisbee. "Try to release it level," he said, as his father looked at a disappointing toss that tilted and sank to the ground just a few yards from his feet, one of only a few awkward moves Dilly Burden had ever made in his life. "And flick your wrist," Wheeler said patiently, standing close by. "Put as much spin on it as you can."

Dilly tried again, and this time it thudded to the ground just short of Wheeler's outstretched arms. "I'll get the hang of it," he said with gusto, always up for an athletic challenge.

"You'll get it," Wheeler said, sending the disk floating back to the younger man with a deft flick. "It's all in the wrist."

Soon, the two men were standing fifty feet apart, flipping the wooden disk back and forth. "It could be very satisfying," Dilly said, still concentrating too hard to smile. "Yours seem to hover in air. Mine sink like pewter plates."

"Wasted hours of working at it," Wheeler said.

Wheeler had brought some cheese, wine, and bread, and a blanket. They sat in the Vienna Woods and talked for hours, relaxed and far from the cares of worlds that now seemed far, far away in time and place.

"Tell me what you did after Harvard," Dilly said.

"I stayed in Boston and studied at a music school. It wasn't there in your time. I studied guitar and played with my band nights. We were called Shadow Self, and we developed quite a following."

"Married?" Dilly cut a slice of the rich yellow cheese and laid it on a chunk of bread.

"Never married. There were a number of women in my life then." He looked at his father warily. "The life of music concerts discouraged monogamy. Things had changed pretty much in terms of sex, and people had many relationships. It was supposed to make you more open and developed. But there was one woman. We saw each other serially. She was a student at Radcliffe, Joan Quigley was her name, from an old Boston family, and serious about school, although she is really the one who encouraged me to go with music and drop out of Harvard." He looked off into the distance, remembering. "She broke me in, freshman year, when I was green and wet behind the ears. For years after that, when my band started doing road trips, she would show up in one city or another. She was married to a stiff and successful lawyer in Pittsburgh, very prominent, who became a federal judge. I don't know how she got away. It was pretty easy to find me in those days. The band was famous, I guess you would say, sort of like Glenn Miller or even, dare I say, Benny Goodman."

Dilly lit up. "Did you know Benny?"

"Everybody knows about Benny Goodman."

"I played with him one summer."

"Everybody knows that too. It's part of the Dilly Burden legend."

Dilly came down to earth. "Oh," he said. "I'm sorry. It was a bit much, I guess."

"I'm not saying we were as good as Miller or Goodman. I'm just giving you an idea of the context." Then Wheeler laughed, the thought of comparing a swing band to full-blown sixties acid rock amused him. "We were popular. And the crowds were pretty big. Fifty, a hundred thousand, easy."

Dilly looked impressed. "Holy cow!" he said, in what had been a trademark.

"Oh yes. Sound amplification got sort of out of hand. Bands were loud and raucous. I don't think you would have liked the music. Or the way we looked. You had to have seen it, but we had hair down to our shoulders, played loud electrified instruments, with bright lights flashing most of the time—strobe lights, they were called—and we wore wild cowboy clothes. Not exactly what you looked like with Benny Goodman."

"People liked that?"

"Well, it was kids mostly, sixteen, eighteen, around in there. The same sort of thing as with Frank Sinatra."

"What happened with the woman?"

"Well, in 1973, she wrote me. I got the letter in Fairbanks, Alaska. She said she had something pretty major to tell me and was sort of depressed. I got on a plane that afternoon and showed up in Pittsburgh. She was more glad than usual to see me." Wheeler looked off into the woods. "I was sort of the love of her life, I guess you would say. She liked me because I was unconventional, and her life was very much the opposite. It seemed to be her destiny she couldn't escape, she said, at the same time she told me how ill she was."

"She died?"

"A year later. She had a congenital blood disease and it caught up with her. It was her death—it took about a year—that changed things. There was a concert in Berkeley, at the football stadium, tens of thousands of people. I wrote a song for her and sang it alone on the stage. I was playing your old Martin guitar, which became sort of my trademark. No one had ever heard this song before, and I never sang it again. It was called 'Coming Together,' and it became, some said, the most famous song of the 1970s. I sang it that night alone on the stage in front of forty thousand people and then walked off and never came back. I became sort of a legendary recluse, I guess you'd say. It all created sort of a mystique. It was all for Joan Quigley." There was a long silence as Wheeler looked off into the distance. "I never really got over her."

"How about your mother?"

"The year Joan was dying, she came out to the ranch and lived with me in the guest house from time to time, until she was too weak to travel. Mother loved it."

Wheeler looked over at Dilly. He was sitting with his hands locked in front of his shins, letting his mind drift. "I guess I told you she never remarried or had any male company to speak of. She was sort of a one-man woman."

Dilly's eyes were closed, and he let go a deep sigh. "She was some kind of woman, Stan. I guess it goes without saying that I was pretty naïve physically when I met her. We did not have a sexual revolution going on in my time. She knocked my socks and everything else off. I know it sounds corny, but I never even came close to knowing what love was until I met her. I was all tied up in knots, and she untied them one by one. She had no constraints."

Wheeler laughed. "That's what a lot of people say about me."

"When I grew up in Boston things were reserved. I mean people were guarded about expressing anything. I didn't think about it because that's the way it had always been. You kept things pretty much to yourself. Not Flora. She hit me like a whirlwind. She unwound my clock, she used to say." Dilly was still looking off in the distance. "She was a great follower of Sigmund Freud. You know he came to London to live in his last year. The Nazis drove him out of Vienna, and your mother was part of the group that prepared the way for him and found him a home. She said he would have loved to get a hold of me, that I was a textbook case of repressed sexual desires."

"Overdeveloped superego," Wheeler added.

"She said that?" Dilly said, smiling proudly as if it was a compliment or a reminder of special moments.

"She said it once."

Dilly laughed. "Look," he said, "I hope I won't embarrass you. I mean it's not the sort of thing a father is supposed to tell his son, but your mother did a lot to unsuppress me. She took it on as her life project, I think." Dilly's eyes were closed, his smile suggesting the deliciousness of his thoughts. "And she was on her way to being very successful when I accepted that last mission in France—" His voice dwindled away.

"She was always so proud of you," Dilly said. "She said you were going to be the first liberated Burden. She said you certainly were not going to get involved in all that silly schoolboy hero business, but that you were going to have a proper combination of family virtues." Suddenly Dilly snapped around and looked at Wheeler for a long moment, perhaps realizing for the first time that the small son he had left in London only a few months ago was now a middle-aged man, older than his father, beside him. "How did you do?" was Dilly's curious question.

"Well, let's put it this way. I don't think anyone would have called me repressed. In fact, Boston and St. Greg's and Harvard tried to have the opposite effect of Flora on you. They tried to get me to wind my clock. I did save the Dover game and get carried off the field."

Dilly looked genuinely impressed. "You did?"

"Yep. They all said it reminded them of you. I was just about flunking out. The Haze was working overtime to get me to be conventional, and I did it. I had this pitch I learned in Feather River called the prongball." He held up his pitching hand. "You wet the inside of your middle finger and apply it to one spot near the stitches, like this." Wheeler held up an imaginary ball between two forked fingers. His father was delighted. "And when it's goopy, the ball pops out from between these two fingers like a watermelon seed. It makes the ball jump around, if you throw it hard enough. It worked against Dover, and it worked against Yale."

"What'd you do against Yale?" Dilly's face was full of interest.

"I came one pitch short of a perfect game. In my sophomore year. It was the prongball and it was jumping all over the place, and the Yale batters couldn't hit anywhere near it. I got two strikes against the last batter." Wheeler paused, sinking into the memory. "There was this bigoted jerk from St. Greg's named Prentice Olcott, about everything I despised in stuck-up Bostonians—"

Dilly interrupted suddenly, "Prentice Olcott. No kidding?"

"No kidding. But you couldn't have heard of him."

"His father went to St. Greg's with me. He tried to be student body president and captain of everything that I was, and was insanely jealous. If your mother thought I was repressed, she would have had a field day on Prentice Olcott." Dilly smiled broadly. "He was—" Dilly restrained himself.

"His son was a real asshole," Wheeler said without reserve.

"So was his father." Dilly had started to laugh. "He was a real—" Laughter was getting the best of him. "I've never said that word. You see, people didn't talk this way in my day."

Wheeler had begun to laugh. "They didn't in mine either."

"But you did."

"Most of the time." Wheeler looked over at Dilly. "You can too, you know."

"I don't know about that."

"Give it a try," Wheeler said, and waited.

Dilly's eyes were watering now, but he still had trouble with the word. "Prentice Olcott was a racist and a bigot," he said. "And a real—" His sides were splitting, and he rolled onto the blanket. "He was a real and roaring asshole."

"It must have been genetic," Wheeler managed to get out, himself rolling backward, off the blanket onto the grass.

"Like father," Dilly said, still convulsed, "like son. Asshole father. Asshole son." Dilly sat up and wiped his eyes, shaking his head. "Whew. I hadn't thought of Prentice Olcott in a long time." He looked over at Wheeler, who was lying on his back, gazing up at the Austrian sky. "Maybe you didn't know this, but when I made that catch against Yale that you say became so famous, there was a lot more riding on it than just a game." The thought stopped him for a moment before he continued. "There was a little kid in the fourth class at St. Greg's when we were first classmen named Silver, Maury Silver, and one day I saw Prentice rubbing his nose in the snow, and I stopped him. Little Maury Silver looked up at me and said thank you with his deep brown eyes. I'll never forget it. The little guy was truly humiliated. Prentice looked back at me as he was leaving and said 'I didn't know you were a Jew lover.' Well, Maury Silver was about ninety pounds, but he loved the Red Sox and knew about everything there was to know about them. Later that spring Maury Silver got hit by a car. His parents buried him in his Red Sox cap. When we were in that game against Yale, it was spring of our senior year. We were ahead three to two, when that batter came to the plate. I thought of Maury Silver and what it must have felt like to have a big first classman hero rubbing your face in the snow, and I thought of those awful words, 'Jew lover,' and I remember thinking I was going to catch that ball if he hit it all the way back to New Haven. You know who the batter was?"

"Oh Jesus," Wheeler said, sitting up.

"Right. Prentice Olcott."

They had folded up the picnic blanket and were back in the open space, now yards apart, throwing the Frisbee. "I forgot to ask what happened," Dilly yelled out across the space.

"To what?" Wheeler said, barely moving to catch the long soaring throw from his father.

"What happened to the pitch."

"Which one?" Wheeler launched a long soaring throw back.

"Your perfect game against Yale."

"I walked off," Wheeler said matter-of-factly.

"You walked off?" Dilly stopped and stared and let the disk drop quietly beside him. "You were one pitch away from a perfect game against Yale, and you walked off?"

"I got to the last pitch and I put down the ball and my glove—it was actually your glove—and took off my Harvard uniform item by item, right there on the mound, picked up your glove, and walked off."

Dilly looked at Wheeler for a long time, at first in astonishment before he picked up the Frisbee beside him, and then as his mind drifted back to thoughts of his brief and happy life with Wheeler's mother, to understanding and respect. "Your mother's son" was all he said.

Dilly picked up the Frisbee and with a quick flick of the wrist sent it soaring across the open space with an absolutely perfect throw. As it hovered over Wheeler's head, about to descend to the exact spot where he stood, the son looked across at his father and saw a smile of absolute satisfaction.

"That's it!" Wheeler called across their special plot of the Vienna Woods.

⁂

On the ride back to the inner city, Dilly sat with the hardwood Frisbee in his lap, picking it up and feeling the smooth surface from time to time, his mind reconstructing the beautiful disk in flight. He said nothing, but smiled contentedly. Wheeler interrupted his reverie. "You know, your words became famous," he said. "Your graduation speech is on a plaque in the main hall of the school, and every St. Greg's boy knows it by heart." And Wheeler drifted into part of it, the part that went "too proud to cheat, too brave to lie." And then he closed dramatically, "For I am a St. Gregory's boy!"

"Good lord," Dilly burst out. "That saccharine thing!"

"The headmaster, Mr. Wiggins, quoted it each spring, on the opening day of the baseball season."

"Charlie Wiggins?" Dilly said with surprise and Wheeler nodded. "You didn't tell me Charlie became headmaster. We used to play on teams together at Harvard."

"Oh, didn't we all know that. He used to tell the whole story of how heroic and self-effacing you were, 'always looking out for the other fellow,' he'd say, usually with tears in his eyes. Then he would recite your speech. There wasn't a dry eye in the study hall, especially with the older people."

"They weren't my words," Dilly said curtly.

"Weren't your words?" Wheeler sounded shocked.

"I explained that at the time, but I guess it got lost in the retelling. I found them in an old book in mother's private bookshelf where no one was supposed to be. I was snooping. The words that caught my eye were handwritten and entitled 'A Gentleman.' I adapted it by plugging in the 'St. Gregory's boy' part, and it made quite an impression when I read it at graduation. Funny—" He paused and reflected. "Mother never commented on it."

"Not your words?" Wheeler said, shaking his head. "Well, let's not tell the two generations of St. Greg's boys who had to memorize it."

Dilly too shook his head. "It is peculiar being a legend. There is much to adjust to, so much that gets embellished." He looked back at the hardwood disk in his lap and gave it a slight flip, then went silent again.

That evening back in his room at Frau Bauer's Wheeler opened his journal to a fresh page and tested his memory by writing out the words he had memorized years ago as his heroic father's graduation speech, only this time substituting "a gentleman" every time he came to "a St. Gregory's boy." He found that he remembered the whole thing, word for word.

40

A Perfect Place for an Assignation

he perfect place for an assignation," Kleist had said with a wink as he led Wheeler through his friend's studio near the Stephans-Platz. When Wheeler had mentioned he was looking for a place to be alone, his artist friend was more than a little enthusiastic. "Einhorn will be gone for four months, to Paris, and would be offended if you did not use it." Kleist laid the key in Wheeler's hand. "I have to apologize ahead of time. It's a little cluttered. Our Secessionist group is using it for storage."

"A place for a little well-deserved privacy," he said to Weezie as he unlocked the door and ushered her in. "Perfect, except that it smells a bit of turpentine and linseed oil."

She walked in and looked around at the loft apartment lit by a large overhead skylight and cluttered with sheet-draped easels, stacks of draped paintings, and the painter's velvet couch in the corner. "This is perfect," she said, taking in a big breath. "It smells like creativity." When she looked back at Wheeler and gave him that smile full of resignation and joy, he could see she was blushing.

"This embarrasses you?"

She put on her courageous face. "I would wish to stay here forever," she said. "It is a place to let one's hair down, to be freed from one's constraints."

"And to quiet one's stern disapproving voice."

Weezie smiled and sighed. "One's Aunt Prudence's voice perhaps?"

"Precisely," Wheeler said, offering her his arm gallantly and ushering her over to the couch where he sat beside her. There was a rosy glow about her, and she leaned toward him with just a suggestion of the release from her Boston propriety for which he had been the catalyst.

"I thought you would prefer this to a perpetual series of cab rides."

"That was very romantic," she said. "A lovely risqué overture. But you are right in assuming that the following movements deserve something more stationary, say like a faded velvet couch in a rustic painter's studio. A place where a proper Boston girl would never consent to meet."

Her freshness made him laugh. As he looked into her eyes, he felt more rich and fulfilled than ever before in his life. Here it was at last, the feeling of oneness he only hoped for. "This is more the way it is supposed to be," he said, and he encouraged her to stay sitting beside him. "A place to settle and be comfortable."

"Oh, I am comfortable," she said. "That I am *so* comfortable with all this is an amazement to me. I cannot decide if I am losing or gaining strength."

"I would vote for *gaining*," Wheeler said lightly.

"I have totally compromised my principles, totally given myself up to lust and desire," she said, frowning and closing her eyes. "And yet, I feel so unafraid. I feel like one of those women in the paintings. I cannot explain it, but for the first time in my life I feel the warring parties have quieted."

"The Puritan side has been vanquished by the sybarite side, I think."

"You make it sound light," Weezie said, smiling cautiously. "I think that is so. Totally vanquished. I am completely grateful to you. I have found rapturous pleasure, that is for sure, but I also have a strong feeling of independence."

"That is my rapturous pleasure, seeing you grow in strength."

"I so hope that pleases you." Then she looked at him quizzically. "Has your ardor been quenched?"

He laughed again. "What a delightful turn of phrase," he said. "Where ever did you find it?"

"It is out of my past," she said, allowing an expectant pause. "Well, has it?"

"Quenched it has been," he said, meeting her eyes. "And so much more."

"I think it is good for the soul when the body's needs are quenched." She said that last word with a look of total contentment, as if just finishing a difficult puzzle. Then she smiled even more broadly. "I had no idea what it all meant," she said, suddenly becoming serious. "I guess you would say that I was pathetically naïve, or innocent, or worse. Now, I cannot believe how quickly I have adapted to the role of sybarite. There must be a term for needing to experience something before knowing how to describe it."

"Aren't you being a little overly analytical?"

"I feel I have to analyze it to describe it."

"And to convince yourself that you have not fallen from grace."

"Oh, I *know* I have fallen from grace. But I asked for it. It is what I wanted," she said without much concern, wistfully more than with any overtone of guilt. "I do feel as if all my backbone is gone. I have been reduced to a sack of feathers." She looked at him with a wild desire in her eyes. "I do love it, and I do not wish for it to stop."

Wheeler smiled and touched her cheek. "Don't you suppose everyone really wishes to find this?"

"And now, I will tell you something shocking." In the pause, she seemed to be deciding if it was too awful to divulge. "Why I came back," she continued. "I thought that if I were going to roast in hell for what I was wanting—" She paused again. "—that I might as well come back to you, and do it right. And now I cannot think of anything beyond the intoxication of complete sensual delight. I don't think I will ever again have it off my mind, nor will I ever eat again. I have totally lost my appetite for any other earthly food."

"Is that bad?"

"I keep thinking, what if everyone decided to say whatever and do exactly what he or she felt like, just did what felt good, not what he or she should do. What would happen to civilization? How would continents ever get discovered or novels be written or heroic deeds done?"

"Do you think people who discovered continents and did civilized and heroic deeds never experienced this?"

"That is what I am trying to comprehend. I don't understand how it all fits together." She released an involuntary shudder.

"To everything there is a season," he said.

"A time to embrace," she followed, it coming as something of a relief. "And a time to refrain from embracing." She thought further on it. "So you are saying there is biblical permission for this sort of thing?"

"I am."

"I think that is stretching things a bit."

"Sounds like permission to me."

"I don't think that is what my aunt Prudence had in mind when she read Ecclesiastes." With that, she rose and walked over to one of the large draped easels. "You know, there is something I have been very desirous of doing." And she reached up and freed the sheet and pulled it from the first canvas. Both she and Wheeler gasped and stared in amazement. There before them was a large brightly colored painting of a totally naked woman, surrounded by color and gold, with a look on her face that Wheeler would later describe as "dreamy ecstasy." Weezie walked over to the first stack of paintings and again pulled off the sheet. This time a man and a woman, both clothed but with the most sumptuous expression toward each other. She moved the painting and found beneath it yet another riot of color. Then another. Then another. Before ten minutes had passed, the two lovers found themselves surrounded by brightly colored paintings, all of them, to one degree or another, radiating an irresistible sensuality.

"These are the Secessionists," Wheeler said.

"I have never been in the presence of such incredible vitality," Weezie said emphatically, her eyes shining.

"And look at this beauty," Wheeler said, pulling the wrapping off one last canvas. They both stood speechless for a long moment, taking in the penetrating green-eyed gaze of a goddess in full golden warrior armor, her brown hair cascading down from her golden helmet over a large golden medallion on her chest, her hand reaching out to hold a golden spear. "This is Athena," Wheeler said when he could speak, "favored daughter of Zeus, born from out of his head, the most magnificent of the deities, beautiful and powerful guardian of ancient wisdom and the whole wonderful city of Athens. You can always recognize her because she has the likeness of the fearsome Gorgon Medusa on her breastplate." He reached out with his hand and touched the gilded paint of the armor. "This is the essence of feminine strength, the beautiful and the horrible." He stopped and looked at her. "You have Athena strength in you. I have seen it and felt it."

Weezie stood staring without speaking for a long time. "Oh, I wish," she whispered.

"You do," Wheeler said. "That is something you must know with absolute certainty, and never forget."

They made long passionate love on the painter's velvet couch, surrounded by the splendor of the paintings, and afterward, under a down comforter they found in a cabinet, they lay naked in each other's arms.

As they were leaving, they did one more tour of the easels. "I think we should keep the covers off," Weezie said. "What do you think?"

"Absolutely," Wheeler said with conviction. And as they stood again in front of the painting of the magnificent Athena, he said again, "She is within you. Most definitely. You must never forget."

Weezie looked into his eyes, languidly at first, and then with a conviction to match his. "I must train myself to remember, mustn't I?"

"You must. She is within you when you need her. She always has been, I suspect. You just haven't noticed."

And as they were leaving, dressed again and proper, Weezie pulled on his arm and caused him to look back with her over the paintings. She spoke, still in awe. "A perfect place for an assignation."

41

The Right Place at the Right Time

he's here," Dilly said excitedly, as soon as Wheeler found him at the café table in the Prater where they had agreed to meet.

"Who's here?" he said.

"Mother, Eleanor Putnam. She's here in Vienna."

Wheeler, caught a little by surprise, probably tried his best not to over-react. "How in the world did you conclude that?"

"Last night, I remembered. The reason Father came to Vienna in 1897 was to study the international banking that became his profession and chase down Mother and ask her to marry him. That was part of their story that for some reason I didn't recall until last night."

"Have you seen her?" Wheeler asked.

"No, but I know she's here. We have to be very, very careful. As much as it would be tempting to approach her, we cannot. Absolutely cannot." He stopped and looked worried. "One thing we know for sure. She is a very attractive young woman." Dilly paused for thought. "And quite a powerful one, you know," he said suddenly. "You would never know it from her demeanor, and she did everything possible not to attract attention, the last thing she wanted. And, as you know, Bostonians never show their wealth *or* their power. But she headed the board of the family invest-ment fund, and it was much larger than anyone suspected. She was, I discovered fairly late in the game, its principal architect."

Wheeler listened with high interest as Dilly began to unwind. Images of his evenings with his grandmother at 6 Acorn Street kept running through his head, the intensity with which she always greeted him, the total attention and affection that radiated from her eyes, the beauty and grace that she conveyed, even in her late eighties. And then the magic of the last night of her life, the waltz; feeling her light and graceful in his arms as they glided so easily around the living room, losing all sense of time, and how she had said with such warm assurance, "Everyone knows how to waltz." And then Mrs. Spurgeon's summoning and the awfulness of finding his grandmother on the floor of her bedroom, and the terrible, unexplainably debilitating sense of loss.

"It was my father who was full of bluster," Dilly continued. "Puffing about how the Burden family had such a tradition, but it was Mother's Hyperion Fund that quietly ran things in a significant segment of Boston culture, with large anonymous gifts to the symphony, the Museum of Fine Arts, the Episcopal church, even the Pops. Harvard University and our old school St. Gregory's were also major secret beneficiaries, as was the Athenaeum and its publishing company."

"Wait," Wheeler interrupted. "The Hyperion Fund supported the Athenaeum Press?"

Dilly noticed the consternation on his face. "You know of it?" he asked.

For a moment Wheeler only stared, collecting his thoughts. "It was the Athenaeum Press," he said finally, "who had sought out and published both Mother's book *Persephone Rising* and the Haze's and my *Fin de Siècle*."

"Mother's hand," Dilly said, letting this new information sink in for a moment, then he continued. "When I was at Harvard Law School, I was doing a study of foundation grants and gifts and kept coming upon the Hyperion Fund, so I investigated. It seems that the fund had made incredibly wise and strategic investments since the beginning of the century. When I dug into the records, I found that the fund had gone from a small infusion of capital in 1900 and converted over the next thirty years into a major financial force in the investment world.

"I interviewed the fund's director, a man named T. Williams Honeycutt, whom I had known for years. I found him infuriatingly private and reserved, willing to answer my questions only in the most brief and cautious way. He was such a typical conservative Boston banker that I could not imagine him being the leader of a financial institution that had made such amazingly wise and sagacious decisions, especially the two stunners. In 1907 and 1929, he had directed the entire fund out of the stock market and into other holdings, thus totally avoiding the two great crashes.

When I asked him questions about that move, he was remarkably unforthcoming.

"After 1929, the fund was back at it, fully invested in the market, again making shrewd choices and again increasing its value by leaps and bounds each year. Again, I asked Honeycutt and again he gave cautious and reserved answers. I was becoming more and more frustrated and less and less willing to give it up. The more Honeycutt stonewalled me, the more the investigative reporter I became." He broke off the stream of exposition. "You know I tend to get a little obsessive about things."

"You were on to something," Wheeler said.

Then he resumed. "I noticed patterns: big gifts to institutions who then made big changes. In 1908, for instance, a large donation to the New York Philharmonic, which they said in an acknowledgment allowed them to pursue the new director, who just happened to be Gustav Mahler. In the same year, a gift to Clark University near Boston, which enabled the large and significant conference in psychoanalysis in 1909. Then, later, a number of personal grants to artists from Europe, all Jewish, who were fleeing Nazi oppression. When I asked Honeycutt for patterns to these gifts, he simply said they were timely and thoughtful foundation decisions. I kept after him, I was relentless, trying to discover how the foundation had been so extraordinarily prescient, and how they had known to plant such strategic gifts in such strategic places.

"Finally, Mother came to me. She told me she would answer my questions, and asked that I stop harassing Will Honeycutt. 'You are driving the poor man to distraction,' she said. 'He is just the fund's conservator,' she said, 'not the decision maker. I have what you want to know, but you must keep it between us.' And she proceeded to tell me that the decisions were all hers, that she was the president of the fund and that it was entirely under her control. Honeycutt was simply the very dedicated and loyal manager. As she spoke, she sat across from me on the couch and I saw her in a totally different light. She looked poised, controlled, and I must say, strikingly beautiful, the embodiment of feminine power, one of the Greek goddesses.

"When I asked her how she had made such fortuitous investments, becoming a financial partner in about ten of the most successful companies in America as they were just starting up—a number before they had even gone public—she just smiled benignly and said she studied hard and had an instinct for it. 'I visited companies,' she said. 'I got a feeling for what areas were the future, like automobiles and electricity and soap products, and I found the right horses to back. I took the train to Detroit in 1902, the year before he founded his company, and met with Henry Ford, and I wrote him a check right then and there. I told him I had faith in his vision. A few years earlier, I made our initial investments in automobile production, first backing a man named David Dunbar Buick, who built an automobile even before Ford, and then Champion Ignition Company, who made spark plugs. Both of these companies later became General Motors, in which we have now a major holding. It was simply the right thing to do at the right time,' she said, very calmly and with matter-of-fact precision, as if it were the most logical thing in the world.

"I asked her how she knew to make these investments, and she repeated that it was just intuition, from knowing how important automobiles were going to be. Then I asked her the big one: how did she know to get out of the market before the 1929 crash? You know what she said?" Dilly looked incredulous.

"Intuition," Wheeler said.

"She looked at me with the most serious and honest expression and said 'I just had a hunch.' A hunch, she said, just like that."

"I guess she was just good at it," Wheeler said, beginning to get a grasp on what he was being told.

"General Motors," Dilly said, shaking his head. "If you had to make one single investment at the beginning of the century, that was it. And she was in on the ground floor."

"And Ford Motor Company," Wheeler said. "And General Electric?"

"Right. She bought the fund's Eli Lilly, Proctor and then Gamble, and General Electric holdings in 1898, when very few people had ever heard of them. In 1919, just after the Armistice, she went to William Boeing and told him she would fund any of his new airplane projects in which he needed help. He was building dressers, counters, and furniture on the side, just to stay in business." Dilly rattled off a number of other names and years. "The remarkable thing I discovered was that the investments came just a year after the company started. Mother would just go to the founders and say she wanted to invest. She was very attractive and very captivating and deceptively shrewd. I don't need to tell you that the returns were enormous."

"I'd add International Business Machines and Hewlett Packard in 1950," Wheeler said. "But you wouldn't know about those."

"Mother probably kept going after I didn't come back from the war, so if those were good investments, she would have bought in. She had an uncanny eye, it turns out. She was still going then, right?"

"Into the sixties," Wheeler said.

"Well, anyway," Dilly said, "you get the idea. At the beginning of the century, everyone was investing wildly, and the Hyperion Fund did not ever buy one share of popular stock. And the more I looked into it, the clearer it became that it was Mother calling the shots. In 1920, she arranged for the fund to give St. Gregory's an endowment for a faculty salary. Did you ever hear how the Haze referred to his faculty status?"

Wheeler paused, searching his memory bank. "A 'funded position,'" he said. "That is even how the headmaster referred to him in public. I had never heard of such a thing and thought it sort of odd."

"So he was for over forty years, an anonymously funded position, supported by a permanent endowment. Funded from guess where."

"And you're saying that your mother set it up."

"After the First War, Arnauld Esterhazy returned from Europe pretty much a wreck. Shell shock, or something. Some said he had been gassed. Mother arranged for the school to give him housing and a part-time faculty position, like the one he had left to go to war, until he recovered. In the beginning, he taught only a few classes of geography to the little boys. He was pretty much a nervous mess, I guess, and didn't reach his full bloom as the Venerable Haze for about ten years." Dilly paused. "Just as I was rising to the upper grades in the early thirties."

"It turned into another good investment, I guess you'd say."

"I guess," Dilly said. "He was certainly important to me."

"And to me," Wheeler said, looking up to notice that like his own Dilly's eyes were filled with tears.

"There is more I need to tell you about Arnauld Esterhazy," Dilly said, suddenly becoming serious. "Christmas 1943, your mother and I took a break from the war and brought you home to Boston. During that visit, I introduced you and your mother to Arnauld. We went out to his 'rooms' at St. Greg's. He was delighted to meet your mother and enthralled by you. You were absorbed in your three-year-old world, of course, and for some reason, as we were sitting and talking, you looked at Arnauld, and because of his prematurely white hair, I suppose, you shouted out, *Grandfather!* and ran to him, climbing up into his lap. Arnauld was overwhelmed. He loved it, and held you, and then suddenly he began to cry. As you know, he could get a bit emotional, but it would usually pass. But this time it did not, and he held you and began to sob. I got up and walked over to him, and put my hand on his shoulder, and I could feel his heaving. At the time, I did not know what it was, but I was deeply touched, as was your mother.

"Later in our stay at Acorn Street, I had a disastrous and fateful conversation with my father, and I became deeply upset, and told your mother that we would be leaving. Mother came to me. She was saddened, of course, but she seemed to know exactly how disturbed I was, and exactly why. She was very serious, and sort of matter-of-fact. 'There is something you must know before you return to England,' she said. 'You must go see Arnauld Esterhazy, and you must go alone.' I called him, and we agreed to meet at the St. Greg's skate house.

"The Haze had grown to love skating," Dilly continued. "I was quite involved in hockey when I was a boy, and I taught him to skate on the Charles River on Sundays during the winters, and he loved going out with me. We would skate and talk, and I must say that he got better and better at it, and after I graduated, he kept it up. During my senior year at Harvard, I was captain of hockey, and one Sunday I organized a team skate from the college to St. Greg's, and I told all the Haze's old students at the college. Together—we must have been almost fifty strong—we skated the hour or so along the Charles, an impressive sight, and arrived at the St. Greg's skate house at noon, the exact hour I told the Haze I would meet him there. What a thrill it must have been for him. Just as he stepped out of the skate house onto the ice of the river, around the bend came fifty college students, most of whom he knew by name. We formed a circle around him and gave him a thunderous *Haze, rah. Haze, rah, rah.* Tears came to his eyes, of course, and to the eyes of all of us, even the hockey players who didn't know him.

"So, now, around the new year of 1944, just a few months ago for me, over forty years ago for you, the Haze told me to meet him at the skate house. We laced on our skates and began to glide along the smooth ice of the Charles River, the fresh clear New England air in our faces. 'I love this,' he said. 'I could go on like this forever.' And then he looked at me, and he said, 'Dilly, dear boy, your mother and I have agreed that before you go back to the war there is something you must know.' And he told me this story." Dilly paused and took a deep breath. Then he recounted to his son exactly what the Haze had said.

Later that evening, alone in his room at Frau Bauer's, Wheeler wrote a detailed record of his remarkable conversation with Dilly. At the end of it, in outline form, on one whole page of his journal, he included the names and dates of the Hyperion Fund's momentously prescient investments.

42

Just This Once

rnauld Esterhazy grew up as the third son in a famous aristocratic family in fin de siècle Austria-Hungary and spent a remarkable boyhood and young adulthood surrounded by art and music and ideas in Vienna. In his young manhood, he spent much of his time in the coffeehouses of the city and became a part of the intellectual crowd that made Vienna famous at that time, a branch of which called itself *Jung Wien*. In 1897, when he was nineteen, he met a young American woman, Weezie Putnam, who captivated him and determined, it turned out, the direction of the rest of his life. When she left Austria and returned to Boston and later married, Arnauld kept up a correspondence. Some years later, after he had completed his degree in philosophy and had spent a few years teaching in the university as an academic fledgling, she encouraged him to come to Boston and take a teaching position in German and European history at St. Gregory's School, from which her husband had graduated.

Arnauld taught for a number of years, and the life of an American schoolmaster agreed with him. In 1914, when the tensions in Bosnia Herzegovina seemed to suggest war, he was preoccupied and torn. If Austria declared war and sided with Germany, he would feel honor bound to return home and join the army, something he deeply did not want to do.

His admiration of Miss Putnam, who now had become Eleanor Burden, had continued, and he greatly enjoyed the evenings on Beacon Hill, when he was invited to dine with her; her husband, Frank Burden, the St. Gregory's hero who had competed in the first modern Olympic games in 1896; their two talented young daughters; and the society of the Boston Brahmins who graced their table. He loved the beauty and serenity of Eleanor's home, the charm of her conversations, and the vision of her loveliness in the formal setting of her elegance. It was an infatuation he had carried with him from Vienna years before, and it remained secretly in his heart. He was sure it would last forever, never expressed and never in any conscious way to be acted upon. Arnauld was certain that he would remain a bachelor all his days and that Eleanor Burden would remain forever his inspiration, his Beatrice, and the love of his life.

He made the fateful decision to return home, and he came to Acorn Street the night before he was to sail for Germany. He and Eleanor dined alone. He could barely keep his hands from shaking, the heaviness of this departure weighed on him so powerfully. He had a premonition that Austria's decision to go to war was absolute folly. The major powers would slug it out in a most ugly fashion and the poor Austria-Hungary empire would be trampled in the process. And yet he felt compelled to return and do his part.

He drank a few glasses of wine and at least for the evening tried to concentrate on Eleanor's beautiful face and forget the cauldron he was about to throw himself into.

"I sail from Hoboken, New Jersey," Arnauld said, as if it was quite a distinction.

"Sooner or later," Eleanor said with a wry smile, "everything ends up in Hoboken, New Jersey."

But the mirth did not last long. "I fear I shall never see you again," he said solemnly to her in the living room after the meal. "My heart is breaking."

She looked into his eyes. "Oh, dear Arnauld, you are such a fatalist." She was doing her best to make light of the moment and perhaps to dissipate the negative energy. "As soon as the unpleasantness is over, you will return here and resume your teaching."

"Do you really believe that?" he said.

She looked down for a long moment. "The future is the future," she said. "However it turns out, there is something you must know and carry with you." She looked into his eyes, about to speak, but no words came, from either of them.

She rose from her chair and walked toward him, holding out her hand, and it gently touched his cheek, wet now from his own tears. She sat beside him and leaned into him, as if to kiss him on the wet cheek, but her lips found his. Arnauld, always the timid one, began to pull away, and

Eleanor, always the strong one, whispered, pulling him back toward her, "No, Arnauld. Just this once," and their lips remained together tenderly. Slowly, she reached for his hand and slowly she brought it to her breast and repeated, "Just this once, Arnauld. Just this once."

She led him to the guest bedroom on the second floor, where he had stayed overnight on a number of occasions, and she undressed him slowly and lovingly, and she helped him undress her. At times when he seemed fearful or tentative, she always guided his hands, and turned them into those of an experienced lover, encouraging him not to hurry, showing him how to enjoy and savor each part and each special sensation. "Gently, gently," she would whisper. "Slowly, slowly." The flickering candlelight of the bedroom lit their bodies in images that would stay in his mind forever, he knew. As much as he wanted to speak and to tell her that this was truly amazing and the fulfillment of all of his dreams of love, beauty, and desire, he said nothing, only waited for her coaching and instruction. At what seemed to his guide and mentor the appropriate time, she led him to enter her, and there he felt for a moment a completeness and connection he never imagined possible, then able to control himself no longer, he exploded.

"We can stay here all night," she said afterward. "The coast is clear."

And so, for just one and only one time Arnauld Esterhazy fell asleep in the arms of the love of his life, thousands of miles away from the events that had ruined his equilibrium. When he awoke, he was alone, in the second-floor bedroom of the Burden home at 6 Acorn Street, Beacon Hill, Boston, where he had awoken enough times before to find it familiar, so familiar in fact that he wondered if he had just experienced a wonderful and forbidden dream. Later that morning, he did indeed leave for Hoboken, New Jersey, and the transatlantic steamer passage to Bremen, Germany.

Exactly nine months later, to the day, when Arnauld was in the middle of the harrowing anguish of war, Frank Standish Burden, Junior, was born, and the legendary life of Dilly Burden began.

43

The Gloves Come Off

igmund Freud would confess of himself that he needed a close friend and a passionate enemy, and there were times when the two were united in the same person. "I always knew how to provide myself with both over and over," the great doctor admitted, late in his life. Those passionate friendships he entered with such intensity, such as with Josef Breuer, with whom he wrote the famous Anna O case, and Wilhelm Fleiss, his Berlin friend whom he was writing regularly during Wheeler's time, all ended in bitterness. And, of course, the most celebrated example of this passionate friendship turning to rancor would come with Carl Jung, with whom Freud would begin an intense father-son collaboration in 1906 and with whom he traveled to America and Clark University in 1909. When the two strong-willed psychologists began to disagree about the nature of libido, the sex drive, their disagreements became so personal and rancorous that they split in 1912, and never communicated again.

Wheeler began to notice the subtle shift in the great doctor's attitude toward him after they had settled into the genial routine of their regular meetings. As Wheeler prepared his journal entries, we can notice more and more care with the sections that dealt with Freud, and we learn that Freud began reading to his American visitor passages from his own writings and from his letters to Fleiss. Suddenly, as the intensity increased and the two men were sharing intimate details, a certain tension began to arise.

The great doctor was vacillating. One minute he affected the objective distance of a scientist, the next he was moving in close as an intimate colleague. When the subject was history or the life of the mind, he was close and personal; when it moved to anything approaching the subject of time dislocation he slid back to his usual distance. For Wheeler, the change seemed to begin in one moment when he told his host about the significance of the stock market page.

"You could make a lot of money with this," Wheeler said, not entirely jokingly, but Freud did not return his smile.

"And why do you say that?" Freud asked, penetrating with his dark eyes.

"Because it really is the future," Wheeler said, tapping his fingers on the page emphatically. The doctor did not budge. Friendship or no, Wheeler realized in that moment and recorded in his journal, "The doctor is simply not going to believe my story, so the gloves are off."

"You really are on to something unique here," Wheeler told his host at the beginning of the next session, and the rest came out in a burst. "What you offer as a scientific theory of the unconscious mind is an inspired vision. You are going to establish forever that childhood determines the course of adulthood. This is not lightweight stuff!" Wheeler's enthusiasm was now unrestrained. "You can see beyond the details. You explore the controversial. You can't help that."

Overwhelmed by this sudden and surprising change of pace, the great doctor began to warm to his guest's affirmation. "You make it sound heroic."

"It *is* heroic. How do you think Heinrich Schliemann found Troy?"

Freud nodded his pleasure at the comparison, and Wheeler continued. "Schliemann found his way through relentless criticism, people calling him an amateur and a huckster. But always he had one vision in front of him. Troy was not fictional. It actually existed, and Schliemann was determined to find it."

"The sexual center is not my invention alone, you know. Charcot planted that seed."

"I know that." Wheeler could see in Freud's eyes that he liked the way his visitor paid attention to details.

"So I am not to blame for that fixation on the sexual."

"No," Wheeler said. "But you are the one who is waving it in the face of the proper bourgeois Viennese."

"I am the messenger who is going to be shot at."

"The hysterics you have been treating have displayed an astonishing array of symptoms—debilitating body pains, paralysis of limbs, depressive moods to intermittent hallucinations. And you know the cause is not physical. Am I right?" Freud nodded. "So, you are seeing early traumatic experiences and sexual conflicts as the cause."

"That is a fair summary."

"These early traumatic experiences of childhood cause the bizarre symptoms of adulthood."

"That is what I am saying, yes."

Wheeler paused, weighing his words. "You are moving the conversation forward in a way that cannot regress. You are bringing to the table the fact that Troy exists. From now on all arguments against that truth will be reactive. A profoundly important step."

"Then you don't disagree with me?"

Freud looked genuinely curious, a signal that, in spite of himself, the doctor was beginning to take his strange guest seriously. Wheeler spoke with extraordinary insight and clarity, as if he, like some ancient mystic, had seen the future. As much as Sigmund Freud knew with absolute certainty that his patient's complex story was an immense fabrication, he was still fascinated by the glimpse into the future that it held, much the way workers on the mental ward learned French history from the man who thought he was Napoleon. *Very perplexing*, Freud would say.

"Quite the contrary. You are very right, and if you stick with the idea, you are going to get what you want."

"What is it that you are so sure I want?" The doctor now sounded a bit impatient.

"What you want is fame for a breakthrough idea."

Freud paused and looked at Wheeler for a long moment, obviously startled. "Then what is the problem?" Freud was now fixed on Wheeler, at once both defensive and expectant. He was really listening, and Wheeler, by Dilly's admonition to have no effect on the present, was moving into dangerous territory.

"The problem is—" Wheeler paused, aware perhaps in this instant that he had gone too far. "The problem is that it is too damned logical. You think you have to abandon the one for the other."

"They cannot coexist," Freud said suddenly, with the first hint of defensiveness. "Children cannot have been abused and also *imagine* the abuse."

Wheeler shrugged. He knew well the problem. Like himself, Freud was given to extremes. In order to take interest in an idea he had to proclaim it as the *only* idea. He needed the extremes, both to attract attention and—more importantly—to sustain his own interest. "Well, that is for you to work out. I am just saying that in your zeal to move toward the most important discovery of your life, you are stating it in the extreme. In your rush to get to Troy, you are digging through the evidence of lots of other civilizations."

Freud glared at him, his mind gripped suddenly by the reality of what he was doing: taking seriously and seeking the counsel and wisdom of a madman.

The narrator must intrude here and point out what may be obvious at this point. Over the past few meetings, since the first sharing of Wheeler's journal, both men had become swept up in the intensity of the conversation, each more involved, to a much higher degree than either wished. Wheeler had definitely gone too far, sharing with the great doctor details of the future he had definitely wished to hold back, and Sigmund Freud, for his part, had fallen in and out of the thrall of his patient's alternative reality in which he clearly had had no intention of believing.

Wheeler, the twentieth-century man, was bringing much to bear. Wheeler's mother, from her distant perch in a California farm in the mid 1950s, had struggled with Freud's ideas and his impact, struggles she had shared with her son and set free in her *Persephone Rising*, often considered as much an anti-Freudian as a feminist treatise. The Haze in his expansive writings had labored over his understanding of Freud's work, a labor Wheeler had picked up in his long preparation of their joint book *Fin de Siècle*. Wheeler could not help sharing what he knew. "Everything has now fallen into place for you," he said to the great doctor. "You have recognized that remembered infatuation with the mother and jealousy of the father are universal, that the Oedipal relationship of the child to the parents is, as you say, 'a general event in early childhood.'"

The doctor nodded cautiously at this point, not certain where the patient's conversation was headed and just who was actually in control. "This is a good summary of my views. But where is this leading?"

"Isn't it possible," Wheeler said, barely pausing, "that your former view, your seduction theory, was actually right?"

"It makes no sense," Freud said quickly, trying ever so slightly to disengage.

"But what if a child is beaten and humiliated with regularity? Isn't he going to grow up perverted?"

"My theory accounts for that," Freud said, now overtly dismissive.

But Wheeler, wound up, took no notice. "The child in Lambach is a case in point. The unrelenting abuse is very real, as is his future menace."

"Ah, the child in Lambach again," Freud said with now just a tinge of sarcasm. "The one you and your father are so sure is pure evil."

Wheeler remained nonplussed. "The one I would like you to meet."

"I do not think that will be necessary."

"That boy in Lambach is going to grow up to be a monster, all because of the humiliating childhood abuse he could not escape. He is mistreated constantly by his father, and abandoned emotionally by his mother, beaten almost every day. He is learning to be obedient and to accept daily punishment with compliance. Most of Germany is accustomed to that kind of poisonous parenting. Faced with the evidence, I don't think that even you would argue that the cause was entirely sexual tension, that he lusted after his mother."

"What exactly is your point?" Freud said. Wheeler could see that his host was equivocating, on one hand ready to dismiss the rantings of his delusional patient and on the other ready to defend himself against the legitimate intellectual attack.

"The unexamined life, Herr Doktor," Wheeler said. "Neither of us has much use or respect for it."

"That would seem obvious, especially considering how we have spent the past weeks."

"Well then, let's do *examine*. I know what you are trying to say, but I am acknowledging it is the first wave of brilliant analysis that will change the world. But it is too narrow."

"Narrow or not," Freud said quickly, "I have told you before, the seductions must be seen metaphorically."

"And I have told you before, the seductions must be literal *and* metaphoric."

The two men found themselves at loggerheads, but highly charged. Each had found his equal, someone he could talk to without slowing down or explaining, and that was both intoxicating and intimidating.

"You are saying that my Oedipus discovery is too limiting?"

"There are other myths, you know."

"I do not see how another myth would be helpful."

"By using the Oedipus myth, the way Jesus used parables, you will get everyone's attention, and will introduce your listeners to great depth, without having to describe your subject literally."

"You are so kind," Freud said, now purely sarcastic.

"But by sticking to that one possibility, you are being too literal, too rational. The problem is that you are about one hundred percent *logos*."

"And not enough *eros*," Freud said quickly.

"Precisely. You are following the rationality of Apollo and ignoring the sensuality of Dionysus. You are saying it is Oedipus or nothing, *either or*. It is childhood drives or nothing."

"You will have to explain."

"Look," Wheeler said after a pause. "Don't you see what you are doing? You are introducing introspection to an age when people don't do much self-examination. This is the rising connectedness to complement the overly masculine dissections that science has brought with it over the past few centuries. This is the rise of the mythic feminine, the connection of all things."

Freud looked genuinely curious for just a moment. "The 'mythic feminine,'" he repeated, liking the sound of it. "Yes. The connectedness to all things," he concluded.

"But why stop short?"

Freud shifted uncomfortably in his chair. "You suggest something different?" he said curtly.

"Why not take another myth now and expand that? Then take many myths. You are being as narrow as the monotheists you criticize. You have broken into the secret temple, but you are not using its full power."

"What other myth do you recommend?"

"Well, why not Orpheus, for instance? The musician responsible for playing the sun up every morning, who loses his lover, Eurydice, to the god of the underworld, separated from his feminine nature, if you will. He is given permission to retrieve her only to lose her forever because of breaking the rules and looking back at her."

"I know my Greek mythology, Herr Burden," Freud said, barely hiding his indignation.

"But the ending. Do you know that in the end Orpheus is attacked by the rageful women of Thrace who are jealous of his attentions, and he is torn apart and thrown into the river?"

Now Freud smiled, following the argument in spite of himself. "Are you saying I should be torn apart by angry women?"

"It will be suggested, believe me." Wheeler paused for effect.

"I do not see how this myth relates to hysteria."

Wheeler didn't even skip a beat. "Stories *are* the unconscious. That's what you are saying."

"What, pray tell, does that say about the roots of hysteria?"

Wheeler was wound up now. There was no stopping. "This story tells the plight of the bifurcated character. The split is what is killing your patients. They need to unite the two parts of their natures, the *logos* and *eros*, if you will. We all have the split, but in their cases the split is debilitating. Orpheus represents both Apollo and Dionysus, both *logos* and *eros*. We are separated from our true nature, and unless we are brought together by physical immersion in real life, we will stay fragmented forever."

Freud suddenly held his guest in his gaze for a long moment. "Very interesting," he said, then paused, collecting himself. "Thank you for the mythology lesson," he said curtly. "But I will stick to my Oedipus analogy, if you don't mind."

"Of course, that is your prerogative. I am just saying that I think it is too narrow, unworthy of the grandeur of your work."

"I think you miss my point, Herr Burden." Freud was now glaring at his visitor.

"I think you miss mine."

"I think—" Freud paused, as if reconsidering his response, aware that he had been on a dangerous precipice, right on the edge of believing his patient's grandiose story. "Herr Burden," he began slowly, pulling himself back to solid ground, becoming absolutely serious. "I know you believe that you are here to dissuade me from moving away from what you call my 'seduction theory' to Oedipus. I appreciate the passion and conviction with which you have pursued your argument. But what you do not see, and perhaps never will see, is that in sharing your ornate and elaborate story, in sharing so openly your journal, you have strengthened, not diminished my conviction."

The compulsive conversationalist found himself suddenly silenced. "Wait," Wheeler said. "You think my story *strengthens* your belief?"

"I do."

"You think that I have concocted this whole fantastic story because I am feeling guilty that I have killed my father to have my mother to myself?" The words had erupted from him out of exasperation and now sat unavoidably before them. Neither man spoke.

The great doctor shrugged, as if to acknowledge the painful and unspoken truth. "The unexamined life, Herr Burden," he said deliberately. "Neither of us has much use or respect for it."

Wheeler shook his head. "I think we have so much more to talk about."

Sigmund Freud stopped him with a movement of his hand. "I think we will call an end to this meeting. We will not need to meet again." Abruptly rising and turning his back to Wheeler, he moved quickly toward the door. "I am sure you can find your way out." As Sigmund Freud left the room, Wheeler was aware once again what a short man his host was.

44

Out of the Dark Corners

hy do I tell you all my secrets?" Weezie said. She was sitting with her legs under her on the shelf in front of the large open window looking out onto the Stephans-Platz. She was wearing a white lace blouse only partially buttoned, with her hair up, the way it had been the night of the opera. "It is as if you are my confessor." Then she smiled and looked back at where Wheeler was sitting in an overstuffed chair, admiring her effect in the morning light. "I should be confessing about the spell our conversations have cast on me. I am totally bewitched."

"Have you never talked this way to anyone before?"

"My friends and I have always been very proper. There were always girls who talked about such things—" She wrinkled her nose in adolescent distaste. "But they were of questionable repute."

"Did you never talk with a young man?"

Weezie recoiled. "Oh, heavens no. One would rather die on the spot than talk to a young man about secret things."

"So you just hold it inside?"

"That is just what one does."

"And what is the result?"

She looked back out the window. "One should not go around talking about feelings. It just is not considerate." She paused. "On the other hand, it does seem to make things better to get them out of the dark corners." She looked back at Wheeler and smiled again. "You see, that is what you have done to me. You have caused me to bring all manner of unmentionables up into the daylight. Shameful. Once they are there, they don't seem to be as important or worth hiding anymore." She readjusted her legs under her. "The strict Puritan voice inside me is losing out to the sybarite, I fear. And all because of you."

"Aren't the two voices giving in to a third?"

She looked at him quizzically for a moment, to be certain he wasn't teasing. "I do not follow," she said.

"You said before that you were inhabited by three people. I'm just saying that your aunt Prudence and your willful child have perhaps stopped warring with each other and have given way to that third self you described. Do you remember how you described it?"

"My mother," she said pensively.

"Exactly. The Puritan part of you—" Wheeler raised his hand to the top of an imaginary diagram in front of him. He moved his hand down to the bottom. "The libertine part—" He moved his hand to the middle position. "And the middle voice, the mature moderator, the authentic one. Strict parent, mature adult, impulsive child: three voices in all of us, actually, and we should try to use the middle one."

"The mature voice I would like to hear always but often cannot."

Wheeler nodded and smiled. "The mature voice, right. And whose voice is it?"

"My mother's."

Wheeler said nothing, only looked at her expectantly. At first, noting his expectation, she looked perplexed, as if unable to guess what should be coming next. Then she closed her eyes and smiled. "Not my mother, actually. My mother's gift to me, the one I have had such a hard time reaching."

"And what is that voice?" Wheeler said softly.

"That third voice, that mature one, the one I want to use. It is not my aunt Prudence with all her *shoulds* and *will nots*, and it is not my willful child with its selfish gratifications. It is just the one real and true voice."

"The authentic one," Wheeler said.

"What a curious way to describe it," she said. "That is precisely it: my authentic voice," Weezie said. "And how I wish to use it all the time."

"You're not alone in that wish."

"But I seem so far behind. So often I feel afraid. I hear that Puritanical voice, and I feel unworthy and afraid. I want so to move beyond."

Wheeler smiled. "And you do that by opening up and talking."

Weezie fell silent and thought for a moment. "I need to open up more. I know that. I would have told no one, absolutely no one, about my meeting with Herr Mahler. And I would have hoped that no one had found out. I was so embarrassed that I would cringe inside every time I thought of it. Now, I have mentioned it enough times that it seems commonplace." She smiled. "What every young girl does, you know: faint in the presence of a great master."

"And you begin to see connections."

"That is the confounding part. I have felt that way before—flushed and dizzy. In college, when the girls would talk about uncomfortable things, and they would take delight in looking at me to see how I was reacting, I felt terrible pressure and would feel faint."

Wheeler was amused. "What kinds of things?"

She looked away. "You know, the things girls in college talk about when they are trying to rattle someone they think naïve and sheltered."

"What kind of things?"

She began to flush. "You know! I know *you* know."

"I have never been a college girl," he said with a gentle laugh. "You'll have to tell me."

"The things that make one blush and faint."

"About what? Radical politics? Women's right to vote? Garish interior design? Going without a bath?"

"No," she said impatiently, "other things—"

"What sorts of things?" Wheeler was boring in, not letting her off the hook.

"You know," she said, now sounding peeved.

"I don't know."

She balked, but then said finally, "Things sexual."

"And why do they make one blush and faint?"

She looked back out the window, and her perturbation fell away suddenly and she became rapt in deep thought, then turned back slowly. "I do not know," she said with great earnestness. "I have never given it any thought."

"And was that what made you faint with Herr Mahler?"

Again, she looked pensive and took a long time to answer. "How curious," she said absently. "I had never thought of it that way."

On certain afternoons when Wheeler knew Dilly would not be there, he brought Weezie to lunch with Kleist's friends at the Café Central. They were more than gracious to her and seemed to like the way she held her own in a discussion of art or even politics. Of course, she had few equals on the subject of music, and her reputation on that subject preceded her because of her already-established association with the music crowd. "They think I am your sweet girl," she said after one such lunch.

"They don't mean it disrespectfully," Wheeler said.

"I think it would be better if we were not seen together in public," she said, "now that we have this new—" She paused, having trouble with the word. "—this new arrangement."

"You are worried about how you are being perceived."

"I know that proper girls, the ones these young Viennese will eventually marry, do not join them in artist's studios for trysts. That role is saved for their shop girls and promiscuous workers' daughters."

"That is the old order," Wheeler said, "for sure. But now there are modern women." He would have told her of Alma Schindler, the well-born and ravishingly beautiful painter's daughter who had numerous affairs before marrying Gustav Mahler, then Walter Gropius, the world-renowned architect, and then finally the writer Franz Werfel, who wrote *The Song of Bernadette*, but in 1897 she was only eighteen years old and still unknown. "I think that young artists in Vienna are the perfect people to understand such 'arrangements,'" he said, just a little defensively.

"It is not only that. I have the feeling I am being watched. There is a young man who keeps his eye on me from a distance, and it makes me feel uneasy, as if he is a spy from back home." She became quiet, lost for a moment in the enormity of what she had committed to with Wheeler. "However, I shall miss very stimulating company," she said finally. "My friends at home talk about frivolities. Your friends in Vienna talk about matters of substance."

"Like the end of the world."

"Well, some of it is a little gloomy," she said with a smile. "I don't know why they do not have more hope for the future of everything. My frivolous friends think that Boston will be there, just as it is now, forever. These people give the impression that they really think Vienna is about to collapse on itself. But it is stimulating, nonetheless."

It was late in the afternoon when she returned to the studio. Wheeler was waiting for her with an anxious smile. "I have a surprise," he said. "Look in the corner, over there." He pointed behind one of the brightly colored canvases.

She walked over and saw two instrument cases leaning against the wall. "A cello," she said with a burst of unrestrained joy, opening the larger of the two cases.

Wheeler opened the other and pulled out a classical guitar. "I found a wonderful old music shop, and the proprietor loaned me all this, plus some music."

Wheeler brought chairs from the sitting room, and arranged them. Weezie sat and straddled the cello, running the bow across the strings and producing a few tentative sounds. "I am very rusty," she said.

Wheeler fashioned a music stand out of a wooden easel and propped onto it a piece of sheet music.

"Oh my," Weezie said. "We are going to be serious about this." She put her cello aside and walked over to her handbag, opened it, and withdrew a small packet, which she unwrapped and revealed a pair of wire-rimmed glasses. She came back to her seat and put them on. "I'm lost without these, not very ladylike," she said, repositioning the cello.

"It's Haydn," he said, "written for cello and violin. It's not quite my style, but I figured I could improvise."

"To improvise," she said with a sigh. "You are not afraid to do that. Me, I am stuck in following the rules. For me, playing music is sticking rigidly to the prescribed pattern, sticking with the traditions."

"Perhaps we can change that a bit," Wheeler said and began playing the notes as written on the page.

Faltering and hesitant in the beginning, both musicians slowly began to reach into their pasts and find that magical flow of the music and of what the other was doing with it. The deep rich tones of the cello slid under and around the fine finger-picking counterpoint of the classical guitar. Both Weezie and Wheeler let themselves travel with the music until they were lost together, far from Vienna or 1897, somewhere out with the stars. At one point, in the middle of their inspired collaboration, Wheeler looked over at Weezie and saw on her face an expression he would later describe as "dreamy ecstasy."

"Will you play me something from San Francisco?" Weezie said, and with the guitar still in his lap Wheeler began the opening chords of the same melody they had been playing. And then he began singing the song that had had its origins in that blizzardy winter night in January 1959, when Wheeler played music with his idol Buddy Holly, and then had run around and around in his head over the years, until that night in 1975 when he came forward with his father's old Martin guitar alone on the stage at the football stadium in Berkeley, California, when it became the legendary "Coming Together," the best-known song of the era.

He had actually sung it one time before the Berkeley concert, to an audience of one, at the bedside of Joan Quigley, the last time he saw her. She smiled a contented soulful smile. "That's beautiful," she said in little more than a sigh and with no trace of her patented sharpness. "Will you sing that for me, when this is all over?"

"Just one time for the world," Wheeler said, his eyes filled with tears. "Then I'll retire it forever."

"One and out?" she said, with barely enough energy to smile.

"One and out," he said. "This time for you."

With what little she had left, Joan Quigley laughed. "That is so *you*," she said, back to her old self.

And now for just the third time in front of an audience, another audience of one, Wheeler Burden was playing the song "Coming Together" that had become a legend, in retrospect his signature piece. Weezie Putnam, leaning on her rented cello, watched him in amazement. "That is one of the most beautiful songs I have ever heard," she said dreamily, lost in the moment of this first lesson in improvisation.

45

Worse Than You Know

ou've been following her, haven't you?" Wheeler said abruptly, on the train ride back from Lambach.

"Who's that?" Dilly said it quickly, betrayed by a twinge of embarrassment, knowing exactly who.

"I knew it."

"Well, I did find her," Dilly said. "And I will admit to standing and watching her a few times."

"Staring? Enough so that she would notice."

"Well, I guess maybe," Dilly said, now looking uncomfortable.

"And I thought you were the one who said we had to be scrupulously careful."

"I didn't speak to her," he said, defending himself. "Or approach her."

"But she noticed you."

"I guess so. She is so darned attractive. I can't keep from watching her."

"Well, you'd better," Wheeler said without humor. "Or you'll blow the whole deal."

Earlier, he had joined Dilly in his small, poorly lighted, and unheated apartment by the canal off Rudolfs-Platz. Wheeler met him there early because Dilly was planning a train trip up the Danube and said that it would mean a great deal to him if Wheeler would come along. When he entered, he found Dilly surrounded by papers on his small unlighted desk. "What is all this?" Wheeler said.

Dilly looked pleased with himself. "Research," he said, lifting a sheet of paper. It was Dilly at his best, the single-minded pursuit of a project until he got what he wanted. Endless trips to the civil service office, enlisting help, handing out coins and bills to bureaucrats, weaving his way through the paperwork of the empire. "Look." He pointed with his patented gusto to the paper in his hand. "I've found an address."

"And what were you planning to do?"

"I don't know," Dilly said. "It was such a big job and I had so little to go on. I didn't really know much about him other than that he was born in a small town within the empire and that he would be around ten now. I knew his father's name was Alois, that he was a petty civil employee, and that the name Schicklgruber was in there someplace. It's funny though—" He pointed to all the papers scattered on the desk. "If you ask enough questions, you begin homing in. Now finally—" He looked down at the paper in his hand. "I think I have it. Alois Hitler in Lambach, retired civil servant, on a pension, near Linz, just a few hours. A train leaves soon. We could be back by tonight."

Wheeler looked dumbfounded. "What about not interfering with history?"

"We're not going to do anything." There was a fierce intensity in his eyes. "I just wanted to know if I could do it. And now I think I have it. We can be there in a few hours."

"Hold it," Wheeler said. It was all going too fast for him. He had experience—the prongball, Oppenheimer's atomic bomb—that proved if you *can* do it you *will* do it, if you have it you will use it. "You think you have found Adolf Hitler. And you want to go right now to see him."

Dilly was terribly serious, a great laboratory scientist on the brink of a cure. "I just need to confirm it. The pension lists don't give the names of children. All I have is Alois Hitler in Lambach. I've done all the research, and now there is only one way to make sure."

Wheeler looked at all the papers that amounted to an enormous number of hours. No wonder he had not seen Dilly more often at the Café Central. "I don't get it," he said, shaking his head. "You are the one who keeps telling me we have to be careful."

Dilly's face became softer. "I was driven by hate. I was going to garrote the little bastard. That's what propelled me here, right out of my Gestapo cell. Well, now that it is real, and now that I have been here in this remarkable city with my son for a few weeks, my mission has become more gentle." Then the hardness came back to his eyes and he seemed overtaken by an enormous shiver. "But we can't forget all the terrible destruction and cruelty. We can't—" He couldn't find the words.

"But what would you actually *do* about it?"

Dilly scrunched up his face. "I don't know, Stan. I actually do not know. Could I actually—when it got right down to it—harm the evil little bastard?"

"Well, let's say you did decide to do something, and there was no Hitler. Then, for starters, there would have been no Lend-Lease, and no bombing of London, and you would never have met Mother or had a son."

"I haven't said I was going to *do* anything. I just want to go take a look. And it would mean an awful lot if you came with me."

"I don't like it. We haven't gone to find the Haze, and we know he is right here in Vienna, easy to find. You don't want to run into Frank Burden because you might breathe a germ on him—"

"I know, I know," Dilly said. "And I've told you that we absolutely could not go anywhere near them, or Eleanor Putnam who is also right here." Wheeler moved back a little in his seat. "I know all that. But that is small potatoes. That is just to make sure that the right people and circumstances come together in seventeen years, and after, so that you and I can be born." He paused again and his face resumed its hardness. "But with Hitler." He rolled his eyes, trying to estimate the effect of that one man's presence. "We are talking about the ruin of democracy and the ruination of cultures and Coventry Cathedral, and millions of innocent lives."

"And it's worse than you know."

The intensity was back in his eyes. "Let's just go see."

"A long train ride on a few scraps of possible evidence. It's a crazy idea."

On the train, Dilly was more excited than usual, an archaeologist on the brink of his great discovery. "I was getting nowhere, and then I happened to run into a retired provincial tax collector who was in Vienna for just one day. The guy was sort of feeble-minded and couldn't stop talking, but he had a photographic memory. It was a lucky break." He fell silent, watching the landscape pass. "What ever happened to all the Jews?" he said. "Did they get their property back?"

Wheeler sat astounded for a moment. "You don't know about Buchenwald and Auschwitz?" he said.

"What are Buchenwald and Auschwitz?"

"The death camps?"

Dilly gave him a blank look. "There were rumors."

"During the liberation, they turned into a lot more than rumors," Wheeler said, incredulous. So Wheeler told Dilly the stories of the Allied soldiers coming to the concentration camps and what they found and what was revealed later from the Nazi documentation.

Dilly looked stunned. "I didn't believe. No one could do that," Dilly said, after he was finished with all the details. "I discounted what was being said. There are limits, after all, I kept telling people. Have faith, I kept saying. You know, when I was in France the time before that last one, I even got in an argument with a girl who worked for the Resistance. She told me the Nazis were gassing children, and I told her she was getting a little carried way."

"Gassing, and worse. The number got up to ten million," Wheeler said, and he told about Josef Mengele and his experiments and some of the other horrors. "When the Allied soldiers liberated the camps, they made townspeople walk past all the bodies, so no one could say it was just made up."

Dilly was silent for a time, shaking his head in shock, and went back to looking out the window. "And you didn't want to make this trip," he said finally.

"You said there were other things you needed to tell me," Wheeler said.

"About finding Hitler, that's all." Dilly was being evasive.

"You said something more."

Dilly did not look at him. "It's about Eleanor Putnam." His head was turned away. "Actually, I knew she was in Vienna from the very first. And I—" Wheeler stared until he looked back at him. "I've sort of been—" He paused. "Well, sort of obsessed."

"More than just watching her?"

"No, just watching." He looked out the window again. "It's just that—" He breathed a great sigh. "I didn't expect her to be so—so beautiful."

"What did you do?"

Dilly looked back apologetically, hesitant. "It's not so much what I did, I guess. More like what I felt. I mean I never went up to her or anything. She never knew I was watching her."

Wheeler did his best to hide his discomfort.

"I guess I sort of have a crush on her," he said, putting his head in his hands.

"You have a crush on your own mother!"

Dilly looked around the train car, mortified. "She just looks so fresh and young. Her eyes are so blue, and her smile—she has an absolutely knockout smile. In fact, lately I really noticed a change." He stopped to find the right words. "Lately, she has looked absolutely radiant. I figure she must be in love. You don't often see a woman that full of life and passion."

"I wouldn't know," Wheeler said, wishing for the conversation to return to something safe, like Hitler.

"She looks like a beautiful flower opening up."

"Music and Vienna," Wheeler said quickly.

Suddenly Dilly turned to him seriously. "I know what is going on," he blurted out decisively, a look of real seriousness in his eye, and a cold sweat came to Wheeler's brow.

"You do?"

"There's only one thing it can be." Dilly's eyes were filled with conviction. "It is love. It's love for Frank Burden."

The train stopped at Lambach shortly before one o'clock. Dilly pulled one of his scraps of paper from his pocket and asked the stationmaster for directions. They walked quickly through the narrow streets of the small town, past a number of important-looking buildings. Dilly stopped dead and pointed. "There it is," he said, his heart beating so hard Wheeler could almost see it through his jacket. "Wait here."

Wheeler watched as Dilly approached the door and knocked. A dark-haired woman in her forties stood in the doorway in her apron, drying her hands with a towel. She looked friendly enough, smiling and nodding, and at one time pointing down the street over Dilly's shoulder. Dilly shook her hand and then turned as the woman closed the front door.

"I told her I was an American painter and was visiting from Munich. I said I heard she had an eight-year-old son, Adolf, with beautiful blue eyes and I wondered if I could perhaps have him pose for a chalk sketch. I said I would give the family a copy."

Now Wheeler's heart was beating fast. "Her name was Frau Hitler?"

"Of course."

"And she has a son named Adolf?"

"He's at school and will be home in an hour," Dilly said nonchalantly. "He walks along that street."

Wheeler shook his head. "Do you think it's the one?"

"We have only to see," Dilly said.

They killed time by walking the grounds of the eleventh-century Benedictine abbey, the only point of interest in the town. But neither could really concentrate. An hour and ten minutes later they were standing at the same spot near Mrs. Hitler's front door when the young boy approached. Dilly walked forward, toward the young man. Wheeler had no choice but to follow. As they drew near the young boy, Dilly said, "Good afternoon, Meister Hitler."

The boy looked perplexed for a moment, then smiled back. "Good afternoon," he said with a smile as the two men passed. Dilly stopped and stood watching the child pass on toward his house. He took a step toward him, then hesitated, looking for an instant like a man on the brink of a monumental decision. "Meister Hitler," he called to him, and the boy stopped and turned.

"I am an artist," he said. "I would like to draw your portrait. I will return."

The boy looked at him quizzically, then nodded and turned and walked on toward his house.

Dilly watched him until he opened the front door and entered. When he turned back to Wheeler, his face was ashen and his hands were shaking.

On the train ride back to Vienna Dilly sat by the window and watched the Austrian countryside pass by. He seemed deep in thought, and Wheeler, doing some deep thinking himself, allowed the silence. The sighting of the child Hitler had had a profound impact on both of them, and now each just sat without speaking. Suddenly, Dilly turned from the window and looked at Wheeler with the old spark back in his eyes. "You know, I've been thinking," he said. "How did you know I had been following my mother?"

46

Dancing over the Precipice

n their way back from the train station, Dilly suggested they drop in to the Café Central to see what was up with the *Jung Wien*. As they entered with a show of his old enthusiasm, Wheeler could see Dilly's patented energy was not what it had been. The day in Lambach and the encounter with the child Hitler had taken a toll, but he was not about to let that stop him. "Let's see what our *Jung Wien* friends are up to," he said as they approached the table where a discussion was in full bloom.

"The Americans have arrived," said Kleist with his old gusto. "We have not seen you for a while," he said, giving Wheeler a wink. "Your energies have been with other projects, it seems."

Claus rose and motioned to empty chairs. "By all means, join us. Schluessler here is telling us what is wrong with the empire."

Schluessler, the scientist, paused in midsentence and acknowledged the newcomers with a forced smile. "This isn't funny," he said. "We are not headed in a healthy direction."

"Oh, it is not as bad as it looks," von Tscharner said, smiling.

But Schluessler was not diverted. "I think you all have your head in the sand. Karl Lueger has hit a nerve."

"Handsome Karl is just rousing the rabble," Kleist said. "His anti-Semitism is a political game, and he knows it."

"It's closer to the truth than any of you want to admit," Schluessler said glumly. "The working people have been maligned and mistreated by all this splendor our fathers have created, the magnificent Ringstrasse, and have pulled together. They are angry and bitter."

"And they are taking it out on us poor Jews."

"Poor Jews?" von Tscharner quipped good-naturedly. "Name two."

"The animosity is at a boiling point."

"It's only momentary," Claus said. "It can't last."

Schluessler looked serious again, becoming annoyed that no one was matching his seriousness. "You Jews let it get out of hand, and now you will pay." There was no good nature in his words anymore. "You control eighty percent of the banks. You run the businesses. You are good with money, and you are good with helping your own kind. You had an advantage and you exploited that advantage. And now you will pay."

"Oh, come, come," Claus added. "You are sounding much too serious for our intellectual circle."

But Schluessler, dug in now, would not retreat. "I am serious. Jews are ruining our city, and the sooner we are rid of them the better."

"A city without Jews. I can't imagine it," Kleist said, now trying to lighten the atmosphere.

"Well, I can," said Schluessler. "And I must say, I look forward to the day."

"You can't be serious. Who would write the music?"

"And the plays?"

"Who would attend their performances?" A nervous laughter erupted from the group.

"I am serious. Deadly serious. Things have gone far enough, and now it is time for change." He glowered at the silent faces around the table. "You mock me, but on this note I am right." He rose suddenly from his seat. "And a lot of people agree with me." Then he suddenly walked away, toward the door, leaving the rest of the table in uncomfortable silence.

"Well," Dilly burst out, "that was a stimulating discussion," but there was no life in his voice.

The two friends needed time to think and talk things out, so they had agreed to meet for lunch at one of the restaurants in the Prater, after which they were going to have "another session with that Frisbee thing," Dilly said.

"That was a bad turn with the *Jung Wien*," Dilly said, looking deeply concerned.

"They have no idea what is in store for them."

"And I suppose we can't warn them."

"No impact," Wheeler said glumly, and at that moment he wondered if Dilly was going to bring up Weezie Putnam again and speculated on how lucky it was that Dilly had not seen them together and how quickly he had accepted Wheeler's "I guessed" when asked how he had known about Dilly's watch on her. Maybe he had seen them and was being discreet, which Wheeler doubted, since that option required an indirection of which the younger man simply didn't seem capable. When Dilly Burden had something on his mind he put it square out there on the table. "There was nothing even remotely resembling subterfuge in his style," Wheeler's mother said of her husband. "He was totally incapable of dissembling, which made him a great spy."

"You may have noticed that my health is not tip-top," he said to Wheeler as they sat down. "Energy's not what it used to be. Those dreadful Germans ground me down." As far as Wheeler could tell, his father was indefatigable, but now it was difficult not to notice the shadows deepening under his eyes and some uncharacteristic moments of breathlessness. But this morning he seemed excited and filled with energy for the outing. He held in his hand a copy of the *Neue Freie Presse*. "Look at this," he said excitedly, slapping the front of the paper with the back of his hand as Wheeler pulled up his chair. "Egon Wickstein's first publication. I remember reading this in 1934 and giving it to my friend Brod Walker. It was the summer after our junior year. We were on a grand tour of Europe."

Wheeler looked down at the morning copy of Vienna's great daily newspaper. On the lower front page, in the usual *feuilleton* spot was Wickstein's essay. "'The Preconditions of Cultural Apex,'" Dilly read. "A little stuffy. But you have to remember he is only eighteen. I think that is swell. We are sitting here with a piece of history in front of us, and we are the only ones who know it." Then Dilly began reading it, a little slowly, translating as he went. "It is a lively piece of writing. You can see that the boy has talent. I remember when I first read it to my pal Walker. I think it was that morning that he decided to make Wickstein his life's work." Dilly looked askance at Wheeler. "He wasn't much of a scholar in those days, you know. More interested in the young ladies and Cambridge alehouses. But that summer discovering Wickstein sort of lit a fire under him." Dilly looked off into the distance, smiling. "And now you say he went on to become one of the ranking Harvard scholars." He gave a satisfied smile. "Brod deserved that. He was an exceptionally good man."

Wheeler looked down at the copy of the *Neue Freie Presse*. "This is my essay," he said, his voice full of ironic amusement, which Dilly at first took as humor. "I'm serious," Wheeler said. "This is my essay."

"You're joking."

"I'm not. I'm dead serious. I pretty much dictated it to Egon the other day in the Café Central."

"That's impossible." Now Dilly looked confused. "This is pure Egon, any graduate student could tell you that. It will be known as his first published work."

"That may well be, but it is pretty much verbatim an essay I wrote at Harvard in 1960, in a philosophy course."

"How did it end up in the *Neue Freie Presse?* By osmosis?"

"No, I told you. I gave it to him. He had that deadline and needed something, so I told him my idea, and he wrote it down."

Dilly stared at his son. "This essay appears as the first selection of the book Brod edited on Wickstein's early works. He gave me a copy when we all came home for Christmas in 1943. And you are telling me *you* wrote it."

"I know it is in Dr. Walker's book. I know it is considered pure Egon Wickstein. That became very clear to me when I nearly got bounced from Harvard for plagiarism for my own essay. I'm just telling you that I gave him the ideas."

"You mean you gave him the subject matter."

"And most of the wording. He was desperate and not being very discerning. The deadline was quick upon him."

Dilly shook his head. "You are saying that if it had not been for you Egon Wickstein might have written his first essay on the tulips at Belvedere?"

"Exactly."

Now Dilly was looking serious, trying to get his arms around something big. "You gave Egon Wickstein the idea for his first published essay. I read the essay to Brod Walker in 1935. Brod Walker used it to found his fascination with Wickstein and became the American scholar who popularized Wickstein in English—" He stopped and his mind tried to sort out the enormousness of it all.

"And there is more. When I originally wrote the essay in freshman year it was for Philosophy one-oh-one, and it was titled 'The Great Catch.' The stuffy title came later. I was trying to figure out on paper why people made such a big deal out of small dramatic events in art and politics and—" He paused to see that Dilly was following.

"And sports."

"Right," Wheeler said. "From the time I got to St. Greg's people were always telling me what a hero you had been and how you have saved this game or that game or had done this or that with a hockey puck. At first I couldn't figure why it made so much difference to all these highly educated and stuffy people. When I got to Harvard, they all wanted to talk about what you had done there, especially in sports. And most of all it was the catch you made against Yale: 'the Catch' everyone called it. So, I wrote the essay explaining why the great catch in general is the highest point of civilization. I used Willie Mays's catch of Vic Wertz's fly ball in the 1954 World Series as my model." He paused. "You've heard of neither of them," he added quickly, then continued. "That essay went on to become 'The Preconditions of Cultural Apex,' the essay whose ideas I gave Egon the other day at the Café Central, and the essay that caused an assistant professor named Fielding Shomsky to go apoplectic and nearly get me thrown out of Harvard for plagiarism."

"What saved you?" Dilly said, beginning to see it all.

"Your friend Professor Walker just sort of buried the whole thing. Lord knows what he thought."

Dilly shook his head. He was struggling, trying to take it all in. "Whatever happened to Wickstein? In 1943, when Brod published his book, he was reported incarcerated somewhere in Germany."

"It's not a good story," Wheeler said grimly.

47

A Magnificent Example

gon Wickstein spent his twenties in Vienna, studying philosophy and then teaching at the university, developing something of a reputation for his sharp wit and his outspoken—some would say abrasive—flair, publishing his *feuilletons* often in the *Neue Freie Presse*, and proving incapable of keeping his opinions to himself. In 1914, at age thirty-four, with some fanfare, he moved to Cambridge University to share thoughts with Bertrand Russell. It was then that he began to distinguish himself and attract attention for his ideas, and in the early 1930s, he published his *Critique of Pure Reason*, now considered one of the finest works of twentieth-century philosophy. Almost before the ink was dry on the first edition in German, the book was put on the objectionable list in Nazi Germany and cast into the bonfires. The following year, his autobiography, *Before Yesterday*, was published and to this day it is considered one of the best descriptions of early-century intellectual and cultural life in Vienna, but still, like its predecessor, a Jewish book, it went into the bonfires. "I must have said something right," Egon was said to have exclaimed upon hearing of the second distinction. But like Freud's early works, neither book sold very well at the outset, or was particularly well-known.

The child Hitler from Lambach left home in 1908 at age nineteen and moved to Vienna hoping to become an artist, sharing the city for five years with Egon Wickstein. Despite a reasonable talent, he failed repeatedly to gain entrance to the Art Academy of Vienna. For five years, he eked out an existence by selling his watercolors and developed a sense of politics and hatred for Jews by watching the master, mayor Karl Lueger. It was then that he learned the power of demagogic oratory and the political uses of anti-Semitism. During this time, it is speculated that he came in contact with Egon Wickstein and developed an intense reaction against him, as he represented all that the young man hated about Jews.

In 1914 Hitler moved to Munich and after humble service as a corporal in the great war helped form the National Socialist Party. It is likely that neither Wickstein nor Sigmund Freud noticed him when he was arrested during the *putsch* and sentenced to four years in prison, only nine months of which he actually served. It was during that incarceration that he dictated his *Mein Kampf* to Rudolf Hess.

In 1938, when tension was rising from Germany, much to the disapproval of his friends and colleagues, Egon returned to Vienna to help. But the surging time of pro-Germanism and anti-Semitism was far greater than any one brilliant philosopher could match. Early in 1938, Hitler invaded Austria and Vienna. His Anschluss, the takeover of Austria, was greeted by hundreds of thousands of cheering Austrians. The Catholic cardinal greeted Hitler in person and pledged the support of Austria's majority Catholic population. The effect on Vienna's Jews was immediate and devastating. They were taunted and beaten, expelled from their homes, their businesses and their properties looted by avaricious neighbors. A large number of lawyers, judges, physicians, and businessmen improved their living standards and their family futures by plundering their Jewish neighbors. At the university, nearly all Jews—forty percent of the student body and fifty percent of the faculty—were dismissed. "Of all the cities under Nazi control," the Haze told his boys, "Vienna was the most debased on Kristallnacht a few months after the 1938 takeover. Simon Wiesenthal, the famous Nazi hunter after World War II, has said that compared to Vienna, the Kristallnacht in Berlin was a pleasant Christmas festival."

During this awful time, when most Jews and political opponents of Nazism were trying to flee Vienna, Egon Wickstein thought it his duty to return, much to the dismay of his Cambridge colleagues and friends. He was one of the major forces in persuading his eighty-two-year-old friend Sigmund Freud to leave and working with forces outside Austria to pressure the Nazis to release him. After much negotiation and the gift of $400,000 to the Nazi Party, Freud and his immediate family were allowed to leave for London, where young psychiatry student Flora Zimmerman, among others, was waiting to prepare a welcome. After Freud's departure, Wickstein and a number of friends meticulously photographed the Berggasse 19 apartment and then boxed up all remaining items that the great doctor did not take himself. They labeled the box "toilet articles" and sneaked it out past the invading Nazi guards, who in a few days had emptied the apartment of all valuables, appropriating them, and erasing all memories of the Jews who had lived there, regardless of any contributions to the advancement of civilization that might have been generated there.

It was clear to all his Viennese friends that Egon was high on the list of undesirables, and many friends interceded and offered him plans of emigration, but Egon refused, saying that Vienna was his home and it belonged to his people, whom he defined as all intelligent book-reading denizens of the café world. Shortly after Freud's departure, Egon was detained for questioning and held for a while at the football stadium, then not heard from again. Over the years, intellectuals from neutral countries around the world tried to pressure the German government to release him, and the answer always came back that Egon Wickstein had engaged in subversive activity and he was safely incarcerated in a concentration camp, being well cared for.

His great fame was not really established until after 1944, when his fate was unknown and Broderick Walker of Harvard University published his collected works, the first of which was a *feuilleton* from the *Neue Freie Presse* entitled "The Preconditions of a Cultural Apex." Then in 1950, the Harvard professor published his monumental biography of Wickstein, a work that characterized Vienna at the turn of the century and put both men on the map.

After scrupulous research into the details of the young philosopher's life, Brod Walker discovered from eyewitnesses exactly how Egon Wickstein met his end. In 1938 he was questioned and detained by the SS and shipped to a prison in Germany where the high command considered what to do with their high-profile prisoner. After a few months of holding this offensive Jew who did not know how to keep his mouth shut, one day an SS officer took him out into the prison courtyard and with his service-issue Luger put a bullet into the brain of one of the century's great thinkers. It was a case, Brod Walker lamented, of a very limited example of human intelligence having ultimate power over a magnificent example. It was said that when Hitler was told of the end of "the offensive Jew," he was greatly pleased.

It was not until the end of the war that Egon Wickstein was declared an official casualty, his martyrdom firmly established. At the time of

Wheeler's visit to Vienna in 1897, there were over 200,000 Jews in the imperial city. By the time the Russians rolled into Vienna in 1945, at the end of the Second World War, there were 127.

In the summer of 1956, Arnauld Esterhazy, then seventy years old, returned to Vienna for the first time since the end of World War I, and for the last time. The opera house, destroyed by a single direct hit from an Allied bomb in 1945, was reopened. Arnauld visited the Dilly Burden memorial in Paris, then went to Vienna for a performance of Wagner's *Tannhäuser*. At the end of the performance, he discovered something very wrong in the reconstructed and refurbished space. He wept for all that had been lost, for his beloved Dilly and for his old friend Egon Wickstein, but it was also for something deeper. The whole performance seemed flat and lacking the vibrancy and vitality he had remembered when Gustav Mahler was conducting and the audience was electric with cultured appreciation. "Something was dreadfully wrong," Arnauld wrote in his notes from the occasion. "One awful and devastating reason: there are no Jews."

48

A Historic Gift

hat afternoon in the Prater, they walked out to an expansive spot of flat ground. Wheeler wanted to show Dilly what the Frisbee could do in the open spaces. Dilly was delighted.

"You're getting the hang of it," Wheeler said, as his partner launched a tilting throw that hit the ground about halfway between them.

"Now this time you are going to have to show me exactly how to throw it. We must not leave until I have mastered it." Mastering for Dilly meant the most thorough analysis of how it worked: exactly how the disk was to be held and released, the aerodynamic sciences that applied, and then some serious study of how to maximize the effects of throwing and catching. Wheeler had never seen anyone as analytical about something that he had always taken for an instinctive act.

After a while Wheeler said, "Let's stop talking about it and throw it."

He stood thirty yards from Dilly and released a throw that soared high and then dropped gracefully to where his father was standing. Dilly nearly failed to catch it, he was so enthralled by the graceful flight. Dilly would have to step forward to make his throws, but Wheeler could see him working with his form, doing practice throws in his mind until he removed from his delivery the quirks that were making the disk roll over shortly after it left his hand. He listened to Wheeler's long-distance coaching, and added intuitions of his own. Soon he was making long, graceful, accurate throws.

"Ready for the real distance?" Wheeler yelled to him across the green expanse of the Prater. He brought his arm back and then swept it forward past his chest with a violent suddenness, putting his full body weight behind it. The disk left his hand from a position below his waist and rocketed

out toward where Dilly was standing, sailing far over his head before slowing and beginning to hover. Dilly, failing health or no, caught by surprise,
at first watched in awe, then with an unbelievable burst of coordinated
energy, he spun, and, without looking up, raced across the grass to a position a good distance away where the disk might fall. At the last possible
moment, he looked up, saw the Frisbee over his shoulder, reached out,
and grabbed it with one sure hand, tumbling as he did and rolling to the
earth.

It was an exquisitely coordinated move.

Wheeler ran over to where Dilly was picking himself off the ground.
"That was fantastic," he said.

Dilly was standing, brushing grass from his suit pants. "I wanted to see
if I could catch it."

"I guess so," said Wheeler, in awe, his heart soaring with love and
pride.

Neither of them noticed the carriage drive up and stop. It was driven
by two white horses, which, after the incident, both men realized were of
superior breeding. But neither the coach itself nor the coachman looked
special enough to attract attention. The glass on the windows was frosted
and difficult to see through. The carriage might have been parked beside
the field where they were throwing for ten or twenty minutes.

Dilly was concentrating on his style, and Wheeler was watching with
fascination the concentration and attention to detail of this remarkable
athlete he had heard about all his life.

They were now standing nearly fifty yards apart, their throws sending
the wooden disk soaring gracefully over the great distance, Wheeler's
throws dropping gently within Dilly's reach, Dilly's coming closer and
closer to his distant target.

Neither did they see the coachman descend from his seat and walk
across the grass to where Wheeler stood. "Please," said the man, pointing
across the field toward the coach, whose door was now open. He began to
walk back, ushering Wheeler. Dilly stayed at his position, watching in
fascination.

As Wheeler approached he had trouble seeing into the coach, and it
was not until he was only a few feet away that he saw the woman in black,
sitting in the coach, waiting for him. And it was not until he was nearly
upon it that he realized that this was no ordinary two-horse carriage.

The woman's eyes followed him as he approached. Now, Wheeler realized that she had probably been watching them throw the Frisbee for some time. She had a look of affection on her pale face, and her eyes were filled with tears. She did not speak, but made it clear that she wished Wheeler to approach. Wheeler had no idea why he did it, but as he approached he knelt on the footrest with one knee.

"I am honored—" he began, but she silenced him with an index finger to her lips. She stared at him in silence.

"You have shown me much beauty," she said, in barely more than a whisper. With a rustle of silk she leaned forward in her black leather seat and extended a hand. Wheeler held out both of his. She placed in his hand a cloth-wrapped bundle about the size of a walnut, and with her other hand pulled his fingers closed on it, holding him there for a long moment, as if hoping to give or receive from him some vital life force. "Take this," she said solemnly. "And live." She looked deep into his eyes.

Wheeler stood rooted to his place beside the road in the Prater as the carriage disappeared into the distance and until he could no longer hear the sound of the horses. He turned and looked back at Dilly who was approaching him cautiously.

"That wasn't—" Dilly said, looking stunned.

They both looked down into Wheeler's hand, at the small packet enclosed in an embroidered handkerchief. Slowly, Wheeler unwrapped the cloth until the contents lay exposed in his palm. Neither man dared breath.

Wheeler's outstretched palm held a man's large gold ring, studded on the sides with small diamonds, each one worthy of being the centerpiece of a necklace or brooch. In the center was a huge emerald.

Dilly exhaled in disbelief. "It's Crown Prince Rudolf's." He leaned in closer to examine it. "It must be worth a fortune."

On the way home in the cab, they discussed what Wheeler might do with the ring to keep it safe, and Dilly suggested entrusting it immediately to a bank. "It is a godsend," he said. "There is enough there to support you for a long time."

"To support us both."

Dilly looked up at him sadly. Suddenly the hollowness had returned to his eyes. "I won't be here much longer, I fear. My stay is of the shorter variety."

"You don't need to go. We can be here in Vienna for a long time. There is no reason—"

"You don't understand." Dilly had a look of quiet patience in his eyes. "I don't have a long time."

Wheeler could not speak. One look at his father's face told the whole story. He shook his head. "But why?" He brought his hands up in a gesture of frustration.

"It was so when I came. It was just a chance for some extra time. An escape from the awful situation I was in."

"You knew that when you arrived?"

"I suspected it. I mean, I couldn't really be very upset. The pain was gone. I hoped desperately for a release from where I was, and suddenly I drifted to Vienna. It has been wonderful. I have seen my father. And my mother—" He paused and looked out the window. "My beautiful mother." Then he looked back at Wheeler. "And you. I have had the luxury of knowing my son as a grown man and seeing what a fine person you grew to become. You have not finished telling me about yourself, about how you have been spending your adulthood. You will have to do that soon." He nodded slowly and smiled. "It has been a happy time for me. I do not mind passing slowly away."

"We can get you some help," Wheeler said desperately. "Vienna is a medical center of the world."

Dilly smiled and shook his head slowly. "How would you describe my ailment, let alone my circumstance?" He placed his hand on Wheeler's. "I think you have to accept what is happening and be grateful for the time we have had. You did not know your father, and now you do."

"How can you just accept it? That doesn't sound like the famous Dilly Burden fortitude. Where is all that legendary willpower?"

"There is no alternative," he said, still smiling. "I was given time." He closed his eyes dreamily.

"I am not just going to let you drift off." But Dilly was not listening.

"I have only one regret, you know—"

"I'm going to insist that we get some help. I'm going to take you to Dr. Freud at least."

"I was hoping to see your mother again." His eyes were still closed. "How wonderful that would have been. The crowning glory of this wonderful dream."

Wheeler gave in finally to Dilly's reverie and watched the Danube Canal pass by out the window on the way back to Frau Bauer's, planning how he could get medical help to this man he had grown to love. It occurred to him in that moment and later that he had grown up with the legend of this man, a legend that had always filled him with awe. Now, he had gotten to know the real man underneath, and his affection had grown and deepened. "I think we came here to get to know each other," he said finally.

Dilly took a long appraising look before speaking. "You know," he said, "I think you are right." He was smiling exuberantly.

That same afternoon Wheeler had stopped in at a few banks on the Kartnerstrasse to find out about depositing valuable jewelry for safekeeping. He had stepped into a small street to take a shortcut, hurrying along, not watching ahead, when he looked up to find a man square in his path. Both men stopped short to avoid a collision. He found himself staring into the angry face of Frank Burden. "You!" the younger man exclaimed.

Wheeler stood motionless. "You stole from me," Frank Burden said, with a look of deep hatred in his blue eyes, his hands beginning to shake.

The two men remained paralyzed for a moment, staring into each other's eyes. And then instinct grabbed Wheeler Burden and he bolted sideways, and in a move he had used scores of times as a famous rock-and-roll icon, he flew into a shop doorway, rushed past the few customers to the back and out through the storeroom to the alley, into a neighboring storeroom, out through the new shop door back onto the street, and gone. For a second time, Frank Burden was left behind shaking with a rage that had now become almost uncontrollable.

49

How Like a Nightmare

he story of the child in Lambach must have become for Sigmund Freud a fascinating and disturbing strand, one that he must have resisted pursuing for fear it might hinder the free flowing of the rest of Herr Burden's complex tale, but one that now, after the meetings were no more, he had trouble getting off his mind.

A child with a sinister future, one of mythic proportion, was the antithesis of Hannibal, Theseus, Oedipus, and Joan of Arc, the heroic savior, one who was destined as an adult to pull the whole world into his hatred. How like the archetypal evil one he must have seemed, like the devil, the Antichrist, Beelzebub. "If man creates a perfect god," he would conjecture later, "man must create a perfect evil." It was a story about which Herr Burden seemed to know a good deal and was eager to discuss. It was clearly detailed consistently in the journal, making for meaty analysis. Freud had discovered that the details of myths and dreams and the delusions of hysterical patients all came from the rich and incredibly imaginative material of the human unconscious mind. And the imaginings he now had before him in Herr Burden's complicated fabricated story were the richest he could imagine.

What he could piece together as summary was roughly this. The child, an Austrian, subject of excessive abuse by his father and lack of success in school, grows up to become the tyrannical and charismatic dictator of a unified Germany in the 1930s. Germany, in the meantime, has suffered humiliation and abuse itself after having lost a war in the early 1900s to England, France, and America. The aged empire of Austria-Hungary has completely disintegrated and vanished. Through the use of fear, propaganda, and violence, the demonic leader rallies his fallen country, stimulates industrial and military might, and returns Germany to a position of international power. Once in control of this power he launches a campaign of world conquest and extermination of an obvious scapegoat, the Jews. His actions cause a global war, world conflagration, and an eventual crumbling of his dynasty, but not before he has caused the systematic torture and deaths of millions of undesirables, mostly Jews. In the end, history books depict him as the most evil of figures.

While in so many ways unbelievable and grandiose, the story, a myth of the future, contains within it some fascinating details, projections of Herr Burden's own fears and uncertainties and grandiosities.

The abusive father of the child of Lambach—no doubt abused himself as a child—was a petty civil servant of questionable lineage. He was born out of wedlock with an uncertain father, possibly a wealthy Jewish employer of the mother. It is interesting to point out here that it is not unusual in the case of mythic heroes for the parentage to appear to be mysterious. Moses and Oedipus were both foundlings, raised as princes. In this case, the illegitimate civil servant subjects his young son to regular beatings and humiliations, while the passive mother submits. The son is scarred by the beatings, but also by the tacit approval of the mother. The father, vile perpetrator of the injustices, is held up by family and society as the subject of respect and admiration. The whole world accepts the outrageous injustices as the normal course in life. The abused child becomes both respectful overtly, as the dutiful child, and resentful underneath. In this case, the mythic child of Lambach represses his monumental rage until he rises to power, with epic consequences.

The child dreams of a rise to omnipotence and the ability to turn on the abusive father, but the child of Lambach's father is dead by the time the boy is fourteen, and the rage, which has now reached such enormous proportions, is further repressed until it can find some legitimate outlet for its release.

That outlet comes only when the adult is proclaimed chancellor of Germany. The rage is released against the scapegoated Jews and against the countries that have been strangling the oppressed Germany ever since the unsuccessful war, with catastrophic consequences that destroy cathedrals, cities, and an entire race.

How like our nightmares is this tale. The repressed rage we feel growing inside threatens to set off a world conflagration. Feeling helpless and downtrodden himself, the abused child responds not with sympathy to the downtrodden around him, but with contempt and systematic abuse in much the same way that a beaten child in turn beats his lowly dog. Ever attentive and ever suspicious, the perceptive doctor would be wondering the entire time how this grandiose story related to the humble childhood of the story's teller.

Much as modern Viennese politicians von Schönerer and Lueger have used anti-Semitism as a rallying call for the masses, Herr Burden's mythic twentieth-century demagogue in Germany and Austria used blatant anti-Semitism to rally millions of otherwise disparate non-Jews to his cause. According to Herr Burden's reality, anti-Semitism became so extreme in Germany in the 1930s that Jews were taunted and beaten in the streets by special police. A Jew coming home with a bottle of milk, helpless to protect himself, could expect to have the contents of the bottle poured on his head by a brown-shirted trooper, in much the same way that a child is helpless before the tyrannies of the abusive but enfranchised parent. Jews learned to submit quietly rather than risk further injury and death.

Then, according to the patient's tale, Jews were rounded up and shipped in cattle cars to extermination camps in Poland, designed as a final solution by the child of Lambach whose hatred has found ultimate and terrifying release. The malevolent leader is quoted at one point as saying, "If the Jews had not existed, we would have had to invent them." But what is anti-Semitism if it is not hatred of the Jew in oneself?

Dr. Freud would have found particularly interesting in the patient's tale that this leader was purportedly unable to have normal sexual relations. He developed such a bizarre set of sexual practices—involving being urinated on before he could attain satisfaction—that he never married or produced children of his own to abuse.

What is hatred but repressed rage at the parent? Here we have a mythic character whose repressed anger and sense of humiliation was so great that it could poison a whole nation and nearly destroy the world. And there is more.

Herr Burden even draws a number of comparisons between this mythical Hitler and the Archduke Rudolf. Claiming to have facts at his disposal not available to the general public in 1897, he speculates on the nature of the relationship between the crown prince and his father, the Emperor Franz Joseph. Apparently, Rudolf, a liberal, wished to lead Austria-

Hungary away from dependence on Germany. He hated the young, belligerent Kaiser Wilhelm, his cousin, and wanted to move toward alliances with France and an embracing of the Slavic influences throughout the empire. The conservative father found his son's overtures offensive and thwarted him, rebuking and humiliating him publicly. Filled with frustration and self-loathing Rudolf killed himself, in the ultimate omnipotent act of self-destruction and revenge against the harsh father. Rudolf's self-hatred is simply hatred of his father?

A sensitive and artistic young man, Rudolf destroyed himself instead of waiting patiently to gain control of the whole Hapsburg empire. The mythical child of Lambach, born humbly, would rise to power on his own initiative and destroy a nation and a race in the process. How similar they are, and how revealing of the damaged psyche of the storyteller.

And what of this child of Lambach himself? Did such a child actually exist? Is there in such a child an innate goodness that is slowly being eroded and reshaped by his base treatment, or does he possess from the start an innate evil that fate and circumstance simply put in the right place at the right time? By age ten is it perhaps too late to change the direction in which his life will run, or would it be possible to lift the child out of his base circumstance and place him in a foster home where love and affectionate attention could perhaps nurture in him compassion and empathy?

Freud must have given much thought to his duty in this case. He knew enough to believe that this Adolf Hitler was in fact a real young man in Lambach and that Herr Burden and a colleague had paid the young man an anonymous visit. If either man wished to do ill to this child of supposed evil destiny, should Freud intercede in the child's behalf?

On the other hand, Herr Burden is faced with an intriguing moral dilemma. According to the patient's tale, both he and his colleague believe that the child in Lambach is in fact the childlike manifestation of the man who will bring so much harm and evil to the world. Imagine having that power and knowledge. Imagine similarly a man of 1897 finding himself in Corsica in 1775 in the presence of the child Napoleon Bonaparte. Could he not save the world much bloodshed and agony by putting an end to the child's life, right then and there? Would he in fact change history, or would another character with similar motives and aspirations, perhaps even worse, rise up to fill the void? Would he have an obligation to allow history to unfold as it was intended without taking any action whatsoever?

For most of us these thoughts are only romantic conjecture, but for someone who believes he has traveled back in time they are part of the awful reality offered up by the unconscious psyche. Knowing that one were in the presence of such a child would give one the potential for real action that the rest of us would treat only in dreams and nightmares.

How, even after the cessation of their meetings, Dr. Freud must have been drawn back involuntarily, again and again, to the conversations with his most unusual guest and the details and nuances of his most unusual journal. And how, completely against his will, again and again, the great doctor must have been compelled to speculate about the inner turmoil that necessitated the creation of such a child and such a complex and haunting tale.

50

Woman of Substance

heeler felt the strongest urge to take Weezie away from Vienna. He proposed that they spend a few days in the nearby resort town of Baden.

"With whom as chaperone?" she said pertly when he first suggested it. Wheeler only looked at her, and she caught herself, blushing slightly. "A proper young lady does not travel without a chaperone," she said quickly, covering her naïveté. Then she looked down. "I suppose the rules of what a young lady does or does not do have been suspended somewhat."

"I don't mean to push you," Wheeler said apologetically. "It's just that Vienna is feeling awfully confined right now, and I would like to get away with you. If you can't do it, I certainly understand, and—"

She cut him off. "I want very much to go away with you. It is just an adjustment, that's all. My head is in two places these days. Part of me is back as a little sheltered Victorian girl from Boston, and part of me is a newly minted woman of substance in a brave new world."

"We could be there in a little over an hour by train. There is a quiet secluded hotel near the baths. And lots of beautiful walks."

"It would be good to leave Vienna for a while. I will have to tell Fraulein Tatlock I am visiting friends of Father. I hope she is not too inquisitive."

Wheeler smiled. "I don't think Fraulein Tatlock was born yesterday." He rose. "I need to make arrangements of my own. I will pick you up in two hours."

She looked sheepish again. "Don't you think I had better meet you at the station?"

"Of course," Wheeler said. "You're getting better at this than I am."

He waited at the station for twenty minutes, watching the large minute hand on the station clock coming closer and closer to train time. Then he saw her enter through the large west door, not seeing him at first, looking around the expansive interior of the station. She was carrying a small suitcase.

"I thought you had stood me up," he said, approaching her.

"I nearly did. Three times I leaned forward to tell the cab driver to turn around."

"I'm glad you didn't." He took her bag. "We will have to hurry."

"I did not know how to dress, or how to look for such an occasion." They were walking briskly toward the platform.

"You have two choices. Blushing bride or bossy wife."

"What about brazen strumpet?"

Wheeler deflected the remark with a gentle laugh. Somehow he could not think of her as a woman of easy virtue.

"I hate being so torn," she said, once they were seated and the train was under way. "I feel like such a featherhead, not being able to make up my mind."

"Between what and what?"

"Between doing what is proper and—" She wrinkled her nose. "And doing this." She was sitting erect, not touching the seatback. "I just wish I would either drop this whole business with you or accept it for what it is. I just keep vacillating back and forth like a reed in the wind. One minute feeling daring and exciting and the next minute overcome by guilt."

"And what are you feeling right now?"

"The latter." She had turned away to hide the tears in her eyes. "I think this is a terrible idea. I have ever since you left the café. I wanted so to tell you I would not be coming. It made me feel low and degraded to carry my bag downstairs at Fraulein Tatlock's and to lie to her about where I was going. I wanted so to send a note to say I would not be joining you."

Wheeler tried to hide the sinking feeling. "I'm sorry," he said. "I didn't mean to put you in a difficult position."

"I just wish I understood it." Impatience crackled in her voice. "Even as I tell you this, I do not find myself convincing. I am not very happy with myself for showing such poor resolve."

He watched her until she turned to him. "I am very glad you didn't turn back, and I think you show excellent resolve."

"Because I choose to do what you want." There was a touch of defiance now in her voice.

"No. Because you do what you want."

"And you think I want to degrade myself."

"No. I think you want to discover yourself."

They rode through the countryside, both watching out the window, she sitting erect and proper in her seat. "How does one sleep?" she said suddenly, catching Wheeler off guard.

"How do you mean?" He looked up to find her blushing.

"In these arrangements," she said. "How does one sleep?"

"The usual way, I suppose."

"I mean if one is proper."

"Well, in that case, I suppose, in separate rooms."

"And if one is a sensualist, how then?"

"Well, I believe sensualists would sleep side by side, without clothing."

She looked down, and Wheeler thought perhaps that she had taken offense. "Would you like separate rooms?" he said, as sensitively as he could.

"That would be a waste of resources," she said properly.

"I could have a portable bed brought to the room."

"No," she said, looking very serious and determined. "I would prefer side by side and without clothing."

They had ascended the path to the Rudolfshof Restaurant at the top of the Thereinwarte, overlooking the town below. "So, here we are in the middle of an illicit rendezvous," Weezie said suddenly. "Do you suppose that everyone seeing us knows what we are doing?"

"Do you notice people staring at us, as if we are something terribly out of the ordinary?"

"Well, no, I haven't noticed that. But one still feels self-conscious."

"Has it occurred to you that perhaps the other people you are referring to are too concerned about their own intrigues to notice anyone else's?"

That made her smile. "You are so good at seeing the lightness in all things. I do so appreciate that." She paused as they walked along. "But still there are thoughts and worries that one cannot keep from revisiting."

"Perhaps those are the ones asking to be reexamined."

"Oh my," she said in a little gasp. "That is awfully modern."

"Well, it is true. Let's try one."

Weezie took a deep breath. "All right," she said, summoning up her courage. "I keep reliving the awful scene with Herr Mahler. I can't seem to get it out of my mind. I cringe when I think of the embarrassment."

"Why do you think you fainted?"

"I cannot say. I just felt a rush in my head, and the next minute I was looking up at Herr Mahler and the maid from the chaise."

"What was happening as you began to swoon?"

"He was showing me his music."

"Tell me the details."

"I had been standing beside him at the piano as he leafed through the sheets of music. He picked up one and began telling me about it, pointing out notes on the melody. I think he was assuming I was far more facile at reading music than I am."

"Did he touch you?"

"He was leaning toward me. I could feel his arm against mine."

"And he was pointing with his finger?"

"No," she said, struggling to recall. "He had picked up a bone and he was pointing with it, tapping the sheet music. I think he was very excited—"

"Wait," Wheeler said. "He was pointing with a bone?"

"No," she said impatiently. "I said his baton."

"Go on," Wheeler said.

"He was tapping his baton on the sheet music and directing my eyes to the lines of melody, and I couldn't focus on them. They began to swim in front of me."

"He was leaning into you, excited."

"He was very intent on having me see exactly what he had tried to do with his music. It was a Hungarian folk piece, and he wanted me to see how he had arranged the counterpoint."

"He was attracted to you."

"No. He was showing me the music." She was looking a little flushed. "I was trying to follow, but I couldn't keep up."

"Think about how he was touching you."

"It was just his arm against mine. Pressing closer so that I would follow his words. I could smell his breath."

"And he leaned closer."

She was looking very uncomfortable now. "His arm was against mine, and I could feel his side against mine. He is not a very large man. I mean he is wiry."

"You felt his leg against yours?"

Perspiration had formed on her brow. "I think we must stop talking." She reached for the glass of ice water.

"You felt him pressing against you as he tapped the sheet music."

"I was trying to concentrate on the music. His words were enthralling. This was the great Gustav Mahler, and he was explaining to me how his melodies worked, and I tried to concentrate on his words, but I couldn't. All I could feel was his breath, and—"

"Him pressing against you?"

"Yes. I wanted to stop. I wanted to see the music, but I couldn't. I wanted to back away, but I couldn't. And my head began to swim and my knees buckled, and—" She stopped, looking puzzled. "His arm," she said suddenly. "I didn't fall to the floor. His arm caught me. His arm had been around me. As I swooned, I felt him catch me. His arm—"

"Go on."

"He had placed his arm around me, and his hand. His hand had slipped around—"

"Go on."

"My head swam. It is not very clear. I can't really remember it very well."

"His hand had slipped around, you said." Wheeler was not letting her off.

She struggled with the memory, fighting through layers of cobwebs. "He tapped the paper with the baton, and his words were getting more and more excited. He pulled me toward the music with his arm around me, and I tried to follow."

"And his hand?"

"His hand had slipped from my shoulder. He was so very much involved in telling me about the music, he was not aware of what he was doing. And I was beginning to swoon, and his hand slipped—"

"Keep going. Where was his hand?"

"It had slipped to my bodice." Wheeler didn't speak. He just watched her running the thought through her head.

"What was going on?"

She seemed to be struggling. "He was excited about the music—" Wheeler wouldn't take his eyes off her. "Herr Mahler was showing me—" Finally, she closed her eyes and pursed her lips. When she opened them, there was in them a new clarity. "Herr Mahler was seducing me."

⟋☉⟋

"Why did I not remember?" she said later. "I honestly did not remember those details. It was like complete amnesia."

"And now?"

"Now they are clear as day. I was standing beside him and he came closer and closer and put his arm around me and I started to swoon. His arm was around me and his hand moved to my bodice."

"Bodice?"

"To my breast." She smiled. "It is all so easy to say now that I have said it before."

"You are a very attractive woman," Wheeler said. "Herr Mahler is a very temperamental and artistic man. He made a pass, we would say in California."

She wrinkled her brow. "But why did I not remember it that way? There are whole sections I just did not remember. And now they are lucid and clear."

"There is more," Wheeler said.

⟋☉⟋

They had acquired a room in a hotel near the river. Weezie had stayed in the café while Wheeler had secured the room under the name Mr. and Mrs. Harry Truman. He and Weezie had walked quickly through the lobby and up the stairs. She sat on a cushion on the window seat where she had been for the better part of an hour. "I keep going back to my aunt Prudence."

"She is an awful woman."

"She meant well," Weezie said quickly in defense.

"I don't think you have to stand up for her. She sounds harsh and cruel and unfair to a child."

"She meant well—" Weezie began again, and then stopped. "She was harsh and cruel." She said it matter-of-factly, as if it felt good. "That is exactly what she was. And it is funny. I have never said that to anyone."

"It feels pretty good, doesn't it?"

"Yes, it does. Aunt Prudence was harsh and cruel and unfair to a child." She paused and looked down, as if knowing that more was expected of her at that moment. "She was dreadfully unfair to *me*." The silence that ensued let the words settle, and then she began a gentle laugh. "And furthermore, she was a—"

"Go on," Wheeler said, smiling at her mirth. "Exactly what was she?"

Weezie ceased her laughter, pulled herself up, and spoke with schoolgirl diction. "She was a witch."

"Are you sure?" Wheeler probed now in mock seriousness.

"Absolutely," she said, throwing her head back, laughing. "She was definitely a witch. She kept a broomstick in the closet."

She told in great detail the incident with the soap, how she had heard the story from the girls at Winsor School and how she had mentioned it at the dinner table and how Aunt Prudence had reacted and the awful taste of soap in her mouth.

"How did your mother die?" Wheeler said suddenly.

"Diphtheria," she said without thinking. Then she looked amused with herself. "You know for years I thought she died from eating chicken at a picnic. I was only eight, you know, and I guess no one bothered to explain it to me."

"Eating chicken?"

"Swallowing a bone. In fact, sometimes I have to catch myself even now. That image was so clear to me."

"Of dying from swallowing a bone?"

"I know it's odd. Just one of those things a little girl misconstrues, I guess. Someone must have said something to me that suggested it."

"What did the older girls say in the hallway at Winsor School?"

Weezie looked puzzled. "They said, 'Maybe she swallowed his bone.'"

"Do you know what they were talking about?"

She looked at him disgusted. "Well, I do now," she said disdainfully. "I didn't then."

"And they said you'd find out soon enough?" Weezie nodded. "And that evening you asked at the dinner table." Weezie nodded. "What did you ask exactly?"

"I told you. I asked what *ardor* meant."

"And your aunt hauled you off to the bathroom for the soap treatment?" Weezie nodded again. "Isn't that awfully harsh for one word? Even the Puritans used the word *ardor* in public." She looked puzzled again. "Put yourself there again. Think about it."

"We were eating roast beef and Yorkshire pudding. I remember that. My father had just said he thought his sermon would be on forgiveness, and the thought just came to me. I asked it."

"How did you say it?"

Weezie closed her eyes tightly. "I put my fork down. I reached for a glass of water," she said slowly. "I said I had a question from school, and my father looked over at me and asked what it was. And I said—" She fought to recall it accurately. "I asked it."

"And exactly what did you ask?"

Weezie paused and looked puzzled for a moment. "You know I don't remember." Then she spoke after another pause, curious about what came out. "I said, 'What is a man's bone?'"

"And that is what sent your Aunt Prudence into a rage?"

"That's it."

"And what did she say when she washed your mouth out?"

"She said that Mother was willful and asked if I knew what God brought her?"

"And you thought she died from eating a bone?"

Weezie shook her head. It was going too fast. "The bar of soap, and the swallowing of the bone and the willfulness, and the picnic," she said in little more than a mumble.

"Your aunt told you. She said God killed your mother."

"She said it was her willfulness."

"You were eight at the time. You heard the older girls' story."

"The dream. I go into the dark basement and my mother is in white at a picnic. She invites me to join her, and then she chokes on the piece of chicken."

"You want to join your mother."

"Yes."

"She is in light, at the picnic, the antithesis of your Aunt Prudence's darkness and black. She calls you to her. What did your aunt say killed your mother?"

He paused.

"Willfulness."

"Keep going."

"The bone the girls were talking about."

"Keep going."

Weezie wrinkled her brow again, then a light came into her face. She shook her head. "Sexual intercourse," she said slowly. "It's the one thing Aunt Prudence never had." She looked up. "The witch made me believe that sexual intercourse killed my mother."

It was now late at night. Weezie had not moved from her place at the window seat. Wheeler was lying on his back sideways on the bed, looking up at the ceiling but listening to her attentively. She had gone over and over the details of how she had structured her own story from the events and from what her aunt had told her over the years. She had pieced together the very complicated sequence of incidents that had led her to believe that her mother's sexuality had been both her great life force and the cause of her death. The force had drawn her toward it and repelled her. It had drawn her to Wheeler. It had drawn her into Herr Mahler's advances and thrown her into a deathlike swoon. It had driven her out of the carriage and away from Vienna that night after the opera. And it had pulled her back.

The puzzle was close to finished, waiting for the last fateful piece. Weezie's face was drawn; her voice was without emotion, as she worked her way in the dimly lit hotel room. She went quiet for a long time. Then suddenly she spoke. "I am ready," she said, and Wheeler rose from the bed and came over beside her.

"I was in bed," she said. She closed her eyes. The words came without expression. "I had been there for over an hour, unable to sleep, thinking about princesses in airy castles. I heard the footsteps on the stairs and thought it unusual because Father had already kissed me good night. The door creaked open and he said my name. I answered. He came over to my bedside, but did not turn on the gaslight. Light from the street came in the window and I could see his sad, careworn face. I was so happy he had come into my room. The times without Aunt Prudence between us, watching everything I said and did, were rare. 'Sugar Plum,' he said, 'I am so very lonely.' I could smell that he had been drinking, and he slurred his words, but I had become accustomed to that in the year or so following Mother's death. I had also become aware of the sadness in Father's face, and I would have done anything for him to make it go away. He touched my forehead, and I felt the sadness in his cold hands. 'I am so very lonely,' he kept repeating. I wanted so very, very much to take away the grief that had sat on him now for so long and that gave him so little reprieve. He lay down beside me and was still for a long time. I did not move, but I wanted to hold him, to make him whole again.'"

She stopped. The air in the room was dark and heavy. Wheeler did not move or speak. She was long past needing any prompting from him. "I hardly knew what was happening. It was not sudden or violent. I only knew that Father had come to me for the first time and the last time. It happened and I knew what the bone was and I could tell that Father knew it had killed Mother. And after he left I knew it would kill me. And as I lay there in the darkness waiting for death I hoped I would see Mother, and I hoped for Father to find peace."

Her hands were covering her face now and she wept, at first softly, and then with a wrenching violence that racked her body. It was some time before Wheeler moved to her and held her in his arms in the dim light of a rented hotel room in Baden in the year 1897. She wept in his arms, at first convulsively, then gently, before falling into a deep and peaceful sleep.

On the train ride back to Vienna they sat across from each other, the only two passengers in their first-class cabin. Wheeler could not take his eyes off Weezie as she stared out the window with a soft smile on her lips. "What are you thinking?" he said.

She turned her head ever so slowly, pulling herself back from a distant reverie. "It is hard to explain," she said, "but for the first time in my life I can remember the golden years with Mother, without the black cloud. It's as if the darkness has lifted."

Wheeler could not help smiling. "That's the way it is supposed to work."

"You did it for me." There was a look of the deepest love in her eyes.

"I didn't," Wheeler said. "And I'm not being humble or coy. You did it for yourself. The hero must go it alone. That's one of the oldest stories in the world. You searched in the corners and found what needed to be found. I just handed you the lantern."

"I love you very, very much."

Wheeler looked a little uneasy. "You know, you're supposed to separate the two—the guide and the lover."

"I think that is too sophisticated for me. I just know I am not the same person I was, and it is only because of you. And what we have shared physically. I do love it so! Too much, I fear. It is such a wonderfully powerful part. I cannot imagine one without the other. You have opened me up, and I love you for that, and I will love you forever. I am absolutely, absolutely certain of that." She refused to look away. "I will love you forever, no matter what you are or what you do or where you go."

For the first time, Weezie was beginning to sense Wheeler's unusual circumstances. For a moment he just looked into her eyes. "There is something I want you to have." He reached into his coat pocket and pulled out the packet in the embroidered handkerchief. "This was given to me by a very special person. I would like you to have it and keep it to remember this time. No matter."

Weezie took the packet apprehensively and slowly and carefully peeled back the layers of fine linen. When she came to the last layer, through which she could see an image of the contents, she let out a little gasp and looked up at Wheeler with an expression he would choose to remember forever, one of love and wonder. "What is it?" she said, lifting the last fold.

The sight of the ring brought from her chest now an almost imperceptible sigh. She held it in her hand like a wonderfully colored bird, examining the details before speaking. "It's incredibly beautiful."

"You'll keep it then?" Wheeler said. "No matter."

Her voice was still more like a sigh. "No matter."

51

The Legend of Dilly Burden

ren't you angry about the way it turned out?" Wheeler said, as they sat in Dilly's small room, Dilly on the bed and Wheeler on a chair beside the bureau. Dilly had not mentioned his condition again, but the dark shadows under his eyes had deepened and he seemed depleted of his usual boundless energy.

"You mean the deception, the Churchill stuff?"

"Well, your own side did turn you over to the Gestapo."

"For a greater cause," he said with a shrug. "They knew I would crack. They knew the Gestapo would believe me because I believed. That was a brilliant strategy—a little diabolical perhaps—"

"A little!"

"—but look at all the lives it saved."

"But you were a pawn. You, the great Dilly Burden, of all people."

"Your mother pointed out that I was a pawn all along. The people of St. Gregory's School needed a schoolboy hero to prove that their narrow way of looking at the world was right and proper. Then at Harvard I played into similar hands, always wanting to prove myself within the system, the system that had been around for three hundred years. My making such a success out of my career made the complacent old fogies even more complacent. God really did go to Harvard. I was a pawn in a huge game, and it didn't really matter what I thought my duty was, the outcome was inevitable. My 'rigid sense of duty'—as your mother called it—was my blinders. It kept me seeing the world the way I wanted it and kept me from looking into the heart of darkness."

"And a cell in Gestapo headquarters changed that?"

"You have a lot of time to think." He looked away. "I kept wondering how they could do what they were doing. Torturing adults is one thing, but I heard they were torturing children! That was it for me, thinking about the children. And then I began thinking about Hitler—the king of the darkness and about finding him as a child. And I thought of my awful last conversation with my father." Dilly went silent for a moment, then looked over at Wheeler. "I told you I had thought of Vienna because of Mother," he said, "but that was not really the case. It started because of Hitler. I reconstructed Vienna in my mind because I wanted to put my fingers around his scrawny little neck and squeeze the life out of him.

"That torture is awful stuff. You've got to do something to keep your mind off it, so I just thought more and more about him and then about him as an eight-year-old child, and then about Vienna. Pretty soon it occupied my every moment, reconstructing the details of this time and place and piecing together all that my mother and the Haze had told me." He raised his hands and gestured out to the world of Vienna in 1897. "I created the Ringstrasse. That was it, the Ringstrasse. I re-created the buildings, the trees, the parks, the music, the food. I began to imagine my father and my mother, as they would have been as young adults.

"It was like a detailed journal in my head. I wrote in it painstakingly page by page every day, giving lifelike details to each person—the coffeehouse intellectuals, the famous men like Freud and Mahler, my father, my mother, and you. I even imagined the story that my mother used to tell about a meeting with Gustav Mahler and how she fainted dead away from the shock."

Wheeler's eyes had not moved from his father's face. He watched him with complete attention. "And pretty soon I couldn't tell fact from fantasy. And pretty soon—"

"You were actually here," Wheeler said.

"Exactly. I had to pinch myself."

"But you were actually in Vienna."

"That's right," Dilly said. "And then I realized how much I had botched it."

"How's that?"

"I should have spent my time calling up your mother. How I would love to see her!"

"And you realize it will not be too long until 1914 when I am reborn—" Dilly continued a while later. He frowned and looked over at Wheeler. "Unless you have fouled that up with all your attention. You know," he said, frowning, "you really should have stayed far away from her."

"You know about that?"

"I know enough," Dilly said.

Wheeler looked down at his feet, but couldn't hold it for long. "It is worse than you think," he said, looking Dilly in the eye.

Dilly snapped his head around and glared at Wheeler, and then saw too much written in his son's face. "Oh Jesus," he said. "How long?"

"Quite a while."

"And how bad?"

Wheeler grimaced. "Pretty deep, I fear."

"Does Frank Burden know?"

"He's seen us together, I think."

"Oh lord," Dilly said, rolling his eyes. "You certainly have a feel for drama."

"There's more." Wheeler looked into Dilly's pale face. "I ran into him. He seemed pretty angry."

Dilly frowned. "That's great," he said in a rare moment of sarcasm. "That'll fix things up just fine." Then he thought for a long moment. "I guess I have created a monster. I just needed a way to get out of my cell at Gestapo headquarters, and look what we have now."

Wheeler became aware suddenly that Dilly was not angry that he and Weezie had become intimate, and the reason was beginning to sink in. "You really think you created all this, that you gave it all life?"

A spark had come back into Dilly's tired eyes. "I did. It has all been my doing." And in that moment Wheeler saw the greatness of the man who had been held up as a hero throughout his life, the father he had never known except in legend. Dilly Burden, the hero of St. Greg's School, Harvard College, and World War II, created his own world. Confronted with schoolboy sports he learned the games with such thoroughness that he dominated them. Confronted with academic subjects, he created new orders. Confronted with music, he played the clarinet in a way few people had heard before. Confronted with the defeat and humiliation of Nazi extermination, he created his own world in the romantic past. Not Vienna as it had been, but Vienna as he wanted to see it.

"And then it became *reality*!" Dilly's eyes flashed now. "I created it all. The city from my mother's stories, from the Haze's lessons, the famous people from books and journals." Now the frown returned to his face. He stopped for a moment and took a drink of water. "But it all started for one reason."

"So you could escape," Wheeler said hopefully, to show he was following. "So you could step out of your wretched cell."

There was a hardness in his face now. "So I could track down the demon child—" He looked away, then returned to Wheeler's eyes. "And strangle him. I surprised myself with the power of my own hatred."

Seeing the pain in Dilly's face, Wheeler offered what solace he could. "You did track him down, and you didn't strangle him."

"When we went to Lambach, I intended to do it. I was going to walk up to him wherever I ran into him and lock my hands on to his neck. I figured he would be dead before you could pry me loose."

Wheeler thought for a moment. "You didn't really intend to do it, though."

Dilly looked puzzled. "How can you say that?"

"You invited me to go along. That was your safety valve, your way of insuring yourself that you would not go through with it."

"On the contrary," Dilly said with simple conviction. "I brought you along to keep reminding me of the reality of what I was doing. I was afraid that when I arrived and saw that he was just a child that I would not be able to conceive of him as the Hitler of history. You were my link with that reality."

"Then why didn't you do anything?"

Dilly shook his head. "I intended to. I tried, but he had too good a defense even my hatred could not penetrate, the ultimate shield."

"And what is that?"

"He was, after all, a child."

Wheeler was beginning a thought. "You were on a mission, weren't you?"

"That's what I've been trying to tell you."

"You had an obligation to do it." Wheeler appeared fascinated, taking in the aura of this man who all his life had been his legendary, larger-than-life father.

"You mean it is all willpower?" Wheeler said, with a flash of insight. "If only you want it badly enough, you can get it, and you wanted out of that awful torture, so you willed all this."

Dilly tried to shrug off Wheeler's directness. "Well," he stammered slightly, "if you put it that directly. Yes."

Wheeler smiled and shook his head. "That's it." And then he repeated, "That's it."

"That's what?"

"The heroics. All my life I've been trying to figure out why my father was such a hero, why he did the incredible things he did." Wheeler tapped his temple with his index finger. "I was trying to figure out what was going on in my father's head. And now I get it."

Dilly looked uncomfortably amused. "Well, you might as well tell me."

"It's a matter of will," Wheeler said. "You really think you can control the world around you. You thought you were responsible for what went on around you. If something went right, it was your doing. If it went wrong, it was your doing."

"Well, that's a bit extreme—"

Wheeler cut him off, a real spark of discovery now burning in his eyes. "You thought it was all up to you. I mean, a lot of people think they are powerless in their lives, and you thought you had all the power." He paused and looked into his father's face, his expression changing to one of compassion. "That must have been a great weight."

Dilly looked away, at first shaking his head slowly. "You are quite something," he said softly. "So like your mother."

"And like my father."

Dilly turned with a quizzical look. "How so?"

"In trying to find out what made my father tick, I was trying to figure out myself. I was always different from the rest of the children. I couldn't just put my hands in my pockets and walk around like one of the guys. I was always getting myself into trouble by doing something crazy. You were the hero, and I was the eccentric, but don't you see, it was the same thing. We both thought we could change the world around us. We both had the same curse."

Dilly nodded slowly. "And you know what it was, don't you?" Wheeler said. "We thought we were omnipotent."

Separately, Wheeler had arranged to meet them in the studio. He told Weezie outright that he had someone he wanted her to meet. He had told Dilly simply to meet him at the studio at eleven in the morning. Since their escape to Baden, Weezie had glowed with a newfound confidence. She seemed no longer to hold him in awe, but to treat him as an old friend, with the utmost deference and respect, but also with a kind of profound intimacy. "You have seen into the darkest corners of my soul," she told him.

"Once you get in there and light a few torches," Wheeler said, "there's not much to be ashamed of, or to be intrigued by."

"Will I soon be so exposed that I will lose all interest for you?"

Wheeler laughed. "I am interested in you fatally," he said, and she told him he had a peculiar choice of words.

"I cannot believe how talking about the dark and sinister things robs them of their power. As soon as I called Aunt Prudence a witch—a bit of an exaggeration, I fear—she seemed to vanish. Herr Mahler made an advance—" She smiled gently. "Or I imagined it—"

"I don't think you imagined it. It sounds as if Herr Mahler made a first-degree move on your breasts."

"And that is not so terrible, is it? My mother was a perfectly normal woman with a bright and cheery extroversion who died sadly by a chance encounter with diphtheria. I can even talk about the other incident—" She looked down.

"You need to call it 'the other incident'?"

"I can talk about it. It's just not until after luncheon." She smiled and then grew wistful. "It was terrible on my father. He never forgave himself." Then her face lifted up. "He could never talk about it. With all that guilt he must have been hounded terribly. If he could have just looked me in the eye and admitted it and told me how sorry he was."

"People aren't that way," Wheeler said. "The worse things are, the deeper they bury them."

She looked at him lovingly. "How did you become so wise?"

Wheeler laughed. "I'm eccentric, not wise. And besides, I didn't invent the idea, you know. It comes from right here in Vienna."

"And it has reached as far as San Francisco?" She looked at him for a moment. "When I ran away from Vienna that morning after the night in the cab, I thought some dark thoughts about you. You seem to know so much and seem to be so open; it is as if you are from another planet or another time. I thought for a while that you were indeed the devil incarnate that Aunt Prudence talked so much about and was ever on the lookout for."

"Why did we ever invent the devil? Doesn't that strike you as peculiar?"

"Still there are things about you I cannot account for. It seems as if you were sent."

"Sent?" Wheeler said, looking surprised.

"Yes, sent. To free me from the dark corners. For the better, I assume."

"I can't imagine who would choose me to send."

"You've had the effect of someone sent."

"Sent by whom?"

"I don't know," Weezie said, squirming charmingly. "By whomever it is who sends. By my guardian angel."

"That settles it," Wheeler said with conviction. "No guardian angel in clear conscience would send me."

"Well, anyway, I feel the recipient of whatever it is people get sent for. I feel—" She searched for the right word. "Blessed." Their eyes met, and Wheeler could not look away.

"Thank you," he said genuinely. "I feel a little blessed myself," and he leaned forward to kiss her.

There was a knock on the door. Wheeler rose quickly and opened it, and Dilly walked in. He was looking drawn and tired but determined to carry on, wearing all over his face the fact that he had no idea what was coming.

"What's up for this morning?" he said, bouncing forward into the room and stopping dead when he came into view of Weezie, standing by the window. Wheeler moved behind him to prevent any retreat.

"There is someone I've been dying for you to meet," Wheeler said cheerfully, before Dilly could say anything. "This is Weezie Putnam from Boston." Wheeler made a gracious sweeping gesture toward her. "My friend Herbert Hoover," he said, "from California, also."

Dilly glared at Wheeler, but there was nothing he could do. He was already fully in the room thanks to the pushing from behind. Weezie had stepped forward with her hand outstretched. She was looking absolutely radiant.

"Hello, Mr. Hoover," she said. "I am so happy to meet you."

Dilly took her hand. "Miss Putnam." He shook it tentatively, his eyes so fixed on her beautiful face that he didn't notice the paintings. "Harry has told me so much about you." Perhaps she could not hear the annoyance in his voice.

"I have told Mr. Hoover about your virtuosity on the cello," Wheeler said quickly. "He was wondering if you would consent to play a bit with him and me. Mr. Hoover is an enthusiast for the clarinet." Dilly frowned, but Wheeler had already moved over behind the easel where he had stored the instruments he had borrowed. "I happen to have the necessary weapons over here."

Dilly forced a smile. "We have a small piece of business to conduct first," he said. "Perhaps we could step out into the hall."

He motioned to Wheeler to follow him out the door, and when they were out of earshot of Weezie, he attacked in a loud whisper. "Listen, fellow, this is not funny." He pointed his index finger at Wheeler's chest. "You are playing with fire here."

"I wanted you to meet her," Wheeler said in his own loud whisper.

"You should be staying far away from her, and I certainly shouldn't be anywhere near her."

"You said you found her fascinating."

Dilly looked as if he might explode. "I really don't believe what you have done. You just think you can do anything you damn well please."

"I don't think I can do anything I damn well please, but I don't like avoiding what is good in life because of unnecessary rules."

"And you call tampering with the future harmless fun, I suppose."

"It won't do any harm for us to spend some time together. She doesn't know who we are. What harm can it do?" He tugged Dilly's arm. "Now come on."

Dilly pulled his arm free. "What harm?" He looked incredulous. "Existence, my friend. That's all."

"What happens happens."

"I see," Dilly said. "You're willing to obliterate yourself. All you need to do is destroy the chance of my being born, and bingo, that takes care of you, no matter who's biological son you are. I am not going to contaminate destiny."

Wheeler looked at him consolingly. "Things are already contaminated. We might as well enjoy ourselves."

Dilly looked exasperated. "Don't you have even a modicum of respect for limits?"

"Come on," he said, pulling him back to where Weezie was standing looking out the window. She turned.

"Is everything all right?" she said. But Dilly was now preoccupied with something new. He stood inside the door, seeing for the first time the riot of color and sensuality in the studio's decorations. He stood transfixed.

Wheeler had found a piece by Vivaldi, written for three strings. Dilly played hesitantly, not wanting to give anything of himself that was not absolutely required by the circumstance. Wheeler noticed that he kept from looking at Weezie. It was so obvious that at one point she looked over at Dilly as they played and made a wry face as if to say, "What is wrong with your friend?"

"Let's improvise," Wheeler said. He picked out the melody on the treble strings of the guitar.

As he played, Weezie picked it up with the cello. Dilly sat immobile. Finally, Weezie looked at him. "Come on," she said with a smile that could have melted Gibraltar, "join in."

The first few notes out of the clarinet were hoarse and raspy, but then he slid into second gear and worked his way through to the refrain. Weezie joined in, and Wheeler began picking out a counterpoint. Suddenly, Dilly raised his clarinet and reached for the third above the melody, and they had a trio going. Weezie caught Wheeler's eye and gestured to Dilly. His eyes were closed. He was lost in the music, and from his clarinet was flowing the popular sweet soft sound that had won him his wings with his legendary Charles River Boys and captured the attention of the legendary Benny Goodman. "Keep it going," Wheeler said, when they came to the end, and they were rolling again.

Weezie, who had never heard such music, kept her eyes on Dilly until he opened his. As much as he did not want to look at her, she had him in her sights, mesmerized by the sounds she was hearing, sounds that hinted to her the directions things would go after Mahler, the exposure that would later anchor her treatise on Vienna music. The "modern" clarinetist, the protégé of Benny Goodman, tried to look away, but it was no good. Dilly Burden smiled back at his mother, who was enthralled, drawn into the musical style she had never even dreamed of. "That's it," she gasped, totally enthralled by the beautiful young man, and the improvisation. "So that is where our music is headed." It came to her in a flash.

That night as Wheeler was preparing for bed he noticed that his journal was missing. He looked for it everywhere. He even walked over to the Café Central to see if he had left it there. Losing it had given him a cold clammy feeling, and he was about to spend an agonizing sleepless night when he remembered very vividly laying it on a table in the studio as he was picking up the instruments to cart them back to the music store.

He rose at his usual hour the next morning and had a short breakfast before heading over to the studio. He let himself in and walked to the table where he knew it would be. There was no journal. A cold terror grabbed at his gut as he turned slowly to the window seat where Weezie had sat that first day, looking like a painting by Vermeer.

She sat gazing at him with a curiously vacant expression. All the color seemed gone from her face. In her lap, opened to the middle pages was his journal.

"Have you read it?" he said, a painfully obvious question. She nodded. "The whole thing?"

She nodded gently and continued her vacant stare. "I stayed up most of the night," she said. "From cover to cover."

52

What Had to Happen

I have to admit it," Dilly said, looking pale and drawn, standing beside the bed in his rented room, "that music was beautiful." He reconsidered. "No, it was better than beautiful." He was picking up steam. "It was jim dandy. It has given me a whole new lease on life."

"I thought you were going to shoot me," Wheeler said, now sitting on the bed beside him.

"It was the right thing to do. Everything is the right thing to do. The future will be the future. For things to turn out as they did, for Mother. This is what had to happen."

"Everything?"

"Everything! She told me that in confidence one evening, when I was in law school, when I was pressing hard for information about the Hyperion Fund's unusual investment history, that what happened to her in Vienna changed her life forever, 'in ways you will understand later,' she said. I'm beginning to understand. And one more thing."

"What's that?"

"You know that old book I found in her bookcase, snooping?" Wheeler nodded. "The one where in 1932 I found that passage about the gentleman that I used in my graduation speech?" Wheeler again nodded. "The one that contained a detailed investment strategy for the twentieth century. I know now what that book is," he concluded and stared at Wheeler until he received a nod. "Mother has to have that book to become the woman she becomes."

Wheeler looked uncomfortable. "Well, *that book* is now safely stored away among my things."

"It's all right," Dilly said, as if having seen a vision. "Don't you see? Whatever happens happens. I was supposed to tell the Gestapo my secret. You were supposed to meet up with Weezie. Whatever has happened has happened." He looked very much at peace.

"You've changed your tune, then?"

"I've realized what has had to be. And now it has. And now you and I are free to go. It will be painful for Weezie, but she will be all right. We, of all people, know that. She will become a great woman."

This was Dilly's famous mind over matter springing into action. He was going to take over and get them both out of this mess. You could see it in the sparkle that was struggling to replace the dull gray that had settled in his eyes over the past few days.

"We have enough clothing, and Dr. Freud has loaned you enough money for us to live for a while, until we can find jobs and build up some reserves. We have your flying disks and a wealth of twentieth-century talents and imagination. We could eventually set ourselves up well somewhere in Europe and earn enough money for the passage to New York, where we would be at home with the language and the geography." He was talking himself into health, not entirely effectively, Wheeler could see. "We could even try our luck as baseball players," Dilly continued, "introducing that prongball thing of yours to the national game. Maybe eventually we could even buy a piece of land in the Sacramento Valley and start a farm. We can even start doing some investing; we both know where to place our money, and what to avoid. Considering our enormous differences of personality, I think we could both be happy and productive with a long partnership."

He pulled a pocket watch from his vest pocket and eyed it, then looked up at Wheeler. "We want to be careful with time. The train leaves in an hour."

Their train ticket from Nordbahnhof was for Budapest, where, traveling with forged American passports as Hoover and Truman, they planned to begin as street performers or perhaps find a band that needed a couple of hack musicians. "We'll be like a Bob Hope and Bing Crosby movie." It was a simple matter of planning, Dilly said, and of exploring all the options.

"I suppose nothing can be done," Wheeler said finally, with a tone of restrained exasperation that brought things back down to earth, at least for a moment. "She will return home to Boston and marry that arrogant prick."

Dilly looked over at him, surprised for a moment. "I would have said it a little more evasively."

"I was looking for a stronger word," Wheeler said. "But my vocabulary failed me."

"He really is—" Dilly paused as if searching his own vocabulary. "—a little severe," he said with a faint smile to Wheeler's back. "Isn't he?"

"What I don't get is the mechanics of it. I mean, how in hell is she going to bring herself to marrying the guy?"

"She just will," Dilly said firmly. "That's all."

"But, I mean, how? What on earth will provoke it?"

"After she had met you?" Dilly said with a kind of nonjudgmental clarity that now caught Wheeler by surprise. Dilly was smiling understandingly.

"I would have said *that* a little more evasively," Wheeler said. He had risen and turned back to the canal scene out the window.

"It will just happen," Dilly said, sitting down on the bed beside Wheeler's packed bag. "That's all we need to know."

"I guess she'll want to shake the memory of all this." Wheeler's heart sank, as he thought of losing her. He gestured with his hands out toward the world of Vienna, a new frustration showing on his face. He knocked the flat of his hand against the window casement.

Dilly shrugged. There was a surprising lawyerlike certitude in his voice. "What am I supposed to say? She's going to get over it and you. She's going to return to Boston. *And*, she is going to marry Frank Burden. Maybe because she'll have a mental collapse and forget this whole nasty business, maybe because she'll figure out that's the only way this story can unfold again, her destiny, you could say. Maybe because she will simply find a way to fall in love with him. Who knows? Anyway it happens, she'll marry the man." Dilly paused and waited. "And it'll be a good thing for the two of us."

"I was really worried that, you know, that he was going to—" Wheeler stopped, more incredulous than concerned.

"You thought something sinister was going to happen?"

"The thought had occurred to me," Wheeler said.

"Well, nothing's going to happen in Vienna," Dilly said. "We're gone for good." He held up the two railway tickets to Budapest.

"Right." Wheeler looked off in the distance, shaking his head slowly. "It's my story anyway, not yours."

"Well, I know some of your story, don't forget."

"And you know what's in Weezie's future?" Dilly nodded, showing suddenly in his eyes a great sadness. "It will be so damned hard on her," Wheeler said, striking the casement again. "She'll get back to Boston, and life will return to normal. You and I will be out of her life, and it will be years perhaps before the first event." There was an abstract emptiness to his voice. "The sinking of the *Titanic*, probably, or who knows?" Wheeler paused, as if noticing something in the street below. "That won't be for fifteen years, so maybe she will have forgotten by then. But some of it will come back—the rising fame of Sigmund Freud, the arrival of Arnauld Esterhazy at St. Greg's, World War in 1914, or—" He looked over at Dilly.

"The birth of her own son."

"It will hit her sometime in there."

"She will always know what's coming."

"Maybe she didn't read very much," Dilly said suddenly. "I mean, maybe she flipped through it quickly."

"Wishful thinking," Wheeler said with a sickening finality. "If you could have seen the look in her eyes, you'd know. You of all people know how persistent she is. She attached to that thing like a lamprey."

"You took it back from her, right?" Dilly said.

"I've got it safely packed away in my bags, I told you that. At least she won't have it with her. You know how damn thorough she is."

A heavy silence fell between the two men, as if for the first time they both realized what it all meant. "If only you hadn't been so detailed in writing it," Dilly said with a sad, almost admiring smile. "She's going to be a damned Cassandra. To know the future and be powerless to do anything about it . . ." His voice dwindled away into the profundity of the thought.

She would watch Hitler grow like an evil flower. The child in Lambach would lose his father at fourteen, become the art student in Vienna, and the political activist in Munich, where in prison he would write *Mein*

Kampf. He would rise to become chancellor of Germany, then spread his hatred throughout the world. Weezie would see all this, knowing what would happen next, knowing how the hate would kill her own son.

Dilly cringed this time. "She is going to have a great effect on the world because of what she is going to know, both the good and the bad. That's what I found out in my law school research. She caused things to happen. Major things." He paused to think. "When you put it all together, it is pretty impressive, amazing even. In 1909, she made the major contribution to Clark University that created the conference that brought Sigmund Freud to America and launched him. A few years earlier, it was Mother who gave *The Interpretation of Dreams* to her family friend William James at Harvard. Around that same time, she arranged the gift to the New York Philharmonic to bring Gustav Mahler for his tenure there, and Mahler's initial fame in New York came from a little book by a pseudonymous author named Jonathan Trumpp, and you know who that was."

At first Wheeler could only stare, letting the words sink in. "Wait," he said suddenly. "What are you saying?"

"Mother was Jonathan Trumpp," Dilly said. "I thought you knew that."

"No!" Wheeler was stunned.

"It's true."

The revelation was still sinking in. "Eleanor Burden," he said slowly, "your mother, the Weezie Putnam who is now here in Vienna wrote *City of Music*, the Haze's beloved 'Little Book.'"

"Yes," Dilly said.

"I can't believe it."

"It's true. The best of well-kept secrets, but I figured it out that year in law school. Mother made me promise never to tell anyone."

Wheeler was still shaking his head. "That Trumpp book was in the Haze's collection, heavily marked up by him. I used it for writing *Fin de Siècle*. I practically memorized it. He used a lot of it in his famous 'Random Notes.'"

"It was pure Mother. The reason she came to Vienna in the first place, I think, published when she returned to Boston. It was a big hit."

"She says she's abandoned it."

"Well," Dilly said, shrugging. "She is going to go back to it." He shrugged again. "Unless you have really fouled things up."

"Right. And you know about her investments and the avoidance of the crash in twenty-nine. Then in the thirties she made the significant gift to Princeton University Press that began the publication of the complete works of Carl Jung, whom she is going to meet in 1909. You know that, right?" Wheeler nodded. "She funded women's suffrage activities, citizen's rights movements, peace movements, anything that promoted introspection and tolerance. And the list went on and on. And there was always a theme to it."

"And what was the theme?"

"That was what I could never get my arms around. It was all Vienna-connected, that's for sure. And it all had to do with introspection, and self-discovery and psychological depth, but that was as far as I got."

Wheeler suddenly looked pensive. "Flora's book!" he burst out. "It was when I was pretty lost in Victor Hugo and baseball and the mythology book my grandmother sent me on my ninth birthday and I totally memorized, so I never really marveled at it. But a representative from a Boston press came to her out of the blue and solicited it. Mother was in her reclusive period, you might say, and she did nothing but pull together all her thoughts, a lot of it from conversations she and I'd had about mythology, and it became *Persephone Rising*. It was beautifully written. I wish you could see it. The book seemed to take off on its own, sort of what they called a cult classic, and you know that it has been credited as the beginning of the American feminist movement."

"Athenaeum Press, a Hyperion Fund creation?" Dilly broke in.

"Right. And my book, the Haze's book, *Fin de Siècle*," Wheeler said. "Same thing. A guy shows up, again out of the blue, again from Boston, and offers me a contract. I always thought that some St. Greg's alum found me, but it wasn't, it was Athenaeum Press."

"And that was after she was gone. Posthumous instructions from Mother."

"It's funny," Wheeler said, shaking his head. "That book is really the reason I'm here. The notoriety I got from it sort of did me in."

"So you see," Dilly said. "It was all the work of one person. She caused it all to happen, always behind the scenes and anonymous, but always the instigator. The list is a long one. She was more of a force than either you or I know."

"She will be all right, then?" Wheeler let out a sigh of great relief.

Dilly stared at him hard. "You know that. You saw her at the end. You know what a force she became."

"Right now, the whole thing feels like a huge mistake."

"I hated what you did," Dilly said, "and I certainly do not want to know the details. But you did what had to happen. You gave her what she needed to have to become the mother I knew and the woman of influence she was." Dilly paused, as if weighing what he was about to conclude. "What has happened has had to have happened, just exactly as it has for Mother to be Mother. We did all this *for her!*"

Wheeler looked into Dilly's face. "We are leaving out one detail, of course."

"And that is?"

"The whole cycle." He looked out at Vienna. "She'll know all this too." With his hand he swept out toward the city. "She'll know that we all end up back here at the end of each loop."

"And that's consolation?"

Wheeler turned back from the window and faced Dilly. There was a look of deep resolve in his eyes. "Isn't it for you?" And then his eyes surveyed his father in front of him, seeing objectively for the first time perhaps how he had wasted away in the past few days. "You don't look so good," he said.

"I think I need to lie down," said the tireless Dilly Burden. "I think this might be it."

53

The Last Burden

e're getting a second chance, you and I," Dilly said, lying nearly motionless on the bed in his small rented room. "That's what we get out of all this, I've concluded."

"I'll buy it," Wheeler said.

"We've had this time together, to find out things. How it all turned out."

"Can you tell me one more then?" Wheeler said. He wanted to take advantage of their newfound candor.

"No limits now," Dilly said, smiling, with barely enough energy to lift his head. "You have blown the cover off my ironclad limits."

"What happened between you and your father that Christmas you came home from London?"

"Christmas of 1943," he said, letting his mind drift. "Funny, it seems so long ago. I brought your mother and you home. You were almost three, and a pretty chipper little guy. We came over by the *Queen Mary*, on its way back from delivering troops. The war was going full-bore, but the Admiralty pretty much insisted that I take the time off. They said I was overworked and needed the rest. Your mother and I had a most wonderful time on the crossing. We sat and read to each other and, when you fell off to sleep—"

"You made marvelous and noisy love on the ship bunks."

"Good lord, you remember?"

Wheeler laughed. "It's all right. Mother told me."

A soft smile crossed Dilly's lips. "Your mother *would* have told you that. She was what we used to call *liberated*." He closed his eyes to savor the moment, and then continued. "I had not seen my parents for a long time, and I was looking forward to showing off my wife and my beautiful son, to them and to Arnauld Esterhazy. The visit went well. Mother was in heaven having us in the house, and she and I had long talks together. She was unusually fond of her grandson, I think. And your mother was for her a happy addition: Flora minded herself and did not bring up some of her wilder ideas."

"Such as sexual liberation and pacifism."

"To mention a few," Dilly said with a smile. "It was not until near the end of our visit that Father and I had our time alone. I think I have told you that my father and I were not very close. There was not any animosity between us, but on the other hand we had never talked about much of substance. He was, of course, very proud of my athletic accomplishments at his old schools, and he often told me stories of how it had been in his day and what the 1896 Olympic games in Athens had been like, but we did not share much in the way of ideas."

Dilly stopped. "Say, I could sure use a glass of water," he said, and Wheeler poured a glass from the porcelain pitcher on the bureau and held it while Dilly drank. "Mighty good," he said, then continued.

Frank Burden and his son retired to the oak-paneled study and closed the door. "I am glad we can have these moments alone," the father said, after Dilly had turned down the offer of a cigar but accepted the brandy. "There is much to talk about. I wanted you to know how much I admire what you have done in the war effort."

"These are extraordinary times," Dilly said.

"I am glad that you are content with a minor role in these last months. I fear things will not be pretty before the peace."

"The peace?" Dilly said innocently.

"The invasion is coming. We all know that. Eisenhower's attack will be enormous, and Hitler's defense will be ferocious. Both sides will exhaust themselves, I fear, and there will be a negotiated peace."

"You think the invasion will fail."

Frank Burden took a long appraising look at his son. "Hitler's defenses are stronger than anyone knows. So much emphasis has been put on air power that everyone has forgotten where his power really lies. It is in the tanks, his Panzer divisions. They are exceedingly mobile and can be

moved anywhere in Europe in a matter of days. That is what the Auto-
bahns are for." Frank Burden looked into his son's eyes. "The Panzer divisions are the key to the whole thing."

"But the invasion force is stronger than anyone realized," Dilly said.

"I'm merely talking strategy," Frank said. "The invading forces will be
successful in the opening days, then the Panzers will attack, right at the
time when the invasion forces are most vulnerable, before the supply lines
are established."

"Are you saying the invasion will be a failure?"

The father could see the look of shock in his son's eyes. "Standish,
Standish, I am just being a realist. I am an American, a patriot, you know
that. But we must prepare for reality. Hitler will sue for peace, and Frank-
lin and his friend Winston Churchill will come to their senses. We will
all come to our senses. The war will be over in a year, and both sides will
lick their wounds and begin the recovery."

"The Germans will stay in France?"

"European borders," Frank said dismissively. "They change every hundred years. Look at what we now call Italy. Look at what used to be Austria-
Hungary."

"I can't believe you are saying this," Dilly said.

"Realism, my son. Simply realism. The new Europe is coming, and we
need to position ourselves. That is why you need to stick to your minor
role right now, and you need to prepare yourself."

"Prepare myself?" Dilly said, not understanding.

"You are being watched, believe me. You have been watched all along:
the football, the music, the catch you made against Yale, that law school
brilliance, now the war heroics. Believe me, my son, people have noticed.
When the peace comes, there will be an international financial community, one of great power and reach."

Dilly stopped him. "Are you saying that Berlin will control things?"

"Not Berlin," Frank said confidently.

"London, then?"

Frank shook his head. "International banking, a new world order, a
new way of doing things. You will be getting the call."

"Wait," Dilly said. "You're losing me. Not London, not Berlin, then
where?"

"Vienna," Frank Burden said. "It is all set. The financial interests are ready to pull together and move there. That magnificent city with its rich history is now free."

Dilly stared at his father, incredulous. "Free?" he said, dreading what was coming next.

Frank Burden tapped his cigar in the ashtray. "In the emperor's Vienna there were two hundred thousand Jews. The Jews controlled everything, the newspapers, the arts, and especially the banks. They had a stranglehold on it all. And now—" He tapped his cigar again. "Now, they are gone. The city is free. We funded him, and he has done his job, a little brutishly, I fear, but the job is done."

"Wait," Dilly said again, struggling to keep up. "You funded Hitler?"

"In the early days, when he was just getting started, there was a group of us who were well positioned. We made him, you might say, and I happened to be in the right position to pull it all together. Without that pulling together of banking interests, he would be—" Frank paused. "Well, he would have remained a former corporal and a failed postcard artist. We got him the money to found his Reich, and we got him the money for his Panzer tanks. It was an investment with enormous returns."

"I can't believe you are saying this," Dilly said, staring in disbelief.

"Look, Standish, no one asked that it turn out this way, but a revitalized and industrialized Germany was an essential part of the formula. We all agreed on that. This is just simple reality. What has happened has happened. I am just advising you to the reality you might not have thought of. I am just encouraging you to keep your head down over there for the next few months. Wait it out. And when it is over, there will be a need for strong leadership. You will be getting a call. My son will be getting the call." Frank Burden smiled proudly at his son. "I know because I know the people who will be making that call."

Dilly could think of nothing to say. "Father," he said finally, "Flora is a Jew. Your grandson is Jewish. The last Burden is a Jew."

Frank Burden looked back at his son with that same matter-of-fact coldness, like a surgeon looking down at an inflamed appendix. "I have no grandson," he said. "You are the last Burden."

After he finished his story, Dilly was silent again, and Wheeler let out a soft sigh. "How horrible for you," he said in little more than a whisper.

"Those were the last words I had with my father. It was at that awful moment that I decided to return to France and the Resistance." Dilly's head rested on the pillow. His eyes were closed and his lips puffed out with each breath. "That was when Mother told me that she and Frank Burden had lived very different lives, 'parallel lives,' she said. That was when Mother told me to go see Arnauld, alone."

A long dark silence descended onto the room. "So you see," he said slowly without looking over at Wheeler, using the compact language of someone who had few words left. "It appeared self-destructive perhaps. A mission of unreasonable risk." He was coming near the end. "Not out of hatred for Hitler but, as Dr. Freud would pinpoint, to kill my father. But it wasn't that. It was partly that I felt obligated to compensate for the awful influence of Frank Burden, granted, but there was more." He fell silent again. Wheeler watched his own father and could see he was losing ground. His head barely came off the pillow now as he made his points, and his eyes became more and more hollow. "You know that your mother always blamed my tightly wound sense of duty, but this time it was more. I wanted to go because of what my father told me, yes. I wanted to go for the most sacred of reasons." Wheeler said nothing, just let him continue. "I wanted to go for my son. I wanted to go for *you*."

There followed another long silence, the two men just looking at each other, too far along now for any shyness. "Thank you," Wheeler said. "It is the missing piece."

"When I found out about my father, I thought the world had ended. Then I found out about the Haze and so very much fell into place for me. But, now, it doesn't seem so important. Now that I have met you, I feel at peace. You are a good man, a tribute to your mother and me. I am so glad we met."

"We've had a chance to see what each of us is like."

"That is why I was sent here," Dilly said in little more than a whisper. "A blessing for me."

"You know," Wheeler said, "I've never told anyone this, but when I edited the Haze's 'Random Notes' in the seventies and eighties I found that the pages of that old loose-leaf binder were all different ages and conditions, and he was constantly changing the contents, over the years adding, subtracting, and consolidating from the boxes of papers in his closet. You could tell the progression of his thinking by the age of the paper. But what nobody knew was that the first page, the front of the Haze's famous 'Random Notes' binder was the oldest and the most yellowed, the one that had been there from the start and had never changed. It was the dedication of a life's work, I guess you'd say. And you know what it said?"

Dilly could barely move his head now. He nodded. "Tell."

"It said, 'To my son.'"

There was a stillness in the room that now had no time or place to it, an air that could only be described as sacred. "That's good" was all Dilly said, but his smile told it all.

"You know I love you," Wheeler said, reaching out and covering Dilly's hand. "I have always loved you, Father."

"That's good," Dilly repeated, then he whispered, "I love you—" He paused to savor the words. "—my son."

"You're slipping away," Wheeler said, his eyes filled with tears. "You don't have to, you know. There is a way—" There was now a desperation to his voice, and he leaned closer.

"It's all right," Dilly said, feeling the enfolding warmth of the hand, still smiling contentedly. "This time I'm trying for your mother."

And Dilly Burden was gone.

PART FOUR

Fin de Siècle

54

A Powerful Resolve

s Wheeler stood at the window, taking in a last look out at the Danube Canal from the second-story window of his room at Frau Bauer's, he felt heartsick about leaving Weezie. Once exhilarated by the thought of roving with Dilly, now he found there only a doubled sense of loss. The walls of his room were stripped bare and all that remained from his stay in Vienna was on the bed, a carpetbag with the few possessions he had managed to collect, including the suit he had stolen from Frank Burden on his first day and the journal, now safely back in his possession, into which he had written his last conversations with Dilly. For one last time Wheeler looked around the room that had been his home for this extraordinary time in Vienna, and his mind wandered as it had so many times back over the events and their causes.

His train ticket, one of two, was for Budapest. Why, he did not know really. It had been Dilly's idea, seeming somehow more appropriate to head east for the time being, rather than to Paris or London. But first, if he showed up, he would travel with Freud to Lambach.

"What good will that do?" Dilly had asked in that last day, when he heard of the invitation.

"I honestly don't know," Wheeler said. "But maybe if we can get him to sense the deprivation the child is being raised in. Maybe that will change things, just slightly."

"Better than strangling the little fellow?" Dilly had said, rolling his eyes. Wheeler had offered the trip in a very precise and narrow time frame. He had no idea of Freud's response. "He must have started believing your reality. If he shows up that's quite a statement: it'll show that he finally understands."

"I don't think he will," Wheeler said. "But at least I offered."

Now alone, Wheeler looked around the room, and so his mind wandered. Dilly's death had come peacefully, as if he had quite literally run out of fuel. Wheeler had to keep reminding himself that this was the second time Dilly had died, and not only was it infinitely more peaceful and comfortable than the first, it also had followed a time in which they both had been granted a very special wish. It was indeed a second chance.

But still it was death. Wheeler sat with the body for a long time and wept, making his peace with the father he had never known. His mind kept drifting to his mother, Flora, and to how much both he and Dilly had wished that she could have been with them in Vienna. And why not? If he and Dilly had traveled, why not she? And what a time they would have had! It also occurred to Wheeler then that had Flora been with them, Dilly probably would have stayed. Instead, his body now lay cold and waxlike on the bed of his small dark rented room, while his spirit ranged out over time looking for his great lost love.

Wheeler had left Dilly's room, dropping an unsigned note in the mailbox of the proprietor of the building, reporting that the man in the second-floor room had died, and leaving it up to the public officials of the city to establish the identity of the deceased. Dilly Burden's expired body was of no use to anyone. "Maybe they will bury me in the unmarked grave beside Mozart," Dilly had said in one of his last bursts of optimism.

With nearly unbearable heaviness of heart Wheeler collected his things to do what he knew he must: leave Vienna without a trace, to leave Weezie, once and for all. She had a new start on life now, and she was resilient and mature. The future had her marrying Frank Burden soon after their return to Boston, and there was nothing stopping that, nothing irrevocable or permanently damaging that had happened; in fact, there was no evidence that said everything was not according to the reality of history.

Except Weezie's having read the journal; that was a problem. Her reaction had of course been almost unbearable to take in. She looked numb and confused, crushed by the weight of what she had read.

"You allowed me to call you by that other name." She looked more sunken than angry. "Even in those moments of the greatest intimacy for a woman."

"I had to."

"Well," she said, considering all the options. "Well, I guess it doesn't change those moments."

"I hope not."

"You know," she said, looking him straight in the eye, with a powerful resolve. "I am known to be very good in times of crisis," she had told him. And all Wheeler could hope was that this would be for her one of those times.

He would never forget the image of her sitting by the studio window with the journal in her lap, her own mind racing with the extraordinary new information that now confronted her. How completely enervated she looked in the face of the awful knowledge. "I don't care about this," she said after a time, after she had collected herself. "I made my commitment to you when I came back to Vienna. We can get any money we need from my family, and we can go anywhere we need to go." Her eyes shone with a bright confidence.

Wheeler did not know how even to begin. "You weren't to have seen that," he said dumbly. "I wrote it for my own sanity. It was incredibly careless of me to leave it where you could find it."

"No," she said, nodding with conviction. "I have become part of this story. It is important that I know the truth."

"What do you make of it?"

"There are only two ways to make sense of it," she said, struggling for self-control. "Other than the fact that it is a remarkably thorough and well-documented record, very hard to disregard. Either it *is* true, in which case its author is some sort of visitor from another time, or it is not true, in which case its author is certifiably mad."

"Which do you think?"

"I honestly don't know," she said softly, "but considering the alternative, I prefer to think it true." As she spoke, incredibly brave and positive, seated erect in the light from the window, Wheeler was overcome by how courageous she was and how much he loved her. It was not for the flow of history that he now feared, but for the emotional well-being of this woman he loved.

"I think you should give me the journal," he said.

"That is possible." She lifted it from her lap, closed it, and handed it to him.

"We should not see each other again," he said, taking the journal and feeling its weight.

She let out a tiny gasp. "That is not possible."

"It is necessary, though."

"I think I would die if you left me now," she said, her eyes now filling with tears. There was more concern than desperation in her voice. It was as if she was stating a fact about the weather or remarking on the color of the wallpaper.

Recognizing at once the truth behind what she said, Wheeler walked over to her and touched her hair. She looked up at him with a new depth in her blue eyes. He pulled her face to his chest and then bent down and kissed her. "What are we going to do?" he said from the bottom of his soul.

"Take me to bed."

☙ ❧

They lay in each other's arms without speaking for what seemed like an eternity, with no need to part, with nothing of the outside world calling them away from each other.

"Your friend Dilly—" She paused and pulled herself up bravely. "The one you say is my son. He is dying, isn't he?" she said.

"I am afraid he is." Finally, he was able to tell her the truth.

She winced. "Is there nothing to be done?"

"It appears not."

"And when you die," she said, her face buried in the nape of his neck, "is that how it will be for you?"

"Who's to say?"

"I will be with you when it happens," she said with a kind of conviction that resonated with the farthest stars.

"When the end comes and it comes suddenly, there is something you absolutely must know," Wheeler said. She moved against him, her bare breasts against his chest, their legs intertwined, waiting for him to continue. "I have waited all my life to find love like this. Will you know that, confidently and completely?"

"I shall," she whispered.

"Promise."

"I absolutely promise," she said, pulling herself even closer.

And it was in that moment that Wheeler knew that he would have to leave her and leave Vienna forever, regardless of the consequences.

55

A Classic Admiration

he decision to leave Vienna had settled on Wheeler with the heaviness of a death, yet he knew that leaving Weezie, allowing her to return to Boston, was the only plausible course now. He walked along the Ringstrasse with a sinking of heart like none he had ever felt before. He headed toward the Café Central for a good-bye visit, one last romantic gesture.

To understand what happened next you need to know one last detail of Wheeler Burden's life. When his band Shadow Self parted company forever, it was not just the abandonment of performance music that called Wheeler. He began a project he had been putting off for a long time: the editing of the Haze's "Random Notes."

The project took him a full ten years, researching details, reading other accounts, interviewing St. Greg's alums, immersing himself completely in the life that his old mentor had lived as a young man. Curiously, the only thing he did not do was travel to Vienna. "I don't want to ruin it," he said.

When Wheeler walked off the stage that last time in front of forty thousand at the football stadium in Berkeley, quite a mystique built up around him, and the world wanted to know what he was up to. "You are more famous for doing nothing," a friend told him, "than most famous people are for doing something." He was working on a secret project, *Rolling Stone* reported; "probably a rock opera," one of his former band members said. "Wheeler always liked that weird music."

Finally, after ten years, he announced that he was finished and bound the manuscript up and sent it to Athenaeum Press in Boston, where the editors had nearly given up hope. Six months later *Fin de*

Siècle by Arnauld Esterhazy was published, and much to everyone's surprise it became a best seller in Boston and the rage of bookstores and coffeehouses around the country. Wheeler began receiving a wave of invitations to speak, and "for the Haze," he said, he began once again appearing in public. These public appearances fueled the sale of the book, which led to more invitations. It was this new notoriety and celebrity that brought about his end. But more on that later; for the time being just know this.

As he walked into the Café Central for the last time, he could see none of the *Jung Wien* sitting at their usual table or anywhere in the café. He had already committed himself to a path toward the table when he realized the solitary occupant was the one person he had tried assiduously to avoid, Arnauld Esterhazy. The young man was sitting alone at a table, reading the *Neue Freie Presse*. He looked up slowly and fixed his eyes on Wheeler in a way that made it impossible for him to retreat. "Herr Truman," he said loudly, "I am reading my friend Wickstein's *feuilleton* in today's paper. It is his second."

"That is good," Wheeler said noncommittally.

"It is very good," Arnauld said. "Although this one is not as good as his first. That first one was a masterpiece. It really got people's attention. I am very proud of my friend."

"Where is everyone else this morning?" Wheeler said, looking around.

"You are the only one showing up this morning, Herr Truman. There has been an eruption in the group. I doubt if we will ever be the same again."

"What is it?" Wheeler said without thinking, and suddenly he and Arnauld were in conversation.

"A cataclysm. It's all about politics. We should avoid politics and religion. They always seem to cause schisms."

"And which was it this time?"

"The mayor. I don't know that we can survive this hideous dissension." Arnauld launched into a description of the heated discussion of Jews and the parts played by the various members. "I don't understand it," he said earnestly, "but anti-Semitism seems to be the driving force of a whole cultural movement. Where does it come from?"

The conversation seemed to do nothing for Arnauld's disposition. If anything, he seemed to sink deeper and deeper into gloom. "And there is more, Mr. Truman."

"What is it?" Wheeler said openly, the previous conversation giving him a false sense of security.

"I am in love with someone who does not love me."

"That can be very painful. I know."

"I am overcome by hopelessness. There seems to be no point . . ." His voice tapered off.

"Often it is not as bad as it seems."

"I feel like ending it all," he said with the kind of artistic fatalism that meant business, and Wheeler's mind raced suddenly to a note he had found among the Haze's papers dealing with that dark self-destructive mood that seemed to lead so many Viennese artists to suicide. He admitted that as a young man he had fallen into such a mood with such dark thoughts, but he had been pulled out of it by the chance encounter with a wise older man who used to frequent the Café Central.

Oh, come on, Wheeler almost said, but caught himself. "What is causing this?" he did say.

"It is the American," Arnauld said with a sigh. "It is Fraulein Putnam."

Wheeler had been dancing around conversation with young Arnauld, leaning away from him as much as he could, but suddenly, taking stock of the situation, he could see a deep fatalism and depression in the young man's eyes, a look that filled him with apprehension. "You are really serious about this, aren't you?"

"Very serious," Arnauld said. "I wonder if it is worth it to go on."

"I would be patient, Arnauld," Wheeler said, and he could see that the young man was now hanging on his every word, leaning on him for an avuncular wisdom that might set the course for the next decade of his life.

"You don't think it hopeless then?"

"Oh my, no," Wheeler said now with conviction, "Fraulein Putnam is very fond of you." He paused, struggling to find the right approach. "You must think of Abelard and his Eloise, Pygmalion and his Galatea, Gatsby and his Daisy."

Arnauld looked puzzled. "Gatsby?"

"Sorry. It is a local California reference," Wheeler said, realizing his anachronism and backpedaling. "A Gold Rush love story." He paused, then recouped quickly. "Think of Dante and his Beatrice."

A spark of hopefulness came into his eyes. "Dante and Beatrice, I like that," he said. "That is very comforting."

"It should be. Yours is a classic admiration. The kind that fuels great art." Wheeler looked at him empathetically. "I see you finishing your graduate studies and becoming a great teacher of young minds. I see you being very successful and winning the heart of a beautiful woman, an American, the love of your life, fathering a magnificent son. I see your writing published to great acclaim. You need to be patient and it will work out better than you can now hope. It will just take time."

"You sound very reassuring." The very impressionable young man was mesmerized by Wheeler's words. He looked immeasurably better.

"Trust me, Arnauld. I know what I am talking about."

"Oh, thank you," he said, tears of relief now filling his eyes. "Thank you," he said, the thought of suicide now far from his mind.

56

The Jew in Vienna

t was time to leave. Sigmund Freud was not going to show up for the offered appointment, a final sign of his firm belief that Wheeler's strange story was only a complex hysteria. And so Wheeler picked up his bag and looked around the room to see that he was leaving nothing behind, nothing he needed for his trip, nothing to prove that he had been there. He turned to leave.

There was no telling how long she had been standing there behind him. She stood stone still, her eyes wide, her hair rumpled. She was holding the small suitcase she had carried to Baden. "You are planning to leave, aren't you?" she said, glancing quickly at the blank walls and the carpetbag on the bed.

Wheeler turned, the life drained from his face. "How long have you been there?" he said almost under his breath.

Her eyes were blazing. "You can't leave. I don't care about all that I read," Weezie said. Her voice was calm and steady, full of that famous resolve. "I don't need to understand. You don't need to explain anything. But you can't leave me." She walked purposefully toward where he stood by the window until she was close enough to reach out a hand to Wheeler. He hesitated for an instant, his eyes darting as if looking for an escape route, but then he reached out his own hand and took hers. "I only know one thing," she said, "and that is how much I love you. And I know that we are not victims of this story. You have taught me nothing if not that."

There was a total calm to Weezie Putnam's eyes, something wondrous and inspiring. "We can leave Vienna together," she said. "You have two tickets, I know that. We can play beautiful music together, and we can read and talk and grow. Nothing is holding us back. We can go anywhere and do anything." Wheeler could not speak, transfixed by the conviction in those eyes, and the love. "But there is one thing I must have. I know that now with indelible certainty." Her eyes would not move from his. They pulled him toward her, and he tried to evade them. "I must be with you, Wheeler. You are my life now, my total love and life."

Wheeler felt he was losing ground rapidly. He began to pull his hand from her grasp, but then took both her hands in his. "It is what must be," he said, penetrating with his eyes. "There are things you simply don't know. You should have never come here."

Her calm resolve gave way to incipient desperation. "I will die without you, don't you see that?"

"You'll be fine," he said, shocked by how unconvincing he sounded.

"I know you love me. Nothing can shake that," she said, her eyes now imploring.

"Of course, I love you," Wheeler said, his hands slipping to her waist, where he could feel her soft warmth. "I love you now, and I will love you sixty years from now. I will love you forever."

Finally, there were tears in her eyes. "Then you must not leave alone. I must go with you."

Wheeler felt lost. "I must—" All his own firm resolve was gone. He looked into Weezie's face.

"Don't you see?" Weezie said. Then she paused and took a deep breath, summoning up all her strength. "There is something I know about you now. You have never finished things in your life. You have been to great heights and you have come to the brink of great accomplishment and fulfillment. And you have always walked away. I know now what you mean to me, but I know also what I mean to you. We are each other's destiny."

He pulled her to him and now could feel himself giving in completely, all traces of propriety and self-preservation gone forever. "My love," he said into her ear.

"Yes, yes," she said. And he held on to her as he had never held on before. This time he was not walking away.

"We will have to hurry to catch the train," he said, sounding like Dilly.

"I'll take the tickets," she said.

As Wheeler opened the front door to Frau Bauer's, turning to help Weezie after him, a man appeared on the sidewalk in his path. "Are you leaving Vienna?" he said, his voice cold and unfriendly. It was Frank Burden.

Wheeler was off guard. "I am going on a small business trip." Slowly, he pushed Weezie away from him.

"No, you're not." Frank Burden's blue eyes stared fiercely. "You are running out."

"Am I not free to leave Vienna?"

"You stole from me."

"I'm sorry," Wheeler said. "I was desperate. I needed the clothes and the money. I can pay you back."

"It's not the clothes and the money," he said, his eyes burning, his body shaking on the brink of control.

"I'm sorry," Wheeler said, putting out his hands in supplication. "What can I do?"

"You have gone out of your way to humiliate me."

Wheeler stepped sideways to be well clear of Weezie, who stood transfixed in the doorway. "It was not intentional."

"Hah," he said, the veins on the side of his neck protruding as he paused. "Don't patronize me." He glared at Wheeler, who put down his bag.

"There has been a misunderstanding. I'd like to talk about it."

Frank Burden's blue eyes narrowed even further. "You don't understand, do you? I won't be embarrassed." The young man flashed a look of pure unmitigated hate. His hand appeared from behind his back trembling, trying to steady the revolver aimed at Wheeler's chest.

"Stop this," Weezie said, taking a step toward Frank Burden, who clicked back the hammer. Weezie froze where she was. Wheeler stepped back. "There is more than you know, Frank," Weezie said, imploring. "You've got to stop."

Frank Burden did not seem to hear and was glaring at Wheeler. The door to the hallway had remained open, and Wheeler stared dumbly. Over Frank Burden's right shoulder from the street side Sigmund Freud appeared, arriving a bit late for his appointment to travel to Lambach. He looked at Wheeler, whose hands were raised waist high. Then he looked at Frank and saw the gun in the trembling hand. He seemed puzzled for an instant, and then, when he saw Weezie's face, he knew all.

"Let's sit down and talk," Wheeler said.

Weezie probably had started her scream, "No, Frank!" an instant before the gun exploded.

57

San Francisco, 1988

t was after midnight by the time he signed the last book, polished off the last straggling conversation, and drove back to Stanyan and Parnassus to the famous ground-floor apartment where he had lived for fifteen years. He was distracted by the reflective state of mind that had settled on him over the past couple of months as he made the rounds of coffeehouses and small bookstores, talking about *Fin de Siècle*. This night had been especially distracting because the signing had been at City Lights Bookstore, a place he had been so many times he could not count, as an observer. Now to be the center of attention again, after his long retreat from the world, had been both exhilarating and unsettling. "They're only coming because you are famous for doing nothing," Joan Quigley would have quipped. He could hear her as if she had been lying next to him naked, blowing the words softly into his ear. "You ought to get a shave and a crew cut and see if they still come out." That theme again, Wheeler would have quipped back. He missed Joan Quigley.

But these appearances were not about him, he would insist, they really weren't, and the results proved him out, more or less. People came out for a combination of reasons, not the least of which were the reviews of the book that called it an important literary event. It was the Haze's "Random Notes" that had occupied him for ten years, but it was not just the book, he had to admit. It was the "papers" that had been left to him in the old man's will and that Wheeler had donated to Widener Library the moment he finished reading the last galley proof from Athenaeum Press. The Haze's "papers" were cardboard boxes full of letters, scraps of paper, fragments of articles, and notes written on everything. It was the scattered brilliance of a truly great mind, he had begun to realize, and the reason it took him so long to pull it together in what was now the published *Fin de Siècle* was first that he wanted to be absolutely true to the old man's thoughts and impressions and, second, he wanted to make sure that he, the editor, understood exactly what this extraordinary observer's thoughts and impressions meant. Wheeler the eccentric athlete, musician, lover, became Wheeler the researcher. "So that's what you've been doing all these years," one of his old Shadow Self band members said to him at one of the signings, in Ann Arbor.

He never finished the manuscript, actually. "This thing could go on forever," he told his mother one day in exasperation, when he was visiting her at the ranch, and then he pulled the last sheet out of his old Royal typewriter, sealed the whole goddam thing in a cardboard box, and mailed it to Boston. "I'm through," he said and went for a long walk with her in the Feather River bottomland. He had made a few changes as the proofs came back to him, but that was pretty much it.

The first review appeared in the *Boston Globe*, timed to meet the date of the book's appearance in local bookstores. Why it had been so positive Wheeler did not know, but it all had something to do with a connection Wheeler had not seen as he was poring over the notes. Arnauld Esterhazy, a young man at a pivotal place and a pivotal time in history, had been witness to the dawning of a new age. He had been born in an antediluvian period and had survived the flood. What he had been teaching his boys at St. Greg's for some fifty years was his own personal wonder at the dawning of a new age. "The birth of modernism," the reviewer called it, and he attributed to the book's editor the compliment that he knew exactly what he was doing.

Wheeler's mother collected the reviews dutifully, and when there were enough of them, coming in now from all over the country, she put them in a big floppy scrapbook. "I didn't understand any of this," Wheeler said to her, holding the collection of writings in his hand. "All I did was pick up the stone and throw."

Athenaeum Press had no budget for promotion or book tours, so the invitations came in spontaneously, mostly from places that had no means of paying airfare or any kind of expenses. "If you happen to be in the area," they often said. And Wheeler, using his mother and his mother's telephone number as his agency, began saying yes and "coming up with the funds." Coming up with the funds meant paying his own way, which was

for Wheeler, the Last Burden and heir to the Hyperion Funds, no problem. That is how the bookstore visits came about, and soon Wheeler was
saying no to big stores and yes to the little ones. "A brilliant strategy," a
reviewer called it later because the crowds were always overflowing out
into the street. "Creating a frenzy," the man called it. Creating a frenzy
was something Wheeler knew something about.

The City Lights signing was a culmination in some ways, for reasons
sentimental to Wheeler, and his reflections on his old mentor that night
were especially evocative. Because of circumstances, that evening became
as famous as his last appearance on the pitching mound or his singing of
"Coming Together" that first and last time at the football stadium at
Berkeley. "City Lights Bookstore could not possibly have contained all the
people who claim to have been there that night," a retrospective article in
Time magazine said years later.

"It has brought back a flood of memories," Wheeler said to the famous
owner as he was leaving that night, and legend has recorded those as his
last words because no one knows if he said anything to the man who confronted him in the alcove of his apartment just about half an hour later.

In that alcove, Wheeler had opened his mailbox as he always did and had
turned to put his key in the front door. He probably was not aware that the
man had come from somewhere in the shadows and was standing just a
few feet behind him. We can only conjecture. He turned and saw the man
then, but he did not become alarmed, just turned slowly to face him.
Wheeler recognized his assailant, although it took a moment to metamor-
phose the scraggly, almost deranged appearance back to how the man had
looked almost thirty years before. The men could have exchanged a few
words, no one really knows, but probably not. The gun was of a large
enough caliber to create a deafening concussion in the small alcove and
knock its victim to the ground, a policeman told reporters. The first bullet
struck Wheeler in the side, which meant that he was not fully turned, but
the force spun him a bit so that the second bullet struck him square in the
chest and knocked him backward into the wall beneath the mailboxes.
Wheeler's last moments were spent in a sitting position, looking up at
where the man had been standing and out into the night of Stanyan

Street. And it is from that position and time and place that this whole story begins.

"If you want my candid opinion," one detective told a reporter off the record, "from the look on his face he knew what was going on. Last thoughts sort of get frozen there, ya know. You see all kinds, some gasping for breath, some surprise, real bad pain, some horror and terror. But you don't see too many like this guy. For what he had just been through, this guy was real peaceful."

What they figured out was that as Wheeler turned around before opening his front door he was surprised, startled even, by the face of a man whom he had last seen as he was walking from the pitcher's mound at Harvard University in 1961 dressed only in a jockstrap. For all this time, apparently, through Woodstock and Altamont and the *Rolling Stone* articles and the famous last song in Berkeley and now—the final blow—the publication of a successful book about Vienna, the man had developed what researchers called a preoccupying and disabling obsession with the celebrity of Wheeler Burden. Now, the man was completely deranged, and from the fatal alcove he walked to Golden Gate Park, and in the center of the Japanese Garden he put the gun in his mouth and blew out the back of his own head.

The man was Wheeler Burden's Harvard freshman philosophy professor named Fielding Shomsky.

58

Esterhazy's Book

 in de Siècle was entirely Arnauld Esterhazy's book, the work of his lifetime, collected and edited by one of his most appreciative students. That is what Wheeler said over and over at his book signings. "This is Mr. Esterhazy's book," Wheeler kept saying. "I just pulled it together into a reasonable whole." It was the Haze's "Random Notes," he told the St. Greg's alumni who showed up at the small bookstores and coffeehouses around the country where he made his appearances. And those who remembered the Haze and his charismatic style smiled and knew it was so. But it wasn't quite that simple, and in the beginning the task of coming up with a "reasonable whole" was for Wheeler a bit daunting. Daunting enough to make the task a ten-year one.

Mr. Esterhazy's "Random Notes" was a loose-leaf binder of about 250 or so pages, but it did not remain static and unchanged over the half century of his reading from it. He was constantly fussing with it. If you actually took the book in hand, which few people ever had the privilege of doing, you saw immediately from the color and condition of the pages that they represented different and interchangeable versions of his thinking, some very old, some very new, some spliced together from both. Over time he would edit and crop and scissor and glue and move ideas around as different aspects of turn-of-the-century Vienna became clear and then outmoded in his view. The version that Wheeler inherited in 1965, at the death of his great mentor, was only the version most recently revised by its author. "Had he lived a few more years—or months," Wheeler would say, holding up the actual binder, "I am sure we would have a different 'final version.'" Any material that was excised from the sacred binder found its way into one of the innumerable cardboard boxes in his closet. Nothing got thrown away. Much of the material in the boxes ended up in the binder, at one time or another, and then back in the boxes. Much of the material was in German and would be translated before being brought forward. Some was in Czech, Hungarian, and the other languages of the empire. It turned out, Wheeler discovered, as soon as he began editing in earnest, that the "Random Notes" was a living document with a huge waiting list.

So as Wheeler began pulling together the version that would come into print and become the lasting memorial to the great mind who had been his and his father's most indelible teacher, he used as his resources all of the "papers," always trying to express each point and offer each illustration as the Haze would have wanted it. And that was no easy task. "Another editor would come up with an entirely different book," he said. At times, confronted with a superfluity of embellishments, Wheeler simply had to write the idea in his own words, always trying to capture that very special way of expression that was Arnauld Esterhazy.

An example of this editor's creative license was the issue of the grand unifying theory that Arnauld struggled with for sixty years. Just what was it all about? Arnauld had been aware that the world of his father's generation had been one of extraordinary growth in Vienna. The aristocracy and the wealthy citizenry, made rich by the industrial revolution, knowing that Vienna's fate was not going to be military victory, had settled for cultural greatness. They had worked together in the second half of the nineteenth century, like in no other European capitol, and built the fabulous city of the Ringstrasse. But at the end of the century everything had changed and the sons of those civic-minded fathers rebelled. The Secessionists in art and architecture, Mahler and Schoenberg in music, Egon Wickstein in philosophy, Lueger in politics, and of course Sigmund Freud in psychology, all led a movement that was more intensely personal, and it overturned the old world.

The world of the fathers had been rule bound, rigid, fixed, and hierarchical. The world of their highly cultured sons, raised in their aesthetics-centered homes, was more interconnected and warmly personal—"more a web of interconnectedness than a ladder of order," the Haze said famously—even sensual and erotic at times. Over the decades, Arnauld struggled with trying to express what he had experienced and seen, and one could see in poring over these papers how he worked at coming up with the unified theory. He read Freud's *Interpretation of Dreams* when it came out in 1899. Newly in America in 1909, he attended the conference at Clark University that brought Sigmund Freud and Carl Jung to world consciousness. He attended New York Philharmonic concerts in 1910 when Gustav Mahler was conductor. He attended the museums before and after the Great War when the Viennese painters Klimt, Kokoschka, and Schiele were featured. He read the works of Arthur Schnitzler. He watched as the "modern" movement spread through Europe and America in the prewar 1930s. All the time he worked on his theory, his "Random Notes," all the time trying to summarize what magical change had taken place in 1897, the year of great change in his life, the year he fell in love with the American Weezie Putnam.

Then in 1955, he came upon a book, one with no overt connection to Vienna or the turn of the century, that "opened his eyes," he said, to the union of thoughts he was looking for. That book took him into the world of classical mythology, a world frequented by all the major voices of his time, and opened up for him the world of the goddess. That book, which had begun by the author's recording the ideas of her eccentric free-thinking ten-year-old son, was titled *Persephone Rising*, by Florence Standish.

It is interesting to note that one section of "Esterhazy's book" *Fin de Siècle* has been singled out over and over again by critics, at the time of its publication in 1988 and over the years since. A close reader can see that that chapter is the one in which the editor took the most creative license, expressing the ideas as if they were a marvelous dialogue between a brilliantly cultured observer of Vienna's turn of the century and his most eccentric and compulsively conversationalist student. It is that chapter that probably best summarizes the Haze's elusive unified theory and that best answers that nagging St. Gregory's question: Why did the Haze leave his "Random Notes" to that strange kid from California?

The title of the chapter was "The Rise of the Feminine."

59

Feather River, 1988

or Flora Burden the story began, not when Wheeler arrived in Vienna, or even when Dilly arrived, but on a spring morning almost one month to the day after the tragic death of her son at the hands of a deranged assassin. For her, the story began with a packet that arrived by one of those overnight couriers for which she had to sign personally. Inside the colorful cardboard envelope of the courier service was a parcel wrapped in an ancient manila envelope with the inscription: "Please deliver to Mrs. Flora Burden, Feather River Ranch, Feather River, California on June 10, 1988." Attached to the envelope was a note from a vice president of the Boston Five Cent Savings Bank.

"Dear Mrs. Burden," it said. "Please pardon the method of delivering this package. It has been sitting in a vault in our bank for a long time, a longer time in fact than anyone currently in the bank's employment can remember. We are following the instructions of the original depositor, who appears to be your late mother-in-law, Mrs. Frank Standish Burden, although there is some confusion as to when exactly she issued those instructions. If you have any concerns or suggestions about the contents of this package, or if the contents raise any specific issues to which our bank can be of administrative service, please do not hesitate to contact me directly. We are completely at your service."

The envelope was old and did indeed look as if it had been recently dusted off after many years of storage. True to the letter of the instructions, the packet had been mailed on the assigned day and arrived at Flora's door a day later, on June 11. "Who can you trust," Dilly used to say, "if you can't trust a Boston bank?"

She was curious but somewhat detached as she slit open the envelope

with the paper cutter on the desk in her study. Inside she found a fine
linen handkerchief alongside a novel-sized book, a well-worn journal,
bound in fine red leather. Protruding from it was a rather thick letter in
longhand, dated June 1959. At first, she thumbed through the journal, but
could make little sense of it, so she extracted the letter and began to
read.

My dearest Flora,

*You will understand as you read this letter and absorb its
contents that I am in a quandary as to how to begin this story. I
know full well how powerful an effect it will have upon you. No
matter how I begin, these contents will be difficult to absorb and
will have lasting effect.*

*I write this not knowing if you will ever read it. You will soon
realize that your reading of it is just one more confirmation of the
extraordinary nature of the leather-bound book you have just
received with this mailing. Let me begin.*

*From the book, you will understand, I received a precise de-
scription of the timing of much over which I had no control, so
my plan was to have this letter arrive exactly one month after
your great tragedy, the loss of your son. My desire is to have some
healing effect on your great grief and to transfer to you at the end
of your time some of the hope that fills my soul at the end of
mine. In short, my dear daughter, if you are reading this, it
means that you will soon understand how all of our lives weave
together in a fatal and continuous and repeating loop, one not
easy to comprehend. This diary should give you the detailed information you need to piece together this complicated intertwin-
ing of lives. In the beginning, I fear, the details will be perplexing
and unbelievable to you, but have faith, dear girl. When you
begin to realize the full import of it, you will be heartened beyond belief.*

*Until you have familiarized yourself thoroughly with the en-
closed journal, the details I include here will have little meaning,
but over time I am sure you will find them essential in understanding how events ended for us in Vienna.*

My role, as it turned out, was to orchestrate that grim ending in Vienna. As you may know, it was in my nature to serve quietly behind the scenes, to make very little public display of decisiveness; however, in this case I was quite forceful, and all turned out for the better. Whether it was actually my role or whether I intruded and irreparably changed the course of history, I did not know for many years, until the birth of my son, your arrival on the scene, and the birth of our magnificent Stan Burden, called Wheeler. I long ago stopped questioning what I should do and started doing what felt right at the time. Here is a rough summary of what happened.

The sad fact is that Frank Burden confronted Wheeler in a wild rage and shot him dead. I was convinced then and remain so today that Frank became overcome with rage and took leave of his senses. He too looked horrified. Shocked as I was, I had enough presence of mind to secure the journal from Wheeler's bag before the police arrived. The Vienna police were known for their severity, and there was much confusion in the wake of the shooting, but no connection was ever made to Frank Burden or the other death in a small hotel room nearby. There were only two people who knew the whole story: Sigmund Freud and I. Connected to the case through Frau Bauer, Dr. Freud, it became apparent, intended to restrict his police testimony to his patient with a severe case of amnesia, whose true identity he had never discerned. After a month of what was awful despondency and grief for me, I was allowed to return home. One of the ways I kept my sanity during that month and on the journey back to Boston was to complete my extensive manuscript on Viennese music and Gustav Mahler.

Frank and I both returned to Boston, and we were indeed married in 1903. We never mentioned Vienna or the events that took place there. I brought with me the journal you have in your hands. Frank made a terrible mistake, that is unquestioned. He went on to become very successful and responsible as a Boston banker. A bit stiff and removed as a father, he nonetheless loved his son's achievements, which sadly confirmed some of his *misguided notions, as had the writings of Lothrop Stoddard and others. He and I rarely discussed ideas, and I suppose we tolerated the other's views because we had to, giving each other quite separate lives. Frank was devastated by the death of his son in the war and never really recovered from it.*

I can tell you that in the first decade of the century, a young Viennese scholar named Arnauld Esterhazy, in his late twenties, was appointed to the faculty of St. Gregory's School for Boys outside Boston. It is no secret that the appointment was made through my arrangements, and the young teacher was a frequent guest in our home. Within this journal you will read of how Arnauld left his teaching position in 1914 and returned to Austria to perform his patriotic duty as a soldier, a disastrous and near-fatal experience for him. Again, I was instrumental in arranging his return to teaching at St. Gregory's School in 1920, where he taught for another forty years, becoming something of a legend and a significant influence on both of our sons. I have added to this journal over the years a few details in my own hand that help round out the story, including the circumstances surrounding my son's birth that have remained a secret all this time.

And by the way, you may know that Sigmund Freud never mentioned anywhere in his writing that in 1897 he had had a strange visitor from America. He never came forward at the time or revealed that he had been witness to a shooting or anytime later that he had been warned of the repercussions of child abuse in Lambach. He remained silent.

As for me, my job done in Vienna, I had my own enormous grief to settle, but of course, knowing what I know, my perspective on the whole matter was markedly different from the rest. I did, in fact, return to America, having lost the love of my life. There was a part of me that never recovered and a part of me that grew and flourished enormously, part realist and part hopeless romantic living in a state of wondrous hope. Such is the gift of love. Jonathan Trumpp never wrote again and his true identity has remained a secret. His volume was published in 1899, and that circulated well through the music world. At the time it was singled out as the principal influence in introducing New Yorkers to Gustav Mahler, who ended his career as director of the New York Philharmonic Orchestra.

I have led a happy life. I have tried to stay out of the way and to have as little public impact as possible. I always played my hand behind the scenes. But you do know that the investments of Hyperion Fund monies were extraordinarily successful. Why exactly you will discover from the journal you now have in your possession. The fund was begun by the very successful investment of monies derived from the sale of an immensely valuable object of jewelry: a ring authenticated by the auction house as having belonged to the crown prince of Austria. It came to me in the handkerchief enclosed here. I chose my stocks and investments according to a simple plan, from one simple page in this remarkable volume. And in the buying frenzy of 1929 I withdrew from the stock market entirely and remained out for a few years, thus avoiding entirely the Great Crash in October of that year.

Shortly after my return to Boston, Sigmund Freud published his Interpretation of Dreams, and I gave a copy, in German of course, to William James, who had been a dear friend of my mother. With the help of Dr. James, the Hyperion Fund made a large gift to Clark University, near Boston, and the conference of 1909 was created, bringing both Sigmund Freud and Carl Jung to this country. I do not need to tell you the significance of that event. Also during that same time, a large Hyperion gift to the New York Philharmonic allowed the appointment of Herr Mahler. Shortly thereafter, the Athenaeum Press arranged for the first translation of Dr. Freud's book into English. You may recall that this same press discovered your magnificent book in 1955 and your son's book in 1975. I do not need to tell you that these and other well-placed projects and investments were made possible by what happened to me in Vienna and the book which I carried away from there.

Where it will go from here, my dear Flora, I do not know.

What I do know is how deeply I feel for you and how greatly heartened I am to know that for all of us life will be an endless cycle. We dream and touch each other in those dreams. As my son, Standish, known as Dilly, would say, we remain eagles.

With the deepest love,

Eleanor, known as Weezie

60

The Rise of the Feminine

t the end of the journal, in one of the passages not in Wheeler Burden's but a woman's neat hand, there is a description of the scene outside Frau Bauer's from which we can construct a picture of what transpired.

Pushing Weezie away from him left Wheeler's arms out to the side and his chest fully exposed. As Frank pulled the trigger and the air was filled with a most awful deafening concussion, the bullet struck Wheeler square in the chest and knocked him back against the exterior wall of Frau Bauer's. He seemed to hang for an instant, staring incredulously at his assailant, and he slid down the wall into a sitting position. The life would be out of him within a few minutes.

The witnesses, their ears ringing, could only stare in shock at what had transpired. With her hands on her face, Weezie let out a scream and then rushed forward and knelt beside where Wheeler had fallen. A grimace had settled onto his face. He looked up at her, confused for just a moment, then calming. He raised his hand. "You must get him out of here," he said in little more than a whisper, pointing at Frank Burden.

For her own stunned and paralyzed moment, Weezie could only stare at the man she loved, and then something seemed to snap inside her, controlling what had to be done, as if in one fateful instant she understood her future and her destiny. Frau Bauer came bustling out the door and stopped in horror, seeing Wheeler on the sidewalk and Frank with the gun at his side. Dr. Freud too looked horrified and stepped away.

Suddenly, Weezie was possessed. Perhaps she had known what was going to happen. However it was, she jumped at Frank, grabbing him by the arm. Frank Burden seemed in a daze, staring at what he had done. "I didn't know—" he began, and she cut him off.

"Do not talk," she said with a fierce authority. "You must listen and do exactly as I say. You must leave Vienna immediately." She handed him one of Wheeler's train tickets. "This is for the Nordbahnhof, for Budapest," she said.

Frank must have been stunned to be addressed this way, by a woman. He took the ticket mechanically and stared at it. "If you are caught in this country, you will be incarcerated and executed," Weezie said. "Or spend the rest of your life in prison. You must leave and not stop until you have arrived back in Boston." Frank nodded yes. He tried to speak, but she cut him off again. "Once you get to Boston, they will not try to extradite you, and you will be safe." She walked him a few steps down the street. "Have you your passport?" she asked, and he nodded. "Now, give me your room key." He reached into his pocket and gave her the key. "You can wire home for money once you get to Budapest. I will pack up all your trunks at the hotel and send them back to Boston. You will never mention this to anyone. Do you understand?" She gave him a shove away down the street. "Now, go," she said finally.

Moments later, far from the scene of the mayhem he had caused one could see Frank Burden hail a cab, climb in, and drive away. Near him, one could see the figure of Dr. Sigmund Freud, walking swiftly from the scene.

Weezie returned to Wheeler, who was sitting at the base of the wall, the life nearly out of him. She knelt beside him and took his hand. She looked fiercely into his eyes. "You cannot leave," she said, as if still in control. "You must hang on."

A slight smile came to his lips. "You are going to accomplish great things," he said.

"I don't want to accomplish great things," Weezie said, her fierceness dissolving. "I want to spend my life with you."

"No," said Wheeler Burden, making an attempt to lift his hand in protest. "This is how it is meant to be."

"Take me with you!" she said now in panic, but Wheeler caught her eyes in his and calmed her with his smile.

"We meet again, you know."

"But you won't recognize me."

"Tell you a secret," he said with almost no breath. "I thought my grandmother most beautiful." He closed his eyes for a moment. "I had a crush on her."

"I'll look forward to it" was all she could think of saying. "Are you in pain?"

"No pain," he whispered. "There was." He closed his eyes and looked as if that might be the end, then they fluttered open. "And, hey—" He focused on her. "Don't forget to send that mythology book ... Edith Hamilton ... ninth birthday. You can write in it—" He was adding more, but his voice faded.

She squeezed his hand. "I won't forget," she said.

"Promise."

"I promise."

"That's good," Wheeler whispered, slipping away.

"No," she said resolutely, squeezing both hands now. He opened his eyes wide, one last time and found hers.

"We will waltz again," he said distinctly.

They exchanged a few last words, Weezie gripping his hands even tighter. And then his eyes closed, and he really was gone.

Weezie knelt beside him with her hands on his for what might have been an eternity, until just before the police came.

61

Fin de Siècle

 rief began descending on Weezie like a thick shroud of night. Much later she would be far enough down the path of self-discovery to know that a good part of it was a revisiting of the major event of her childhood, the death of her mother, which she had not been allowed to feel. But right now she was struggling for breath, afraid to stay awake because of the devastating sense of abandonment, and afraid to drop off to sleep because of the arrival of the terrifying dark figure that rose up and hovered at the foot of her bed, ready to enfold her in its embrace.

In many ways she had been sheltered: she had led a life of privilege and had never endured the hardships of poverty or physical violence or racial prejudice or war. She had come to Vienna in search of something she didn't know or understand, and in her experiences with the culture and the relationship with one man, she had opened herself to great inner depth but also to unbearable vulnerability. "I feel as if I have given it all to you: my body, my honor, all my dark parts," she had said to Wheeler while sitting up on the studio couch, draped only in a sheet. "I have fallen completely in love, and that love has allowed you to carry all that for me."

Wheeler had smiled at that. "That I do willingly," he said. He was standing beside one of the most striking of the Secessionist paintings, the one of the goddess Athena, she with the fierce eyes and bright helmet.

"And what if I lose you?"

"Oh, my dear," he had said, fixing his eyes on hers, "my part as guide is only temporary, while you are beginning to explore the dark corners. Soon you will be going on your own, converting the paralysis to strength. You will discover this powerful goddess here beside you, her strength indelibly within you, expunging all those dark memories, to make them a positive part of your new self." He had smiled then, running his fingers over the thick gold paint of the grimacing Medusa medallion of Athena's breastplate. "Her great strength is within you, always was, always will be. You must never, never forget that."

But now he was gone, and the sense of loss seemed unbearable. She had lost his protection, and no powerful goddess was rising up to save her. She could feel the dark parts returning in waves surrounding her, swallowing her up, with no guide and protector to turn to. She could not come close to finding that power of Athena that had seemed so accessible to her while this one great love of her life was beside her. "Take me with you," she had said to him in those last moments, as she felt his spirit slipping away, sliding down to the underworld, and his eyes had fluttered open one last time and he had raised only two fingers this time to keep her where she was.

The devastation was complete, and as she lay awake at night, unable to sleep, she gasped for air, feeling herself pulled deeper and deeper into the void that overcame so many in this city of suicides. She did not know what the bottom was, but she felt herself being drawn down, down. Even images of her mother in her white dress and her inviting smile could not help. She was utterly and completely devastated.

In the midst of despair and doom, some tiny spark of hope flared up, at least momentarily, some "self" she had barely acknowledged in her life, some inner power of survival trying to come to her rescue. Somehow, she knew she had to save Frank Burden and return to Boston. She had no choice. And yet while in the throes of this paralyzing and enveloping grief, she knew what she had to do.

She had been questioned at length by the police at the scene of the shooting and waited until the coroner's wagon came and removed the body. The police agent could see her despair, the enormity of the grief that now had her in its grip, and he escorted her back to Fraulein Tatlock's, where he took her passport. "We need you to stay in Vienna," he said.

Barely able to speak, she told the kindly Fraulein Tatlock what had happened in front of Frau Bauer's. "Who did it?" Fraulein Tatlock asked.

"I do not know," Weezie said.

And somehow, despondent and shocked as she was, that very afternoon, after the police left, Weezie picked herself up and walked to the Hotel Imperial and let herself into Frank Burden's room, and fighting off numbness, she collected all his belongings and packed them into his large steamer trunk. Inside the trunk, she found currency from other European countries in marked envelopes. With those funds she arranged to pay what remained of his hotel bill, and she instructed the hotel to ship the trunk back to Frank's Boston address, leaving a significant tip for those who accomplished the task. By late afternoon, there was no trace of Frank Burden anywhere in Vienna.

With an even greater heroic effort, she scheduled an appointment the next morning with Sigmund Freud and arrived at Berggasse 19 precisely on time. She and the great doctor were the only witnesses to the catastrophe. She knew she had to speak with him personally, and she knew exactly what she needed to say, to give his great mind a mystery to solve: that was the way. As she entered the room, she noticed how short a man he was and how his piercing eyes seemed to take in everything. He showed her to a chair beside his desk, and she sat.

"How may I help you, Fraulein Putnam?" he said graciously.

"I have something very complex to tell you."

"I am quite good at dealing with human complexities, you may have heard."

"Good," she said. "We have never met, but I think perhaps you had heard of me before our unfortunate meeting yesterday in front of Frau Bauer's." Dr. Freud nodded the acknowledgment in the least demonstrative way. "Unfortunately, I knew Mr. Truman very well, as you know. You will have to excuse me if I seem a little incoherent during this meeting, but the event of yesterday has left me with little to hold on to."

"You have my sincere condolences," he said. There was a tone of more than usual empathy in his voice. "And perhaps I may render you some form of relief."

"Please do not misinterpret my visit, Herr Doktor. I am not here for myself."

"Then what do you want from me?"

"I am here to try to protect someone who has been wronged, and I think you might help."

"I see."

"A young man named Frank Burden has come to Vienna to seek me out and to ask for my hand in marriage. I deeply regret that I have become greatly distracted by my very strong and very sudden feelings for the man we both saw killed yesterday. I am deeply ashamed of my actions, and I fear I have ruined myself and most likely ruined my chance to honor Mr. Burden's offer. You know well of the standard held in Vienna for young women who wish to marry young men of promise, and the same standard holds in my native Boston. By my passionate involvement with Mr. Truman and by my devastation at my present loss I have brought things to ruin, I fear. "

"Perhaps the situation is not as dire as you think."

Weezie kept her eyes locked on his. "Oh, I fear that it is."

"And where does my assistance come in?"

"I need to tell you that a few days ago a man came to me, a man from San Francisco. He provided some shocking information. It seems that he was a business partner of Mr. Truman, and because he felt he had been betrayed, he wanted me to know the truth, to protect me, he said. He told me that Mr. Truman was a very experienced and well-traveled confidence artist and that he was out to get my money and that this man and Mr. Truman were in the process of victimizing Frank Burden also. I need to add here that Mr. Burden and I are both from very wealthy Boston families." The moment she began telling this part of the story, she could see the thoughts whirring through the cerebral doctor's mind.

"And what is this man's name?"

"He is Mr. Robert Dilly."

Dr. Freud took a moment to process the information. "How did you react to this Mr. Dilly's information?"

"Not well, I fear. I knew of Mr. Dilly because I had met him before. He is quite an accomplished musician, as is Mr. Truman, and we had played some music together, which I now see was part of the plot to draw me into their confidence. Because I was desperately and shamefully in the thrall of Mr. Truman, I decided to disregard Mr. Dilly's information and follow my seducer wherever he went."

"You know that you are not the first woman to have found herself in such a position," Freud said. His attempts to comfort were touching.

"As for Frank Burden, they had befriended him also and were in the process of enticing him into an investment. They had acquired his hotel room key and were about to steal from him some personal papers that would allow them access to his private dealings and his bank account."

"And you believed this story?"

"I did. Mr. Dilly acknowledged that Mr. Truman was indeed from San Francisco, but he had traveled through Europe for many years, victimizing young American travelers. He said, by way of example, that he and Mr. Truman had just recently traveled to a town near Vienna because Mr. Truman had fathered a child some years ago, and the mother was asking that he provide some funds for the child's schooling. Mr. Truman borrowed money from Mr. Dilly to pay the woman, and Mr. Dilly feared that in traveling to the town Mr. Truman intended to do the child harm, although nothing transpired on the trip. Mr. Dilly had recently discovered that Mr. Truman intended to leave Vienna with me and the money they had inveigled from Frank Burden."

Freud looked concerned. "And Frank Burden discovered the plot?"

"I don't think so," she said. "Why do you say that?"

"Why then did he show up at Frau Bauer's with a gun?"

Weezie gave Dr. Freud a look of seemingly genuine confusion. "I do not follow," she said.

"Mr. Burden, why did he come forward?"

"I am still not following." She paused, summoning all her courage to look hard into the doctor's face. "You have never seen Frank Burden," she said. "Have you?"

"I have not," Freud said.

"He is slightly overweight, slightly portly, and has balding red hair."

Now it was Dr. Freud who looked confused. "I assumed—" he began.

"Oh, my goodness," she said. "That was not Frank Burden," she said emphatically. "That was Mr. Dilly."

"And I saw you approach him and take something from him. What of that?"

"I told him he had better depart quickly—I don't know why I said that—and I demanded that he give me the key to Frank Burden's room."

Freud needed a moment to think. "You mentioned an illegitimate child. You don't happen to have a name and the name of the town."

Weezie shook her head. "I am sorry, but that was a detail I wasn't able to absorb. The whole story came as quite an enormous shock to me." She looked very distressed, then suddenly remembered. "Wait a moment," she said. "I wrote it down." And she opened her small handbag and began fingering in it. "Here it is," and she handed a slip of paper to the doctor.

He took the slip and examined it, and she could see his head whirring. "Adolf Hitler," he said, "Lambach." He paused and looked up at her and said, almost under his breath, "Very interesting." Weezie said nothing. "And now what do you want from me?"

"Dr. Freud, you are astute enough to see that I am in very grave despair. I intend to extract myself from this very disturbing situation as soon as the Viennese police will allow. I intend to return to Boston, to recover my equilibrium, and to marry Mr. Burden, if that is still a possibility. He had nothing to do with this frightful mess, and it is very important to me that his name not be dragged into it in any way. I know that Frau Bauer will tell the police of your close relationship with Mr. Truman, and I know they will come to you for information."

Freud nodded. "The police have already contacted me, and we have an appointment this afternoon."

"Then, I have come none too soon. I know also that in the complicated story Mr. Truman told you that Frank Burden seems to be implicated, and I assure you he is not. To be quite selfish about it, the best outcome for me is for Frank to return to Boston, and for him not to hear anything about the death of the unfortunate Mr. Truman." She did her best to fully collect herself. "I cannot stress that strongly enough."

"So you want me to leave any mention of Mr. Burden out of my story to the police?"

"That is all I can ask. I will leave him out of mine, and I can only implore you to leave him out of yours."

Dr. Freud thought for a moment. "I think that can be done."

"I thank you more than you can know," she said and after some brief parting conversation she prepared to leave.

"I know this has been a great shock to you, Fraulein Putnam," he said at the door. "If there is any way I can help, I hope you will return."

"Thank you. You are very kind," Weezie said. "But I intend never to bother you again."

Her conversation with Dr. Freud seemed to have served well its purpose—the police never made the connection to Frank Burden—but that fact brought little relief. The darkness settled on her more and more, and she sank deeper and deeper into despair. She stayed in her room and left only to take long walks by herself. Fraulein Tatlock expressed her concern by bringing food to her room on trays, but Weezie ate little. At night, she slept only briefly and then fitfully, the dark figure visiting so menacingly and with such regularity that she would cry out. This went on for almost a week, endlessly. And then one night something very strange happened. She had slept soundly for what must have been two hours; then the dark figure came to claim her, and off to the side of the bed she saw something glittering and stirring, and the black figure retreated, hung back, then vanished. Beside her bed was the figure of the goddess, with her fierce eyes, gold helmet, and medallion of the petrifying Medusa. She said nothing, only smiled, powerful and confident, and pointed across the room to the table where there sat a neat stack of blank papers and a fountain pen. Slowly, painfully Weezie rose from the bed and moved to the table, sat down, picked up the pen, and began to write. Suddenly, all the words they had spoken about Vienna and music and Gustav Mahler and the waltz, some his, some her own, began pouring out of her. She wrote that night for what must have been two hours, and then she walked back to bed and fell asleep, and just as she was falling away, she glimpsed the goddess standing over her, beautiful, wise, noble, and tall, and somehow she knew that that figure would be with her for the rest of her stay in Vienna and for the rest of her life.

Weezie's own questioning by the Vienna police continued as an ordeal, forcing her to stay in this city that now held such painful memories. It began at the scene at the time of the murder when Weezie told them quite honestly that she and Mr. Truman had been close, and she gave them her address at Fraulein Tatlock's. Finally, after three weeks of periodic questioning, in which there had been no mention of Frank Burden, they returned her passport and said she was free to leave the city. The last night she was sitting with Fraulein Tatlock, thanking her for all she had done, and the cheerful lady looked at her and said, "Was it Frank Burden?"

Weezie was caught totally by surprise. "What on earth makes you ask that?"

"The descriptions."

Weezie paused, looked the old Viennese in the eye, and took her hand and squeezed. "It is very, very important that you not think that."

And Fraulein Tatlock said, "I understand." And years later, when Eleanor Putnam Burden heard that there were rumors, she conjectured that Fraulein Tatlock had been the source, certainly not Sigmund Freud.

She bid a tearful farewell to Fraulein Tatlock and left, first by train to Paris, then by boat from Le Havre. During her month of forced stay and the passage home, she wrote continuously on music and Vienna and Gustav Mahler. In New York, on her way back to Boston, she stopped by the *New York Times* office and handed an editor the lengthy manuscript.

"Something of significance?" he said with a smile, remembering Weezie's promise in going to Vienna in the first place.

Weezie shrugged. "Catharsis," she said. "Jonathan Trumpp has written his last."

The editor weighted the manuscript in his hand. "This is a whole book," he said with an amazed and a proud smile.

"I wish it titled *City of Music*," Weezie said with authority.

⚬◎⚬

When Eleanor Putnam returned home, she was rarely called Weezie again. As time passed, she could recall the memories of her time in Vienna and with Wheeler Burden with poignancy, then joy, then inspiration. She could even revisit the fateful last moments outside Frau Bauer's as she knelt beside him, this remarkable man who was the love of her life. As time passed, she remembered less and less the awful feeling of loss and more and more the beatific smile and the last words that held her entire future.

"We will waltz again," he had whispered, words she now cherished above all others.

"I have an enormous responsibility," she had said at the end, holding his hands, struggling to gain control, struggling to find that Athena strength he had said was within her all along.

Wheeler's eyes were fixed on hers, and he could muster only enough strength to nod.

Her eyes were filled with tears now, but they shone with the ancient fierceness that came up from primordial fires. "You must know this," she said, squeezing his hands. "It seems too much—"

"You are up to it," he said with what breath he had left.

"Too much—" She paused. "But I can do it. You must know this, Wheeler Burden, the love of my life. You must know that I *am* up to the task, and I can do it."

He smiled at her. "I know," he whispered.

"I can do it for you. For all of us."

"That's good" were Wheeler Burden's last words.

This time around.

Author's Note

This novel is a work of imagination, but it is grounded in history. It had its beginnings over thirty years ago when a friend introduced me to *Wittgenstein's Vienna* by Allan Janik and Stephen Toulmin, and he and I began theorizing about transporting ourselves there. That was the year I was in graduate study at Stanford University, and I began dabbling in research about the period, choosing the fall of the year 1897, somewhat arbitrarily, to home in on. By happy accident, 1897 proved to be a fascinating choice, as Vienna in that year was on the brink of profound cultural changes that would lead to what we call the "modern" movement in politics, art, and culture. The ubiquitous coffeehouses, descendants of the actual Kolschitsky's Blue Bottle, were the undisputed center of intellectual life. A group of artists and architects calling themselves *Jung-Wien* (Young Vienna) and Secessionists were preparing their rebellion against the classicism of their industrialist fathers. And the political scene was becoming fractious and splintered. A Stanford European history professor gave me a fascinating essay by Carl Schorske called "The Transformation of the Garden," and I was off and running on a delirium of research. During the spring term of that school year, I submitted the first rudimentary version of the story of Wheeler Burden's miraculous dislocation as an independent study for a visiting professor from Rutgers named George Levine.

Over the years since then, as I expanded, refined, and embellished the story, finishing a draft every five years or so, real historical events began weaving their way into the plot I was inventing as I went. I became grateful to many sources, among the best being the Janik and Toulmin book and Schorske's 1982 masterpiece *Fin-De-Siècle Vienna: Politics and Culture*, which eventually served as a model for the Haze's magnificent "Random Notes" and Wheeler's subsequent bestselling *Fin de Siècle*. Among the many other resources I found were *The Eagles Die: Franz Joseph, Elisabeth, and Their Austria,* by George Marek; Ilsa Barea's classic *Vienna; The Viennese: Splendor, Twilight, and Exile,* by Paul Hofmann; *Freud: A Life for Our Time,* by Peter Gay; and *The First Moderns: Profiles in the Origins of Twentieth-Century Thought,* by my Princeton classmate Bill Everdell. Over time, more and more real-life events began to dominate the background of my story.

Sigmund Freud's discovery of the Oedipus myth is real, of course, and it happened in October of 1897, just as Wheeler would have arrived in Vienna. The great doctor gained world fame after his visit with his young protégé Carl Jung to Clark University in 1909, and he really did leave Vienna in 1938, escaping the Nazis in a negotiated deal, and spent the last year of his life in London, where he would have been welcomed by a committee of disciples and followers that could very well have included Flora Zimmerman.

Also in 1897, Gustav Mahler had just been given his post as director of the Vienna Opera, a position he held until 1907, at which time he took a position with the New York Philharmonic. During the period of the novel, modernist Arnold Schoenberg, in his twenties, a friend of Mahler's, was beginning to attract attention, and could have been part of Wheeler's *Jung-Wien* experience and would probably have been mentioned in *City of Music.* Composer Alban Berg was only twelve at the time.

Egon Wickstein is a fictitious character whose life trajectory represents many lives of the time. But he is based at least in part on the real philosopher Ludwig Wittgenstein, who grew up in Vienna and served in the army in the Great War, but left for good for Cambridge, England, in 1929, escaping the entire Nazi occupation and persecution. Wittgenstein is generally considered to be the most significant philosopher of the twentieth century.

The glorious sensual paintings in the assignation studio could have been a reality, but their appearance in 1897 is a bit of an anachronism. The riotously colorful and sensual paintings described, suggestive of the works of Gustav Klimt, Egon Schiele, Koloman Moser, and Oscar Kokoschka, would have actually been from a later time period, early in the next century. The magnificent Klimt *Athena,* painted in 1898, became the symbol of the first Secessionist show, which opened in the spring of that year. Alma Mahler would perhaps have been a member of the young artist group Weezie befriended, but she was only eighteen at the time, so she is missing from the story.

On Sunday, November 28, 1897, resulting from the calamitous and dire regional tensions of the time, mounted soldiers did indeed attack the crowd of marchers outside the Viennese Parliament with drawn sabers, causing much bloodshed and death, as described.

Mark Twain, arguably the most famous American to Europeans, lived with his wife and two daughters at the Hotel Metropol for an extended stay, arriving almost concurrently with Wheeler. The description of his Concordia speech of October 31, 1897, is accurate. That and other aspects of the great American's stay in Vienna are described in Carl Dolmetsch's splendid "Our Famous Guest": Mark Twain in Vienna, which is also an excellent description of fin de siècle Vienna. The reason for the Clemenses' visit was to allow Clara to study piano with famed teacher Theodor Leschetizky.

The incidents surrounding World War II in England and France are for the most part historically accurate. Coventry Cathedral received a direct hit in a horrendous bombing raid the night of November 14, 1940, and was reduced to rubble. The allies did indeed plan an elaborate hoax to deceive Hitler and hide invasion plans, and it is likely that a number of resistance spies working in Northern France believed it to be true. In the period directly following the invasion, Hitler held his formidable panzer divisions in Calais. The reason has never been ascertained, but it was definitely a decisive contribution to the Allied success. William B. Breuer's Hoodwinking Hitler: The Normandy Deception is an excellent source for this material.

The headmaster of Noble and Greenough School, Dedham, Massachusetts, in the 1930s and 1940s, Charles Wiggins, wrote a legendary description of a gentleman that is known to generations of the school's students and alumni. That description is my model for Dilly's famous graduation speech, which Wheeler wrote into his journal. Buddy Holly did indeed part from his Lubbock friends, the Crickets, and moved to Greenwich Village. He died in a small-plane crash in Clear Lake, Iowa, on the night of February 3, 1959, Wheeler's second year at St. Gregory's. Governor Goodwin Knight, NBC newsman Chet Huntley, and my Princeton classmate Joel Rosenman, the cofounder of Woodstock, are historical figures who influenced Wheeler's life. The disastrous Altamont concert did take place in December 1969, as described, and it is the subject of the excellent documentary Gimme Shelter.

In a project of imagination as long-lived as this one, fiction and history do tend to blend together, sometimes rendering the author unable to remember the difference. Such is the case for me here. Over the years, it has been difficult for me to think of Buddy Holly without his early-morning session with Wheeler Burden, or Winston Churchill without his paternal attachment to Dilly, or Sigmund Freud, for that matter, without the influence of Wheeler's journal entries. We can only imagine the individual actions, decisions, or conversations that could have changed history, and perhaps did. It is those imaginings that have fueled my passion for this story over the course of four decades.

Beyond the many historical references that have contributed to this novel, there are numerous friends and associates to whom I am indebted, beginning with my friend Steve Cohen, who in 1974 introduced me to the splendid *Wittgenstein's Vienna* and launched with me the idea of traveling there. Wheeler Burden, of course, came to life over the years and developed an identity all his own, but the details of his story were enriched by three influences. Much of his early life comes from my growing up on a prune and almond farm in Northern California and my journeying east to Boston for prep school. His middle years with baseball and music were inspired by my friend, another Princeton classmate, Doug Messenger. And his rock-star success, from Woodstock through Altamont and Berkeley, is inspired by another friend, David Crosby. To Doug and David I am grateful.

The novel's discovery and success after all this time came about thanks to an extremely fortuitous sequence. My basketball friend Milt Kahn recommended a gifted freelance editor in New York named Pat LoBrutto. Pat was invaluable in helping me see and develop a unity within my story that had evaded me for thirty years. Pat recommended the manuscript to an extraordinary literary agent, Scott Miller, at Trident Media. Scott recommended it to my very talented and attentive editor, Ben Sevier, who presented it beautifully and passionately to his team at Dutton, and suddenly the project was on its way to becoming a book. The faith and enthusiasm that Dutton has shown for my novel has been overwhelming and heartening beyond words. During the long and arduous process of converting manuscript to book a number of people played key roles. I am indebted to Randall Klein at Trident; Brian Tart, Trena Keating, Erika Imranyi, Lisa Johnson, and Rachel Ekstrom at Dutton; and my readers Mike and Bobbi Wolf, Louis Sanford, Mallard Huntley, Susan Coats, Jano and David Tucker, Beth Clements, Barbara Kimmel, my sister Hannah, and fellow writer, Dan McCaslin, a Schorske buff. To this list I add Jim Davidson, a friend and patient advisor. My children, Nan Pickens, Paula Edwards, Kirsten and Bruce Edwards, sharp and perceptive readers all, lent loving support along with timely and wise commentary. And of course, my wife Gaby, ever the attentive and well-read English teacher and editor, read the manuscript aloud and attended to each page with devoted care.

Since this is a life work, I feel obligated to express my gratitude to influences over my lifetime of loving history, fiction, and stories. I am grateful to Sydney Eaton and Timothy Coggeshall, my English teachers when I myself, at my "St. Gregory's," was rough-hewn from the California provinces. During those years, I was profoundly influenced by my own legendary headmaster, Eliot Putnam, and deeply grateful for friendships, especially those of Mike Deland and Jim Wood, who lent names and details to this story. In my years as an English teacher I fell in thrall of Mark Twain, Arthur Miller, J. D. Salinger, F. Scott Fitzgerald, John Irving, and Pat Conroy; and during those years in school I have been fortunate to know and call as friends a number of distinguished writers. In this regard, I am grateful to Max Byrd, Barnaby Conrad, Oakley Hall, Richard Ford, and Beth Gutcheon. Also during those teaching days, I had the luxury of colleagueship with a number of very special teachers and lovers of the literary dialogue, among whom were Stan Woodworth, Joe Caldwall, Ed Hartzell, Bill Nicholson, Barclay Johnson, Katherine Schwartzenbach, Cathy Rose, and Barbara Ore. Late in my career, my experience at Pacifica Graduate Institute enhanced and deepened this novel in both obvious and subtle ways. I am grateful to my Pacifica teachers and classmates in general and to Dennis Slattery, Bobbi Wolf, Al Smith, Bill Drake, and my wonderful photographer JoAnn Carney in particular.

It is a great personal sadness that my mother and father are not alive to see this lengthy project come to fruition, as they were the ones who encouraged all four of their children to make the most of the superb education they provided and to pursue a life of learning and books and service to others. Deepest gratitude also goes to my three wonderful children: Nan, Bruce, and Paula have been a joy and inspiration to their parents from the moment of their births. And for her encouragement, inspiration, support, and unconditional love, I wish to express my boundless indebtedness to my wife, Gaby. This book, the fulfillment of life aspirations too complicated and numerous to describe here, satisfies at least one very simple and expressible goal: the enduring fifty-year dream of dedicating a novel, my own "something of significance," to her.